CLEMHORN
NADIR

(Book 2 of the Clemhorn Trilogy)

A Novel of the
Cross-Temporal Empire

Andrew J Harvey

ZMOK
BOOKS

Clemhorn: Nadir by Andrew J. Harvey
Cover image by
This edition published in 2023

Zmok Books is an imprint of

Winged Hussar Publishing, LLC
1525 Hulse Rd, Unit 1
Point Pleasant, NJ 08742

Copyright © Andrew Harvey/Winged Hussar Publishing, 2023
ISBN PB 978-1-958872-17-8
ISBN EB 978-1-958872-18-5
LCN

Bibliographical References and Index
1. Science Fiction. 2. Steam Punk. 3. Alternative History

Winged Hussar Publishing, LLC All rights reserved
For more information
visit us at www.whpsupplyroom.com

Twitter: WingHusPubLLC
Facebook: Winged Hussar Publishing LLC

CONTENTS

Prologue 9
Chapter One............... 10
Mmbuto é Line April 1980 (96AE)

Chapter Two............... 15
Fort Larsa — Etu Line April 1980 (96AE)

Chapter Three............... 33
Mmbuto é Line April 1980 (96AE)

Chapter Four............... 52
Naisre — Mainline May 1980 (96AE)

Chapter Five............... 58
Bathre — Mmbuto é Line May 1980 (96AE)

Chapter Six............... 71
Ngoni — Mmbuto é Line May 1980 (96AE)

Chapter Seven............... 85
Neu Stuttgart — Etu Line May 1980 (96AE)

Chapter Eight............... 104
Leolie — Etu Line June 1980 (96AE)

Chapter Nine............... 107
Rufiji — Mmbuto é Line September 1980 (96AE)

Chapter Ten............... 120
Leolie — Etu Line June 1980 (96AE)

Chapter Eleven............... 126
Iller River — Etu Line June 1980 (96AE)

Chapter Twelve............... 143
En route to Rufiji — Mmbuto é Line October 1980 (96AE)

Chapter Thirteen............... 150
Leolie — Etu Line June 1980 (96AE)

Chapter Fourteen............... 154
Rufiji — Mmbuto é Line November 1980 (96AE)

Chapter Fifteen............... 158
Rufiji — Mmbuto é Line November 1980 (96AE)

Chapter Sixteen.. 171
Heidleberg — Etu Line September 1980 (96AE)

Chapter Seventeen.. 182
Unknown location (near Detroit) — Mainline November 1980 (96AE)

Chapter Eighteen... 185
Unknown location (near Detroit) — Mainline November 1980 (96AE)

Chapter Nineteen... 195
*Choququirau — Mmbuto é Line (Charleston, COA, Mainline equivalent)
December 1980 (96AE)*

Chapter Twenty.. 208
Unknown location (near Detroit) — Mainline January 1981 (97AE)

Chapter Twenty-one.. 224
Rufiji — Mmbuto é Line March 1981 (97AE)

Chapter Twenty-two.. 233
Leolie — Etu Line June 1981 (97AE)

Chapter Twenty-three.. 242
Le Havre — Etu Line June 1981 (97AE)

Chapter Twenty-four... 252
Dar es Salaam — Mainline May 1981 (97AE)

Chapter Twenty-five... 262
Carthago — Mmbuto é Line July 1981 (97AE)

Chapter Twenty-six.. 266
Rufiji — Mmbuto é Line July 1981 (97AE)

Chapter Twenty-seven.. 280
Le Havre — Etu Line August 1981 (97AE)

Chapter Twenty-eight.. 294
Milano equivalent — Mmbuto é Line February 1982 (98AE)

Chapter Twenty-nine... 307
Milano equivalent — Mmbuto é Line February 1982 (98AE)

Chapter Thirty... 317
Western hemisphere — Etu Line August 1981 (97AE)

Chapter Thirty-one.. 325
Leolie — Etu Line February 1982 (98AE)

Chapter Thirty-two.. 330
Habesh — Mmbuto é Line July 1982 (98AE)

Chapter Thirty-three.. 339
  Rome — Mainline February 1982 (98AE)

Characters... 342

Glossary.. 346

First families of the C-TE (95AE)... 352

Lines of the C-TE (95AE).. 353

For Debbie

PROLOGUE

After eighty years of total war, the remnants of humanity on the Nayarit Line struggled to survive in sealed domes, surrounded by radioactive wasteland and genetically engineered viruses. It was in the last, desperate years of the war that the first trans-temporal portal was developed at Chiqu, a small research facility on the west coast of North America. As the domes finally failed and civilization collapsed around them, Iapura led fifty-three survivors from Chiqu to found a new empire on a parallel Earth; an Earth where, in 1884, Russian and English armies faced each other across America's Great Plains, totally unprepared for the technology of the invading Nayarit.

Over the next ninety years Iapura's Empire expanded steadily across a series of parallel Earths, absorbing and conquering until it included over fifty-four separate time-lines. Finally, however, with its technology stagnant and its ruling Council riven by dissent, the death of Manet, First Leader of the Cross-Temporal Empire (C-TE), plunged the Empire into civil war.

After Miro's surprise attack shattered the Progressive alliance the Clemhorn family struggled to re-establish itself, and to prepare for a rematch. But Miro's new allies would make that task all the more difficult.

CHAPTER 1

Mmbuto é Line
April 1980 (96AE)

The smell of cypress rose around Donald as he stepped through the portal. Behind him, light from the portal spilled into the darkened forest as a diesel generator hummed quietly in the background. Taking a deep breath, he paused for a moment, relieved that once again he'd survived the transfer. He knew the fear was irrational, but that didn't make it any less real.

"Leader?" It was Hastings, the Engineering Group Leader who'd been in charge of establishing the new base.

Donald jumped, startled out of his reverie. "Yes Hastings?"

Hastings made a small motion with his hand. "If you could, sir. . ."

It took Donald a moment to realize what he meant, then, embarrassed, he stepped aside, out of the way of those following him through the portal.

Tsitsho, the Clemhorn Force Leader of the 48th Light Infantry was the first through, and the rest of her detachment in their light blue uniforms and blue kepis quickly fanned out around her into the area the engineers had cleared around the portal.

"Tsitsho," Donald said, making the introductions. "This is Group Leader Hastings."

"Group Leader," Tsitsho said, saluting. "Where do you want us?"

"You're going to be spread a bit thin with only a hundred troops. . ."

"Closer to fifty," Tsitsho said, interrupting. "We're still down half our strength from the attack this morning."

"Fifty," Hastings said, accepting the correction.

Donald frowned. "I thought we'd lost thirty for the entire Battlegroup?"

"Most of the fifty are just wounded," Tsitsho said. She looked at Hastings.

"The priority is the bunkers and getting someone out to cover my engineers still finishing the outer trench line," the engineer said. "The main trench can probably be left till the rest of the Battlegroup comes through."

Tsitsho looked thoughtfully at the three earth-work bunkers built around the edge of the cleared area. Revetted with sandbags and timbers from the cleared vegetation, all three bunkers faced towards the portal. "I don't suppose you know what we could expect?" she asked Donald.

Donald shook his head. "Not a thing, sorry. The last contact with this line was almost a hundred years ago. It's probably safe to assume that if there is any contact it will be hostile. Apparently our last contact didn't end very well."

In fact, from what his father had told him, their response had involved both biological and nuclear strikes before the line was 'sealed'.

"All right," Tsitsho said decisively. "A squad for each of the bunkers. The rest can help you finish the outer lines."

"They shouldn't have much more to do," Hastings promised. "My aide will serve as your liaison," he added, indicating the individual concerned who acknowledged his new role with a nod.

"Thank you," Tsitsho said. "Leader, with your permission I will see about getting everything set up."

"Of course, carry on," Donald said.

The throaty roar of a second generator starting up disturbed the night and Donald was almost blinded by the glare of lights from the top of a mast erected next to one of the bunkers. Blinking away tears he turned back to Hastings. "And now, as I'm supposed to be in charge of this side of the evacuation, you'd better give me a quick tour."

The tour took less than fifteen minutes, but by the time it was finished Donald was almost relaxed. In the twelve hours they'd had, the engineers had managed to achieve a minor miracle.

In addition to the three bunkers, tents had been set up to house the troops and equipment that would be coming through shortly. The entire area was ringed with a deep trench, reinforced by a breastwork of sandbags. Fire lines had been cleared, and the removed vegetation had then been used to strengthen a series of fire-pits that provided interlocking fire along the entire line. A further, outer, trench was still in the process of being constructed, but barbed wire had already been strung along its length and a series of small minefields gave further protection.

"It's impressive," Donald told the engineer sincerely.

"Thank you."

"Leader." It was Tsitsho.

"Yes?"

"I just wanted to let you know we were in position."

For a moment Donald stared at the portal hanging like some enormous soap bubble in its frame. "Okay," he said. "You better tell them to start moving everything through."

The next couple of hours quickly degenerated into a blur as he worked to prevent the area around the portal from disintegrating into chaos. Everyone was aware of the time limit that pressed relentlessly upon them, but it was still well after one o'clock before the last of the 48th, including the wounded, and their supplies had come through. Almost immediately bits of furniture started to come through the portal, and Donald realized that his father must be stripping the campus of everything that could be moved, with no regard to its value or purpose. The flow continued until the first, faint light stained the horizon with the hint of the new day, when with nothing else to pass through, Conrad and their father finally stepped through the portal.

Wearily the World Leader surveyed the chaos of boxes, crates, desks and cabinets that littered the ground around them. "That's it," he said. "Close the portal."

"What about the Dynands?" Donald asked. The university on the Mainline had been held by a combined force of Clemhorn Light Infantry and a Battlegroup of Dynand regulars. A lot of the supplies that had come through had been Dynandian, but so far the only troops through had been from the 48th.

"Yes, what about the Dynands?" Defella said as she stepped through the portal. Her light green uniform was stained with dust and smoke, and the feather she normally wore in her bonnet was missing. The two Dynand troopers who followed her through looked just as exhausted, but the muzzles of their machine pistols lazily covered the techs standing uncertainly next to the portal's controls with calm professionalism.

The World Leader sighed and rubbed his forehead. "I thought I made it quite clear you were to remain and surrender with the rest of the army."

"You were deserting us."

"No."

Defella snorted. "I spoke with my mother by telephone an hour ago, just before she returned to Dynand. She told me we were to return with our shields, or on them. If your insist we remain we will defend the University until we are overrun. Frankly I would prefer to live but. . ."

The World Leader stared at her angrily but she glared back at him Finally his shoulders slumped and he shrugged. "As you will," he said. "Bring them through."

"Sergeant," Defella said.

"By the twos. Quick march," the Sergeant bellowed, and a moment later the wail of Dynand bagpipes filled the air as a piper led the first of the Dynands through the portal. For a moment, as the Dynand marched past him, a swagger still visible in their steps despite their exhaustion, Donald could almost believe his brother's promise that they'd be back. Indeed he had to believe, because if he didn't it would mean that he would never see Matija again, or his unborn child.

Actually, he thought with a tired smile, what Conrad had said was 'that there was no way that he was going to let a snot of a Raputa think he'd beaten a Clemhorn,' but that was close enough.

CHAPTER 2

Fort Larsa — Etu Line
April 1980 (96AE)

Ivy leaned back in her chair, stretching her neck and trying to work the kinks out of her back. The staffing report she'd been trying to complete stared sullenly up at her. Who'd have thought there was so much paper work involved in running such a small Fort?

Her fingers played with the key that hung from the fine silver chain around her neck as she gazed out of the window. Outside winter dragged on, shadowing her mood. She glanced down at the key, which served as a constant reminder of Jon's letter which still lay, unopened, in the bottom drawer of her desk.

There was a knock on the door. "Yes Daniels," she said, recognizing her 2IC's knock, happy for the interruption.

"We've just received a message from Continental Headquarters," Daniels said, poking her head around the corner of the door. "Etu's been placed on Orange Alert."

"The whole line? Do they give a reason?" Ivy asked, holding her hand out for the message slip, her interest piqued. Generally an alert applied only to a county, or at most a continent. Ivy had never heard of it being applied to a whole line before.

"Afraid not."

"It has to be Miro," Ivy said, looking at the message. Unfortunately it didn't offer any clues.

"Well if anyone was to know it would be you. After all, you're the one with the contacts."

"Thanks," Ivy said dryly, handing the slip back to her. She was unwilling to admit that she'd been doing her best to ignore the nagging of her conscience to respond to her mother's weekly letters. Besides, her mother very rarely discussed politics in her letters. Most of the time they concentrated on the minutia of daily life at Leolie, plus the latest on what had been happening to her brothers and cousins. "All right, you'd better make sure the other Troop Leaders know."

"Did you want to delay the departure of Marsha's Troop tomorrow?"

Ivy shook her head. "No, not without more information. I'm still worried about the reports we've had of Pegoni raiders in the area."

"Of course." Daniels gave a cursory salute and left to track down Marsha and Yellow Elk.

Ivy looked down at the unfinished report on her desk. It would be easy to just leave it for the moment, maybe go for a walk down to the village or something. She'd been doing a lot of that recently. No one would complain. She poked the report with her finger; after all she doubted anyone was actually ever going to read it. She got up and moved round to the window. Outside someone was trying to sweep up the untidy mush of partly melted snow that had turned the red sawdust surface of the parade ground almost black. She frowned up at the overcast sky. It might mirror her mood perfectly but that didn't mean she had to like it. Where the hell was spring?

Outside the soldier had finished sweeping and with a sigh she picked her fountain pen up and returned to her paperwork.

The next day, as the fort's bugler sounded reveille, Ivy strode briskly across the parade ground from her quarters to where her three Troops waited for morning inspection. The Third, Marsha's, was already mounted, the horses fidgeting quietly in the cold.

The sun had been up for just under an hour but her breath still steamed before her in time with her breathing.

"All present and accounted for, Force Leader," Daniels reported, coming to attention.

"Thank you," Ivy said, returning the salute. "You may dismiss the parade. I don't want to hold up departure."

Daniels saluted and turned back to the Force. "Sergeants, dismiss the parade."

As the first two Troops headed back to the warmth of their barracks Ivy made her way over to where Marsha was waiting at the head of her Troop. There was little to see of her Third Troop Leader under the completely un-regulation beaver hat and scarf she was wearing. With the flaps from the hat pulled down and the scarf wound round her face only the tip of her nose was showing.

"Feeling the cold?" Ivy asked with mock solicitousness.

Marsha grunted and Ivy didn't bother to hide a grin. She hadn't really been expecting more of a response. Marsha could make a tree look talkative at times.

"Don't push yourself," Ivy told her seriously, looking up at her. "I don't want anyone injured."

Marsha nodded.

"And with the alert I want you to maintain hourly radio contact."

"Of course, Mother."

Ivy snorted. If anyone was the mother it was Marsha. As far as she'd been able work out from the paperwork she'd been doing yesterday this was

Marsha's third term, which meant she had to be at least forty-five. Compared to her own twenty-four years that was almost ancient.

"Take care," Ivy said, stepping back to slap Marsha's mount on the rump.

As the last of the twenty-five mounted infantry in Marsha's Third Troop rode out through the fort gates Ivy turned to see Daniels waiting for her. She raised an eyebrow. "Well?"

"I'm going to take my Troop out for a run after breakfast. I was wondering if you wanted to join us."

Ivy considered the question. Maybe it would be good for her, but she shook her head regretfully. "Sorry, I wouldn't mind but I've got to finish the accounts for the packet boat this afternoon."

"You'll get fat," Daniels said warningly.

"Unlikely," Ivy said with a pensive smile. She'd lost ten pounds over winter.

Ivy was still trying to balance the accounts later that morning when there was a knock on her door.

"Enter," she called.

It was Trooper Monahan, the largest trooper at the fort, and the beads in his hair clicked quietly as he crossed the room to hand her a message slip. "This just came in, Leader. It's from the Fort Leader at Krath."

Krath was one of the small Troop-sized forts that ringed the Alps, about fifty miles north-east of Fort Larsa. She scanned the message quickly. One of his scouts reported sighting a large raiding party of twenty guerrillas moving in her direction.

She looked up at the map pinned on her wall. Marsha wouldn't be strong enough to take them on by herself, but maybe. . .

"Trooper, get this encoded and send it to Leader Marsha at once." She scribbled a message explaining the situation, and ordering her to slow her march until Ivy and the rest of the Force could join her.

Monahan saluted, and turned to go. "And hurry," she told him. He broke into a run.

She went to the door, where she could see Sergeant Horsing sitting on the stoop polishing some gear, his ginger hair glinting in the sun.

"Sergeant," she called. "Sound assembly."

He nodded and bellowed an order. A moment later the bugle rang out, and troopers started to pile out of everywhere and assemble in the square. There weren't many of them and Ivy remembered that Daniels' Troop were out on a run.

"Sergeant Horsing, get someone after Daniels and call them back."

"What's happening?" Yellow Elk, her Second Troop Leader asked, stepping up onto the verandah.

"Krath spotted a large group of about twenty raiders," she said, handing him the message slip. "Marsha's not strong enough to take them on by herself but with our help we might be able to get them all." The effect of losing an entire raiding party might, perhaps, make the Pegoni think twice about sending more of them in future.

She returned inside to check the map again. She'd need a couple more autogiros, but there were two other forts in addition to Krath which might be in a position to lend them to her. She scribbled off a message to all three Fort Leaders and went back outside to find someone to take it to communications. She was just wondering what had happened to Daniels when the first of her Troop ran back through the large double wooden gates and into the fort.

As Daniels read the message Ivy checked her watch. "It's eleven now. I'll give you twenty minutes to have everyone saddled and ready to go. Daniels, detail a squad to look after the fort, but I want everyone else. I think it's about time we gave these raiders a taste of their own medicine."

The two Leaders saluted and turned back to their own troops, which within moments were scattering in all directions. She checked her watch again. She still needed to brief Lieutenant Williams, the fort's aviator. The autogiro was going to be crucial if this plan of hers was to have any hope of success. At least she didn't have to worry about packing, or saddling her own mount, which gave her a little extra time. Rank did have some privileges after all, she thought with a grin.

The entire garrison were mounted and waiting for her as she opened the door and stepped down onto the wooden porch at precisely twenty past eleven. Not bad, she thought as she walked to where Archos was holding her mount.

"Ready?" she asked, as she swung herself up into the saddle.

Daniels nodded.

"Move out!" she ordered.

Both Daniels and Yellow Elk brought their horses up level to hers as they passed through the main gate.

"So what's the plan?" Daniels asked.

"I've ordered Marsha to slow down," Ivy explained. "We should catch up with her shortly after midday. I've asked the Fort Leaders at Krath, Hague, and Montague for a loan of their autogiros. Once we've got a precise location of the raiding party from them the whole Force moves to engage them." Her hands demonstrated what she meant.

"The terrain's going to make it difficult to locate them," Daniels pointed out.

"Which is why the autogiros are so important."

Yellow Elk frowned.

"What?" Ivy asked.

"I don't really like using the autogiros. As soon as the raiders see them they'll know they've been spotted. It'll give them the opportunity to split up and try to escape."

Ivy acknowledged the point with a shrug. "Unfortunately I can't think of any other way to make it work. As Daniels said, the terrain's going to make it impossible to locate them without the autogiros. But I'm not sure what else can we do — we can't just let a raiding party waltz around unopposed."

"We could undertake a punitive raid," Yellow Elk said. "At least it would teach them a lesson."

Ivy conceded the old argument with a shrug. "And as I've explained, Continental Headquarters won't authorize one. They're too worried it will trigger a full scale war, which is something we can't afford at the moment."

"And we can afford this," he said, his gesture encompassing the two Troops riding behind them.

"Apparently."

Ivy refused to allow Yellow Elk's words spoil her mood. This was the first real opportunity to get out of the fort since she'd learned of Jon's death, and the first opportunity to strike back at the Pegoni who had been a constant irritation since her arrival at the fort. The sky was a perfect washed-out blue, and the day was finally starting to warm up, but that would probably change once they entered the forest canopy.

A large stag startled by their passing paused for a moment on the skyline to watch them, silhouetted against the dark green of the conifers behind him. Ivy's fingers itched for her rifle, but his antlers were still developing. Give him another couple of months and he'd be a worthy target.

They caught up with Marsha's Troop just after midday, and together the full Force made camp that night about ten miles into the Alps.

By morning Ivy's mood had turned bleak again. She'd spent a sleepless night, worried about whether she was doing the right thing. And now, as she studied the map while the rest of the Force stirred to life around her, she'd almost convinced herself that the whole thing was going to be a waste of time. That might be bad enough, but given the assistance being provided by the other three forts, it was going to be a very visible waste of time.

"What's it looking like?" Daniels asked, handing her a mug of fresh coffee as Ivy pored over the map.

"Not good," Ivy admitted, straightening up to accept the mug.

"So what's wrong?"

"The raiding party was spotted by Krath, here." She indicated the spot on the map. "Unfortunately there are at least three routes they could take to get down to the Danube from there, and we simply can't afford to cover all three. If we do that we lose our numeric advantage. Basically, if the autogiros can't find them we're stuffed."

Daniels frowned up at the thick canopy overhead.

"Yeah, I know," Ivy said. "It's going to be difficult to locate them in this."

"Well, we didn't think it was going to be easy," Daniels pointed out.

No, but she didn't know it was going to be so difficult, Ivy thought. "It's just that. . ." she trailed off, realizing she couldn't say that since Jon's death she'd wondered if she was up to the task. Maybe she should just resign, but then what would she do? She'd never wanted any other career apart from the army since she was ten.

"Leader."

It was the communications officer, flimsy in hand. Ivy took the message slip. "Oh great, just what we needed," she said.

"What's wrong?" Daniels asked.

"The line's been moved to Crimson status." It was the highest alert level possible. What the hell was going on?

"Do we head back?"

Ivy considered the question. It was tempting, an excuse to give up without losing face. Was it something Jon would have done though? And if they gave up now could she live with the consequences, knowing what she did of how the raiders operated? She shook her head, deciding she couldn't.

"Not yet," she said, checking the message again. "There's no indication of an actual attack. Let's push on."

That day saw them moving even further into the mountains. The terrain was so rough now, the forest so thick that for most of the time the Force had to walk, leading their mounts. Ivy's mood got progressively worse as they struggled up the valley and by six thirty, an hour before sunset, she was on the verge of calling the whole thing off as a wild goose chase. Under the trees it was already almost too dark to move, and the autogiros still hadn't seen any sign of the raiders. The toe of her boot connected with something hard, and she swore as she tripped over another tree root.

"Force Leader." It was the radio operator.

"Yes."

"Lieutenant Williams for you."

"Clemhorn here," Ivy said, taking the microphone.

"We've located them," the aviator said, pitching his voice to carry over the noise of the autogiro's engine and rotor.

"You're sure?" Ivy said. Maybe this wasn't going to be such a wild goose chase.

"Positive, there's about fifteen of them. I can't be more precise because I didn't want to let them know they'd been spotted."

"Understood, where are they?"

"About five miles nor, nor-east of you." He gave the grid reference and Ivy reached for her map.

"Roger that," she said once she'd located it on the map. "All right, you and the other autogiros better head back the Fort. We'll see you again about an hour after sunrise."

"Wilco."

"What do you think?" Daniels asked, who had come up while she was talking to Williams.

Ivy showed her the map. "It's too far for us to reach tonight, but we can set up camp here, and leave the horses when we move on at first light. What do you say, ten, ten-thirty?"

Daniels nodded thoughtfully. "Probably. Is it a good idea to leave the horses though?"

Ivy shrugged. "We're going to move faster without them. At the moment all they're doing is slowing us down."

"True. All right, we camp here?" she asked looking around.

They were in the middle of a dense copse of fir. There was little undergrowth, just a thick layer of pine needles and the rich aroma of pine sap.

"I think so," Ivy said. "We need to be able to set the camp so it's secure for tomorrow. If we're going to do that we can use the extra light — not that there's much of it."

"I'll get everything set up then," Daniels said.

***

"Leader." Ivy came awake from a light doze later that night to the soft touch of a hand on her shoulder. It was the radio operator, which probably meant it wasn't good news.

"What is it?" she asked, unzipping her sleeping bag just enough to check her watch in the shadowed light of the kerosene lamp the signaler was carrying. One o'clock. Wonderful, she thought sarcastically. Thanks to nerves she hadn't actually been able to get to sleep until twelve.

"A message from Leolie, for you."

"For me?"

"Yes Leader."

From Leolie? She took the message slip with trepidation as the signaler held his kerosene lamp up for her to read by.

It took her a moment to piece out the message in the uncertain light of the lamp, and even when she'd finished it she had to re-read to actually make sure she'd understood.

"What is it?" Daniels asked, her face peering out from under the shelter of her bivouac on the other side of the fire.

"It's from my mother. Gods, I can't believe it. We've lost control of the Mainline, and Leolie is presently under attack. I've been ordered to return to Continental Headquarters where I'm to resign my commission and take up the position of Continental Leader."

She looked at the trees that hemmed in the camp, their canopy blocking out the sky. "Damn! It's going to take forever to get back." The whole Empire was falling apart and she was stuck out here in the boonies. She should have ordered the Force back when the line was moved to Crimson.

"If I may make a suggestion?" Daniels offered.

"Of course."

"It would be faster for you to take the autogiro back to the fort."

"I agree, if it could land anywhere."

"We passed a rock plateau large enough to take it earlier today. The autogiro could pick you up about ten, and then have you back to the fort by lunchtime."

"Thanks Daniels, you're a lifesaver." Ivy uttered a silent prayer for 2ICs. She was turning back to the signaler to tell him her reply when she heard a single shot from somewhere on her left and froze. What?

A second later she was scrambling out her bag and reaching for her rifle. She'd been wearing her boots loose laced in her bag and was just pulling them tight when a second shot rang out, followed almost immediately by the quick rattle of automatic fire from Marsha's direction. Oh gods, they were under attack.

The signaler had turned his lamp down but Ivy's night vision was already shot. Goddammit, why couldn't they have attacked fifteen minutes ago? Then again, maybe she could have wished for them to do it after breakfast.

"I'll go and see what's happening," Ivy told Daniels, as she finished her laces. Grabbing her rifle she cautiously started towards the firing that, unfortunately, did not appear to have lessened.

A flare burst overhead, and the forest exploded into stark contrasts of white and black. The dense forest canopy overhead cut out a lot of the light, but there was still enough to see by and Ivy took advantage to move quickly to where she remembered Marsha had set up her tent. The shadows moved disconcertingly around her as the flare slowly descended.

The horses on a line to her left were pulling uneasily at the rope. The one closest seemed particularly nervous and as it reared, Ivy dropped to one knee, her rifle automatically coming up to her shoulder as she realized that two shadows she'd thought were tree roots were actually moving, rising to their feet. The thin edge of a hatchet glinted in the guttering light of the flare and Ivy reacted instinctively, her finger squeezing the trigger, then moving the aim point and firing again just as the flare guttered out overhead.

She remained where she was until another flare burst overhead. The horses were still there although even more obviously spooked and it looked as if both raiders were down. The question was, where were the sentries? She started forward and almost stumbled over a body. She crouched, and took a quick look. Well that answered that question.

She heard someone moving behind her and pulled back into the shelter of a tree.

"Leader?" It was Sergeant Horsing.

"Here, Horsing," Ivy said keeping an eye on the horses.

"Daniels sent me to keep an eye on you."

"It looks as if they were after the horses. Cover me. I need to calm the mounts or we're going to lose them."

Carefully Ivy moved forward, trying not to further spook the horses. The second flare was already starting to gutter out as she reached the line and moved quickly to the most frantic of the mounts, speaking soothingly as she did so.

She'd successfully calmed the five most hysterical horses before she found the first raider, stumbling over his body as she made her way down the line. Well that was one raider who wasn't going to be doing any more raiding she thought, satisfied.

She couldn't see any sign of the second raider, and she waved Horsing over, relieved to find McKenzie and Donogh were with him — well that solved one problem.

"You two stay here and make sure no one walks off with the horses," she said to McKenzie and Donogh. "Once I've spoken to Marsha I'll try and get someone to assist you. Sergeant, let's go."

She reached Marsha's position without further interruption, slipping into the foxhole next to her Troop Leader just as Marsha was about to let off another flare.

"Hold the flare," Ivy said. "We might need them later."

Marsha carefully lowered the flare-pistol as the flare slowly descending overhead sputtered out and died, leaving them in impenetrable, stygian night.

"Can you get a squad over to help McKenzie and Donogh with the Second Troop's mounts?" Ivy said. "There were a couple of raiders trying to cut them out."

"Hrak?" Marsha called.

"I heard, Leader."

Marsha's first Sergeant headed off with a squad.

"What happened?" Ivy asked in the abrupt silence as the firing broke off, straining to make out anything through the darkness.

"Not sure," Marsha replied honestly. "It looks as if we've lost our sentries, and the mounts. If Keyriss wasn't such a light sleeper we'd never have even known they were here."

"How many did you get?"

"No idea, probably not as many as we should have."

Ivy nodded. "It looks as though they got Yellow Elk's sentries. Almost lost the mounts as well." She suddenly swore.

"What?" Marsha asked.

"We were set up. There must have been two groups. We thought we were tracking them but really they were tracking us." Damn, how could she have been so stupid!

Marsha swore as well.

"I'd say that's it," Ivy said with a sigh, when nothing had happened for five minutes. "Let's see what the damage is. Put a flare up."

Marsha raised the pistol and, warned by the sudden sputtering, Ivy covered her eyes against the glare of the rocket. A moment later the flare exploded overhead and once again the forest was thrown into stark contrasts of light and dark.

Marsha gave a shrill whistle and circled her arm into the air. Five troopers broke from their foxholes and moved forward cautiously into the surrounding forest.

"I better check with Yellow Elk and Daniels," Ivy said. "Give me your report when you've finished your recce."

"Will do," Marsha said.

Ivy rested her hand on Marsha's shoulder for a moment, before hoisting herself out the foxhole and heading back to her command post. Horsing fell in beside her. "What do you think?" she asked.

"We were lucky; it could have been worse."

"Yeah. It was a real crapshoot and we just got crapped on," Ivy said bitterly. Gods, she'd been suckered in real good. "Tell Yellow Elk I want a sitrep."

Horsing cast a look round but things looked pretty quiet and he nodded, peeling off in the direction of the Second Troop.

"What's the situation?" Ivy asked, as she reached Daniels' foxhole.

Daniels looked up. "We're missing Hercules. He was on the flank with the Second Troop."

Ivy tried to hide a wince.

"What's Marsha's situation?" Daniels asked.

"We'll find out in a moment. She's still checking."

Another flare burst overhead just as the last one guttered out and a moment later Ivy heard someone moving quietly over the dried pine needles.

"Leader?"

"Here Horsing. What's the situation?"

"Yellow Elk said they've lost four, and Rachel's missing."

Ivy's stomach clenched at the news, and for a moment all she could remember was lying semi-concussed on the ground after the disaster with the paddleboat, as the two raiders prepared to rape her. Damn, damn, damn!

"How many did we get?" Daniels asked.

"So far they've found only the one body."

"Ivy?" It was Marsha.

Ivy looked round, wondering just how much worse the night could get. "What's the damage?" she asked.

"Four dead, three wounded, and we lost half the mounts."

"Anyone missing?"

"No, why?"

"It looks like they picked Rachel Huron up," Daniels said.

Marsha swore.

"Yup, just the perfect end to a perfect night," Ivy said. "Okay Marsha, I want you to get a team together — make sure you include Jules." He was their best tracker. "Your job's to get Rachel back. I don't want her to be in their hands any longer than she has to be. Let me know as soon as you're ready to leave. In the meantime I better get that message off to Continental Headquarters, and see about arranging for the autogiro to pick me up."

"I'd forgotten about that," Daniels admitted.

"I wish I could," Ivy said.

"Pardon, am I missing something?" Marsha asked.

"Just before the attack we received a message from Leolie," Ivy explained. "I've been promoted to Continental Leader and ordered to return to headquarters. Apparently the line is under attack and we've lost control of the Mainline."

There was stunned silence at her announcement.

"I'm leaving you in one hell of a spot," Ivy told her two Troop Leaders. "Unfortunately I don't have any choice."

"Of course not," Marsha hurried to reassure her.

Then why didn't she feel that, Ivy wondered.

It was shortly after mid-morning when Ivy reached the plateau where Lieutenant Williams was waiting to take her back to the fort by autogiro. Daniels and a short squad of five accompanied her to the top of the hill.

"I'll arrange for immediate replacements to be dispatched as soon as I get to headquarters," Ivy told her 2IC.

"You may have bigger problems than one understaffed fort to worry about," Daniels said.

Ivy nodded. She wanted to disagree but she had the feeling Daniels was right. "Keep me informed about Rachel." She looked at the squad clustered a short distance away. "And look after them for me, Daniels."

"Of course. It has been a pleasure working with you," Daniels said, coming to attention and saluting.

Ivy returned the salute, tears pricking at her eyes. "Thank you. The pleasure has been mutual," she said sincerely.

Her eyes were still stinging as she climbed into the autogiro behind Williams. As soon as she was buckled in, Williams revved the engine and, dropping the clutch, launched them into the air.

Ivy watched the squad disappear below her, before leaning back and closing her eyes. She wished she could have stayed, at least until she'd had a chance to redeem herself. Maybe a new chapter of her life was starting, but it seemed the last one was closing on complete and utter failure.

CHAPTER 3

Mmbuto é Line
April 1980 (96AE)

"Conrad."

"Yes Papa?" Conrad looked up from the box of ammunition he was itemizing. The Dynand he'd been working with stepped back to give them space and for a moment Conrad was distracted by the hint of her breasts under her loose shirt.

"Donald's just radioed in," his father said, ignoring his son's temporary distraction. "He's about ten miles up the coast and he thinks he's found us a base. A deserted castle if you can believe it."

"Good," Conrad considered the chaos that still surrounded them. "The sooner we get this stuff under cover the better."

"The problem is that it's next to a not-so-deserted city. I'd like you to take another squad up to reinforce him. Donald's probably the closest we have to a First Contact Specialist, but I'd appreciate your views on the tactical situation."

"Of course."

His father placed his arm round Conrad's shoulders and drew him aside, lowering his voice. "And we have a problem. We've just lost both of the generators."

"What happened?" Conrad said, appalled. Without the generators they couldn't power the portal.

"Someone tried filling them up with gasoline instead of diesel."

"How did that happen?"

His father shrugged. "Apparently that's the only fuel we brought with us. And the person who did it wasn't aware of the difference. Kaito thinks he can fix one of the generators, *if* he can get a new supply of diesel."

Conrad shook his head. They just weren't getting a break.

"So you understand why it's imperative we establish good relations with the native culture," his father told him.

Which explained why, cold and wet, he was now carefully working his way around the foot of a steep hill early the next morning, and doing his best to avoid brushing more water down his neck from the sodden branches overhead. He paused for a moment to listen to the crash of waves against the unseen cliffs on his left, then froze as their forward scout lifted his arm in warning.

He let out a soft sigh of relief when Donald stepped forward from the shelter of a giant oak.

"Hello Conrad."

"Donald, you look like hell," Conrad said undiplomatically. There were deep shadows under his brother's eyes, and his skin looked like chalk.

"I haven't been sleeping well," his brother admitted.

"I don't think anyone's had a decent sleep since we got here," Conrad told him.

Donald didn't look convinced.

"So where's this castle you've found us?"

"It's this way," Donald said, turning and leading them up the hill.

It was a difficult climb through the dense vegetation and native heath that covered the side of the hill. Some of the bushes had leaves that were as sharp as barbed wire and Conrad, sucking a particularly painful cut on the back of his hand, was almost ready to suggest a breather when they suddenly broke out into the open.

"Will you look at that," Conrad's Dynand Squad Leader said softly, as she stared up at the massive walls that crowned the top of the ridge.

Conrad nodded silently. The derelict fortress facing them was huge. Behind its massive, outer brick-wall, which must be at least forty, forty-five feet in height, there were at least three more, each one larger than the one below.

"Think it'll do?" Donald asked dryly.

"I'm impressed," Conrad said sincerely. There were obvious signs of damage, the thirty-foot tree growing out of the top of the closest battlement for one, and in places the outer brick had simply disintegrated and washed away, leaving the wall's core of soil exposed, but none of that affected the sheer grandeur of what remained.

"Come and have a look inside," Donald said.

Once through the enormous gatehouse, which was almost as wide as the wall was high, Donald led them along the broad avenue that wound, corkscrew fashion, up the hill towards the central keep.

"So, how long has it been deserted, do you think?" Conrad asked.

The limed surface of the avenue was covered with a thick layer of mulch that muffled their footsteps as they approached the final wall.

"Two, three hundred years," Donald guessed. "Well before we contacted the line."

"What do you think happened?"

"I've no idea. There's no sign of any damage. But just wait till you see the view from the top," Donald said, pausing in front of the entrance to the keep that towered at least eighty feet over them.

"Is it safe?" Conrad asked nervously, looking up at the narrow steps built into the keep's inner wall.

"Safe as houses. Come on, I'll show you."

The muscles on the top of Conrad's thighs were screaming when they finally reached the top of the stairs. The sentry, positioned there, saluted smartly as the three of them appeared around the top of the steps, Conrad returning the salute with a grimace.

Donald grinned. "You need to get out more, Conrad. You're getting unfit."

"Thanks," Conrad said. Luckily for his male ego, his Dynand Squad Leader seemed to be moving just as stiffly as she moved past him, towards the edge of the battlement.

"My god, will you look at that!" she said.

Conrad followed the Squad Leader across to the edge of the battlement. The clouds had started to lift and across the Hellespont, only two miles away across the strait, the continent of Europe was emerging from the drizzle that still layered the far coast.

Below them, spread out along the shore facing the narrow strait, was the city Donald had reported finding. Automatically Conrad lifted his binoculars to his eyes.

"How many people?"

"Forty, sixty thousand?" Donald guessed.

Conrad nodded. From the look, that sounded about right.

The city stretched along one side of a harbor that was enclosed within two protective moles. On the land side, the city was protected by two deep ditches and a series of low earth embankments, reinforced by five brick redoubts. On the top of each redoubt Conrad counted six cannon, with what he assumed was their ammunition neatly stacked beside them under the protection of tarpaulins. Two short, stubby forts overlooked the harbor, with at least another thirty cannon each.

"The fishing fleet's out," Donald said.

Conrad nodded again. The harbor was nearly empty, with only two fat-bodied merchant ships, and three large galleys tied up at the quay. All of the galleys carried masts, the largest had three and what looked like about thirty-two oars.

"Have a look at the central plaza," Donald suggested.

Conrad shifted his glasses to the center of the city and its huge plaza, perhaps a hundred yards across. "Ah, I see what you mean," he said. The surface of the plaza was made up of hundreds of colored slabs, laid out in a gigantic map of Africa. Around the plaza was a series of low, flat buildings.

The most impressive building took up one entire side of the square. He suspected that building housed the city's administration, possibly a palace.

"So, what do you think?" Donald asked.

Conrad surveyed the road that snaked out from the town and along the coast, passing just below them. "I think we need to go and meet them."

It took about two hours to reach the road, by which time the clouds had lifted and the sun had started to dry out the puddles. Reaching the road, Donald immediately bent over to inspect its surface. As he did the five Dynand accompanying them took up a loose defensive position around them.

"What? Conrad asked, wondering what had caught Donald's attention.

"The line's not that advanced, no motorized vehicles."

"How can you tell?" Conrad said, looking down at the surface of the road, which appeared to be made up of densely packed two-inch broken stones

"The road. It's only been Macadamized, not sealed. It's a good surface, but it wouldn't hold up to motorized transport."

"Is that good or bad?"

"You tell me," Donald said, standing up, and brushing his hands off against the back of his trousers.

"Company," Conrad said warningly, as a small boy leading a flock of goats appeared over the crest of the hill in front of them. The boy let out a yelp as soon as he saw them and promptly took off in the direction of the city, deserting his flock.

"Do we wait here?" Donald asked.

Conrad shook his head. "Let's try and get a little bit closer," he said, waving the squad forward.

"I wish we didn't have to use the Kelsor Virus," Donald said, as they started towards the city. "It's just too damn dangerous getting it as an adult."

"We don't any choice," Conrad pointed out. "Not if we want to avoid another Decimation." The problem was that among the Empire's inhabitants the virus was passed from mother to unborn child through the bloodstream — in effect, everyone in the Empire had been inoculated before birth. Unfortunately that meant there hadn't been any reason to improve the method of transmission.

"That doesn't mean I have to like it," Donald said.

"Once we've established contact, how long do you think you'll need to create a basic vocabulary?" Conrad asked.

"Two, three days? I should have a better idea once we start but as I understand, it normally takes a day to get a basic vocabulary of five hundred words, and three days for the full thousand."

"That's running it pretty close."

Donald nodded. "I know."

"Leader," their radio operator said, holding up the radio's handpiece. "It's for you." It was the Squad Leader Conrad had left at the citadel.

"Thanks," he said, taking the handpiece. "Yes Daniella? Conrad here."

"Leader, there's about two hundred infantry moving out in your direction from the city."

That was quick, he thought; there was no way the goatherd could have got back to the city by then. "Roger that. All right everyone, we've got visitors. Parade ease!"

The five Dynand snapped to attention, then relaxed into parade ease, rifles held loosely across the body.

Donald quirked an eyebrow at his brother before coming to ease as well, hands held comfortably behind his back as they waited.

For once Conrad didn't feel the need to try and second guess himself. He'd done everything he could, and now all he could do was wait.

It didn't take long for the infantry they'd been warned about to arrive. They were wearing a uniform that consisted of a short-sleeved white linen shirt with a long, scarlet breechcloth that reached to the knees, sandals, feathered headdress, and bandoleer. Each soldier, about half of whom were black, carried what looked like a long, breech-loading flintlock, probably rifled.

The soldiers moved smoothly into a loose cordon around them, about twenty yards away, before coming to a halt.

"What now?" Donald asked quietly.

Conrad shrugged. "We wait, I guess."

Nothing seemed to happen for quarter of an hour, and Conrad was just wondering if he shouldn't try and do something when the radio operator handed him the radio handpiece.

"Conrad here."

"Another group has left the city in your direction," Squad Leader Daniella reported.

"How many?"

"Nine. And there's a boat leaving harbor."

"One of the galleys?"

"Affirmative. It's the big one."

Conrad frowned. Now why would they do that?

It didn't take long for the second group of nine to reach them, and when they came to a halt on the other side of the cordon they studied one another with interest.

Of the nine, five were guards, dressed and armed exactly as those already surrounding them. The other four, dark skinned and wearing ornate robes with bright, geometric patterns, were unarmed. One of the four was a young woman, and quite a fetching one at that.

"Donald, they're all yours," Conrad said, his eyes temporarily leaving the young woman to consider the three men who had accompanied her. Two were late middle aged, possibly merchants or senior bureaucrats, but the third was considerably older and looked to be in his late seventies. Despite his age his eyes were a bright and very disconcerting blue.

"Thanks bro," Donald said,

"You're the first contact expert," Conrad reminded him.

"Hardly that," Donald said with a snort. "Now I wonder where they're going," he said, as half of the soldiers surrounding them formed up and began to move off down the road.

"Probably to see if they find out where we came from," Conrad said. He turned to the radio operator. "You better warn Squad Leader Daniella to keep her head down, and ask her to relay the warning to my father."

"Well, I guess I better make a start," Donald said, as the radio operator bent to her task. Dumping his pack on the ground he pulled out the first of Seagul's first contact books. Opening it to the first page and holding it so the others could see he started to walk towards the group.

Conrad's attention switched back to the girl, who appeared to be studying him with intently. Seeing him looking at her, she lowered her eyes. A moment later she looked up from under her lashes, and seeing him still watching gave him a soft smile. Unabashed, Conrad continued to watch her. She had flawless, deep ebony skin and her hair, pulled back into a tight bun on top of her head, was held in place by two slivers of bamboo with small, silver handles. She was wearing a long, white cotton dress, inlaid with a fine golden thread that glinted in the sun.

Her attention was fixed on Donald for the moment, and the book he was holding. Turning her head she said something to the eldest of the group standing next to her. He nodded once, before moving forward to meet Donald. He was a small, wizened man with short, white curling hair that was worn cropped close to his scalp. Now closer, Conrad rapidly increased his age upwards.

They met about halfway between the two groups and Conrad watched Donald show him the picture on the first page.

"Man," Donald said, and flipping to the second page, "woman". Riffling the rest of the book's pages Donald indicated the size of the task facing them.

The elder turned and said something excitedly to the others, before holding out his hands for the book. After flicking through the pages he turned and there was a quick discussion between him and the young woman. Finally, something seemed to be decided and as the others withdrew back to the city he squatted down, and patting the ground next to him indicated that Donald should join him.

"Conrad," Donald said. "I'll need your help."

Conrad tore his gaze off the departing girl and back to the task in hand. With a sigh he moved forward to squat down next to his brother.

"Just think how much easier it would be if you could speak her language," Donald pointed out, opening the book back to the first page.

"I've never found that much of a problem," Conrad said.

About an hour later another party arrived from the city, with a large cart hauled by oxen. The cart carried a large, silk pavilion, and once it had been erected a short distance away, outside the cordon, the old man, whose name turned out to be Chengerai, indicated they should move to it.

"Leader."

"Yes, Kurslow," Conrad said, acknowledging the squad's medic as they made their way across to the pavilion, the outer cordon of soldiers keeping their distance as they moved with them.

"They may know who we are."

"What do you mean?" Conrad said, trying to keep his voice level.

"I've been watching, and they've been quarantining us, no one within sixty feet."

"Except him," Conrad said with a nod towards Chengerai.

"Who I suspect has entered quarantine with us."

"Thanks," Conrad said. So they suspected who they were. . . unfortunately he didn't know if that would make it easier, or not.

They'd bought stools and carpets out to line the pavilion and two servants waited to greet them, watching them approach with scared, nervous eyes. Oh yes, they knew who they were.

The translation progressed quickly and not even dusk stopped them as oil lamps were lit. Finally, at around ten, Conrad called a halt. "We need to take a break. Trying to learn a new language always gives me a headache. Tell Chengerai we can start again in the morning."

"Morning, yes," Chengerai said, without bothering for Donald to translate. "Food here. Learn again tomorrow." He grinned at them, then got up and gave them a small bow. "Talk good tomorrow."

"So how do you think it's going?" Conrad asked, as he unrolled his sleeping bag next to his brother's in a corner of the pavilion. Chengerai and the two servants were setting up their own camp beds on the other side of the pavilion.

"Good," Donald said. "We've covered most of the first five hundred. Tomorrow we'll get straight onto the medical terms. We'll need Kurslow for that."

"I'm impressed with Chengerai's memory," Conrad admitted, who was struggling to keep up with the old man.

"Almost eidetic," Donald agreed. "They've probably got an oral tradition."

Conrad hardly seemed to have got to sleep before the smell and gentle pop of frying fish woke him. The sun was barely above the horizon, and rain dripped unpleasantly down the pavilion's waterproofed walls.

"Breakfast," Chengerai said cheerfully.

"Shouldn't he still be asleep?" Conrad grumbled to Donald, struggling free of his bag. "He's old enough to know better."

"He's only seventy-five."

"Then you'd have thought he should have learned more sense by now."

"Diseases wait for no man," Donald said pleasantly.

"Thanks for reminding me."

More furniture had arrived during the night and breakfast, fried fish, bread, fruit, and cold meats had already been set up on a low table. In addition to the furniture, there was also a new arrival. A woman wearing a red gown and carrying a small, solid stethoscope on a gold chain around her neck, stood waiting next to the table. Oh yes, Conrad thought, Chengerai was very good. His guess was confirmed when Chengerai introduced them.

"Donald, Conrad, this is medic Amaka."

"We are pleased to meet you," Donald said.

Chengerai translated and Amaka bobbed her head politely, eyes fixed on the ground.

"Take food," Chengerai said, gesturing at the table.

Breakfast was quickly finished and seating themselves on the carpet in the center of the pavilion Donald started on the medical terms. The translation proceeded quickly and by eleven they had enough for Donald to explain about the Decimation, and the Kelsor Virus.

"You talk Council," Chengerai said, as soon as he understood.

"That would be good," Conrad agreed.

"I talk for you."

"Chengerai," Kurslow interrupted. "Until people have been inoculated we need to keep the contact between your people and ours to as little as possible."

"I see good," Chengerai said. He said something to Amaka who nodded. "You here, I go." He disappeared for only five minutes, however, and when he returned the lessons continued.

Conrad had expected it would be the Council which would approach them but an hour later a shout from one the soldiers brought Chengerai to his feet. "We go city," he announced.

The city appeared eerily deserted as they approached, with no one on the walls or, when they emerged through the main gate, anyone on the streets.

"No cheering crowds?" Donald whispered quietly, out of the side of his mouth.

"No anyone," Conrad replied, wondering what it said about the organizational ability of the society they now found themselves in. At least it boded well for getting the virus distributed — if they could persuade them to!

They were led along the main road towards the center of the city, across the deserted plaza to the palace. Without stopping, they were ushered inside, then marched through a series of steadily smaller courtyards until an enormous double wooden door finally blocked their way. The door was opened on their approach and in the courtyard beyond they stopped.

In the center of the courtyard was a small pond and fountain. Around it, the ground was covered with a deep layer of freshly raked pea gravel. Several low, stone benches were set around the fountain while the courtyard itself was surrounded on four sides by a covered walk.

Raising his eyes, Conrad immediately spotted the soldiers, long rifles in hand, positioned on the roofs around them.

"Donald, Conrad, Kurslow, come me," Chengerai said. "Others stay."

Conrad reinforced the order with a nod, before turning to the radio operator. "You better let Squad Leader Daniella know what's happening."

"Is good Princess is here," Chengerai said, as he led them through the maze of interlocking courtyards and open passages. "Else Council talk, talk, talk."

Conrad didn't know what Chengerai's position actually was, but it was obvious he had a lot of pull as they were shown straight into see the Council. The Council, of five, were seated behind an open U-shaped table in a small, circular plain white room. The young woman, whom they had already met, and who Conrad presumed was the 'Princess', was seated on an ornately carved wooden stool at the head of the table. Stationed like statues against the wall behind them were the ubiquitous guards.

A bench was set up across the open 'U' of the table facing the Council, and on Chengerai's gesture Conrad, Donald, and the two medics seated themselves on it.

Settled, Conrad studied the five other members of the Council. Two had been in the party that had met them outside the city, merchants or senior bureaucrats he'd thought at the time and he saw no reason to change his opinion. The other three, two of whom were female, seemed cut from the same cloth. Conrad almost felt at home, he'd been facing and outmaneuvering similar councils for the past ten years.

But then there was the Princess. Just who was she? He thought Chengerai had said she was visiting, but from where? It was obvious the others deferred to her, yet she was considerably younger, and among the others at the table she stood out like a fresh rose in a bowl of wizened prunes.

His eyes moved to her face to find that she had been studying him, and seeing him looking, she quickly shifted her gaze to Chengerai.

"Chengerai?" she said, turning her hand palm up.

"I translate," Chengerai said quietly before rising to his feet and bowing deeply. "Princess, members of the Council. These are Leaders Conrad and Donald Clemhorn and medic Kurslow, Death Walkers, from across time."

The room erupted into chaos as the guards started forward defensively and the Councilors recoiled to their feet. Only the Princess remained motionless. For a moment the world seemed to hold its breath, and then the Princess shook her head. "Peace," she said and slowly, hesitantly the Councilors settled back into their seats. The guards were more reluctant, and it was only after an imperious wave of her hand that they retreated back to their positions against the wall.

Donald shot his brother a glance and Conrad shook his head warningly.

"Is this correct?" she asked Conrad, Chengerai translating.

Carefully Conrad rose to his feet and following Chengerai's example bowed deeply. "Chengerai tells truth Your Highness."

She glared at Chengerai. "And you have brought them before us — why?"

"Because while their breath brings death, they carry the protection against that same death in their blood."

Which was as neat a way of describing it as any Conrad had heard.

"And why are you here?" she demanded turning back to Conrad.

Conrad considered the story he and his father had agreed on and instantly dismissed it. He didn't think anything but the utter truth would convince the Princess.

"Highness, my people are not the same as those who came through the portal a hundred years ago." Which was true enough as far as it went, as according to his father the entire expeditionary force had been wiped out. "We are refugees and seek your aid to reclaim our throne."

"And what do you offer for this aid?"

"Knowledge."

The Princess tapped her nose thoughtfully.

"Highness," Chengerai said.

She turned her gaze on the old man and raised an eyebrow.

"I brought this matter to the attention of the Council because the matter is urgent."

"Urgent?"

"For the protection they carry in their blood to work, it must be given now."

"How can we know if their protection is in fact protection, and won't kill us?" a councilor asked.

"Oh hush Petra," the Princess said. "We have them within our grasp. There is no reason for them to create such a story other than for it to be the truth."

"Highness," it was the councilor furthest away from them.

"The Lord Kimana," Chengerai whispered.

"Our safeguard during the time of the plagues was always to shun those who carried the death. Why should this be any different? Remember they admit to being Death Walkers."

"And if they do carry death on their breath then we are all dead. However, we had agreed that unlike the people of the Feather Serpent we would talk to these people."

"Highness, you still cannot be considering this." This time it was one of the two female Councilors. "At the very least we must test the truth of what they say."

Kurslow had been listening to the translation of the debate with increasing unease and lurched to his feet. "If you wait it will be too late. The virus, the protection, will only work if it is given before any symptoms appear. After that the protection works in fewer than fifty per cent of cases. Inoculations need to start now."

If Conrad hadn't been watching he'd have missed the Princess's look towards Chengerai, or the very slight roll of his head in response.

"Enough," she said, rising to her feet. "It is plain that if you listen to these people you would know this is not a trap. I will be the first to be inoculated." She stumbled over the unfamiliar word before recovering. "Chengerai, bring the strangers, I will be in my rooms."

"Who is she?" he asked Donald quietly as Chengerai gestured for them to follow him.

"Linele is daughter to the High King," Chengerai said. Despite his age, he seemed to have ears like a bat. "Long may he reign."

Conrad felt himself a little worried where his thoughts had been leading him. A high Princess indeed.

The Princess was waiting for them when they reached her room, seated on a low stool; and giving Conrad another hesitant smile indicated they should seat themselves on the ground beside her.

All settled, she turned to Chengerai and asked him a question.

"The Princess wishes to know what is needed," Chengerai translated.

Kurslow unlatched the lid to his medical kit and was just about to open it when Conrad dropped a hand on his shoulder.

"Wait," he said. Conrad had been watching the three guards standing behind the Princess. It was clear they were on edge, and he wasn't sure what their reactions to the kit's contents, particularly the scalpels, might be.

"Chengerai." He passed the kit across to the old man. "If you could?"

"I need a needle, a vial, and the strap," Kurslow said.

Chengerai passed him the three items he pointed out and quickly, and efficiently he found Conrad's vein and took the required sample.

"Now the hypospray," Kurslow said withdrawing the needle. Unhappily Conrad inspected the small bubble of blood that formed over the hole; he hated needles.

Amaka leaned over interestedly as Chengerai handed Kurslow the small, pistol-shaped injector. "How does it work?" she asked.

"It injects the required sample through the skin using high pressure," Kurslow said, as he transferred the vial into the back of the machine. "This vial gives it about a hundred shots, and there's no risk of cross contamination. The alternative is to simply to make two cuts and bind them together. This is much more efficient." He locked the lever into place and looked up at the Princess. "Right, I need your arm."

Conrad winced at the lack of title.

Good-naturedly she pulled the sleeve of her gown up.

The medic swiped the Princess's arm with an alcohol swab, held the injector against the skin and pressed the trigger. There was a soft 'whfft' and as he withdrew the device the Princess studied her arm. Apart from a slight redness there was no other sign of the injection.

"Is that it?" she asked as Chengerai held out his arm.

"That's it," Kurslow said, as he prepped the old man. "The important thing to remember is that you have to rest for the next couple of days, and take plenty of water. The problem is that you're not only taking the virus that will help you into your blood, but also any other number of diseases. You're going to be running a fever and the gods know what else for about a week. Don't tax yourself."

The Princess said something to Chengerai, who nodded. "The Princess wishes to know if what you have done is truly necessary?" he asked.

Conrad looked up at her. "Truly necessary," he said. "Without it, perhaps nine-tenths of you will die."

She nodded, satisfied at his tone, without waiting for Chengerai's translation, and said something to him.

"The Princess will order you be provided with all the assistance you require," Chengerai said. He frowned at his arm. "How long?"

"Before you start feeling its effects? Perhaps an hour or so."

Chengerai nodded. "You will need more than one injector?"

"We have more," Conrad said reassuringly.

The Princess said something, and rose to her feet.

"You must follow her," Chengerai said. "She will give the necessary orders."

CHAPTER 4

Naisre — Mainline
May 1980 (96AE)

Arnold studied the ceiling above his bed, as he had done every day for the past five months. This morning, it was as though he saw it through fresh eyes, and his gaze shifted to the reason for that change, the plain, green baize-covered Movak Scripture that had rested on his bedside table for the past week. Last night had been the final revelation, however, and for the first time he felt he understood the reason for what was happening to him.

Movak taught that life was the furnace in which one's soul was prepared for the afterlife, and now Arnold knew that the troubles that had affected him — Nedo's death, his own breakdown — had been sent to prepare him. His soul had been heated in the fires of torment before being quenched like a brilliant sword in the hospital's electrical therapies, and he was now ready for God's work.

Reaching across, he picked the book up, opening it to the passage he had marked last night.

Let my word be carried forth unto all the worlds of God — until all know my name. For when that has happened the gates of heaven will be opened and all the true soldiers of the faith will be brought home.

How had Movak known? How could he have known? The prophet had been born six-hundred-and-fifty years ago. The son of a Moorish conquistador and an Incan Princess, the only way he could have known of the time-front, and its myriad, separate worlds, was if God had truly spoken through him.

The click, click, click of shoes in the corridor outside disturbed his concentration and Arnold recognized Doctor Harris' distinctive step. What had brought the good doctor down to this end of the hospital this early in the morning? He normally didn't turn up until evening rounds. Arnold replaced the book on the stand as the door opened.

"Good morning Arnold," the doctor said.

"Herr Doktor," Arnold said politely. "What can I do for you?"

"You have visitors."

"Oh?" He hadn't had a visitor for over a month, and to tell the truth hadn't really missed them.

"It's Petro Raputa."

"Petro?" Despite himself he felt his interest tweaked. "What's Raputa doing here?"

"Perhaps you could ask him yourself."

Arnold considered the matter for a moment, before swinging his feet onto the floor and sitting up. "Where is he? The visitors' room?"

"No, my office."

Petro wasn't alone, and both he and his companion rose to their feet as the doctor opened the door and waved Arnold in ahead of him. Petro's companion was a small man with the coloring and the nose of a Mayan. He wore a turban and a dark blue, almost black uniform. Petro was wearing his black and silver house uniform. Seeing the two of them standing together made Arnold think of two ravens come to pick over his corpse. Had they come for him? Both wore their side arms in closed holsters

Doctor Harris started to close the door but Petro stopped him. "If we could have some time alone?" he said.

Doctor Harris looked unhappy but nodded, closing the door behind him as he left.

"Arnold, good to see you," Petro said as he removed his kepi. His normal shoulder length white-blond hair had been cut back to finger length, and he ran his fingers through it, unconsciously brushing it back from his forehead. The diamond eyes on the two silver jaguars he wore on either collar flashed coldly in the light. "Take a seat. I'm sorry it isn't under better circumstances."

Arnold shrugged. "It's not your fault. Who's your friend?"

"General Mullah Hssan of the Etehad Sho'mali," the stranger said with a small bow, his English almost lost in his accent.

"Peace be on your family," Arnold said, taking a seat.

"And yours. I hear you have been studying our faith?"

Arnold shrugged. "I don't suppose I have you to thank for the Movak Scripture that turned up in my room a week ago?"

The Mullah smiled. "It is the responsibility of any believer to spread the word of God."

"Let my word be carried forth unto all the worlds of God until all know my name," Arnold quoted.

The Mullah raised an eyebrow. "Exactly."

Arnold looked at Petro. "What did you want to see me about?"

"How do you feel?" Petro asked, as he placed the file he was holding on the desk and Arnold felt a sudden flash of anger as he realized the file was his. The anger must have shown in his eyes because Petro glanced at the file. "We have a job for you. I needed to see whether you're up to it."

"And am I?" Arnold asked.

"You tell me."

"It depends on the job."

"World Leader of Etu."

Arnold's mind stalled for a moment. He could actually feel everything stop, before suddenly lurching into motion again. For an instant his mouth tasted of buttered copper, something he hadn't experienced since they'd finished the electro-shock therapy. God not again, he couldn't go through that another time. His tongue buzzed with the sensation and he tried to relax. Carefully he took a deep breath and released it slowly.

"Why me?" he asked. "I'm sure there's a lot of people more qualified."

Petro was watching him carefully. "Not as many as you think. We need someone who can keep the line quiet, someone I can trust, someone who can work with our allies." He nodded at the Mullah.

"You need the Clemhorn name?"

"It would help," Petro admitted.

"And you trust me?"

"Is there any reason I shouldn't?"

Was there? He'd never understood Conrad's distaste for Petro. His own experience had left him with the view that Petro was no worse, and certainly no better than many other scions of the ruling houses.

He looked down at the signet ring he'd been unconsciously stroking. Just what loyalty did he owe the family who had left him here? He certainly wouldn't do a worse job than Conrad, and there was a fair chance he'd do a much better one. Certainly he'd do it with a lot more flair. And then there was the fact that if he refused the offer the Raputas would simply offer the position to someone else and Nona's legacy would be lost.

"No," Arnold said. "If I give my word I will keep it."

"That's what I thought," Petro said, satisfied. "But just in case, General Mullah Hssan will serve as your liaison with Etehad Sho'mali forces on Etu, and your link with Naisre."

"My commissar in other words."

Petro conceded the point with shrug. "Hssan, do you want to say anything?"

The Mullah leaned forward. "Arnold, what is your view of the Movak Scripture?"

"It's a pretty amazing book."

"It would be impossible for the word of God to be anything else."

Arnold gave a short nod. Perhaps here, at last, was someone who would understand what he had been looking for, and more importantly — found. "It seems to talk directly to me, to explain what happened to me."

"In the fires of the furnace let your soul be cleansed and strengthened," the Mullah said.

"For only then will you be ready to hear the word of God," Arnold finished for him.

The Mullah nodded. "I'm impressed. Perhaps we could talk further about this. My role will also include supervision of the missionary work undertaken by my master's forces on Etu. I would be honored to work with you on deepening your knowledge of the faith."

"The honor would be mine," Arnold said. Something had been niggling at him and he turned to Petro. "Do you have any word on my family?" he asked.

"Nothing on your father or either of your brothers. We suspect they're together. We're not sure about your sister at this stage, but your mother has been arrested and is presently in our custody."

"Will that be a problem?" the Mullah asked, studying him closely.

Was it? "No," Arnold said, deciding.

"Let's go then," Petro said, standing up. "My father will need to take your oath but I imagine you could be back on Etu tomorrow."

"If I could make one suggestion," the Mullah said quickly.

"Of course," Petro said.

"I believe, given Arnold's interest in the faith, that I would like him to meet my master, the Caliph. It would mean it would be a week before he could get to Etu, but I don't necessarily see that as a bad thing."

Petro considered the Mullah for a moment, before nodding. "Agreed."

"Just like that?" Arnold said, shocked by the rapidity with which everything was occurring.

"Just like that," Petro confirmed with a smile. "That is one thing that you will learn to appreciate about the Raputas, once we make our mind up, things happen."

CHAPTER 5

Bathre — Mmbuto é Line
May 1980 (96AE)

"How is she?" Donald asked, as Chengerai came out of the room.

"Better. There is no sign of the fever's return and she rests comfortably."

Beside him, Conrad let out a deep sigh of relief. Standing up he rolled his shoulders, trying to relax them. "I'm going for a walk," he announced.

Donald watched him go with a small smile, feeling some consolation that he wasn't the only one suffering because of his love life. The thought of Matija, and their unborn child, still ruled his thoughts, but at least he was starting to be able sleep through the night again. There was no question, that the past three weeks had been particularly hard on his brother as Linele had fought off the effects of a reaction against the virus.

Not that it had been easy for any of them, he thought, and he still didn't know what would have happened if she had died. The Mmbuto é was a mercantilist culture, a society where everything was subject to the market, and its laws of supply and demand: but despite their apparent rationality Donald had detected a streak of fanaticism to their relationship with the High King, and his family. At least the Princess' reaction had been delayed for a couple of days, allowing them to finish inoculating the city's population.

"I suppose this means the quarantine will be lifted soon?" Donald said.

Chengerai nodded. His English had improved to such an extent that it seemed impossible he had been studying it for only three weeks. "The Council was only waiting on news of the Princess."

"I'm sorry," Donald said, genuinely regretful that their arrival had caused so much trouble.

"It's all in God's hands. Besides, the death toll has been less than the last outbreak of plague we had, and it will certainly rid us of any trouble from the barbarians to the north."

"That's one way of looking at it," Donald admitted.

"It would be wise to remember that from the Council's point of view it is the only way of looking at it," Chengerai pointed out. "Everything must be shown as either a profit or a loss."

"I'm afraid I'll never be able to understand how everything in your system has a price," Donald admitted. "Although, perhaps not everything," he said, with a significant look towards the Princess' door.

"No, perhaps not everything," Chengerai agreed, following his glance.

"So, how much longer do you think it will be before the Council agrees to allow us to leave for Rufiji?" he asked, referring to the High King's capital. His father had been trying to negotiate a departure date for over a week now.

"They agreed earlier this morning. I need to speak to the World Leader, as the Council has asked you to travel via Ngoni. There have been reports of a new plague in Egypt and we are eager to see how effective your Kelsor Virus is against it. In addition, the Princess has suggested that I accompany you."

"That would be useful," Donald said. His own skills in the language were still very rudimentary. Besides, he genuinely enjoyed the company of the old man, who had been a warrior in the great wars of northern conquest before (in his own words) taking up the role of historian-scholar, and general layabout in his retirement. He now drifted from place to place in an attempt to see as much as he could have of life before the gods took him home.

They found Donald's father in the suite that had been set aside for them in the far northern corner of the palace.

"How is she?" he asked, coming to his feet as they entered the room.

Donald hid a small smile, there was only the one 'she' that everyone was concerned about.

"The Princess has broken her fever and sleeps normally," Chengerai said.

Donald was not surprised to see the relief on his father's face.

"Do you want any assistance to transport your stores?" Chengerai asked.

"That would be appreciated," the World Leader said. "The Council has just given us permission to use that disused fortress you discovered," he explained to Donald. "There are a couple of conditions on what we can do there, and they've insisted on having observers stationed there, but that won't cause any problems. We are only what we claim to be," he pointed out to Chengerai.

Chengerai turned the palms of his hands out. "I am merely a teller of stories for children," he said. "What do I have to do with the decisions of Council?"

The World Leader snorted and Donald could not stop a grin appearing on his own face. Chengerai might indeed be a teller of children's stories, but that was not all he did. The Mmbuto é was an oral culture, and the role of an historian was an important and influential one. They were the gatekeepers of history, and a good one, such as Chengerai, was deeply respected for his knowledge, and advice.

"Chengerai was just saying the Council has agreed to let us leave for Rufiji," Donald said. "They've asked us to go via Ngoni though."

His father nodded. "I'd heard — they've got the plague. Conrad and I need to stay on for a couple of days to finish organizing things here, but I'd like you to lead the first team, Donald. You'll have Kurslow and Defella. We'll follow on in a week or so. That should also make the Council happier." Donald realized he was referring to the fact that the two could be considered as hostages. "But the sooner I've had the opportunity to meet with the High King, the better."

Chengerai nodded. "The Princess has asked me to travel with you and I have negotiated passage with one of the merchants on your behalf. The Captain is eager to leave as soon as the quarantine is lifted."

Now, as the ropes were cast off and the crew unshipped their oars, Donald could see other vessels also starting to ready themselves for departure. The crew members carried the Kelsor Virus in their blood and, with instructions on how to spread it, there would be no further delay.

The boat they were traveling on normally carried wine south, and manufactured goods north, but on this trip it was carrying wool for the Egyptian looms. There was little room for passengers, so the three of them were quartered with the crew.

After stowing his pack, Donald returned to the deck, hoping that the feel of the spray against his face would lift his mood. Unfortunately the sky was leaden and it seemed that with every step on this journey he was traveling farther from Matija. He was dispiritedly watching the fort on the northern mole disappear into the distance behind them when Defella joined him. She was still wearing her light green uniform with its woolen bonnet, but had rolled up the legs of her trousers and swapped her boots for sandals.

"Looks like the Captain's trying to make up for lost time," she remarked, as the crew tightened the sail.

Donald nodded. "The quarantine must have played merry hell with his schedule. At least wool isn't something that's going to spoil."

There was a silence as both watched the wind fill the canvas, sending the ship surging ahead. "You know, I sailed on one of these once," Defella remarked. "Or at least something very like it."

"On Dynand?"

"Yes. When I was eighteen, I worked my passage from Kernowek down to Ikhaya — that would be from England down to the Cape on the Mainline."

"And what was it like?" Donald asked.

"The happiest time of my life," she said simply. "For just over a month I had absolutely no responsibilities."

"Not quite the same as now?"

"No, not quite the same," she responded with a tight smile as her gaze returned to the horizon.

Donald gave a small sigh.

"Thinking of home?" she said.

Donald nodded. "I just wish I knew what was happening there."

"At least I know my family is safe," Defella said.

Donald nodded. Following the coup Defella's mother was the World Leader of Dynand and the rank would give them some protection. Matija didn't have that advantage — all she had was her anonymity.

They continued to look out over the sea until Defella looked up at the rapidly graying sky and shivered. "I hope that isn't a storm coming up."

"Do you think it might be?" Donald asked.

"I'm not sure. Come on, let's head below, I'm getting cold."

Unfortunately Defella's fears concerning the storm proved correct, and they were woken shortly before midnight by a sudden change in the pitch of the boat.

Groggily, Donald realized he could hear shouting on deck, and that Defella was climbing out of her hammock. "What is it?" he asked, still half asleep.

"I'm just going to find out," she said. "Stay here."

Fat chance, Donald thought, as he swung his feet out the hammock and followed her on deck. As he stepped out into the cockpit, the hatch was torn from his grasp by the wind. Rain lashed his face, and a sudden gust made Donald flinch under its force. By the time he'd managed to latch the hatch closed behind him the rain was so bad he could barely make out Defella talking with the Captain, even though he was less than ten feet away.

Now he knew what a drowned rat must feel like — Donald thought — the water was freezing and it was almost impossible to keep his balance. The boat lurched as a wave broke over its bow, water pouring down the deck to tug at his feet, and through a break in the rain, Donald got a clear view of their surroundings for the first time. His stomach clenched as he saw the size of the waves that towered over the boat on all sides, their blue-green depths frothed and lathered with white. Beside them, the boat seemed a mere toy.

Behind him, the hatch crashed open as two more crew appeared on deck. Donald pressed himself back into the shelter of the wall out of their way, then once they had passed, struggled to relatch the door behind them as water swirled about his feet.

The hatch finally secured, he turned back to watch in horrified fascination as the full fury of the storm vented itself against the ship. Overhead, the wind shrieked through the rigging as sheets of pelting rain swept back and forth across the exposed deck and waves crashed over its stern, plunging it deep under the surface.

Defella had finished her shouted, and probably completely misunderstood conversation with the Captain, and was working her way back towards Donald when an enormous wave broke over the side of the boat. For a moment, she disappeared under its mass. Donald opened his mouth to call for help, but even as he did so, the wave retreated, water pouring off the deck in a flooding cascade. Defella emerged unscathed from the chaos it left behind it, hands securely wrapped around a rope.

"I thought you were staying below," she said, clambering down next to him.

"What did the Captain say?" Donald said.

She shrugged. "It's a bad blow. He wanted me out of the way."

Donald had just started to turn, to open the door, when he felt the boat lurch badly and heard Defella swear.

"What's wrong?" he demanded, but by then he'd also seen the mainsail, which had been heavily reefed, flapping in the wind, threatening to split itself against the mast. More importantly, it had also caught the wind and was dragging the boat round.

One of the sailors had already seen the danger and was struggling to reef it back in but the wind was too strong for him. With an oath, Defella vaulted out of the cockpit and a moment later was struggling to help him.

Goddamn, Donald thought and followed her out into the full force of the gale. The wind hit him like a physical blow and he staggered, slipping on the deck to land hard on one knee. He gritted his teeth against the pain and grabbed a rope to pull himself up again as water swirled around him, trying to spill him across the deck. As he was straightening up he saw another wave rearing over the boat, almost overreaching the top of the mast. He screamed a warning to the two working on the sail, but his voice was lost in the wind and as if in slow motion he could only watch as the wave broke over the side of the boat. He didn't even have time to take a breath before he was slammed back against the deck by the solid wall of water that crashed down on him. It buried him under its weight, pounding him against the deck, and he held onto the rope he had in his hands for dear life.

He could feel his fingers starting to lose their grip and there was nothing he could do. He was out of breath, his lungs burned, and the cold weakened his grip. Had the boat foundered? Surely it should have surfaced by now. Then suddenly, with a lurch, it broke back through the surface of the water, and coughing and spluttering, he lay stunned on the wood as water streamed away from him on all sides. His lungs still burning, he tried to push himself back to his knees, only to discover that his left hand wouldn't respond. He peered through the rain at the flapping sail but both Defella and the sailor had disappeared.

Another sailor appeared, almost lost in the sleeting rain, and Donald forced himself the rest of the way to his feet and staggered over to join him. A moment later Defella reappeared, hauling herself to her feet, and between the three of them they were able to control the sail enough to lash it down again. Once it was secure Donald had just enough energy to lean exhaustedly over the edge of the rail, and to peer out into the raging storm for any sight of the missing sailor. There was nothing. Just the sleeting rain and the heaving ocean.

Defella rested a hand on his shoulder, and when Donald tiredly turned his head to look, she glanced at his arm then jerked her head back to the cabins. Donald resisted the obvious order for a moment before heading below with an exhausted nod, knowing there was nothing more he could do. By the time Defella pulled the hatch closed behind them he was trembling with cold and the beginning of shock.

"What's happening?" Kurslow demanded, one hand braced against an overhead beam to steady himself against the heaving deck, his head bent to avoid banging it on the ceiling.

Chengerai peered at him from out of his hammock. His small, wizened face was pinched and drawn, and Donald had the strange, unbidden thought that for the first time since he'd met him, Chengerai looked his age.

"It looks like Donald's broken his arm," Defella said.

Is that what he'd done, Donald thought foggily. The boat lurched under a wave and he stumbled against the wall. His left arm slammed into the beam and he barely stopped himself from shrieking.

"We need to get you out of those clothes," Kurslow said.

Donald nodded dumbly, and started to pick uncertainly at his jacket with his right hand, but his fingers, numbed by the cold and the rain, didn't seem able to respond. His hand started to shake and he looked at it, puzzled. What was he supposed to do now?

"Here," Kurslow said, helping him, as he started to shiver violently.

A moment later his wet clothes were puddled on the floor and he was wrapped in a scratchy but dry woolen blanket, and starting to feel warmer for the first time in what seemed ages.

"Now sit," Kurslow said, as he and Defella helped him back into the hammock. "Right, let's have a look at that arm."

As his fingers gently probed at the injury Donald simply collapsed.

Donald watched the wave rearing over the boat as he screamed a warning to Defella. He felt the wind blowing the words back in his face, then watched the wave break over the side of the boat, smothering him under its weight.

The water was crushing him against the solid wall of the deck, burying him under its weight, pounding him against the solid surface of the wooden deck, and once again he could feel his fingers starting to slip on the rope.

He woke, gasping for breath and frightened by the intensity of the dream.

"Good morning Leader." It was Kurslow looking down at him. The expression of concern on the medic's face told Donald it hadn't been a dream.

"How's the ship?" he asked. From the lack of pitching the storm had passed.

"In good shape according to the Captain, and thanks, in part, to your actions in tethering the sail," Chengerai said.

Donald raised his arm and peered at the inflatable half-cast that covered his forearm. "What happened?"

"You fainted, luckily. Made things much easier for us to set the bone. It looks like a clean break so you'll need to keep the cast on for only six to eight weeks. Your father asked to speak to you when you were awake."

"Oh," Donald said, swinging his legs out of the hammock, then pausing to collect his balance.

"Take your time," Kurslow said. "There's no hurry."

Donald looked around doubtfully. "Where's my clothes?"

Kurslow reached back into the hammock beside him and produced Donald's spare uniform. "You may need some help to get dressed," he suggested.

Donald considered the cast dubiously, and nodded. "Six weeks you said?"

"At least," Kurslow said cheerfully.

***

The storm had blown them well off course, and it took them a couple of days longer than planned to reach the mouth of the Nile, and the port of

Ngoni. The black plague flag was flying as they entered the harbor around noon, the stench of death riding the wind to greet them even before they berthed.

The small party was escorted directly to the Chairman's palace, disturbing him in the middle of his solitary lunch. Despite the hour, four braziers were burning in the room, adding a bitter, citric stink to the stench of the charnel house from outside.

"Chengerai, you old goat," the Chairman said, rising to his feet. A tall, rather stout man, his dark face was masked with a heavy white, swirling tattoo. "I wondered who'd been stupid enough to break the quarantine. What are you doing here?"

"Come to save your miserable hide," Chengerai told him with a grin, grasping his arm. "Tenda, this is Donald Clemhorn and medic Kurslow."

Tenda acknowledged the introductions with a puzzled nod.

"I have a message for you from Linele, in the voice of the High King," Chengerai said, reaching into the small satchel he carried and pulling out the clay tablet Linele had pressed her seal into before they left. The date was still operational to one month in the future.

"You were trusted that long," Tenda said, looking at the date.

Chengerai looked offended.

Tenda slapped him on the back. "I was only joking. What's the message?"

Chengerai closed his eyes, clasping his hands together in front of his chest. "To the Council of Ngoni, greetings." Donald tried to hide his start at the sound of Linele's voice issuing from Chengerai's mouth. "Know that the one who stands with Chengerai has a remedy for the plague, and is under the protection of the High King. Act as he wishes, and provide all assistance to facilitate his passage to the Capital. Linele, in the voice of the High King."

Tenda suddenly looked hopeful. "Really? A remedy," he said.

Chengerai opened his eyes and gestured for Donald to speak. Donald nodded. "My companions and I carry a defense against the plague in our blood."

"But there are only two of you," Tenda pointed out. "And I doubt your white blood is thick enough to dilute for the entire city."

"The crew of our boat also carries the defense," Chengerai said. "If you could call your medics together we will discuss with them how best to distribute it."

"Of course, I'll do it straight away." When he returned Tenda carried three flagons of wine. "You'll join me in a toast? I had been wondering how long I had before the plague visited me and mine, and now you bring me news of relief."

"It is not without its perils," Donald warned him. "Some do not survive the treatment."

Tenda looked at Chengerai thoughtfully. "If this old man can take it, then so can I."

The inoculation proved a massive task, the first part of which was to protect the medics themselves. Luckily it seemed as though the effect of obtaining the virus from the native crew had diluted any adverse reaction. Only one of those inoculated suffered any complications, and Donald suspected that in her case it was because she had already been infected with the plague.

As soon as the medics had been protected, the team moved out into the city to begin the inoculation of the general population.

The city was a warren of small alleys and crooked side-streets, all filled with a sweet, sickly stench. Donald immersed himself in the task, wondering as he did so whether he was undertaking some sort of penance for the gassing on Dontfrey, when he had been unable to help.

For a time it seemed that nothing would stem the plague, that the entire city would become a charnel house; but gradually the battle tilted in favor of the living, and slowly the mood of the city began to lighten in response.

On the fifth day, the Council lifted the quarantine and the city came out to inspect its wounds. The day after that, the ship bearing his father, Conrad, and the Princess berthed in the harbor.

CHAPTER 6

Ngoni — Mmbuto é Line
May 1980 (96AE)

Conrad worked his way across the deck towards his father, trying to stay out of the way of the crew who were preparing to make harbor. "Can you see Donald?" he asked his father, peering at the horde who appeared to be waiting for them on the pier.

His father shook his head. "Not yet, we're still a bit far away."

"Your radio is certainly a useful device," the Princess said, coming to stand beside them.

"If you like welcoming committees," Conrad said sarcastically.

"When the alternative is to wait on board until one is gathered, your radio is a great asset," she said calmly. "It would be unthinkable for the daughter of the Living God to land without being met formally."

"A catastrophe," Conrad agreed solemnly, to be rewarded with a dazzling smile.

A couple of minutes later the boat berthed at the pier with just the merest of thumps.

Chengerai and a tall, grizzled man with one of the most complete face tattoos Conrad had ever seen were the first on board.

"Chairman Tenda," Linele said politely.

"Princess, welcome back to Ngoni," Tenda said, pressing the palm of his right hand to his forehead and bowing deeply. "World Leader," he said, turning to Conrad's father and giving a slightly shallower bow. "Your son has told me a lot about you."

"Sir," Brian said with a polite nod of his head.

"I hope to be able to talk with you before you depart; this idea of parallel histories fascinates me."

Conrad watched his father's eyes glaze as he struggled to remember the words. "I would be honored," he said finally.

Conrad shared a grin with his brother who had just stepped on board, Defella close behind him. Their father's lack of language skill was standing joke between them. Then his eyes caught sight of the cast on Donald's arm and he frowned, wondering when Donald had done that, and more importantly why he hadn't said anything about it on the radio.

"Chairman Tenda," Linele said. "I trust my rooms are ready. I would appreciate the opportunity to refresh myself before you brief me on the situation."

"Of course, Princess. I shall escort you personally."

"Chengerai," she said, acknowledging the wiry historian before sweeping ashore, quickly followed by her maidservants and guards.

As the last of the guards disappeared towards the Chairman's palace, Brian pulled his youngest son into a hug. "What happened to your arm?"

"I broke it during the storm."

Defella gave a snort. "He broke it saving the boat during the storm."

Donald shrugged, embarrassed. "If anyone saved the boat it was Defella."

His father looked backward and forward between the two of them, then obviously decided it was going to be too complicated to get to the bottom of it just then. "You're okay though."

"Kurslow said it was a clean break. I just have to wear this thing for another five weeks." He scowled at the cast to demonstrate what he thought of that idea. "So what are we doing now?"

"Linele is going to arrange a boat for us," Conrad said. "She felt that her father, the High King, should be told of events as soon as possible."

"And this has now been done," Chengerai said, re-joining them. "We will be leaving tomorrow."

***

The next day, shortly before dawn, their galley slipped out of harbor on the morning tide. Around midday it entered the entrance to the Mombesi Canal, and, eager to get a better view of their progress, Conrad joined his brother at the bow.

"Feeling better?" Donald asked, as Conrad clambered up the short staircase to join him.

"A little," Conrad said, who in hindsight thought he had probably drunk a little too much of the millet beer at the reception the previous night. "You could look better. How are you feeling?"

Donald shrugged. "I'm all right."

"So tell me," Conrad said.

"Tell you what?" Donald said, avoiding his brother's eyes.

"Whatever's been bothering you since we came through the portal."

For a moment, Conrad thought Donald would dodge the question, as his eyes never left the low-lying sand-flats that lined the edges of the canal, but finally he gave a sigh.

"I'm going to be a father."

"Oh." Conrad wasn't sure what he had thought Donald was going to say but it wasn't that. "Who? Ah Matija?"

Donald nodded.

"Congratulations," Conrad finally remembered to say.

"Yeah, sure," Donald said bitterly.

Conrad raised an eyebrow. "What's bugging you?"

"Well, just look at us. Do you really think we're ever going to get back, that I'll ever see Matija again?"

Conrad considered the question seriously; somehow he didn't think Donald would accept a flippant answer.

"Well?" Donald demanded.

"Yes, somehow or other, we will."

"Because, what did you say, you're not going to let that snot of a Raputa think he's beaten a Clemhorn?"

Conrad gave him a small smile at having his own words fed back to him. "There is that," he admitted. "But really, I think it's because we owe the Empire. I know without it we wouldn't be who we are. And I know that I gave my oath of loyalty to the Empire, and I intend to honor it."

"My brother, the patriot," Donald said dryly.

Conrad admitted the jibe with a shrug. "Besides," he said, "Miro cheated, and we shouldn't let him get away with it."

"And now the real reason comes out."

Conrad pulled a face, not prepared to admit, even to himself, the depth of his patriotism.

"It's hard, though," Donald said.

"I know," Conrad said, putting an arm around his brother's shoulders. "But it won't be forever."

"Well, let's hope not."

"So, where are we?" Conrad asked, looking out at the dunes that lined the canal, stretching off in both directions as far as the eye could see.

"The Mombesi Canal," Donald said, apparently just as happy to change the subject. "Chengerai said it was built five hundred years ago by the Ngoni Free Trade consortium to link the Mediterranean and Red Seas. The Consortium went bankrupt but the Canal was taken over by the State. Apparently it's been a nice little earner ever since."

"Five hundred years ago?"

"That was my reaction," Donald admitted.

"I'm impressed."

"Just wait till you see the Nile-Congo Canal then."

Conrad's face must have shown his confusion.

"You haven't heard? Somehow they managed to run a canal up the entire length of the Nile to Lake Victoria, and from there, to put a tunnel through to the Congo."

"Now that what would be something to see," Conrad agreed.

It took them just over a day to reach the Red Sea, and once free of the canal they settled down to the long, hard slog along the east coast to their destination at the mouth of the Rufiji River, twenty days away. Despite the opportunity the trip gave him to explore his developing relationship with Linele, an opportunity he was amused to find was always carefully chaperoned, Conrad found himself champing at the delay. His frustration was not improved when, upon arriving at the mouth of Rufiji, he discovered they still had another twenty-four hours to get through the mangroves that lined the river's delta.

"Glaring isn't going to make us go any faster," Donald said with a smile, joining him at the bow.

"No, but it makes me feel better," Conrad said, slapping at a mosquito. He inspected the smear of blood on his arm before flicking the remains of the mosquito off. "How much longer till we reach the port?"

"Chengerai said we should almost be there."

Conrad wrinkled his nose. "Gods, this place stinks."

"It's a swamp, Conrad, it's supposed to smell. So how are you and Linele getting on? You seem to have spent a lot of time with her during this trip."

"What else was there to do?" Conrad said, hiding the deepening attraction he felt for the dusky Princess under a veneer of humor.

Donald's eyes suddenly widened.

"What?" Conrad said, looking up to see what had attracted Donald's attention, and finding that the galley had finally managed to struggle free of the mangroves and was gliding across an enormous expanse of open water towards a city that rose out of the river like the tiers of a wedding cake.

A massive, outer wall of enormous, dark-gray granite blocks enclosed a harbor that must have been at least a mile across at its widest. Most of the blocks must have weighed more than thirty tons, and yet they were placed with a symmetrical precision that left Conrad wondering how the builders had managed it. Inside this wall an inner second barrier separated the harbor from the city proper, which rose up on either side of the river in a series of white marble layers.

The water in the harbor was black, its surface a perfect millpond, reflecting the palms planted around its perimeter. Brightly colored canvas awnings provided shade from the sun, in a rainbow of colors that rose through the tiers.

"What do you need those for?" Conrad asked Chengerai, as the galley backed oars to bring them into the quay, pointing at the cannon protruding through the embrasures of the two immense towers on either side of the harbor mouth.

"Pirates," Chengerai said. "From Malagasy. They were all but wiped out a hundred years ago, but they've become steadily bolder over the last couple of years. It's probably time for the High King to be thinking of another campaign."

"If they aren't provided with the virus then there wouldn't be any need for a campaign," the World Leader pointed out.

Chengerai looked thoughtful.

A customs official boarded the boat as soon as it was secure, and upon recognizing the Princess, salaamed deeply. "Your Highness, we were not told of your arrival."

She nodded. "Is the High King here?"

"Yes Highness," he replied, his eyes still fixed on the ground. "He arrived a fortnight ago."

"Good," she said. "This galley is under quarantine. No one is to leave, or to board the ship until I have spoken to my father."

"Highness?" he said, looking up.

"We came from Ngoni and there is the possibility we have brought the plague with us."

"But you weren't flying a warning," he said. To Conrad it sounded as though he was more concerned at the breach in regulations than at the actual possibility of plague.

"There are no cases among us," she told him, "which is why I must speak to the High King at once. Captain."

The galley's Captain stepped. "Highness?"

"We should be back by nightfall, make sure no one leaves before I return. Chengerai and the World Leader will accompany me."

"Princess?" Conrad said hesitantly.

She looked at him for a moment then nodded. "Conrad and medic Kurslow as well."

With the royal guard formed up about the small party they started the long walk up the hill towards the palace. Around them Rufiji's crowded streets seemed to pulsate like something out of the fabled south and the legends of Prester John. Bantu warriors from the Congo in ornately embroidered loincloths and ostrich headdresses pressed shoulders with Phoenician traders from the deep south in their long white robes and curled beards. Broad-nosed women from the Arabic peninsular peddled fruit and nuts from street stalls, and everywhere silver and gold glittered in the tropical sun. A sudden, dazzling flash of light from what seemed a solid wall of gold bracelets hung across the mouth of an alley caused Conrad's eyes to water.

Despite the crowd that filled the streets they progressed quickly, people moving back out of their way to prostrate themselves on the ground before the Princess.

"Is it always like this?" Conrad whispered quietly out of the corner of his mouth to Chengerai, as silence seemed to wash before them, stilling the conversation as the crowds parted around them like a wave.

"Always," came the murmured answer.

"I'm surprised at how clean everything is," Brian said quietly, as he stepped over a deep channel filled with clear, running water, cut into the center of the road.

"Oxen aren't allowed in the main streets between dusk and dawn," Chengerai said. "And street sweepers operate throughout the night."

"I'm impressed," the World Leader said.

"You should be, given the cost to the public purse," Chengerai said.

Conrad noticed Linele's mouth twitch in a quickly suppressed smile.

They finally emerged from a shadowed street, overhung by tall buildings, into a huge plaza thronged with people. The palace, a massive four-story edifice behind a facade of red and white checked marble columns, faced them across the square, taking up two sides of the plaza. Four colossal fountains occupied the plaza's corners and mobile stalls had been set up next to them selling crushed ice and fruit juice. Conrad's mouth watered, as it had been a long, hot walk up from the boat, but the Princess led them past without stopping.

The Captain of the Guard was waiting for them with a small honor party of ornately garbed guardsmen. Each Guardsman wore a long saffron kilt with a heavy cuirass over a dark blue, sleeveless jacket. Long greaves covered their shins and they wore an open-faced styled helmet with a single red and white dyed ostrich feather. In addition to the halberds each carried, they wore a sword and small pistol slung from a wide utility belt worn over one shoulder.

Conrad wondered what they were. The guards looked Mediterranean in origin with olive skin rather than the deeper black of Linele's own guard.

"The Carthago Guard," Chengerai said quietly.

"Ah," Conrad said. Carthago, located on the Mainline equivalent of Cape Town had been settled by Carthagian refugees from the Punic Wars almost two and half thousand years before, and according to Chengerai had been part of the Mmbuto é for nearly five hundred years.

After checking them for weapons the additional guards fell in around them, escorting them into the palace.

Conrad's first sight of the High King was of a young man wearing only a long leopard skin breechcloth and a heavy gold necklace sprawled across his throne, talking languidly to one of his courtiers in a crowded courtyard shaded by a number of tall, overhanging eucalypts. The courtyard was arranged in a series of raised tiers, which flowed upwards towards the throne.

As the Princess appeared, conversation abruptly stilled and one of the guards leaned forward to whisper something in the High King's ear. The High King, startled by the interruption, looked up and Conrad was shocked to realize that the High King was only about eighteen, considerably younger than Linele, his presumed daughter.

"Welcome daughter," the High King said. "Chengerai, I see you have decided to grace my court with your presence again."

"Majesty," Chengerai said, giving a deep salaam. "The splendor of your form is so great that I fear it has dimmed my eyes and I will have to be led by the hand for the rest of my life."

"Always the perfect courtier," the High King said, laughing. "I've missed you, you old scallywag."

Chengerai said nothing, but Conrad knew he was pleased.

"And daughter, we did not expect you back so soon. Who are your companions?"

"Father, may I request the opportunity to address you in private? Urgently."

Conrad thought he might be the only one to realize how nervous she was.

"Of course," the High King said, raising an eyebrow enquiringly. He gestured and the courtyard immediately started to clear. "Now what is it that cannot be discussed in open court?" he asked once everyone had left except for the guards.

"Father, you asked who my companions were. May I introduce World Leader Brian Clemhorn, his eldest son, Conrad, and medic Kurslow of the Cross-Temporal Empire."

"Cross-Temporal?"

Chengerai coughed. "It appears, Majesty, that our musings on the Death Walkers were correct. They did come from a place across time."

At the mention of the Death Walkers the guards started forward protectively but the High King held up his hand, freezing them in place.

"And these are they?" For someone as young as he was, Conrad found the High King's total impassivity frighteningly impressive.

"Not precisely, Majesty. You remember that we have theorized that there are other places where history took a different path from here, for example, where your great-grandfather fell at Bantu and the Empire remained divided."

"Or my father did not suffer his accident? Yes, I remember our discussions. You told me they were barren logic without the means to prove their existence."

Chengerai nodded. "And so it was until now, but these people come from an Empire which consists of several of these 'Lines', as they call them."

"The title of World Leader would appear to be of some importance," the High King said, and Brian inclined his head in assent. "But the size of your retinue does not seem to match that importance," he continued.

Conrad's father started to speak but the High King held up a hand to stop him. "That can wait. You requested to speak to me as a matter of urgency?" he said to Linele.

"It is the plague, my father. They carry the disease on their breath."

"And you brought them here," the High King said to the Princess, his tone suddenly that of tempered steel. This time he did not raise his hand to halt the guards who moved protectively in front of him. "Why?"

"Oh, Father of the Empire," she said dropping to her knees, and touching her head to the floor. "Perhaps I was wrong, but although they bear death in their breath they carry life in their blood; a remedy already proved at Bathre and Ngoni."

The High King watched her impassively for a moment before transferring his gaze to Chengerai. "Is this true?"

Chengerai went carefully to one knee next to the Princess and dropped his head. "It is My Lord. And there is this, that the remedy does not need to be provided to our enemies."

The High King nodded thoughtfully. "Then this is a matter for the Council to discuss." He raised a hand. "Captain."

"Majesty." The Captain of the Guard snapped to attention.

"Arrange for the plague flag is to be raised and the city gates closed. Then request the Council to attend me."

The Captain bowed low and hurried off on his mission as the High King transferred his attention back to the group in front of him.

"Daughter, please show your guests somewhere they can wait. Chengerai, stay; I want a full report." Linele immediately rose, offering her arm to Chengerai who struggled back to his feet.

It was four hours before Chengerai appeared to tell them of the Council's decision; four hours during which Conrad's mind had driven itself in circles, thinking of everything that could possibly have gone wrong.

"The Council has agreed to allow you to inoculate the city," Chengerai said as the three of them came to their feet. "The gates will remain closed until that has been achieved, then arrangements will be made to spread the virus throughout the Empire."

Conrad let out his breath.

Chengerai grinned at his obvious relief. "The Council also discussed your fate," he said.

That didn't sound good, Conrad thought.

"And?" his father asked.

"We will provide shelter for you and your troops, but will provide no other assistance, at least for the time being."

"For the time being," the World Leader prompted.

Chengerai smiled and shrugged. At least that still left the chance of assistance at a later date, Conrad thought.

"Thank you," the World Leader said.

"Don't thank me," Chengerai said. "The Princess was most expressive. It appears she has developed a personal interest in your welfare." He glanced at Conrad.

"Chengerai," Conrad said, eager to ask a question that had been puzzling him. "How is Linele older than her father?"

Chengerai looked confused for a moment before understanding dawned. "The High King is the Princess's mother's brother."

"Her uncle?" Conrad said.

"In your tongue, yes."

"Is her mother's husband dead?" Conrad asked.

"Of course not. He's the High King's Agent in Mombasa."

"Linele is her mother's eldest daughter?" Kurslow asked.

"Yes."

Kurslow's smile creased into a broad grin at Conrad. "That makes things interesting," he said.

"Why?" Conrad asked.

"The Mombuto trace their descent through the female line," the medic explained. "That means one of Linele's sons will be the next High King."

Oh great. Just what he needed to know, Conrad thought.

CHAPTER 7

Neu Stuttgart — Etu Line
May 1980 (96AE)

Ivy was met at the airport by the Military Governor, whom she'd met a couple of times before. A small, squat man, he was clearly uncomfortable, which Ivy couldn't help comparing to the stifling contentment he had shown the last time they had met.

"Governor," she said.

"For you," he said nervously handing her two message slips. The first was from Daniels; they'd found Rachel's body. Ivy's stomach clenched in anger at the news. Damn the bastards, she thought, if there was one thing she was going to do it was make sure they paid for that. She took a breath, releasing it slowly before turning to the second slip, which was from her mother. Leolie had fallen, and her mother had ordered all forces on the American continent to surrender.

Ivy shook her head. America fallen? She suddenly realized that the date-time on the top of the slip made the news at least twenty-four hours old.

"Have you have had anything more recent from my mother?" she asked.

The Governor shook his head regretfully. "That's the last information we have."

"Have you informed the other European Commands?"

"Not yet. I felt you should be told first."

"I've been told now," she said shortly, "so don't you think you should."

He nodded.

"I want a message drafted to all Force Leaders and above informing them of what's happened," she continued. "Then I want a briefing in an hour's time with your HQ staff on our present situation."

He nodded again, and Ivy wondered if he was turning into one of those nodding dolls she had possessed as a child.

"Can you get someone to show me where I'm billeted?" she said. "I've been in the field for nearly a week and need a bath."

"I've arranged for you to stay at our house," he said. "I hope that's all right?"

She remembered how claustrophobic it had felt when she'd stayed there last time and mentally cringed. At least it wouldn't be for long. "Of course," she said.

The Governor must have phoned back to the house because there was a bath waiting for her when they arrived, and a clean uniform was laid out for her when she finally emerged. The uniform certainly helped her confidence, and the fifteen minutes she'd spent soaking had given her time to plan how she was going to tackle the briefing. Doing the last button up on the fresh uniform, she felt as prepared as she'd ever be. Giving one, last look at her reflection in the full-length mirror, she made a totally unnecessary adjustment to the front of her tunic and headed downstairs. 'Clemhorn Victorious' indeed, she thought.

The Governor was waiting for her at the foot of the steps. "Leader," he said, holding out two new shoulder tabards with the gold and silver wreaths of a Continental Leader.

Instinctively her hand went to the two stars on her shoulder. How could she have forgotten?

"I thought you might not have had time to update your uniform," he said.

"Thank you," she said sincerely, already starting to swap them over.

The conference room, in which the briefing was to be held, was just off the main staircase. There was the sound of scraping chairs as everyone stood as she entered.

"Leaders," the Governor said. "I'd like to introduce our new Continental Leader, Ivy Clemhorn."

The entire room snapped to attention, and nervously nodding to those there, she took her place at the head of the table.

"Thank you. Please be seated," Ivy said.

There was a fresh shuffling of seats, but once everyone was settled she nodded at the Governor. "Governor?"

Nervously he cleared his throat. At least she wasn't the only one suffering from nerves.

"Three days ago enemy forces from across the temporal front attacked America," he said. "The information we have is that they used three portals and now control, as far as we can ascertain, the entire American continent."

There was a soft murmur at the news, although all there had already heard aspects of it before.

"Obviously, there are difficulties in gaining information concerning the situation," he continued, "but as more information comes to hand it will be distributed."

"Leaders," Ivy said, standing up. "I requested this meeting to allow us to meet each other, and to discuss the defensive arrangements we now have to take. I believe I may have met most of you at the dinner the Governor put on in my honor four or five months ago," she said, looking round. "I would like to say that my promotion was both unexpected and, under the circumstances, not terribly appreciated."

She felt a little better when she saw the smiles that greeted the joke. "I also want to say that I have a responsibility to my father, the World Leader, and have no intention of letting him down."

There were nods of agreement at her words.

She cleared her throat nervously before continuing. "While we know little about those who attacked us, the speed, and success of their initial assault indicates they know a lot about us, and our military positioning. Therefore, the first thing we need to do is to disrupt that knowledge. I want all our radio codes changed as soon as possible, and all five sub-continental headquarters will need to be moved."

"Including us?" someone said.

"Yes. I thought Heidelberg?"

"Chegos, any idea how long that will take?" the Governor asked.

The Leader to whom he'd addressed his question was a small, compact man with dark skin and fair hair.

"About a week," Chegos said after a moment's thought.

"You have two days," Ivy said.

Chegos looked unhappy but nodded his agreement.

"Leader," one of the officers asked.

"Yes Leader. . .?"

"Davies, Group Leader Davies. About ammunition. With the capture of North America we've lost our factories. How long can we hold out without ammunition?"

Ivy shrugged. "I don't know," she admitted. "But you're now responsible for finding out. And you can draft an order for my signature immediately, restricting the firing of weapons to combat situations only."

She turned to the Governor. "We are going to have to establish our own factories as soon as possible. Who do you suggest for it?"

"Battlegroup Leader McDonald," he said indicating a sharp-looking, balding man sitting next to him. The officer concerned smiled nervously at her.

"I'll need a preliminary report by tomorrow morning," she said.

He grimaced, but nodded.

"Right, one other thing," she said. "If we're serious about holding Europe we're going to have to do something about the Pegoni, and quickly, otherwise we could end up fighting on two fronts. I am aware of the reasoning that has prevented us from launching punitive raids in the past, but the situation has changed. To tell the truth I have nightmares at the thought of the Pegoni aligned with Dontfrey and armed with modern weapons."

There were mutters of agreement from around the table.

"Can you arrange a parley?" she asked the Governor. "Let's see if they want to talk first."

He shrugged. "I can try."

"Davies, as well as checking our stocks of ammunition, I want you to check on fuel, and gas. If the Pegoni don't want to parley we'll have to force them to the negotiating table, and quickly. We simply can't afford to have Aris running free if the enemy attack us." And if there was one thing she was going to do it was make damn sure that Rachel's killers paid for what they did.

There were a number of answering nods.

She hoped she'd done the right thing ordering the transfer of the headquarters to Heidelberg. They were going to have enough problems without the disruption that was going to cause, but if she was right they didn't have much choice. She would give anything to be back at Fort Larsa where she had to worry about only a hundred people, rather than the hundreds of thousands who now depended on her.

As she expected, the next few days were absolute chaos. While CHQ's shift to Heidelberg took priority, planning the campaign against the Pegoni didn't stop, and a plan was quickly developed which appeared to have a good chance of success.

On their last day at Neu Stuttgart Ivy called a meeting to sign off on the plan. The table had already been moved out of the conference room, and without it the room had an echoing, half completed feeling.

Group Leader Davies took the podium in front of the large map of Central Europe pinned to the wall behind him. A map case leaned against the corner, ready to take the map as soon as the meeting was over.

"Leaders," he said, as the grandfather clock in the alcove just outside the door chimed the hour. Officers were still drifting in but Ivy had quickly developed a policy of starting briefings exactly on time, whether everyone was there or not. There simply weren't enough hours in the day to waste them waiting for people to turn up.

"The plan we've developed involves a joint offensive into Pegoni territory from both north and south, with a heavy use of incendiaries. We'll be using five Battlegroups. The 101st and 103rd have already started to concentrate at Fort Trat (the tip of his swagger stick indicated the fort in question, near Mainline Ulm), where barges will convoy them, via the Danube and En, into the Engadin. We estimate it should take about nine days to reach our jumping off point." Once again he circled a point on the map, this time at the foot of the Alps.

"From the south, we'll be using most of the Italian Corps, specifically the 72nd and 87th mounted, and the 105th Light Infantry. The Corps is presently converging on Verona where it will commence an advance up the Adige River through the Brenner Pass." The tip of his stick marked the path they'd be following.

At the mention of the 72nd, Ivy wondered how Force Leader McKenzie had taken news of her recent promotion to Continental Leader. He'd commanded the fort where she had served as a raw Troop Leader, fresh out of the Academy, and had made the two years she'd served there an absolute misery. She hoped he'd choked on it.

Group Leader Davies tapped the map with his stick. "Our intention is to duplicate the impact of General Kaledin's 'March to the Sea' during the Mainline's Second War of Austrian Succession. His campaign ended up burning a front of fifty miles across three hundred miles of Georgia and forced England to the negotiating table."

"Kaledin had what, ten times as many troops as us?" someone said.

"Which just means we'll have to work all the harder," Ivy said to welcoming laughter. "Seriously though, we anticipate the use of autogiros and incendiaries will give us a big advantage. I want you to remember though, that the plan is not to conquer the Pegoni, but to break their strategic, economic and psychological capacity for war. Which frankly, to my mind, is a much easier task." She indicated Davies was to continue.

"The Battlegroups will live off the country. They'll be operating light to allow them to move quickly. The autogiros will enable them to strike further, and faster than would otherwise be possible. We estimate we can destroy 75% of this year's harvest and reduce their livestock by 50% within a month."

A Force Leader held up her hand.

"Yes, Leader?" Davies said.

"Do we know where Aris is?"

"Our best intelligence places his summer base in the Innsbruck area."

"How good is that intelligence?"

"Probably not very good," he admitted. "But our strategy doesn't depend on Aris."

"Five Battlegroups are going to be a bit difficult to replace if we lose them," someone pointed out.

"More like impossible," Ivy agreed, "so let's make sure we don't lose them. Now we do have some good news." She looked at the Governor.

"Yes," he said. "Two days ago three supply ships arrived from America. They each carried a full load of arms and ammunition. Apparently they were dispatched just prior to the ceasefire. In addition, Battlegroup Leader McDonald believes we can be producing enough ammunition to be self-supporting within a month. We'll still have a problem with weapons, but even that may be resolved within the near future. Apparently there is a lot more capacity than we had anticipated."

Ivy checked her watch. "Leaders we've all got our orders. For those of you accompanying me to Heidelberg, our convoy leaves in under an hour."

"Leader, if I could see you for a moment?" the Governor said quietly as those in the room started to disperse.

"Well?" she asked, when they were alone.

"Two things; firstly the kommandos' reconnaissance team we discussed embarked for America this morning. They should reach Fort Orange in fifteen days."

"Thank you." Then perhaps they'd have some real news about what was happening. "And the second thing?"

The Governor cleared his throat nervously, and if Ivy hadn't thought it impossible, she might have said he was embarrassed.

"My wife and I had the honor of meeting your mother when the World Leader presented me with the Order of Honor." His hand touched the small silver cross that hung from the ribbon around his neck. The medal was normally presented to bureaucrats for long service, and she had always thought it a pretty empty award compared to those issued for military service. The obvious pride in his voice made her silently vow to never question its value again. "Your mother was kind enough to draw my wife into a conversation after the ceremony. It is a kindness I have never forgotten. I pray the kommandos find her unharmed."

"Thank you," she said. Oh Mama, if only! It was a prayer she uttered every night.

Standing, he turned to go, then paused and turned back to her. "Leader, if I may speak plainly. I have to say I doubted your mother's decision to name you Continental Leader, but the last week has proved me wrong. You are truly your father's daughter."

Giving a small bow he left, leaving Ivy to stare dumbfounded after him.

Now, as her autogiro circled the landing area at Zuoz in the Engadin, and she looked down on the twenty barges that formed half of the largest force assembled on the European continent since the invasion fifty years ago, she wondered just how much of her father's daughter she was. Because if she failed, there wasn't going to be any way of recovering.

Corps Leader Cudomix, wearing his usual neatly trimmed beard and an open three-quarter length coat, was waiting to meet her as she landed. "Continental Leader," he said with a broad smile as she clambered out of her seat. "And to what do we owe this unexpected visit?"

"Cudomix, it's good to see you again." The Corps Leader had been one of her instructors at the Academy, lecturing on military history. "I thought I better come up and see what's actually happening." She didn't feel the need to explain that worry at the delay had meant she hadn't slept the night through for over a week.

"Well, come up to my headquarters and I'll explain. I don't suppose there's any word from America?"

Ivy shook her head, remembering that Cudomix had family there. "I'm sorry," she said, as he guided her up the slope towards the village where it overlooked the river, his staff quickly falling in behind.

He shrugged deprecatingly. "I presume there's still no sign of enemy activity?"

"No." And the uncertainty of what that might mean gnawed at her stomach like a cancer.

"Let's hope they give us time to finish this first then."

"Amen to that," she said. It was precisely the fear of what would happen if they were attacked while still entangled in the Alps that brought her awake in a cold sweat several times each night.

"Have you heard anything from the envoys?" she asked.

"They got a message back last night. Their chiefs refused our offer of parley."

"Not totally unexpected."

"No, but still unfortunate."

"Certainly, for them. When do we move out?"

"We've had the autogiros out since seven this morning. The rest of the Corps moves out tomorrow." He shaded his eyes, looking south into the valley, towards the mountains. "You should just be able to see the smoke." He looked back towards one of his aides. "What's the damage so far?"

"Susch, Zenez and Poute are still burning, and there's significant civilian movement on the roads moving south."

"Good. And Ofen?" Ivy asked. It was the largest of the four towns in the Engadin.

"We're keeping it for the 101st," Cudomix said. "They'll burn it out when they leave. It's been a dry spring; the incendiaries have been more effective than we anticipated."

Ivy nodded. She paused for a moment, looking south. Yes, she could just make out three columns of smoke in the faint haze that now overlaid the mountains, and there was just the faintest scent of smoke in the air. It was, she decided. . .disquieting. There seemed something very wrong with the whole idea of setting fire to this picture perfect postcard of the Alps.

They'd reached the entrance to the village, and the squad of infantry filling their water flasks at the fountain next to the main gate snapped to attention as Cudomix led them in. Ivy returned the salute without really noticing as she gazed around in interest.

"The houses look larger than I was expecting," she said. The two- and three-story buildings with their thick stone and masonry walls and funnel-shaped windows were considerably bigger than she'd anticipated.

"The bottom floor is a stable," the Corps Leader said. "And there's two or three families in each building as well. As big as they are, I understand they can still get a wee bit crowded in winter."

Ivy nodded. It was a very pretty village, she thought, as they made their way up the main, cobbled road towards the Chief's residence at the center of the village. She pictured the village on fire, smoke pouring from the thick thatched roofs, flames licking up the timber framing, and shivered. Unfortunately, no one had ever said war was pleasant.

At dawn the next day, as the first of the autogiros lifted off from their earthen runway, the Corps moved out of the village. Within an hour, new columns of smoke had started to rise into the crisp air, and by the time the first giro had returned there were another six pillars marking the sites of former villages.

By dusk, later that day, twenty separate columns of smoke rose into the air, marking their path. The thatched roofs, tinder dry, burned readily, and the hot easterly winds had soon fanned the flames into the surrounding forest. As night fell, the mountains were lit by a deep, ruddy glow, and the stink of smoke filled the valley.

The smoke from the fires permeated the food at dinner that night, destroying Ivy's appetite. Knowing she had to eat, she forced herself to take small mouthfuls of each dish. She had just taken another sip of her water to try and wash away the taste of the smoke when a messenger appeared and handed Cudomix a message slip.

"What is it?" Ivy asked, leaning over to see.

"From Aberthol, the 101st are under attack," he said, passing her the slip. He checked his watch. "The autogiros should be refueled. Get them loaded with tear gas and into the air," he told the messenger. "I'll be down in a couple of minutes. It's a couple of days earlier than we anticipated but let's see if we can't show the Pegoni why it's such a bad idea to try and take us on."

It was at times like these Ivy regretted that her father had refused to sanction the use of Blistering Gas. With luck the tear gas would be sufficient, especially as the Pegoni wouldn't be expecting it. And it would certainly be safer for her own troops.

As Ivy and Cudomix entered the Corp's Command Center, Cudomix still munching on an apple, three staff officers were studying a map laid out across a trestle table. Behind them, hidden behind a blanket strung across the far end of the room to cut down on the noise, Ivy could hear the soft crackle of the shortwave radios.

"What's the situation?" Ivy asked.

"It's too early to say, Leader," the senior staffer said, looking up. "We're just waiting on a sitrep. The autogiros should have just finished their first run."

A radio operator appeared from behind the curtain with a message slip, and looked around uncertainly until Cudomix held out his hand for it. The Corps Leader read it.

"Good news?" Ivy asked.

"Very," he said, handing her the slip.

'Pegoni disorganized by tear gas. General attack ordered,' she read. "So now we wait?" she said, handing the slip back to him.

"Now we wait," he confirmed.

Two hours later, Ivy was making herself an ersatz coffee of roasted rice, peas, and chicory when Cudomix came over to join her.

"I don't know how you can stand that stuff," he said.

"Well it was impossible to get real coffee in Italy, and after a couple of months I suppose I just got used to it." She stopped, and looked at him suspiciously when he couldn't stop smiling. "What?"

Wordlessly, he handed her a page ripped from a message pad.

"Are you sure this is right?" she asked, after she'd finished reading it.

He nodded. "I confirmed it personally."

"Two hundred raiders killed and seven hundred prisoners?"

He nodded again. "And just five dead and twenty wounded of ours."

"We did it," she said softly, not really believing it.

"You did it," he said with a smile. Behind him the command center was filled with excited conversation as others became aware of the extent of the victory

Suddenly Ivy felt a sense of fierce elation at the news. She could do it! Even their own losses merely seemed to emphasize the size of their victory.

"And those casualty figures are firm?" Ivy asked.

"Absolutely."

Ivy whispered a silent prayer of thanks to the deities. She looked at the coffee mug in her hand and placed it back on the table. "I think we deserve something a little stronger than coffee," she said.

"I agree, and if memory serves me right we liberated quite a nice sour whiskey when we took this place."

Ivy froze, remembering the cranberry mash whiskey she'd had when she first met Jon.

"Ivy?" Cudomix said, suddenly worried.

"I'm all right, just remembering a friend."

"Dead?"

She nodded.

"Well there'll be more of those before this is finished. Still want the drink?"

Ivy nodded, thinking she'd need something to help her sleep.

When she woke at dawn the next day, the stink of ash filled the air. Relentlessly she continued the attack and by dusk the entire southern horizon was alight and the fires had started to link. The 103rd were making good progress in their advance on Innsbruck, and in the south the Italian Corps were already halfway up the Brenner Pass.

To the Pegoni it must have seemed like a hurricane descending on them. Ivy's only problem was that their stocks of fuel and gas were starting to run dangerously low, and if the Pegoni didn't seek to parley soon Ivy would need to order the autogiros grounded. As time continued to press, her doubts as to the wisdom of chancing everything to this single throw of the dice re-emerged.

"Leader?"

Ivy looked up from the latest report on fuel stocks. They had enough for only one more day, and Cudomix had prepared an order for her signature, grounding the craft. Not that there was much left to burn, she thought sourly. The entire Alps were on fire, the mountains shrouded in a single, massive cloud of smoke that hid the horizon and filled the air with ash.

"Yes Cudomix," she said.

"We've just got a report from the 101st. They've captured a party of chiefs, including Aris. They're seeking to parley."

"Thank the gods," she said sincerely. "Can you arrange for a giro to get me out there?"

"Already done. We leave at dawn."

The next day, in the strange half-light of the fires' shadow, she and

Cudomix were escorted into the 101ˢᵗ's main camp by Aberthol, the Battlegroup's commander. The Battlegroup's First Force was drawn up in parade formation on either side of the gate while directly facing them was the party of six Pegoni chiefs. To one side of the group, with his hands bound with hide, was Aris. There was no mistaking him. Although unremarkable in height, he possessed a certain boldness of appearance that would have made him stand out in any crowd.

One of the chiefs had obviously been elected as a spokesman and, glancing uncertainly at the others, stepped forward.

"Continental Leader Clemhorn," an officer said, translating his words for Ivy. "We bring you Aris Arcaos as demanded, and beg you to leave our lands and people to ourselves."

Ivy shook her head. "The demands were quite clear," she said. "You will supply hostages from each village. They will be kept safe, and returned to you once your good faith is assured. You will also return all prisoners and equipment captured, and observers will be dispatched to make sure that you are not keeping anything back."

"You may keep your weapons," she said, aware of how difficult it would be to collect them anyway, "but you will not raid Clemhorn lands. If you do the mountains will be scoured until only the stones remain."

"But Lord," one of the chiefs started.

"There will be no buts," she said sternly, knowing from his tone that he was going to plead for something. Then, more placatingly, she added, "I am aware of the damage we have caused, and I am not immune to the cries of your children. Grain will be provided to keep you through this winter, but you will not raid my lands ever again! Agreed?"

One by one the chiefs gave their assent.

"You may go," she said. "My envoys will go with you to arrange the hostages."

Aris remained where he was, his eyes not leaving her face, as the other chiefs were escorted out of the fort.

As the last of the chiefs disappeared through the gate, Ivy turned to the Battlegroup Leader. "You may dismiss the troops," she said.

Aberthol snapped a salute and as Ivy turned away, she could already hear the order being passed down the line.

For a moment she studied Aris, but his face remained totally unreadable as he returned her gaze levelly. Just what was she going to do with him? Despite the situation he still somehow managed to convey the impression of a king receiving a guest rather than a prisoner with his captor. Ivy was struck by the knowledge that to have him executed would be a monstrous waste. Unfortunately, it was one she might still have to order. Under normal circumstance he could have been shipped to America where his obvious talents could have been put to use, but now. . .

"Leader Clemhorn," he said suddenly. "I am pleased to have finally met you."

"You speak English?" she said, surprised.

"A little," he admitted, though having heard him Ivy doubted that was the case. His accent was flawless.

Oh yes, executing this man would be a monstrous waste.

"Leader?" It was Battlegroup Leader Aberthol.

"Yes?" she said, unhappy at the interruption.

"I've been informed the First Group will be ready to leave within three hours."

She nodded. The rest, including herself, would follow as soon as the rest of the 101st had returned. Cudomix had already given the orders for the 103rd to follow as soon as the three Italian Battlegroups were in a position to take over from them. She took a moment to consider whether she could be so lucky that Force Leader Jules McKenzie would have got himself killed during the advance. Unfortunately, that was highly unlikely — the Italian Corps had suffered even fewer casualties than the 101st and 103rd.

"Thank you Aberthol," she said. "Carry on."

He paused, uncertainly. "Should I order the gallows prepared?" he asked finally.

She stared at him in disbelief.

"For. . ." the Battlegroup Leader indicated Aris with a nod of his head.

She shook her head. "Aris will be coming with us. Arrange for him to transferred to a barge, and make sure he is well secured."

For a moment he looked as though he was going to say something, then simply gave a curt nod and went to attend to his orders.

"And then?" Aris asked.

"That would depend on you," she told him.

"I cannot turn my back on my people."

"Though they have turned on you," she said.

He stared at her silently.

"There is a wider world out there than you could possibly imagine," she said. "It is one that could find a fresh use for your talents."

He shook his head. "No. For me there will only ever be the Pegoni."

"It is regretted that they did not feel the same for you."

He looked at her levelly, his eyes perfectly flat. "It was by my orders that I was brought to you."

For a moment she was too shocked to do anything, and then slowly a smile forced its way onto her lips as she realized that even in defeat he might still have managed to outwit her, and that the power of the chiefs would remain.

"You realize you are leaving us little choice in what we do to you," she pointed out.

He shrugged disclaimingly.

"You will not try to escape," she said. "The guards will have orders to kill, and I suspect many have ample reasons to hate you."

"I would not presume to make your task any easier," he said, which was not particularly reassuring.

"I wouldn't expect anything else from you," she said with a wry smile. "Carry on gentlemen," she told the two guards standing either side of him.

As she turned away she found the Corps Leader studying her impassively. "You disagree?" she asked.

Cudomix shrugged. "It's not my decision to make. I can understand why you want to keep him alive, but it's not going to be a popular decision."

"I can live with that."

"Good." He drew himself up and saluted. "With your permission, Continental Leader?"

"Of course. And Cudomix, thank you."

"My pleasure."

CHAPTER 8

Leolie — Etu Line
June 1980 (96AE)

"*Today God has delivered our enemies into our hands and has smote them onto death,*" Arnold said, looking down from the top of the hill on what remained of Leolie.

"*So shall suffer all the ungodly* — verse 2154," General Mullah Hssan responded.

"I know you warned me, but I still hadn't quite expected the destruction to be quite so — total."

Here and there a single building still stood, untouched, surrounded by rubble, but little else of Leolie remained. On the far side of the former city the deep green of what used to be the commons was now covered by the holding area of the concentration camp. The camp was almost deserted now, most of those it had held there having already being released or moved onto the more secure camps on the Etehad Sho'mali's own line.

"What happened?" Arnold asked.

"They refused to surrender."

"They were given the option?"

"Of course."

He had thought he might be upset, but instead he felt a fierce elation, a proof that God had finally revealed itself to him, choosing him as its servant to bring others to the word.

Behind him he could sense the nervousness of their bodyguard as they scanned their surroundings from the top of the Personnel Armored Carrier. He remembered the splendor of their line, and the marvels he had seen, all mobilized in the service of his God.

He felt the Hssan's eyes on him and turned a questioning gaze on him. "Yes?"

The General Mullah considered him levelly for a moment. "I was asked to present you with a gift if you proved worthy." He snapped his fingers and held out his hand. His aide, who had been standing behind him, reached forward and placed a small package, wrapped protectively in a simple green silk scarf, in his open palm. Kissing it gently he held it out to Arnold.

"What is it?" Arnold asked, accepting it carefully. Warily he unwrapped the scarf to find a small book, its unmarked leather cover tanned and polished to a smooth, golden-yellow.

"It is a copy of the Movak Scripture in the original Arabic. Its cover is made from llama hide prepared by the ulema Acacatili, a disciple of Movak himself."

Arnold fingers reverentially stroked the skin and the Mullah's eyes brightened at the gesture.

"Thank you," Arnold said. To say anything more would merely deflate the significance of the gift.

"The Caliph was impressed with the learning you demonstrated during your audience with him and asked me to present the gift to you at an opportune time."

"And this is the time?"

"It does seem to underlie the certainty of our cause," the Mullah said with a nod towards the remains of the city, a small smile on his normally stern countenance. It was a smile that didn't quite reach his eyes.

Arnold reverentially pressed the book to his forehead before carefully rewrapping it in its scarf and placing it with the other version in the small satchel he now carried at all times.

"Where is my mother?" he asked.

"At the house."

He nodded, savoring the power that had been delivered into his hands.

CHAPTER 9

Rufiji — Mmbuto é Line
September 1980 (96AE)

Conrad rested his elbows on the railing, watching the African shore disappear into the distance behind them, taking the time to catch his breath for what seemed the first time in months. They'd accomplished a hell of a lot in the last three months, but the pace had been frenetic. Compared to the last couple of months this present mission was going to be a doddle. Which would probably mean there wouldn't be enough to do to keep his mind off Linele. Now there was a confusing woman — or perhaps it was just the way he thought about her that was confusing, he realized with a sigh, as he remembered his last conversation with her.

He'd been stowing the last of his belongings in his duffle bag when there'd been a knock on his door. "Come in,' he called without turning round.

"Do you have everything?"

He turned, surprised, to find the Princess looking uncertainly around the small room.

"I do now," he said. "I'd been starting to worry I wouldn't get to see you again before I left."

For a moment she simply looked at him before covering the space between them to wrap her arms around him.

"What's all this about?" he said, carefully returning the hug. "Malagasy isn't all that far away, and I'll only be gone for a couple of months."

"Be careful."

"I always am."

They'd stood that way for what seemed an eternity to Conrad, his concern slowly turning to desire as he became aware of the pressure of her body on his. Finally she pulled away from him.

"You should not keep my father waiting," she said, brushing her lips across his and then, just like that, she was gone.

And now, just when his mind should be fixed on the mission, Conrad found that he couldn't shake the memory of her body against his, and that last kiss which had promised so much.

He cursed, and swung round to look at the four galliots on the port bow. Smaller, and lighter than the galleass which served as his flagship, under sail they were easily keeping up with the assistance of the offshore breeze. Strung out behind them were the three merchant tubs that carried most of the marines. He suspected that Linele knew exactly the effect the kiss would have on him, but that didn't make it any easier to bear. It was going to be a very long two months!

The ship heeled over as it caught the full force of the offshore breeze and he smiled, as he felt the deck flex under his feet. Five ships didn't seem much of a force to go up against the entire Malagasy navy, but if their intelligence was accurate, one would have been enough. The plagues had struck Malagasy eight weeks ago, and those merchants who had visited the island reported whole cities depopulated and deserted. Now he commanded the fleet of five at the High King's instructions to ravage the island.

He wished he could have brought the 48th, or even the Dynands, but he could appreciate the sense in using native troops. The sooner they got used to each other the better. His thoughts were suddenly disturbed by the arrival of the marines' commander, Colonel Ferai. The Colonel was missing an eye, and his entire upper torso, presently bare from the waist up, was covered in white tattoos. He had hands the size of miniature hams, and while Conrad thought he was probably fractionally heavier than the Colonel, there was no way he would ever get into an arm wrestling competition with him.

"Yes, Colonel?" Conrad asked politely.

"I was wondering if you would care to join the men for exercise, sir? We were just about to start."

Conrad hid a smile; he'd wondered when they would start testing him. "Of course."

Although crowded, the gun-deck, which ran over the rowers' heads, was just large enough to hold the ship's full complement of fifty marines. Placing Conrad front and center of those waiting to begin, the Colonel continued up to the poop deck.

Looking up, Conrad noticed that the rigging was crowded with crew, eager to watch their new admiral in action, and with the following wind there was no need to have oars crewed so he had a full house. So — no pressure, he thought with a small grin.

Three large, bronze drums, each about the size of a fifty gallon container, had been set up on the poop deck, and as the Colonel climbed up the steps to join them, Conrad stripped off his shirt and threw it over the barrel of the nearest canon.

As the Colonel stepped up onto the deck the three drummers commenced a quick conga rhythm. For a moment Conrad was stunned at the combination of volume and enthusiasm that the drummers demonstrated, but when he noticed the marines starting to limber up in time to the music he quickly moved to copy them.

Three minutes into the first set Conrad decided he was hopelessly out of shape. The last three months might have kept him busy, but they had also kept him from exercising, and he quickly decided that the best he could hope for was simply to survive. The calisthenics themselves weren't any tougher than he had expected, but the speed with which they were done to the relentless beat of the drum, lifted them to a whole new class of self-induced torture.

Somehow he managed to keep up with the others, and when the Colonel released them he even managed to walk off the deck without collapsing. Every muscle in his body throbbed with pain, but the honor of the Clemhorn name had been maintained. Clemhorn victorious indeed, he thought dryly, though it had been a near run thing.

They made port at Majanga, at the mouth of the northern two rivers that trisected Malagasy, at dawn on the seventh day. The port had been the center of pirate activity on the island, but the stench of death which drifted out from shore when they were still some distance from the harbor suggested to Conrad that that situation was now firmly in the past.

Conrad joined Captain Rashid and Colonel Ferai on the poop deck as the small fleet maneuvered closer into shore. Rashid was a small, dapper Phoenician from Carthago, the equivalent of Mainline Cape Town.

"It looks promising," Conrad said. Actually, through the binoculars, it looked more than promising with the only sign of life on the quay being some scavenging dogs. There were several bodies lying on jetty, almost bloated beyond recognition.

"I count ten ships," Captain Rashid said. "No sign of life."

Conrad nodded, agreeing on the count. One of the ships appeared to have slipped its mooring and now lay stranded on its side on the sand, but the others still drifted at anchor.

"Lot of sharks though," the Colonel said.

Conrad hadn't noticed the sharks until the Colonel pointed them out, but they were pretty noticeable once that occurred. He shivered. He hated the thought of sharks and from the fins there must have been at least twenty.

"Good eating," the Captain said.

Conrad wondered if the Captain was referring to the sharks, or to what had brought them in from the sea. Regardless, the conversation wasn't getting them closer to their goal. "Bring us into the middle of the harbor, Captain," Conrad said.

The Captain nodded. As the galleass breached the harbor mouth the stench seemed to lift in intensity and one of the marines suddenly dashed for the side as he lost his breakfast. Conrad grimaced in sympathy, but things were likely to get much worse, especially for those who had to go ashore.

With all eight ships of the small fleet anchored in the middle of the harbor, their captains, and marine commanders, joined him on board the *Thandiwe*, the flagship.

"Well gentlemen," he said, when they were all assembled in the Captain's cabin. A detailed, hand-drawn map of the city was laid out on the table in front of them, held down with a set of silver paper weights. "Things appear even better than we hoped for, and I think we can afford to alter our plan somewhat. Captain Rashid, I want you to divide the crews and pick out three of the best ships in the harbor. Clean them out and we'll take them back as prizes. We'll burn the rest when we're ready to go." All present looked happy at the thought of the prize money the three ships would bring.

"Colonel Ferai," he said turning to the Marine Commander. "You are to land your men and quarter the town. Your primary goal is to locate the treasury, but once that's done I want the town stripped bare. We're burning it tonight so you won't have long. I suspect everyone who can has already fled, but be careful. And warn your men not to touch the bodies."

One of the marine commanders snorted, and Conrad smiled.

"Stranger things have happened. There's too much risk of infection so make sure everyone is warned; they need to remember Kelsor Virus doesn't actually make us invincible."

"Ferai, it's all yours," he said, indicating the map.

Ferai studied the map for a moment.

"Cheng, you'll land your men here and cover this area." He indicated the northern section on the map before them. "Tendani here. I'll take the south. Remind your men of the bar regarding individual looting. They will be searched on their return. Any questions?"

There was silence.

The Colonel looked at Conrad and nodded.

Conrad smiled. "Thank you, gentlemen, I want everyone back by dusk. We'll start burning the city then so make sure you are. Now, on your way!"

He waited for a couple of minutes before following them on deck.

Marines from the *Thandiwe* were already filing into their boats, while those on the other ships could be seen waiting anxiously for their own orders. By the time the first of Ferai's marines had scrambled ashore, quickly splitting into three columns and moving into the city, the others had started to disembark.

With the marines ashore, the boats were then freed to ferry the crews chosen to staff the three prizes. Once that was accomplished there was nothing to do for those left until the marines returned, except to swelter in the hot sun. A slight breeze struggled in from the sea towards the close of the afternoon, but it provided little relief from the cloying stink of death that surrounded them.

Finally, at dusk, the marines started to appear back on the quay with their booty, and the sailors were kept busy ferrying them back to the ships. Soon piles of gold jewelry, silver goblets and plates covered the deck of the flagship. On top of one, a marine had macabrely placed a skull, encased in silver, its two large ruby eyes staring sadly back at the city.

Conrad was standing on the poop desk, watching the last of the marines file on board, when Ferai appeared beside him, the white tattoos that covered his face gleaming evilly in the soft light of the hurricane lamp. With him was one of the marines' senior sergeants.

"We have a problem," Ferai said shortly, with a nod towards the Sergeant.

That didn't sound good, Conrad thought. "What?"

The Sergeant came to attention, ramrod straight. "Admiral, sah. Two marines have been found with unlicensed booty, sah."

"What booty precisely?"

"Two rings," Ferai said.

Conrad looked at the piles of loot that covered the deck and almost laughed at the absurdity of the matter. Ferai's face, however, was fixed in a frown and Conrad wondered why they were taking it so seriously. Suddenly he made the connection and grimaced.

"What is the punishment?" he asked.

Ferai looked at the Sergeant. "Sergeant," he prompted.

"For contravention of Article 45 of the Military Regulations — unauthorized retention of booty — the penalty is garrotal — sah."

Conrad felt sick. "No alternative?"

"No sah."

"No chance of commutation?"

Ferai shook his head, and as Conrad stared into the Colonel's impassive face he felt the abyss stir beneath his feet. No, there wouldn't be an alternative, the Mombuto took their contracts extremely seriously, and never more than when money was involved.

"Arrange it," he said..

"Admiral. . . " the Colonel paused uncertainly, but Conrad was in no mood to make it easy for him and simply stared at him.

The Colonel cleared his throat. "The execution needs to be public, as a lesson for the troops."

"Do it then," Conrad said. He spun on his heel and headed below. Damn, why didn't their Sergeants double check before they were allowed back on board, and why did they have to be so stupid?

Two hours later, in the guttering light of a row of pitch torches set up along the edge of quay, Conrad stepped ashore out of the small punt that had brought him from the flagship. In front of him, in full sight of the fleet, a platform had been erected around two posts. An iron collar, at approximately neck height, hung loose from a peg at the back of each post. In the still of the night the city's perfume of death smothered everything under its heavy scent.

Two more boats tied up behind him and from each a small squad brought forward the two convicted prisoners. One must have been about eighteen, while the other was probably about twenty-five, twenty-six. The younger one was visibly trembling and the two soldiers on either side had to support him as they led him up to the posts.

Efficiently, perhaps almost kindly in the case of the younger convict, the two were tied to the two posts and their arms fastened behind them, facing the fleet.

There was no doubt the scene had a certain barbaric horror about it, Conrad thought. The flickering light from the torches reflecting off the dark waters below the quay, while in the harbor the ships of the fleet rode at anchor, their masts lit by the half-moon, low on the horizon. Conrad winced at the sudden onslaught of heartburn that sent a searing surge of pain across his chest.

The two soldiers who had been chosen to act as the executioners stepped forward to adjust the collar around each of the two prisoner's necks. The younger threw a beseeching glance towards Conrad but Conrad ignored him, trying to look through the scene so he wouldn't have to think about what was about to happen.

There was a lever set at the back of each collar, and when everything was ready each of the executioners took hold of their lever in both hands and paused, looking towards the Colonel.

Ferai glanced at Conrad and he nodded. Get it over with, he thought. The Colonel made a small cutting gesture with his finger and the executioners started to turn the lever, drawing the collar tight as their assistants threw a black cloth over the prisoners' heads.

A convulsive pressure of the arms and a heaving of the chest were the only visible signs of the struggle that must be occurring under the cloth then, almost simultaneously, both men slumped forward against their ropes. After a pause of a few seconds, one of the executioners peeped behind the cloth and after giving another turn to the lever, removed the cloth. The dead man was slightly convulsed, the mouth open, eyeballs turned into their sockets.

Ferai nodded at the second man and his executioner followed suit.

"I want the Sergeants of those men placed on charge," Conrad whispered angrily to Ferai. "I don't care what it is, but anyone with half a head on their shoulders should have checked their squad before they went through the official check."

Ferai nodded, and though his face remained impassive, the muscles around his neck tightened.

Conrad glanced over to the two prisoners, now being removed from the garrotte and almost gagged. Angrily he clenched his teeth; now was not the time to demonstrate any sort of weakness. Taking the moment to look back over the city he swallowed down the taste of bile.

"Burn it," he commanded.

"Are you sure?" Ferai asked. "We've probably only skimmed a fraction of what it's worth."

"For what purpose? What we've got now is already more than enough to make each man in the fleet rich several times over. Burn it."

Ferai looked as though he wanted to argue but finally he simply nodded.

For a moment all Conrad wanted to do was to get away from everything, but he was stuck there, surrounded by the stink of death and his own responsibilities. He swallowed convulsively as his stomach heaved. Instinctively he started to make his way along the harbor towards the deeper seclusion of the dark. Two guards moved unobtrusively to follow and Conrad waved them back. After about five minutes he had reached a space out of reach of the light from the torches and leaning forward against the wall emptied his stomach over the cobbles at his feet. It didn't even seem to add to the stink of the city. Gods, he wished he was home.

By the time he returned to the wharf, the first of the warehouses was already alight, and within thirty minutes the entire port area was afire. Flames leaped high into the sky, and for a time the night was as brightly lit as day. As the marines returned to their ships, their task of arson complete, Conrad ordered the fleet to stand farther offshore in case of drifting embers.

By dawn most of the fire had burned its course, though greasy smoke still lolled skyward from a couple of places within the city. In the harbor itself two of the ships they had fired still sputtered away, but of the others there was nothing to see. Satisfied with the night's work, Conrad ordered the fleet to start south.

Two days later, as he was pouring over a map of the coast with Captain Rashid in his cabin, there was a knock on the door.

"Come in," he called.

It was Colonel Ferai. "Admiral, may I speak to you?"

Conrad looked at the Captain, who shrugged. "I'll see to the change in orders," Rashid said.

"Take a seat," Conrad said, gesturing at the chair on the opposite site of the table. "Do you want a beer?" He had been surprised to find that the Malagasy brewed quite a decent maize beer. In hindsight, given the quality of their drinking water, maybe it shouldn't have been that much of a surprise.

"Perhaps later."

Conrad took a mouthful of beer and savored it for a moment. "What's the problem?" he asked when he thought he'd made him wait long enough.

"The men don't see why they should continue, now we've achieved what we were ordered to do."

And have the booty, Conrad thought angrily. For a moment he simply studied the pale liquor in his glass, watching the bubbles rise to the surface. Finally he looked up. "Colonel, our orders were quite clear. We were to ravage the entire west coast for as long as our supplies hold out. The entire west coast," he repeated. "Not just Majanga."

"The men don't see it like that."

"Then you will have to explain it to them, won't you," Conrad said bluntly.

Ferai looked uneasy.

Conrad sighed. "Colonel. The High King's orders were quite explicit. He also quite obviously placed me in charge of this expedition. Are you prepared to question him? Because if so, I am sure that he will expect you to have some very good reasons for doing so. Now I may be fairly new to this line, and to the Mmbuto é, but the fact that the troops feel unhappy is probably not going to impress him very much at all. Don't you agree?"

"Yes, Lord," Ferai said, lowering his eyes uneasily. "You understand why I had to raise the matter though?"

"I would expect no less," Conrad said smoothly. It was indeed the Colonel's job to keep him informed of what the men felt. He wasn't supposed to necessarily agree with them though. Conrad tapped the map laid out on the table that he and the Captain had been studying. "So how long do you think it will take us to finish the job?"

Ferai studied the map. "It's probably only six, maybe seven days straight sailing to the Cape. But having to stop and burn every port we come to? I don't know, maybe another five or six weeks."

Conrad nodded. "That's what Captain Rashid estimates so we've decided to split the fleet into three. That should allow us to finish the job in about half the time. I've also asked the Captain to arrange for the prizes to be dispatched. Do you think that will satisfy the men?"

Ferai considered the matter for a matter, before nodding. "Definitely."

"Then let's do this right. I want the High King to be able to see the smoke from our fires from his palace."

The Colonel smiled, a wolf's grin that fitted evilly over his face. "It feels good to be repaid on these pirates," he said, standing up. "I'll tell the men. You won't have any more problems with them."

Conrad hoped he wouldn't have any more problems with the Colonel either, but held his thoughts to himself.

CHAPTER 10

Leolie — Etu Line
June 1980 (96AE)

Arnold closed the English version of the Movak Scripture that he had been reading in its plain green cover, and placed it carefully on the desk in front of him, making sure it lined up with the edge of the desk and the pad next to it. The desk was bare except for a pad of writing paper, unused; two pencils; and the smooth, golden brown leather-covered version of the Scripture sitting next to the version he had just been reading.

His fingers gently caressed the brown leather. It wouldn't be long before he could read it, he promised himself. Indeed, only yesterday Mullah Hssan had congratulated him on his progress with his language studies. Slow consolidation, that's what was needed. He adjusted the pad a fraction. He had never understood how his father could ever find what he had been working on in the chaos that had covered his desk, or where it had all come from. Delegation, that was the trick — there must have been something wrong with the man.

He checked his watch, not long now. He stood up, went and stood by the window, looking down on the front terrace. Below him a small squad of the Mullah's guard marched across the gravel in lock step. Their dark blue uniforms and turbans looked almost black in the dappled shade from the giant oak that shadowed the main drive.

On the far side of the terrace, a Squad of Clemhorn Mujahideen was getting lectured by an Etehad Sho'mali officer, their turbans marking them as the nucleus of the new Clemhorn army. There were so few of them though. If the Mullah could just get more released from the detention camps, Arnold was sure he could persuade them to join the new Corps, but for the moment all he got was platitudes. Well, if the Caliph wanted his help he had no choice. He knew the Etehad Sho'mali were stretched on their own line. Another two regiments had just had to be rotated back there, but they ran the risk of losing everything they had gained if they didn't give him the troops he needed.

There was a knock on the door, and he turned back. It was Abbas, the General Mullah's tame guard dog, a slim, deadly man, with cold, unblinking eyes and the politest manner Arnold had ever seen. It couldn't be the easiest of tasks to be prepared to lay down one's life for someone you might be ordered to kill at a moment's notice, Arnold thought, and yet Abbas managed their relationship with the utmost of courtesy.

"Leader, your mother."

"Thank you Abbas." He frowned as his mother entered the room. She really didn't look well. There were dark circles under her eyes, and her normally blond, bobbed hair was showing streaks of gray. He was disappointed at the lack of care she had shown to her appearance. Her hair looked as though it had been given the barest of brushes. One should always try to keep up appearances, no matter what the situation.

"Hello Mother, please take a seat," he said, indicating the chair on the other side of the desk. "Abbas, could you arrange for some tea and biscuits?"

"Of course, Leader."

Arnold ignored his mother, returning his attention to the terrace where the nucleus of his new Clemhorn army was now double-timing it back to their barracks.

"Shall I serve?" Abbas asked, flagging his return with the tray.

"Please," Arnold said, taking his seat.

After placing the tray on the desk, Abbas poured the tea. "Milk?" he asked.

"No thank you," Arnold said.

His mother shook her head.

Abbas placed an iced biscuit next to each cup and with a short bow took up his normal position next to the door.

Arnold took a sip of the tea. Perfect. The Mullah had introduced him to Tieguanyin tea during his visit to the Sultan Line. It had a pleasing, amber color in the cup; and a pleasant, slightly fruity flavor. He had already started to investigate planting and growing his own.

His mother took a small bite from her biscuit and followed it with some tea.

"How have you been?" he asked. "You don't look like you've been sleeping well."

"Not very well, no."

"You should get out more, try and get some exercise."

His mother raised an eyebrow and pointedly looked at Abbas.

"Oh, don't mind Abbas. He's as much for your protection as anything else."

His mother made a small sound of disagreement, but took another sip of her tea. Replacing the cup in its saucer, she looked at her hands for a moment before raising her eyes. "I don't suppose you have any word on your father?"

"No."

"Your brothers?"

"Nothing."

Her lips twitched. "Ivy?"

The tea in his mouth suddenly tasted of hot buttered copper and he frowned. He looked at his cup doubtfully, but it didn't look any different. He took a sniff, but it smelled the same. Suspiciously he placed the cup back on its saucer.

"Ivy still seems to be refusing to accept the inevitable," he said. "Perhaps you could speak to her. Persuade her to surrender?"

She shook her head.

"There will be only one result to her intransigence. By choosing to stand against us, she has chosen to pit herself against the one true God. She risks not only her life but her eternal soul."

"Your god."

"There is only one God."

"And Movak is his prophet?"

"Exactly."

"Your sister doesn't seem to have been doing too badly so far."

"That is shortly to change, in fact may already have changed."

She frowned. "What does that mean?"

There was a knock on the door, and Arnold checked his watch. This was probably the news he'd been waiting for.

"Good afternoon General Mullah," Arnold said, getting to his feet as Hssan was ushered in.

"Leader, I thought you would like to know that our forces have seized Neu Stuttgart."

"Any word on my sister?"

"Not yet."

"My thanks General."

The General looked questioningly at Arnold's mother who was still sitting, staring out of the window. Then, with a nod to Arnold, he withdrew, pulling the door closed behind him.

"I think I would like to return to my room," his mother said when the General had gone.

"You could stop all this, you know," he said.

"So could you, but you won't. You're too full of hate."

Arnold looked at her. How could he convince her? He didn't hate her, in fact he didn't hate anyone. If people simply accepted the faith, that would be the end of the matter. Why couldn't she see that the war was over?

His eyes drifted to the Movak Scripture sitting on the desk between them, and as though guided, his hands opened the book.

And in the solitude of the desert, Allah lifted the stones from Chalchihuitlicue's ears and spoke to her and she heard and prostrated herself before him.

And so God had spoken to him. Reverently, he closed the book and gently lifted it to his lips. Placing it back on the table he looked at his mother who looked levelly back at him.

"Well?" she said. "I suppose your god has spoken to you?"

"Actually, he has."

"And what did he say?"

"That you will hear his message."

She raised an eyebrow but Arnold ignored it. Obviously the desert was just an allegory; what was important was the solitude. A memory came to him of the storerooms at the back of the house, dug into the hill. He had accidentally got himself locked in one of them when he was five. He remembered the silence and the utter absence of any light. Yes, that would do.

"Abbas, I have a task for you," he said.

CHAPTER 11

Iller River — Etu Line
June 1980 (96AE)

Ivy leaned against the rail of the top deck as the paddle-wheeler churned its way up the Iller River towards the Danube and Ulm. The hot, summer sun beat down relentlessly out of a clear sky but at least the mist thrown up by the paddles provided some relief from the heat. A sudden eddy stirred the air, bringing with it the stink of burned coal.

A large stand of oak among the forest of beech and pine on the far shore caught her eye. In the middle of the stand a single, massive tree towered over its companions, its crown blackened from a lightning strike. Nearby a beaver's castle blocked a slow moving creek, its owner taking a moment from his ongoing maintenance to peer shortsightedly at the passing convoy.

Raincloud would have loved this, she thought. He'd often talked about taking a trip down the Danube. Her eyes stung abruptly and angrily she squeezed them shut, refusing to cry. When she opened her eyes again they were caught by the sight of the tattered Clemhorn flag hanging limply from the stern flagpole, the double-headed Mayan eagle lost somewhere in its faded golden folds. Talk about an omen, she thought. Straightening up, she shadowed her eyes to get a better look at the four barges strung behind the steamer, like ducklings on a string. Behind them was another steamer, the first of the remainder of her little fleet.

"Leader?"

Ivy looked over the side of the rail to see Corps Leader Cudomix standing at the bottom of the ladder looking up at her. Despite the heat he was still wearing his heavy, dark blue three-quarter length coat.

"Afternoon, Cudomix," she said in greeting.

"May I join you?"

"Of course, come up."

The Corps Leader hauled himself up the steps. "Ah, I see why you're up here," he said, as another breath of wind swept some of the cooling mist across the deck.

"Was there a reason you wanted to see me?" she asked.

"Nothing special. I thought I'd just take the opportunity to find out what your plans are."

Ivy leaned back on the rail, looking out over the dark green of the forest lining the far shore. What she wouldn't give just to be able to swim ashore and disappear into the forest, never to be seen again. "You and me both."

Cudomix shadowed her pose, resting his arms on the rail next to her. "Never doubt yourself, Ivy. You've done well so far. I see no reason why you won't continue to do so."

Ivy sighed deeply. "I'm not sure what my plans are," she admitted. "Aris is safely on his way to Elba, and the Pegoni are handing their hostages over as agreed. But I don't know what I'm going to do until I've got more information, or Miro attacks."

"Leaders?"

Both of them looked over the rail to see one of the communications officers peering up at them.

"Yes?" Cudomix asked.

"A message from the Leader at Neu Stuttgart. They're under attack."

"It looks like you've got your wish," Cudomix said softly.

For a moment Ivy simply looked out over the convoy behind them, the Clemhorn flag momentarily lifting in a gust of wind. All right, she'd got her wish; now what was she going to do with it? Suddenly she smiled. Goddamn it, she had them.

"My thanks," she said turning back to the aide. "Ask the Group Leaders to come aboard immediately."

"So, what do you have in mind?" Cudomix asked with an answering smile as the aide disappeared with his message.

"I need to speak to the Military Governor at Heidelberg. We're less than a day from Ulm at the moment. If we coordinate our forces, we should be able to crack them like a nut in a vise." Her hands demonstrated what she was thinking.

"It won't be easy."

"Of course not. But if we're going to have any chance we have to counterattack before they have the opportunity of establishing a proper bridgehead. We have two Battlegroups in this convoy, and maybe another one around Heidelberg. That's over seven and a half thousand troops, plus artillery. The situation couldn't have been any better if we'd planned it."

"If I could make a suggestion?"

"Of course."

"Coordinating a simultaneous attack with all three Battlegroups might be overly ambitious. And even if you manage it, it means holding off any attack for at least twenty-four hours, possibly forty-eight, which will give them the chance to reinforce their bridgehead."

"What do you suggest, then?"

"Order the Heidelberg forces into an immediate counterattack. I know Battlegroup Leader Whitaker. The 5th are good troops. He'll have them knocking on the door within twelve hours, if you give the word. He may not break the door down but he's sure going to mess up their plans for a party."

Ivy winced. She knew what the consequences of that order would be, but what choice did she have? Cudomix was right. "All right, I'll see to that. You better start planning our own movements."

Cudomix smiled. "Now, that wasn't too difficult was it?"

"Not yet," Ivy admitted. She waved towards the ladder. "After you."

***

An autogiro circled overhead before coming into land, and Ivy cowered as another artillery shell slammed into the farmhouse she had taken over as a base. She could smell the thatch starting to burn, and hear Jon's voice calling her name. Jon! Startled, she started to rise to her feet even as the thatch collapsed on top of her, burying her under its weight. The smoke was stronger now and she could hear the crackle of the flames. Frantically she tried to claw her way free, but the straw was too heavy and the smoke was already suffocating. She could hear Jon anxiously calling her name and then she woke up, heart pounding, not knowing where she was.

"Leader?"

For a moment the voice meant nothing; she was still lost in the chaos and the bloodbath of the nightmare, then gradually she became aware of the mattress against her back, and the steady pounding of the paddle wheel just outside her cabin.

"Leader?" Louder this time, and this time she recognized the voice as that of her orderly.

"I'm all right Sharea," she said to relieve the anxiety she could hear in her orderly's voice. "Just a nightmare. What did you want?"

"The Corps Leader asked me to wake you. We've received news from Neu Stuttgart."

Already? She checked the clock. It was only 11.30. "Where is he?"

"In the saloon."

"Tell him I'll be there in five minutes."

As Sharea closed the door behind her, Ivy sat up, and swinging her feet over the side of the bunk, she put her head in her hands. She could still smell the burning thatch; feel the weight of it against her chest. Damn! Rubbing her eyes, she stood up and then splashed some water from the bowl on the nightstand on her face. Taking a deep breath she looked at herself in the mirror. Her eyes were puffy and her hair looked like a miniature haystack. It was a good thing she wasn't trying to impress anyone, she thought. She pulled on her shirt and started to dress.

Five minutes later, her hair hidden under a kepi, she stepped out onto the deck. It was cool out of the cabin, and she was thankful for the jacket she'd put on. Phosphorous gleamed on the water, but the rest of the boat was in shadows. As she walked quietly along the deck to the saloon at the other end of the boat she was surprised by light spilling from a cabin window, muffled laughter coming from inside. From the voices, there must have been at least four people there, and she paused for a minute remembering times, that felt like a century ago, when as a junior officer she had been able to join such groups. Now she could very well be responsible for sending them to their deaths. Well, she'd wanted the promotion, she just hadn't expected it to happen so quickly.

The sentry on duty outside the saloon came to attention, and as she opened the door, Cudomix looked up from his discussion with a Troop Leader who looked a little worse for wear. A stained first aid dressing was wrapped around his forehead and his right arm was strapped to his chest in a sling. A staff officer was just preparing a fresh mug of coffee in the corner.

"Ah, Continental Leader," Cudomix said. "May I introduce Troop Leader Cadete."

The Troop Leader started to salute before realizing that his broken arm made that impossible.

"At ease Troop Leader," Ivy said quickly, pulling out a seat and joining them at the table. The staff officer put a mug of coffee at her elbow and she nodded her thanks, wishing she could remember his name. She knew he'd been introduced to her.

"Leader Cadete was stationed at Neu Stuttgart," Cudomix said, and Ivy dragged her attention back to the matter at hand. "Whittaker ordered him flown here as soon as he arrived at Heidelberg with the remains of the Force that had been left there. He thought you needed to hear what happened first hand."

"Please," Ivy said.

The Troop Leader nervously adjusted the bandage that held his broken arm. "Our Force was ordered to hold Neu Stuttgart after the rest of the army pulled out," he started. "The enemy launched their attack at noon from a portal somewhere near the middle of the town, probably from the Governor's palace. We lost half the Force in the first two minutes. It was a massacre — they were wearing some sort of body armor and our bullets were useless against them. The Force Leader had stationed the autogiros some distance away, and they managed to get into the air to cover our retreat. Not that it did much good, all three were destroyed within minutes of getting airborne."

"How?" Ivy asked.

"Possibly some sort of rocket? I do know that one of them was destroyed at about half a mile. Ten of us did manage to get out in the confusion though."

Now Ivy knew why they had been so successful in America.

"Anything else?" she asked.

"Yes Leader, I regret to inform you we were unable to detonate the demolition charges."

Demolition charges? "I didn't order demolition charges," Ivy said.

The Troop Leader shrugged. "Someone did, Leader. We spent the first week preparing them. The whole city is wired with explosives."

Ivy looked at Cudomix, who shook his head. He didn't know either. She wouldn't be surprised to find out it had been the Governor. It struck her as something he would have done. Damn, why couldn't people tell her what they were planning.

"We have to close that portal," Cudomix said.

"I'm not sure how," Ivy admitted. "Given what Troop Leader Cadete has said, I'm not sure that even six Battlegroups would be enough, let alone the three we have."

"We could send in a small kommando force," Cudomix said. "Try and take out the portal with a shaped charge. Once the portal is closed we'd have a little more time to plan something."

Ivy nodded thoughtfully. A large enough percussion charge could overpower the gate, regardless of which side it was set off on.

"The problem is getting through their perimeter," the staff officer pointed out.

"How about autogiros?" Ivy suggested. "If they come in at night without engines and auto-rotate down they might not be spotted."

"Your pardon, Leader," the staff officer said.

"Yes Griffiths," Ivy said, finally remembering his name.

"If we took their engines out and towed them into position they could carry two or three troops each."

Ivy nodded. "That would make it a one way trip, but yes, it could improve our chances."

"Leader," Troop Leader Cadete said hesitantly.

"Yes?"

"If the charges are still in place, blowing them might take out the portal. Their initial attack seems to have been centered on the Governor's palace, that was the first area we lost contact with, and there's at least a ton of explosives in the basement."

"A ton?" Ivy said, looking accusingly at Cudomix.

The Corps Leader shrugged. "Obviously someone thought that using the munitions stored in the city would be easier than trying to remove them. We did have an awful lot stored there."

Which sounded suspiciously like an understatement if ever she'd heard one, even half a ton of Trinitrotoluene would easily overpower the gate. There was one problem. "Wouldn't they have discovered and disarmed the explosive by now?" she asked the Troop Leader.

"Possibly not, Leader. Our Force Leader insisted we camouflage everything. The explosives in the palace are set up behind a false wall. It seemed unnecessary at the time, but now. . ."

"How were you going to set the charges off?"

"Radio detonators with a time delay of five minutes."

"What's their range?" If it was good enough they might not need to use the giros.

"We tested it at about seventy-five yards."

Damn. Oh well, back to Plan A. "We're going to have to move quickly," Ivy said, looking at Cudomix.

The Corps Leader nodded. "We should be at Ulm in another hour, but it's fifty-six miles to Neu Stuttgart. That's at least fifteen hours, probably closer to twenty-four if you take into account the chaos we're going to create disembarking at Ulm."

"What about the 5th?"

"I got a report from Whittaker half an hour ago. He'll be in position to start engaging the enemy in about six hours."

Which was six hours more than she'd been told. "Okay, let's do it. Leader Griffiths, you're responsible for getting me those autogiros."

He nodded, and started writing something into his note pad.

She looked at Cudomix. "I want to be at Neu Stuttgart by dusk tomorrow." She checked her watch. "Sorry, dusk today. No excuses."

"We'll lose a lot of troops if we push them that hard."

"We'll lose even more if we don't and that portal's reinforced."

Cudomix nodded. "I'll get everyone awake."

"Gentlemen." Ivy nodded. "I'll leave you to it."

***

Now, as her escort trotted down the road, she found herself wondering if Cudomix hadn't been right, and she was pushing everyone too hard. The weather was hot, at least ninety degrees, and the pace she'd set the army was killing.

Sweat ran down the back of her neck, soaking her uniform, as they passed two dismounted infantry, leading their mounts by the side of the road. Both horses were hobbling, possibly lamed by the hot work after their close confinement on board the barges. They were losing too many horses like that, she thought. A moment later they passed a light artillery piece that had lost a wheel. Its crew, stripped to singlets, were trying to fix it while the gun's four horses were standing, heads down, too exhausted to do anything but simply stand.

They passed another squad of mounted infantry collapsed by the side of the road, taking its ten minute break. Ivy acknowledged the startled salute of the Troop Leader as he recognized her, the rest of the Troop barely stirring as she passed.

A minute later Ivy's mount splashed through a creek over a graveled ford, deeply rutted by the artillery cannon and limbers. The bodies of two horses were pushed to one side of the ford. On the far side the road rose steeply, and a Troop of soldiers struggled to assist a gun up the steep slope. The four horses trying to pull the cannon were unable to manage the weight, and even as she watched one of the horses collapsed and the weight of the cannon pulled the others back. With an oath, the artillery captain stepped forward and fired a single shot into the horse's eye.

"Captain," Ivy called.

"Leader?" the artilleryman said uncertainly, coming over.

"We just passed a canon back there which has lost a wheel. Get someone back to get their horses up here to help. I'd rather we had one canon rather than miss out on both of you."

"Of course, thank you, Leader."

"Just keep them moving," she said. "We've still got a long way to go."

He nodded, and as he turned back to see to his orders Ivy heeled her mount forward over the ford. On the far side she dismounted, then hauled the horse behind her as she scrambled up the slope. At the top she looked back for a moment, to where the army straggled out behind her in its mad rush forward.

"Keep them moving," she told the Force Leader at the top, pulling herself back into the saddle. Between her legs her mount felt like a furnace.

She reached Cudomix' command post at Kraman, five miles from Neu Stuttgart, around nine that night. Dusk was just falling and behind her, as far as she could tell, the army still stretched all the way back to Ulm, fifty miles away. This was turning into a massive debacle.

As she eased herself out of the saddle in front of the inn that Cudomix had taken over for his command post, an aide handed her a cold pasty.

"Thanks," she said. Eating was the last thing she wanted to do but she forced herself to take a bite and almost gagged on the cold fat. Somehow she managed to keep it down.

"Where's the Corps Leader?" she asked, taking another bite.

"Leader Cudomix is inside, Leader," the aide said, taking charge of her horse.

There was a water trough with a bucket next to the door, with a scrap of towel hanging up next it and she looked at it thoughtfully. Her camisole, under her jacket, was soaked with sweat. Shucking her jacket off she dunked her head into the trough, coming up with a gasp. The water was cold! After scrubbing away the worst of the day's march she quickly dried her hair on the piece of towel. After replacing her kepi, she shrugged herself back into the jacket, shivering as it forced the now clammy camisole back against her skin. Much better, she thought. Her trousers still stank of horse, but there wasn't anything she could do about that. Now if only getting the rest of the army into position would be as easy. Bracing herself, she stepped up onto the inn's porch and through its double doors.

Cudomix came to his feet as she entered the main room, and instantly the background noise stilled as everyone came to attention.

"Carry on," she said. "So what's the situation?" she asked as the noise quickly built back to its original level.

Cudomix shrugged. "Not good. The 101st is almost into position, but they've lost fifty per cent of their strength en route, and the 103rd is still spread out between here and Ulm."

Ivy winced at the news. They'd probably pick up a lot of the laggards over the next couple of days as they straggled in, but it was going to put a massive hole in their order of battle.

"And the 5th?" she asked, referring to Whitaker's Battlegroup.

"They've been engaged for the past six hours. Whitaker's being careful not to push too heavily."

Ivy frowned. The 5th should have engaged fifteen hours ago, although if they had they would have been out of ammunition by the time the 101st and 103rd were ready to launch their own attack.

"How's he going?"

"Surprisingly well. The enemy don't seem intent on pushing back at this stage, although they could just be waiting for morning."

"So what time do you think we'll be ready to go?" she asked.

"Two, three at the latest."

"AM?"

He nodded.

Ivy's stomach knotted at the thought of what would happen if the kommandos failed in their raid. If they couldn't set off the explosives, given Troop Leader Cadete's report on the enemy's effectiveness, she'd be lucky to escape with a Force.

Later that night the knot had turned to a steadily gnawing pain in her stomach, and seeking a change from the tobacco fug that filled the operations center, she stepped outside onto the porch that ran along the front of the building.

Taking a deep breath of the fresh air, she checked her watch. A quarter to three. Only fifteen more minutes to go. With a start, she realized she'd been awake for twenty-eight hours, and had only had two hours sleep in the last forty-eight. Still, it wouldn't be much longer. An aide appeared with a fresh mug of coffee but she shook her head; her stomach was already awash with the stuff.

She checked her watch again. The kommandos should have landed about five minutes ago. They had only managed to strip the engines out of six giros, but each now carried three soldiers with their equipment. She could only pray that eighteen soldiers would be enough, because if it wasn't they were going to be in a whole lot of trouble.

Overhead, the sky had a slight overcast, with the promise of rain later that day, but for the moment the stars were still visible, twinkling dimly in the increasing haze. Behind her, light spilled out of all the inn's windows, witness to the activity that had filled it for the past twelve hours.

Suddenly a massive explosion from the direction of Neu Stuttgart caused her to spin round as fire lit up the horizon. She checked her watch — ten minutes early.

"What the hell happened?" she demanded, as she burst back into the operations center just as another, even more massive explosion rocked the ground. Instinctively she glanced behind her but there was nothing to see.

"We're trying to find out," Cudomix said.

A smaller series of shocks rocked the building, followed a moment later by a third, massive explosion that she felt as a physical blow through her entire body. The Battlegroup Leader was holding a radio to his ear, trying to make sense of the chaos. He nodded once. "Go, go!"

"What happened?" Ivy demanded again.

"We don't know. It may have been the kommandos. I've ordered the attack to start."

Just how much explosive had the Governor used?

As though to punctuate Cudomix' words the first salvo of artillery broke out from the north, quickly followed by answering echoes from the east, west, and south.

"How long before contact?" she asked.

"The Scouts are already in position. The main units are still moving up. Ten, fifteen minutes. We didn't want them too close in case the enemy detected them."

A coms officer interrupted him and he took a moment to read the message she had given him.

"What is it?" Ivy asked.

"Scouts from the 103rd report mines."

Ivy nodded. They'd been expecting that but the Pegoni had taught them how to handle mines and the engineers would already be preparing their rockets. She pictured the splutter of fire and the rockets surging over the field to embed themselves in the walls of the city. A moment later, clearance mines would be attached to the ropes they towed, and pulled out over the mine field by means of the pulleys now embedded in the wall. The engineers would light the fuse, and fire would streak out along the ropes to ignite the mines below them, even as the scouts began to move forward over the broken ground.

Another massive explosion rocked the night, and the tempo of artillery fire seemed to lift in response. There was now a ruddy glare from the direction of the city. What was happening?

"The wall's down," Cudomix reporting, looking up from the table. "The scouts are entering the city."

Ivy nodded. The wall had never been designed to stand against artillery; maybe she'd have to do something about that in the future. Among the deeper roar of the guns she could now hear, in the distance, the softer crack of the mortars and the stutter of automatic fire. Another series of explosions rocked the city, and she felt the tremor through her feet.

"Continental Leader," her radio operator said, alerting her to a message he had in his hand.

"Yes?"

"Message from Force Leader Hadlow, she thinks she's reached the remains of the portal."

"Can she confirm?" Ivy asked.

Cudomix raised an eyebrow and Ivy nodded, understandingly. Given the explosions it would take forensics to make sense of anything remaining.

"Any word on the kommandos?" she asked Cudomix.

He shook his head.

"So what's the status?" she asked, crossing over to look at the map.

"The 103rd have just reached their assault positions. They should be entering the city within minutes. The 101st are about five minutes behind them."

"Any resistance?"

"Some, but we seemed to retained the element of surprise."

"And the 5th?"

"Much tougher, but the enemy don't seem to be responding in any sort of organized fashion."

Ivy nodded. That was pretty much what they'd expected. Whittaker's Battlegroup had already been engaged with the enemy for the past twelve hours. It was to be expected that the resistance they'd be facing would be stiffer. The sound of the canon was now an almost continuous pounding in the background.

"The 103rd have entered the city," Cudomix told her.

Ivy nodded her thanks. After the debacle of the march everything finally seemed to be settling down.

"I'll have that coffee now," she told the aide.

When it arrived, she moved back to the door. In the direction of the city the horizon was now a ruddy glow. Glancing up, she realized that the stars were no longer visible behind the thickening cloud.

"Leader?" someone said, and Ivy realized someone was waiting to enter the room. Stepping back out of the way, she followed them back to where Cudomix was in discussion with his staff.

"It looks as if we took out their fuel dump in the first explosion," Cudomix told her, looking up. "And Force Leader Hadlow believes we also took out their armory."

"Nothing like putting all your eggs in the one nest," Ivy said.

"Lucky for us," an officer muttered under his breath.

Ivy hid a smile, which given the way she was feeling, was harder than she had expected.

"Ah, good," Cudomix said, reading another slip an aide had given him.

"What?" Ivy demanded.

"The 101st are entering the city. Only sporadic resistance."

At the news, she felt an enormous grin appear on her face. Cudomix smiled back at her, and with a shock she realized he'd been as worried about the attack as she had been.

"I want the city destroyed, not a single stone is to be left standing," she said. "Let's not leave them any clue what happened."

"Of course Continental Leader," he said.

Ivy took the gentle dig in good humor; after all she had won.

CHAPTER 12

En route to Rufiji — Mmbuto é Line
October 1980 (96AE)

Defella savored a deep breath of the sea air as the galley plunged through the strengthening seas. The shoreline on their right disappeared then reappeared in time to the galley's rise and fall on the waves.

The air was heavy with salt and the threat of rain, although the absence of any wind meant that the galley's single lateen sail had been lowered to the deck and they were under oars, the rowers sweating with the intensity of their task. Behind them, in the distance, she watched the clouds crowding the top of the cresting waves.

"How much longer before the Captain decides to beach?" she asked Kaito as he joined her on the forecastle. At least that was one advantage of a galley, you could always just run it up on the beach to avoid a storm. And the one she was watching develop in the distance looked like a doozy.

"He's not going to. Too many reefs along the shore along here so he's decided to make a run for the harbor at Tanga."

"Are we going to make it?" she asked.

"He seems to think he can."

"He does remember we've got the only portal on this line on his galley," Defella said, wondering once again what had been so important that they'd been ordered to bring the portal and their two useless generators down from Ngoni with all possible speed.

"I'm sure he does," Kaito reassured her.

"Well, it's his neck if he screws up."

"Which I'm sure he's all too aware of."

Defella scowled and Kaito grinned at her, before turning to watch the rowers at their task below them, as they kept to the steady four and a half miles per hour, every hour, a pace they could keep up all day if necessary.

Kaito's attention seemed fixed on something specific below and, following his gaze, she frowned uncertainly.

"Are you checking out that rower?" she asked. He was certainly worth checking out, she thought — his muscles flexing with each pull on the oar.

Kaito started guiltily.

"It's all right," she assured him. "He's certainly worth watching. I just didn't think the Mainline accepted those who preferred. . ." She trailed off uncomfortably.

"Their own sex," he offered. "They don't. And frankly I've got no idea of what the situation is here."

"Oh," she said.

"Look, it doesn't matter. I've never. . ." He made a helpless gesture.

"Why?" she said. "I mean, it's rare for men on Dynand, but it's not unheard for a man to take a heart companion. Although, of course, it is much more common for women."

"Why?" Kaito asked. "Oh, of course, the shortage of men."

"For many women they must either share a husband, or do without," she said matter-of-factly. "But, never?" she prompted.

Kaito flushed. "I've always been too busy. First there was my PhD, then for the last couple of years I've focused on the new portal substrate. And you?" he asked diffidently.

She sighed, and took another look at the rower that had first piqued their interest.

"As you, I have never. . ." She gestured helplessly. "Probably because I have never found a woman I am attracted to in that way. And as for men. . .on Dynand sex between a woman and a man is exclusively for the purpose of a child."

"Really, I find that hard to believe," Kaito said archly.

Now it was Defella's turn to look embarrassed. "Well, there are stories," she admitted. "But I have always been taught that I must save myself for my husband. And potential mates have been difficult to find recently."

Kaito sniggered. "*That* is an understatement."

"So, tell me about Donald?" she said, taking a breath.

"Donald?"

"Well, he was your flatmate."

Suddenly Defella found Kaito's gaze fixed firmly on her face and she flushed. "I meant — "

Kaito simply shook his head. "He's intelligent, loyal, romantic, and gorgeous," he said. "And yes, so you don't have to ask, he likes girls, worse luck for me. But why Donald? I'd have thought Conrad would have been more your cup of tea."

"Conrad?" she said, genuinely surprised. "He's a little too much up himself for my taste."

"You noticed? Don't get me wrong, I like the big oaf, but modesty's not exactly one of his strong points."

She giggled. "No, it's not." She was interrupted by the arrival of her Sergeant.

"Looks like we're going to get wet," the Sergeant said, joining them at the rail.

Defella lifted her head and stared at the clouds rapidly darkening behind them. "I *really* hope the Captain knows what he's doing," she said, looking over to the aftcastle where the Captain was discussing something urgently with the First Mate. The First Mate nodded, and stepped forward to the edge of the deck. Removing the cover from the large drum fixed to the edge of the rail, he picked up two mallets and started a measured beat, matching the existing stroke. After four strokes he paused and for a moment the crew rested their oars out of the water as the Captain stepped forward.

"All right, me boyos," he called. "No one wants to get wet, let's lift the beat."

The First Mate sounded a faster beat, and on the third stroke the Captain's voice, a startlingly rich tenor, rose over the boat, driving it forward in time to the drum.

Once I had a star-eyed maid
I was content with her to lay
"It's a shanty," Defella said, delighted.

Although, rather than singing the chorus, the crew simply hummed it.
In the comfort of her bed
Let me lay until I'm dead
"Sergeant, tell Giselle I want to see her," Defella said.

The Sergeant gave an evil smile. "Aye, Ma'am," and swung herself back down the stairs, taking them two at a time.

"Who's Giselle?" Kaito asked.

"You'll see," Defella said.

It wasn't long before Giselle's blond hair appeared over the top of the steps.

"Leader?" she said. "Sergeant said you wanted to see me."

"I did," Defella said. "Do you recognize the tune?"

Giselle cocked her head, listening. Then a dazzling smile lit up her face. "It's Haul Away'. Or the tune is, anyway."

"Want to give it a go?"

"Of course." Stepping up to the rail she waited for the next hummed chorus and then a glorious contralto voice soared out over the boat.
Once I had a brown-eyed man
I was content with him to lay
The Captain looked up, startled, then with a nod they swapped verse for verse, racing the storm, sending the galley surging across the water as the rowers strained in time to the beat of the drum. Behind them, the storm grew steadily darker, while the white tops frothed at their feet until they finally breached the breakwall and brought the galley into the safety of Tanga

just as the first drops of rain splattered down around them, and Giselle's glorious voice brought in the last verse.

And now I've seen the world
Brown-eyed man, I'll rove no more

Defella had the feeling the crew would have applauded if they had had the energy, but instead they could only rest on their oars as the wharf-rats hauled the boat ashore and snuggled them into the shelter of one of the long boat sheds that ran down to the beach.

Five days later, the galley struggled free of the mangroves that guarded the entrance to Rufiji's harbor, and slid across the mirror-smooth surface of the open water towards the city that rose out of the water in tiers before them.

Under the steel-sleet sky the dark-gray granite blocks that enclosed the harbor looked almost black, while the city's white marbled stone seemed leaden and lifeless.

"A bit duller than what I'd expected," Defella said.

Kaito nodded. "And now we find out what they wanted us for," he said.

Defella snorted. "What they wanted you for. Me, I'm just the security."

"Don't be catty," Kaito said.

Defella pulled a face at him.

It wasn't until the next day that Defella found out what they'd been called south for.

"You can't be serious!" Defella demanded of the World Leader.

He held his hands out placatingly.

She glared at Donald. "Explain to your father how stupid this idea is."

"It was my idea, Defella," Donald said.

"We're not ready, yet."

"We have to find out what's going on. We can't make any sort of plans without knowing what is happening on the Mainline."

"And why does it have to be you?"

"Because I'm the only one with any real experience of the Mainline, other than Papa, Conrad, and Kaito. And I'm the most expendable."

Her heart skipped at that, and she noticed his father wince.

"Expendable!" She glared at him. "If you want expendable send me."
She bit off the comment that she wanted to make about him being a male and that it wasn't his job, as she suspected that wouldn't help.

"It won't work, Defella. We're planning to contact Melanie Seaforth. She used to be Papa's factor on the Mainline until she resigned to follow her partner to South Africa. The last we heard she operated a cross-line import-export business out of the Cape, and still handled a lot of Clemhorn business. But she doesn't know you. It has to be me."

"And how are you going to power the portal?" she demanded, glaring at Kaito. "I thought the generators were stuffed until we can get some diesel?"

"The motors *are* stuffed but we can still use the alternators if we power them with a water turbine."

She threw up her hands in disgust. "Fine, fine. Do what you want. You're going to do it anyway."

CHAPTER 13

Leolie — Etu Line
June 1980 (96AE)

Arnold was studying an obtuse piece of text in the original Arabic when there was a knock on the door.

"Yes Abbas?" he said politely, looking up to see his aide standing patiently by the door.

"General Mullah Hssan to see you," the aide said, stepping aside to allow the Mullah to enter.

"My apologies for interrupting, Arnold," the Mullah said. "But we have just received news from Europe." A tic in the corner of the Mullah's left eye was spasming erratically.

"Please, take a seat," Arnold said, gesturing him towards the visitor's couch in the corner as he closed the book, aligning it with the edge of the desk. "We'll have some fresh tea," he told Abbas.

"Of course," Abbas said, having also picked up on the Mullah's stress.

"I assume it's bad news?" Arnold asked.

The Mullah nodded.

"How bad?"

"The entire expeditionary force was destroyed."

The edge of Arnold's vision wavered as the taste of buttered copper flooded his mouth. Not now, he thought, clenching his fist hard enough to drive his nails into his palm. For a moment the pain allowed him to concentrate. "What happened?"

"We're still trying to find out. What we do know is we lost the portal about 3 AM. It took six hours to get another one established, and by the time we got a reconnaissance group through, your sister's forces were in control of the city."

"How did that happen?"

"It's possible the city was mined before your sister evacuated it. When the mines went off we lost the portal, munitions dump, and main barracks."

"And you walked right into it?"

The Mullah nodded as Abbas placed a new pot of tea on the table.

Arnold waited until Abbas had poured a cup for the Mullah and withdrawn. "How long before we counterattack?"

General Mullah Hssan shook his head. "We can't. Supreme Command ordered the immediate return home of two more regiments yesterday. They were the last of my reserve. I spoke personally to General Mullah Acahuana but he confirmed the order. I understand the move is the first in a phased six month return of all of our forces to Sultan."

"And how, exactly, does the Caliph expect me to conquer Europe, let alone hold the rest of the line without an army?" Arnold said bitterly.

The Mullah pressed a finger against the bridge of his nose. "I made that point and he assured me that Leader Miro would be providing replacement troops."

"Troops who have no understanding of the word of God, nor of the mission we are committed to!" Unable to sit there any longer and listen to empty platitudes Arnold stood up and made his way across to the window. Outside, the wind rattled the glass, a forerunner of the storm building on the horizon.

Rush, rush, rush. God's word was like water wearing down a stone, a slow relentless movement that nothing could stand against, and yet without an army even God's word was powerless to impose its will.

Arnold felt as though his brain was going to explode from the pressure, as decisions piled ever higher, threatening to topple over and flatten him beneath the weight. Suddenly the pressure eased and he heard the sound of bells, pealing as though in celebration. Startled, he looked round, but the Mullah remained seated, staring unseeing into his tea.

"Perhaps, with your support," Arnold said, "we can convince the First Leader that the troops he supplies are, shall we say, more positive to our aims. The Malac Line for example." He remembered the World Leader's first son, George, as being an officious prig, but Malac's main culture had certain similarities with Sultan's own.

The Mullah considered the suggestion for a moment, before nodding.

"However, even Leader Miro's reserves are not unlimited," Arnold said. "We need to further expand the number of my Mujahideen."

"Expansion? To how many?"

"Two Battlegroups initially, perhaps ten in total."

The Mullah winced, but nodded. "I will see what I can do."

"We will need additional trainers, equipment, etcetera."

"Of course."

"I point out that you could reduce the cost of training new troops if the Caliph was prepared to release all Clemhorn prisoners of war."

The Mullah nodded again. "Perhaps you and I should speak to Leader Miro," he offered.

"I think that would be best," Arnold agreed.

Abruptly the bells fell silent, and in the stillness and peace that followed he felt God's presence descend on the room.

CHAPTER 14

Rufiji — Mmbuto é Line
November 1980 (96AE)

Conrad searched the crowd waiting for them on the quay as the fleet worked its way into the harbor, but there was no sign of Linele's sedan chair. Disappointed, he was about to return below when he caught sight of Donald at the end of pier, and a moment later, Defella. He'd almost failed to recognize Defella; her natural golden tan had turned almost black in the African sun, and with a hat covering her hair she looked like a local. There was no mistaking her bright green hair, however, when she took the hat off and threw it exuberantly in the air.

"Donald, Defella," he called, waving happily.

The two waved back and Conrad found his eyes drawn to the movement of Defella's breasts under the thin fabric of the sari she was wearing. Quickly he returned his gaze to his brother. If Linele had been there he had a feeling his life expectancy would have been severely shortened.

"Long time no see, bro," Donald said as they came on board, pulling his brother into a hug.

"Likewise," Conrad said, returning the hug. "I wasn't expecting to see you though," he said, turning to Defella, to be momentarily distracted by her sea-green eyes. "When did you leave Ngoni?"

"About a month and a half ago," Defella said. "Your father asked me to accompany Kaito down."

Conrad nodded and looked at his brother enquiringly, wondering what was so important it needed Kaito.

"A lot's been happening while you've been away," Donald said simply.

"So where's Linele?" Conrad asked with pretended nonchalance, as he waved them towards his cabin. "I didn't see her on the quay."

"Apparently the daughter of the High King is not to be found in such places," Donald told him with a broad grin. Obviously he had not been taken in. "She's waiting for you at the palace, and I wouldn't keep her waiting long. She's had a very touchy temper for the past two weeks."

Conrad smiled at the news. "I'll remember that," he said, holding the cabin door for them. "Take a seat and tell me what's been happening."

"Quite a lot," Donald said, as he took one of the benches that gave him a spectacular view out of the stern windows that spanned the entire width of the ship. "But the most important thing is that Papa has finally got the High King and the Council to allow us to recruit mercenaries."

"How did he do that?" Conrad said. When he'd left for Malagasy the Council had been dead set against the proposal.

"Father agreed to the High King's request for you to lead an expedition to America."

"Me!"

Donald nodded. "It seems to make sense as you'd been Continental Leader there. The Mmbuto é are supplying ten ships with marines and settlers, and father's agreed for you to take the some of the 48th."

"And when am I leaving?"

"In three weeks."

"And what will you be doing while I'm getting seasick?" Conrad asked to hide his disappointment at the news that he wouldn't have long with Linele before he had to leave again.

"He'll be on the Mainline," Defella said. It was obvious that she did not approve.

"Kaito's got the portal working?"

"Almost," Donald said. "The diesel engines proved irreparable but Kaito's worked out a way of driving the generators using water. Defella and I went and had a look last week. He's nearly finished assembling the turbines, and using the existing dam at Ojwang has cut down the time he needed by almost by a quarter. He's constantly complaining he's a physicist, not an engineer; but I think he's secretly enjoying it. He did study engineering for three years before he transferred over to physics, and he's probably always been a frustrated engineer at heart. He's even managed to develop a proof of concept for a homebuilt AC Generator. Luckily this line had already developed wire drawing, so he didn't have to worry about that, but he's still got the patents office working almost continuous overtime. If we can't get home we're going to be very, very rich."

"And the Mainline, how did you persuade Papa to let you go?" Conrad asked.

"With great difficulty," Donald admitted. "But someone has to do it if we're to find out what's been happening since we left. And it just happens I'm the best person for the job."

"Perhaps," Conrad conceded, wondering how much of his brother's determination was due to the possibility of seeing Matija again.

"Anyway, my job's probably going to be a piece of cake compared to yours. Linele has managed to wrangle a place on the fleet with you."

Conrad stared at him for a moment, before he realized his mouth was still open and closed it with an audible snap.

Donald grinned at his reaction.

"How did she manage that?" Conrad asked finally.

Donald shrugged. "You know her better than me," he said. "I'd watch your step, that woman has marriage in her eyes."

"And who's to say I don't?" Conrad said, hoisting himself to his feet. "Come on, we better start making tracks, or there won't be anything left of me when Linele's finished to lead an expedition with."

CHAPTER 15

Rufiji — Mmbuto é Line
November 1980 (96AE)

Donald sat, dangling his feet over the stern of the barge, listening to the sound of the frogs that filled the African night around him. Behind him, he could hear the steady creak from the harness of the two horses towing the barge as they plodded along the towpath. The scent of the savannah, grassy and filled with dust, mingled with the faint hint of stagnant water from the canal while phosphorescence rode their wake across the surface of the water. Overhead, the stars seemed so close, so bright, it was as though he could just reach out and touch them. For a moment it seemed as though the war belonged to some other time.

He scratched at his beard irritably. He'd begun to hate it, but it was necessary as a disguise, meager though it might be.

In the distance a lion roared his challenge to the night, while on the far bank tsetse traps were stretched tautly between the trees, their blue cloth black against the night.

His new beard itched, and he scratched at it again. Unfortunately, no matter how much he hated it, he couldn't get rid of it until he got back.

He turned round as he heard someone approach, and looked up to see Defella looking uncertainly down on him. "Is it all right if I join you?" she asked.

"Of course," he said, patting the wooden deck next to him.

She sat down, leaning back against him to look up at the stars. He froze, feeling her smooth skin press against him.

"It's beautiful," she said.

"I was just thinking that," he said, shifting his arm slightly to make her more comfortable.

"I still think it's a stupid idea."

He nodded. "I know. And I hate portals, particularly experimental ones, but someone has to go, and I'm the best person for the job." Besides, it was the only way he'd see Matija.

They stayed that way for some time.

"Can I ask you something?" she said finally, so softly he had to strain to hear.

"Of course," he said, watching as a fish broached the surface of the canal by their feet.

"Do you like me?"

He looked at her in surprise. "What isn't there to like?" he said, with a smile.

"I'm serious."

"Of course I like you."

"Enough to marry me?"

He froze. Where had that come from? He liked her, but he'd never given her any idea that it was anything stronger. At least he didn't think he had, had he?

Sensing his shock she pulled back from him.

"I'm sorry if I misunderstand your feelings," she said. "I had thought. I mean, I, Normally I would ask my mother to speak to yours but. . ." She gestured, opening her hands to indicate the situation they found themselves in. Her normally piercing green eyes were like deep pools in the shadowed darkness of her face.

"I am honored," Donald said, "but. . ." He paused uncertainly. He didn't want to hurt her, he liked Defella too much, and he had the idea he could do it quite easily at the moment.

She started to stand up, but he put his hand on her shoulder to stop her.

"I'm sorry, Defella, I can't. I'm already engaged."

"Oh." She slumped.

"Her name's Matija."

There was a moment's silence, filled only by the soft creak of the barge's timbers.

"I had hoped to be your first wife," she admitted. There was an uneasy silence. Donald started to say he was sorry, but was interrupted. They both stopped.

"No, go on," he said.

"If Matija," she stumbled over the name, "would have me I would accept the position of second wife. My mother would not be happy, my status is. . .I am sure I could persuade her though."

"I'm sorry," he said, hearing the pain and distress in her voice. "I can't."

"Why? If you prefer I will speak to Matija."

"It wouldn't change things. Matija would never agree to a second wife."

"She will keep you to herself. What sort of woman would expect that from her man?" Defella demanded.

He shook his head, sensing the chasm between their cultures was too deep to bridge.

"Why won't she share?" Defella asked pulling away from him.

Donald's heart almost broke at the anguish in her voice.

"Because we're not Dynand," he said softly, knowing he had to try to explain. "On your line you've had to. There have never been enough men. But on ours. . ." He paused. "She would never understand," he finished.

"But you could ask her? She might understand."

Donald thought of Matija; quiet, shy Matija, and shook his head. "I'm sorry."

He watched Defella's chin come up, as she pulled her shoulders back, and he could sense her pulling back from him, both physically and mentally. "I'll leave then."

He could feel the pain in her voice and wanted to tell her to stay. But doing so wouldn't achieve anything. So instead he simply watched her walk away, wondering if he could have done anything differently.

Now, as he nervously eyed the portal, he was still wondering if he could have, should have, done anything differently. The problem was he didn't think he could have. He genuinely liked and respected Defella; her quick intelligence, her quirkiness, even her green hair, but then there was Matija, and their unborn child. If there hadn't been there wouldn't have been any question about his response to Defella's offer, but there was.

He felt his father's hand on his shoulder. "You still want to go do this?" he asked.

"Yes, Papa."

His father didn't look happy, but they'd been over this so many times by now that there was nothing more to say. Someone had to go.

The portal shimmered. Uneasily, he glanced at Kaito who was monitoring it, but he appeared unconcerned.

"I still wish you'd take someone else with you," his father said. "Defella for instance."

Donald glanced at Defella who was standing next to the portal. She returned the glance, stony-eyed.

"I've got Maku," Donald said, referring to the scout who'd be accompanying him to Cape Town. "We'll be fine."

His father shook his head unhappily, but they'd been through this as well. "You have the letters?"

Donald nodded, patting his breast pocket reassuringly.

"Take care," his father said.

"I will. Tell Conrad I hope his trip goes well."

His father pulled him into a hug, then without another word stepped back out of the way. Donald looked at Defella but she ignored him. With a sigh he nodded to Kaito, braced himself and stepped forward through the portal.

It was hotter and muggier on the other side of the portal. The five Makua Scouts who'd now been there a week watched him dispassionately from the far side of the camp fire. There was a soft inrush of air behind him and he knew the portal had disappeared. They were on their own, unable to return until Kaito turned it on again in a week's time.

Maku, the senior scout, gave him a broad smile from the far side of the fire.

"Right," Donald said, checking the lightening sky towards the east. Dawn was almost upon them. "Let's make a start. There's no sense in waiting around."

The river was less than fifty yards away and with the six of them, it didn't take long to finish loading the small lateen-rigged sailboat they'd brought through the portal with them. Then, bidding farewell to the two scouts who were to stay behind and guard the camp, the others pushed off into the current for their journey down to the sea.

They passed their first village sometime after midday, but soon passed more as they approached the mangroves that lined the coast. Donald was amused by the interest they attracted as they passed each village, possibly because they seldom saw a white man in this part of the country.

When they finally broke free of the mangroves they raised the sail and followed the coast north. With a strong offshore breeze it took them less than twenty-four hours to reach the natural, sand-lined harbor of Dar es Salaam.

Leaving Moniga to guard the skiff, Donald went ashore with Maku and Ade to book passage for himself and Maku to Cape Town, and to secure somewhere for Moniga and Ade to stay until their return. They were successful on both counts, and with the steamer due to leave on the evening tide, Donald and Maku bade the two scouts farewell at the small, rundown warehouse they'd rented near the wharf. As rundown as it was, the rest of the village wasn't any better.

"And you'll both be okay?" Donald asked the two scouts, slightly concerned at leaving the two of them alone on the Mainline without supervision.

Ade nodded. "Moniga will return to the portal and report on your safe departure, then return here. Our language is close enough to make ourselves understood. We will be fine to wait your return."

"Stay safe then," Donald said.

Maku grasped their arms in farewell, and together he and Donald headed back to the wharf where they would catch a lighter out to the steamer.

The *Sea Queen* was a thousand ton tramp steamer that had seen better times. Its paintwork was peeling, its superstructure covered in rust. Its Captain wasn't much different — a Dutchman, with minimal English, who communicated mainly in grunts, and spent much of his time in his cabin, leaving the running of the craft to his First Mate. They were the steamer's only passengers and, as none of the crew spoke either English or Slav, they were left to their own devices, leaving Donald too much time to worry about Matija and the baby.

It seemed a long trip, the steamer stopping at every port between Dar es Salaam and Cape Town, but finally it pulled into its berth under the looming grandeur of Table Mountain, and Donald and Maku were free to disembark.

"Try not to gawk too much," Donald told his companion with a grin, as Maku came to a dead-halt at the foot of the gangway, stunned by his first real sight of the Mainline in all its technological confusion and chaos. Not that Donald blamed him, he'd been away only seven months and he felt overwhelmed as well. Not too overwhelmed to pull Maku out of the path of an approaching truck, though.

Maku gave him an embarrassed smile. "Where to, boss?" he asked, pulling himself together.

"Let's see about the diamonds first."

Maku nodded.

The buyer's office for the Western Diamond Trading Company, one of the largest firms in the Cape, was situated on the fifth floor. Upon stepping inside the foyer, they were immediately shown up to the buyer's office.

"Mr. MacKenzie," the buyer said, rising from his seat and shaking Donald's hand. "I'm glad to meet you. I believe you wish to sell some diamonds?" He ignored Maku.

"That's right," Donald said, affecting the accent of someone who had been in the Cape for a number of years. "Twenty stones, perhaps two, or three million roubles."

The buyer pursed his lips. "That much. Do you have them here?"

Donald nodded and pulled out the small leather bag he had been carrying around his neck. He undid the tie and poured them out onto the table.

The buyer raised his eyebrows at the number and size of uncut stones. Even rough-hewn as they were, it was obvious they were worth the price Donald had quoted.

"Do you mind if I ask where you got them?" he asked.

"From Bongassou," Donald replied, which was close enough to where they had actually been mined. "I had a mine there until the Portuguese authorities closed it down. There was some difficulty about the situation and I was forced to trek out to Mombasa by foot."

The buyer nodded. "A difficult trip," he said sympathetically.

There was no need to say more. The Portuguese guarded their treasures with an almost fanatical zeal, but so long as the diamonds had not actually been stolen the firm would not inquire further.

"Do you mind if I test them?" he asked.

"Of course not," Donald said, settling back.

The buyer took out a small wooden box, which contained the necessary testing equipment. Each stone had to be tested individually, but finally the tests were completed and the buyer leaned back in his seat and surveyed Donald shrewdly. "Genuine," he announced, "and good quality, too."

"Did you believe they might be otherwise?" Donald asked.

"Not really," the buyer admitted. "You said two million roubles?"

"I said two to three million roubles," Donald said. "I trust you to give me a fair price."

The buyer looked at the notes and calculations he had been scribbling down as he worked. "I am sure that you would be aware of the situation that has occurred as a result of the war," he said. "Unfortunately, the market has been fluctuating quite wildly recently, and it is possible the stones could be worth anywhere between two and four million roubles."

"However. . . " He shrugged. "Perhaps if we were to give you an advance of say, one million, with an undertaking to pay you the rest when they have been cut and their value ascertained. By that time the market may have stabilized and we would be able to give you a fairer valuation."

"An undertaking in writing."

"Of course, I'll just call someone to draft it. And will a bank check do?"

Donald looked doubtful. "I would prefer cash. I don't have a bank account."

"A check would be safer and we can open an account for you in a couple of minutes," the buyer assured him.

It was obvious to Donald that the buyer did not want him to go until an agreement had been made, afraid he would take the stones elsewhere.

He nodded. "Agreed," he said.

It took only half an hour for the buyer to arrange for the money to be deposited in a special account, and for the contract to be typed up and signed; then, after shaking hands, Donald left the building with Maku feeling quite pleased with himself.

"Right," Donald said. "Let's see about the hotel."

With the money from the diamonds there was no trouble in booking a suite at the Grand Mariner which, unlike its name, was neither grand or on the harbor. Donald had considered booking into the Ritz, but given that he was attempting to keep a low profile had decided against it. There was too much of a risk that someone might recognize him, even with the beard. Still, the Mariner's rooms were functional, if rather spartan, and the bed was certainly of a good size.

Now came the most crucial part of the mission, making contact with Melanie. Waving Maku to the only chair in the room, Donald took a seat on the bed, picked up the bedside phone and dialed reception. "Put me through to Universal Imports, please. Melanie Seaforth," he said when the phone was answered.

There was a click then Melanie's voice came over the line. Donald had only met her the once, but there was no mistaking her voice; low and husky.

"Yes? Melanie Seaforth speaking."

"Melanie, it's Donald. You used to work for my father. I need to see you."

There was a pause.

"Donald?" she said doubtfully.

"Yes, that's right. My father said you might be able to help us. We need some information."

"Donald," she said, her voice suddenly brightening. "Of course. Why don't you come over?"

"Is it safe?" he asked.

"Of course, just tell the secretary you've got an appointment with me. I'll tell him you're expected."

"I'll be there in about thirty minutes," he said, checking his watch. Her offices were only a block and a half away.

"Can you give me ten minutes?" he asked Maku, as he replaced the handset.

"Of course."

As Maku closed the door behind him, Donald looked at the telephone, then picked it up and phoned Matija's number in Charleston. The phone rang for a couple of minutes without answering, and he was just about to give up and try again later when it was picked up.

"Hello, Matija?" Donald asked.

"Who's this?' the voice asked. It sounded like Professor Maras, Matija's father, but Donald wasn't sure.

"Donald."

"I'm sorry, Donald. Matija's dead." There was a click and the line went dead.

The handset fell from his nerveless hand.

Dead. How could she be dead? What was he to do now? But the answer he kept coming back to was that there was nothing he could do. Round and round his thoughts swirled until they were finally interrupted by a knock on the door.

Donald glanced at his watch and blinked when he realized fifteen minutes had passed.

"You said ten minutes, boss," Maku said, poking his head round the door. He stopped when he noticed Donald's face. "Are you all right?"

"I've just had some bad news," he admitted. He sighed, picked the handset up and replaced it on its rest. "Come on, we better not keep Melanie waiting."

***

Melanie's business must be doing well, Donald thought, as they checked out the building from across the road, given that Universal Imports took up all three floors of the building in front of them. "Ready?" he asked.

Maku nodded, patting the revolver he had in a shoulder holster under his shirt.

"Let's go then," Donald said, leading the way across the crowded street.

"Leader Clemhorn," Melanie said, when they were shown in, standing up and coming round her desk to greet him, ignoring Maku who stepped back to stand next to the door. No, there was no doubt business was doing well, Donald thought, taking in the dark tailored, 100 per cent wool suit she was wearing.

"How are you?" she asked.

"Well enough," Donald said shaking her hand, and taking the seat she indicated.

"Does anyone else know you're here?" she asked, returning to her own seat.

"No," Donald said.

"Good," she said, seeming relieved. "Now, what can I do for you?"

"My father needs information. We've been out of contact with the Mainline for seven months and we need to know what's happened."

She shrugged. "That's rather a difficult thing to answer just off the cuff." She looked nervously at her watch. "Where do you want me to start?"

"How about with you?" he suggested. "Business looks like it's going well."

She nodded. "Quite well," she agreed. "Taxes are high, though. The First Leader has quite a debt to pay off from the war so we're struggling a bit, but we're not badly off. And of course we've been able to capitalize on the links we'd established with your brother to increase our business with Etu."

"My brother?"

"You didn't know. Arnold is the new World Leader."

"Arnold?"

"Yes. He converted shortly after the invasion."

"Converted?" Donald said, starting to feel more and more confused.

She smiled. "Apparently Leader Miro managed to contact a predominantly Muslim timeline. In return for the First Leader providing access to the portals and some additional payment, they supplied him with the military aid he required."

Donald nodded, hence the additional taxes, and of course he had met the military 'aid'.

"And Arnold's conversion?" he asked.

She'd started to say something when her phone rang. "I'll just take this," she said, picking up the phone. "Yes?" She listened for a moment, then nodded. "Fine, show them in."

The door opened behind him and Donald turned, surprised, as a soldier dressed in the dark blue, almost black, battle armor he recognized from the attack on the University at Constantinople stepped through the door. He carried an assault rifle but Maku was already moving, a knife clenched in his hand, and with one thrust forced the blade up under the armor. In the hall, Donald caught sight of a second soldier and frantically threw himself backward, hand scrambling for his own pistol.

He heard Melanie shout "No!" as he landed on the carpet, then three shots in quick succession from the hall caused Maku to stiffen. Donald watched him look down at the blood pumping out of the hole in his chest. He looked up at Donald, gave a regretful smile, and collapsed.

Donald's pistol was stuck, caught up in the tail of his shirt, and he looked up in time to see another two soldiers step into the room. Carefully he raised his hands.

"You should never have come," Melanie said, staring horrified at the two bodies that lay sprawled across her carpet. "The war's over. Why did you come?"

CHAPTER 16

Heidleberg — Etu Line
September 1980 (96AE)

The battle at Neu Stuttgart had occurred almost two months ago, and with no further sign of enemy activity, Ivy was feeling steadily more confident of being able to hold the continent. Or at least of making any further invasion a very expensive activity indeed.

Small factories were still being established all over Europe to manufacture arms and ammunition and finally, output was starting to ramp up. More importantly, the news concerning the Pegoni remained positive. Her primary need now was for information about what was happening in America and on the Mainline.

She was staring moodily at the ceiling, chewing thoughtfully on her bottom lip, wondering if there was anything else she should be doing, when there was a knock on the door.

"Come in," Ivy called, swinging her boots off the desk.

The door opened and her aide poked her head around the corner. "Governor Metztli for you, Leader."

"Show him in, Marley. Good evening, Governor, what can I do for you?" she said, rising from her seat to take his hand.

"I thought you might like to know we've had news from America."

"At last!"

He smiled at her enthusiasm. "Force Leader Tepin arrived at Brest last night from America. I've asked for him to report direct to CHQ. He should be here tomorrow."

"Good."

"Apparently he's brought one of your mother's adjutants back with him. As I thought you might like to speak to them personally about your mother, I've asked the Force Leader to bring them with him."

"Thank you Metztli," she said, genuinely pleased by the gesture.

"My pleasure, Ivy," he replied with a smile.

And that was why she was now waiting impatiently in her office for them to arrive. They were late and, with a General Staff meeting scheduled for ten, if they didn't arrive soon she wouldn't have the opportunity to speak to them beforehand. There was a knock on the door and she looked up eagerly.

"Force Leader Tepin and Squad Leader Raincloud to see you, Ma'am," Marley said, ushering them in.

Raincloud? Ivy checked as she started to rise from her seat. For a moment she swore it was Jon who had stepped through the door, before realizing he was too young.

"Force Leader Tepin," Ivy said, recovering quickly, and reaching out to shake the hand of the blond, blue-eyed Viking, who was standing uncomfortably in front of her. "I'm pleased to see your mission was a success."

"And Squad Leader Raincloud," she said, turning to his companion. "Welcome to Europe. It is Lonce isn't it?"

Lonce nodded uneasily.

"Your brother often spoke of you," she said in explanation. "Please, take a seat," she said, gesturing to the chairs already set up around the coffee table. "Marley, some coffee please."

"My report Leader," the kommando's Force Leader said awkwardly, placing the thick, typewritten report he'd been carrying on the table between them.

She nodded. "I'll get Marley to copy it when she returns, but in the meantime why don't you give me a summary of what happened?"

"Perhaps it would better if you heard from Squad Leader Raincloud," Tepin suggested. "Given that he witnessed the invasion."

Ivy turned her attention to the young Squad Leader. God, he looked so young. "Squad Leader?" she prompted.

Lonce cleared his throat uneasily. "The enemy attacked simultaneously via three portals at Lincoln, Macrow, and Leolie. I was at Leolie with your mother when they launched their attack. It was a massacre; Lincoln and Macrow fell almost immediately. Leolie held out for seven hours before your mother ordered us to surrender. Not that there was much of it left to surrender by then."

There was a moment's silence. It was not unanticipated, but hearing it first hand was still difficult.

"What was their strength?" she asked finally.

"Your mother thought perhaps fewer than five Battlegroups in the original attack."

"And my mother, how is she?"

"When I last saw her she was in good health."

"Where is she now?"

"Under house arrest at Leolie."

Oh Mama, she thought sadly. "You said there were only five Battlegroups involved in the original attack," she said, dragging her thoughts back to the situation being discussed. "What's their strength now?"

Lonce shrugged. "I'm not sure. Most of the Etehad Sho'mali have been replaced by Hocawi and Malac Battlegroups." Ivy recognized the two as Lines as belonging to Miro's Conservative faction.

Ivy looked at the Force Leader.

"Seven," Tepin said definitely.

"Corps?"

He shook his head. "Battlegroups."

"Only seven Battlegroups? To hold all of North America?"

He shrugged. "The militia have been disarmed and the regular troops, what remains of them, are still in concentration camps, many off-line, and make excellent hostages. And with your mother under house arrest and your brother established as World Leader, seven are more than enough."

"My brother?"

"Arnold."

"Arnold!" She looked at him, stunned. Arnold! She felt a surge of anger at her brother's treachery.

"I see," she said coldly. She hoped her mother would be all right. With Arnold in charge, she should be, but there was there was something about the situation that made her feel uneasy. She checked her watch. "My thanks for your time, Leaders. Unfortunately I have another meeting to attend. I will speak to you again shortly. Marley will show you your quarters."

***

A week later Ivy surveyed the members of the Council gathered round the table and fumed. The Council had been debating Force Leader Tepin's report for the last five days and still hadn't decided what to do. Maybe she should just hand everything over to Arnold, she thought bitchily.

The building they'd appropriated to serve as temporary headquarters in Heidelberg was barely large enough for its function. Built in fake Tudor as a hunting lodge, its walls had been decorated with the heads of animals shot by those staying there. She'd had them cleared out of the room they were using for the Council meeting, but their shadows were still visible on the heavy wood paneling where they'd been hanging.

The room was really too small for everyone gathered there, and if it wasn't for the rain now falling outside she'd have ordered the windows opened. As it was, the atmosphere was thick enough to cut with a knife. It was obvious she wasn't the only one frustrated by the constant argument as she caught Cudomix' gaze. Because of the warmth his usual three-quarter length jacket was unbuttoned.

"Now," he mouthed.

She nodded, and as the Battlegroup Leader who had been speaking seemed to be running out of steam she leaned forward quickly.

"Leaders," she said. "We've been debating this issue for a week now, and you're still no closer to coming to a decision. You know my position, we can't remain on the defensive if we are to win this war. We have to attack."

Perhaps fewer than half nodded their agreement.

"You've all read Force Leader Tepin's report," she continued. "There's only seven Battlegroups on the entire American continent. In a week we could raise double that from the militia."

"All of whom have been disarmed," one of the Leaders pointed out.

"So we arm them," she said.

"And what of your brother, Arnold?" another asked. "Who's to say the militia won't follow him?"

"My mother," Ivy said. "And with the militia raised we could have the entire line back in our hands by spring."

"But what's the good of that?" someone asked. "If they simply open another portal and try again?"

"Assuming they did, we know they don't have limitless resources," Cudomix said.

"Neither do we," someone else pointed out.

"Leaders," Ivy said. "Please remember we are not fighting this war by ourselves, and that we have a responsibility to my father to prosecute the war to the limit of our ability."

There were more answering nods from around the table.

"Now, Corp Leader Cudomix and I have discussed the problems of transporting our troops across the Atlantic, and believe we have a solution. As you are aware, the problem with steamers is that they have a top speed of less ten knots, which makes them sitting ducks against my brother's auto-giros." They certainly should be aware, Ivy thought bitterly, they'd pointed it out enough times to her. "Airships, on the other hand, have a speed of eighty-five miles per hour and a ceiling well above an autogiro. They also have the advantage of being able to attack inland targets."

"And where do we get airships from?" one of the Italian Leaders asked.

"Leader Griffiths," she said, indicating the staff officer who had organized the stripping of the engines from the autogiros used in the successful attack on Neu Stuttgart.

The young staff officer cleared his throat uneasily. "My research indicates we could build fifty within six months. Hydrogen powered, of course, helium is too difficult to acquire. It increases the risk of fire but means each should be able to lift over a hundred tons."

"Where are you getting the engines from?" someone asked.

"We strip them from the autogiros."

"And the skin?"

"Linen coated in some form of paint, or perhaps rubber. The bags will be made out of ox-guts reinforced with cotton fabric. It's an approach that has been used on the Mainline."

"Will fifty be enough?" Leader Gllanz asked.

Ivy started to sense victory, Gllanz had been one of her strongest critics, and if he was prepared to discuss details she was almost there.

"More than enough," Ivy said. "In fact we need only twenty, enough for one Corps plus arms and ammunition for three more. The major problem as I see is secrecy. If they found out what we were doing — well hydrogen is very explosive."

The Governor looked around the table, and most there gave him an imperceptible nod.

"Airships it is then," he said.

"Good," she said. "We'll use the west coast shipyards; they've already had some experience working with linen and metal. Griffiths, get things rolling."

Griffiths nodded and made a note on the pad of paper in front of him.

"And that, Leaders, is that. We'll meet in a fortnight to discuss progress," she said.

Ivy remained seated as the room emptied. Was she right? Was she sending a lot of people to their deaths simply because her ego wouldn't accept her brother might have a better claim to be World Leader than she did?

She shook herself fiercely. No! If she started to doubt herself then the war was as good as lost. And she had only been speaking the truth when she said they had a responsibility to Papa to prosecute the war to the limit of their ability.

***

A month later, Ivy was reading Griffin's latest progress report on airship construction when she was interrupted by Marley's knock on the door.

"Leader, I'm sorry to interrupt you, but there's a Sergeant Horsing here who says he has something of yours."

Horsing, here? "Show him in," she said, getting to her feet.

"Sergeant, what are you doing here?" she demanded, pleased to see the tall, burly Sergeant as he was shown into the room. Somehow even his mere presence made the room seem smaller. His ginger hair was longer than it was the last time she had seen him.

"As I was bringing down two squads from Fort Larsa, Daniels asked me to give you this, and to thank you for her promotion."

"She deserved it," she said, taking the small package he handed her, wondering what it was. "Please, take a seat. Can I get you something to drink?"

He shook his head and sat down cautiously on the edge of the chair, placing his kepi neatly on his lap as he did so.

"It's good to see you," she said. "How is everyone?"

"Good."

"And what did Daniels say when she heard I was stripping the garrisons?"

He shrugged, avoiding her eyes and obviously unwilling to repeat what she'd said.

She suppressed a smile. "And you brought what, two squads?"

"Yes, it was all we could afford."

"I know, things are difficult everywhere. But we need at least two Corps for the invasion, and another Corps in case my brother tries to establish another portal."

He nodded, uncomfortably. "At least we don't have to worry about the Pegoni," he offered.

"No," she agreed; at least that was still working. "Did you have a good trip?"

"Passable. There were a lot of craft on the river."

"I've been trying to keep them dispersed. But as soon as we get some on their way, more arrive."

He said nothing and Ivy suddenly wondered why she was discussing matters of strategy with a mere Sergeant, unless it was because she considered him a friend.

"Do you have a job?" she asked.

"Not yet. I was just about to get my orders."

"Good," she said, a thought striking her. "I need a batman, and a friendly face to keep me sane. Marley!" she called out, and when her aide appeared. "Arrange to have Sergeant Horsing transferred to my personal staff as my batman. You better get him a room as well. We're a bit crowded," she explained to him, "but it will only be for another week, then we're off to the coast."

"Of course," Marley said. "Sergeant if you'd care to accompany me, we'll see about those orders."

"I'll see you in the morning," Ivy said, as Horsing reached the door.

He glowered at her before stomping off after Marley.

Ivy grinned to herself, just as her eyes caught sight of the package he'd brought. Hesitantly, her hand reached for her pocket knife, wondering what was in it.

She sliced the string and folded back the brown paper, to find the wooden box that contained Jon's letters. She remembered leaving it in the locked drawer in her office at the fort. She reached for the key but it was no longer round her neck. Of course, it hadn't been for some time, and then she saw the key in the wrapping.

Lifting the lid off carefully she found the letters, and underneath them the last letter from Jon, still unopened. Hesitantly she lifted it out of the box. It had been eight months, but the pain of his death still hurt every time she thought of him. Perhaps it was time though. She opened the envelope and slid the letter out.

6 January 96 AE
Bapaume, France
Mainline

Dearest Ivy

I dreamt of the coyote last night. For my people he is the one who calls us home from the land of the living. I hope I am mistaken, after all the coyote is a trickster, but I cannot go to the Shadow Worlds without telling you of how I feel.

I miss you so much. I read your letters each night, trying to take comfort in the details you provide me of your life. But it is a pale imitation of reality, and I miss your breath on my face, your body in my arms.

I was honored to serve as your father's aide, and the coming battle is one that I serve in, while not necessarily joyfully, at least with the certainty that what we are doing has to be done if our children are to ever see the kind of life that your father and your grandfather want to bring us.

Know that my love will never leave you, and that the hunting grounds cannot keep me from you. That I will be with you in spirit, in both your happiest times, and during your times of deepest despair. That when a breeze touches your cheek it will be my breath, and when a cool wind fans your face it will be my spirit passing by.

Think gently of me, my love. I wish we had had more time together and that I could have seen our children born and grow up with you. That is my only regret, that we were not given the time to grow old together, learn-

ing in each other's company as any couple has a right to do.

My dearest Ivy, our time together was short but brought me more joy than I had a right to expect. If my time is over then so be it, but yours must continue. Face life with a brave face my love, as a true warrior.

I remain your loving servant

Jon

Once again she felt tears silently well from her eyes, but this time not with the agony she had felt when she heard of his death. Carefully she refolded the letter and replaced it in the box.

"May the spirits lead you home, my love," she whispered softly, as she closed the lid of the box.

CHAPTER 17

Unknown location (near Detroit) — Mainline
November 1980 (96AE)

Arnold paused to adjust his cravat before nodding to the guard to open the door. As the door was opened, Donald, who was lying on the cell's single concrete bunk, looked over.

"Wait outside," Arnold told the guard. This was Clemhorn business.

Donald swung himself up to Arnold as the guard closed the door behind him.

"Hello Arnold," he said. "What are you doing here?"

Arnold shrugged. "As I was at Naisre on Council business, Petro asked me if I could oversee your questioning, and as it was on the way home…"

"Petro Raputa?"

"Yes." Arnold studied his brother. He'd changed, no longer the bookish scholar of less than twelve months before. There was something in his eyes that reminded Arnold of the dead look he'd seen in the eyes of other veterans of the war. Well, he was not the same person either. . .

And you said yes?"

"Of course." He looked around the cell with distate. "I'm sorry we couldn't provide you with accommodation more in keeping with your station."

Donald gave a wry smile as he glanced round the bare six foot by six foot room with its single, small, window and covered slop bucket. "It's pretty much what I was expecting."

Touché, Arnold thought. Trying to project an image of calm superiority, he leaned back against the door. "How is Papa?" he asked.

"Good," Donald replied.

"And Conrad?"

"The same."

"Good, good. And Ivy?"

"Ivy?" Donald looked puzzled. "Isn't she on Etu?"

"Of course, it's just I thought you must have seen her recently." It was obvious he must have, Ivy couldn't have destroyed the portal at Neu Stuttgart without help.

There was a pause.

"How's Mama?" Donald asked finally.

"I'm not sure. I haven't seen her for a while." Arnold mentally calculated how long it had been since he had last seen her. Had it really been five months? He must remember to ask Abbas how she was.

"Where is she?" Donald asked.

"At the house."

"And you haven't seen her for a while?"

"No, she is confined to her room. Once she has accepted the one true faith she will be released."

"Arnold, I swear, if you've harmed her!" Donald said, starting to rise to his feet.

"No," Arnold said, suddenly angry. Didn't Donald realize who was in charge! "You will not threaten me! My God has chosen me to do his will and with him beside me nothing shall prevail but his word." His forefinger jabbed Donald's chest, emphasizing each point, forcing his brother back onto the bunk. "That is something you would do well to remember, brother!" He almost spat the last word.

"God has ordained this war as a way to cleanse his enemies from the earth. You deserted me, left me in the hospital, but then he called me. Demonstrated his power in the force of his arms. Promised revenge against those who attacked me and killed Nedo. You deserted me. But that's no longer important for I now serve God's will. Stability *will* be restored to the Empire!"

"Will be? I thought Melanie Seaforth said the war was over?"

Arnold made a dismissive gesture.

Donald stared at him. "I'm sorry about the hospital," he said finally. "We thought it was safer to leave you there."

Arnold looked at his brother. Sincerity. . .perhaps? "It doesn't matter now. He called my name and I answered him. Since then I have sought to do his work. All I ask is that you accept him in your heart."

Donald shook his head. "I can't."

Like mother, like son. Arnold paused for a moment, considering, but his thoughts echoed distantly in the cold solitude of his mind. "Well, what's past is past," he said finally. "I had hoped that you would come to God of your own free will. But as it appears you won't, we will have to try another approach. I have to return to Etu for a couple of weeks, but I will see you again on my return."

He turned to knock on the door.

"So what happens now?" Donald asked as the guard opened the door.

Arnold ignored him; he would find out soon enough.

CHAPTER 18

Unknown location (near Detroit) — Mainline
November 1980 (96 AE)

The building stank of fear and disinfectant. Rajko stopped as the guard leading them down the corridor paused outside a cell door. The door, a dark, bilious green, had a large 'eight' scrawled over its hatch in white chalk. Rajko idly wondered why chalk had been used instead of paint. Given what he knew of the building, perhaps it was so the chalk could be wiped off, thus destroying any evidence of those the cell might once have housed.

His shoulders tensed at the way his sister stood so perfectly controlled behind him as they waited for the guard to unlock the door. The guard had to jiggle the key when it refused to turn all the way, but finally got it to move, and leaned into the heavy iron door with his shoulder to open it. With the door open Rajko could now hear the shallow, broken breathing of the cell's occupant. He glanced back at his sister.

"We'll see him by ourselves," she said.

The guard was taken aback. "My orders are that I'm to –"

"We'll see him by ourselves," she said, her control starting to fray.

The guard considered her black and silver uniform with its insignia of a Dontfrey Battlegroup Leader, started to open his mouth to argue, then, catching sight of Margaret's face, simply nodded.

Wise man, Rajko thought. As the insurrection on Dontfrey had ground on, and Margaret's Battlegroup had found itself fighting an increasingly bitter civil war, his sister had become less inclined to either negotiate or take prisoners.

"I'll need to lock you in," the guard said.

"Of course," Rajko said quickly, before Margaret could start to argue.

She glared at Rajko, then stalked into the cell ahead of him. Rajko followed her and the guard slammed the heavy door behind them.

There were no windows in the cell, just a single recessed light in the ceiling. Two, simple, concrete plinths without mattresses lined the two side walls and served as beds. A single, covered bucket had been placed by the door to serve as the toilet.

"Donald!" Margaret exclaimed, crossing to the far plinth in three strides.

Rajko frowned as he realized that what he had thought was a pile of blankets was actually his cousin, propped up against the wall, wrapped in a blanket, his eyes closed, shivering.

"Donald," Margaret repeated, her hands cradling Donald's bloodied and bruised face.

A slow burn of anger ignited in Rajko's chest — this was not right!

Donald peered at them through eyes almost too bruised to open. "Hello Margaret," he said in a whisper so soft that Rajko could barely hear it. "You took your time getting here."

"We came as soon as we heard," Rajko said, needing to defend Margaret, if not himself. "Neither Arnold or the First Leader exactly advertised your presence."

Donald started to laugh before letting out a gasp of pain.

"What?" Margaret demanded.

Donald winced. "You've just spoiled my surprise for Arnold."

"Surprise?"

"Yeah, before he left he said he wanted to talk to me again. I was going to piss him off by dying before he got back. Here, can you help me sit up?" Donald was struggling to sit up further by himself. Margaret put an arm around him to help, and as she did the blanket slipped from Donald's shoulder. At the sight of the bruising that covered his chest and stomach, Rajko swore.

Margaret froze, before turning back to Rajko. Her face was white with anger. "Rajko, either you get him out, or I will. And if I have to do it, no one is going to like the result."

Rajko grimaced, wondering if their parents knew just how brittle Margaret had become. If she fulfilled her threat, or even just lost her temper, the consequences could be catastrophic, not only for her but also for the rest of the family.

"All right, you stay here and look after him. This might take a while."

Margaret glared at him.

"We have to do this right," he said, "otherwise we're not going to get him out."

"I meant what I said," she warned him. Her voice was tight with anger.

"I know," he said, resting a hand on her shoulder. He started to put a hand out to Donald then, remembering his bruises, allowed it to fall back to his side. "I'll be as quick as I can," he promised.

He half expected to find someone had died by the time he got back, two hours later. Though whether it would have been Margaret, or the guard, he hadn't been sure. Perhaps his warning to the guard as to whom he would be speaking had persuaded him to demonstrate some sense and not try to evict Margaret.

"All done," he said exhaustedly, as the guard let him back into the cell. Neither Donald or Margaret appeared to have moved, and although all Rajko had done was talk on the phone he was drained.

Margaret glanced significantly at the door which the guard had closed and locked behind them.

"Give them a chance," he said. "The First Leader's Personal Secretary was just on the phone to the Governor when I left. Oh, and here they are now," he said brightly, as he heard the key in the lock.

"Leaders," the Governor said as he entered the cell. He gestured the orderly who had followed him in to push the wheelchair over to the bed. Obviously the Governor's temper had not improved, Rajko thought.

The orderly efficiently helped Donald into the wheelchair then pushed him out of the cell.

Margaret rose to her feet, alarmed. "Where — "

"To the infirmary," the Governor interrupted. "I'll see you there," he told Rajko, before following the orderly out.

Margaret started to follow but Rajko held up a hand. "What?" she demanded, irritated.

"You've been recalled," he said.

"What? That's ridiculous. The Corps has just gone into winter quarters."

"Unfortunately, the rebels don't seem to be operating on the same calendar. They've just recaptured Broken Arrow."

"You've got to be joking! How the hell did they manage to do that! We only kicked them out of there three months ago."

"Come on, we can talk on the way out. There's a car waiting for you."

"Rajko!" She started to protest, but he was already hustling her out of the cell. He didn't stop until they were outside and he allowed her to pause for a moment at the top of the steps.

"Are we getting reinforcements?" Margaret demanded, eying the vehicle waiting for her at the foot of the steps.

Rajko shook his head. "What you've got is all you get. I tried, but. . . " he gestured helplessly.

"Rajko. The army is all but fought out. My own Battlegroup is at fifty per cent of its normal peacetime strength."

"I know that Mags, but things are difficult across the entire C-TE at the moment. There's five Lines in overt rebellion, and even more who are simply ignoring the First Leader's decrees. "

"So he continues to bleed those who still do his bidding," she said, her eyes glinted with tears of frustration.

"Come on," Rajko said, placing a hand on her arm and guiding her down the steps. He wasn't ready to face Margaret's accusation.

"And Donald?"

"Safe for the moment. If only to ensure our continued good behavior."

Margaret paused at the foot of the steps, a mulish expression on her face as she considered what Rajko had said. "Then our esteemed First Leader had better take good care of Donald or he will find out exactly what my Battlegroup is capable of, half strength or not," she said finally.

Rajko decided to ignore the comment. It wasn't that he didn't believe her threat, it was because he did. The 501st had proven itself time and again against what appeared to be impossible odds. And from what his father had told him, the entire Battlegroup would walk through fire for her.

"Make sure you take of yourself," he said. "I worry about you."

"Yeah, well I worry about myself as well," she said, and with that she was in the car, and the door closed behind her.

Now what did she mean by that, he wondered, watching the car pull away. He looked up at the building behind. And just how was he going to ensure Donald was kept safe, given Miro's intentions for his cousin?

***

Two weeks later he was still no closer to a solution.

The guard outside the infirmary came to attention as Rajko approached him.

"Morning, John. Is my cousin awake?" Rajko asked.

"He was ten minutes ago, sir."

Rajko held up a ten pound note between two fingers. "Can you make sure we're not disturbed? I've been recalled to the capital, and I'd like to say my farewells to my cousin, without someone looking over my shoulder."

"Of course, sir," the guard said, making the note disappear.

Inside, he found Donald propped up in bed, eyes closed, listening to the some folk music on the radio, his fingers keeping beat on the coverlet.

"You're looking better," Rajko said.

"Feeling better," Donald admitted, opening his eyes and giving him a careful smile. He shifted to sit up a little more and winced. "You're here earlier than normal."

Rajko propped the pillows up behind Donald, before he took the plastic visitor's chair and plopped it down next to the bed. "I've been recalled to Naisre. Some sort of political disaster that needs my attention. I'm not sure I'll be back before they shift you."

"Shift? Where to?"

"A POW camp on Sultan. I tried to get you released on your personal recognizance, but Miro wouldn't hear of it. I'll keep trying though."

"Sultan?" Donald said uncertaily.

"An advanced line. Split off from ours just over a thousand years ago. Islamic — which explains the name."

"They're Miro's allies?"

"Yes. I tried to get you released into my care but Miro won't consider it until you provide the coordinates of the line your father is on."

"I wish I knew it," Donald said dryly. "It might have saved me a whole world of pain. Or perhaps not. They seemed to be intent on causing pain whatever I said." He winced at the memory.

"You don't know it then?"

Donald shook his head. "Papa and Kaito were the only ones who knew them."

Rajko studied Donald. He was holding something back. Donald probably didn't know the actual coordinates, but that didn't mean he didn't know something, some hint that would have allowed them to start identifying the line's coordinates. He resolved to keep that piece of intelligence to himself. There was more than a kernel of truth in what Donald had said about his questioners enjoying the pain, he had seen the medical reports. There could have been no other reason for some of what they had done. Besides, if Margaret ever found out . . . No, far better to play dumb.

He pulled out a cigarette case from his breast pocket and slid the catch up to the left. As he did so, he could just make out the soft hiss of static on the edge of his hearing. He placed it on the small table beside the bed.

Donald raised an eyebrow.

"It's a white noise generator. If there's a bug in here it shouldn't be able to hear us," Rajko explained. "Borrowed it from a friend in Imperial Intelligence."

"That's not really like you," Donald said. "You've normally played a straight bat."

"Times change. So shoot, I'm not sure how long we've got."

"What?"

"Questions. I presume you have some. I had a letter from Margaret yesterday. Posted before she left the Mainline." At least she had had the sense to post it while she was still on the Mainline, he thought. Miro's paranoia was getting stronger all the time, and with any correspondence from Dontfrey getting opened by the censors, the risk was all the greater. "She insisted I answer any questions you have, as she couldn't stay to answer them herself."

"So Margaret was here? I thought she was, but I wasn't sure."

"She was visiting at Naisre when we heard of your capture. We came as soon as we heard."

"How is she?"

Rajko remembered her brittleness. "Unhappy she couldn't stay. Unfortunately, her Battlegroup got yanked out of winter quarters and she got recalled. So — questions," he reminded him.

"You're still fighting? I would have thought the revolt would have been over by now. I mean . . ." Donald gestured helplessly.

"You mean now Miro's won he could have sent the full might of the C-TE against the rebels. Crushed them." He shook his head. "No. We're having to do it the hard way, village by village." He remembered the look on Margaret's face before she left. "The First Leader is still having a certain amount of difficulty in restoring his control over a number of Lines," he explained with a tight smile. "It appears the legitimacy of his claim was severely affected when he broke the Edict."

"At least half the Lines that had been loyal to your grandfather are still refusing to accept him," he continued. "Most are simply ignoring him, although a number are in overt rebellion, Clyde for example. I presume you're aware of the bad blood between Miro and the McArthurs."

Donald nodded. The McArthurs controlled Clyde, and Hayden McArthur, the youngest son of the World Leader, was one of Conrad's closest friends. As a result, Conrad had told him about the trouble between Petro, Miro's son, and Nyree, Hayden's sister-in-law, and Nyree's attempted suicide.

"The First Leader's new allies, the Etehad Sho'mali, appear to have their own troubles as well which has meant he has been forced increasingly back on his own resources. Unfortunately, this has meant he's had to increase taxes, which is making him unpopular, even with those who welcomed the end of the war. Even Arnold is having difficulties."

"Arnold?" Donald said bitterly. "According to my father's former factor it was all settled on Etu."

"In America, perhaps," Rajko said. "But Ivy still holds Europe."

"So that was why Arnold asked about Ivy. And my mother?"

Rajko shook his head. "I don't know. Arnold has virtually cut off any communication with the line. I only know about Ivy because she beat off an attack on her base by the Etehad Sho'mali, and they report direct to the First Leader. It was quite remarkable, she completely annihilated two regiments of their crack troops — about the equivalent of a full Corps."

"Good for her," Donald said.

There was a knock on the door. "Just a moment," Rajko called. Standing up, he slid the catch on the cigarette case to off and replaced it in his pocket. "Look after yourself," he said, holding out his hand. "I'm not sure when we'll see each other again. But rest assured I'll try to get you home as soon as possible."

"Thanks for your help, Rajko," Donald told him sincerely. "But if I could just ask one more favor?"

"If I can."

"Check on Mama for me. Arnold seemed . . . strange."

"Of course." Rajko promised, thinking that 'strange' really didn't cover Arnold's recent behavior.

CHAPTER 19

Choququirau — Mmbuto é Line
(Charleston, COA, Mainline equivalent)
December 1980 (96AE)

It was after midnight in America, but Conrad still couldn't sleep. He was going to be a father! It was a concept that just wouldn't let him get to sleep — it kept running round and round in his mind like a startled rabbit. Linele's even breathing filled the room from deep within the pile of thick blankets on the bed next to him, and raising himself on one elbow he looked down at her wonderingly.

To tell the truth, he still had a problem getting his head round the whole concept of fatherhood, he thought, as he allowed his head to fall back onto the pillow. His eyes tracked over the faint remnants of the murals that had once covered the ceiling without really seeing them. Not that he wasn't happy about the news, it was just that he had never really thought it would happen like this. Or that he would feel about someone the way he felt about Linele. Maybe he was finally starting to grow up, he thought with a wry smile.

Hesitantly, he reached out an arm to hug her. He froze when she stirred, but she simply pulled his arm in tighter around her and with a happy grin he settled himself in beside her.

He was disturbed early the next morning by a rap on the door. What now, he thought irritably, blinking his eyes against the light that had leaked in around the sheets covering the window. Leaning over the edge of the bed he checked his watch lying on the floor next to the bed. Half seven, great, less than six hours sleep. Once upon a time he wouldn't have even noticed the lack of sleep, but now if he didn't get his eight hours he'd be exhausted for the whole day. Not that he regretted getting to sleep so late, the sex had been fantastic — but it would have been nice to have had a longer lie in. He grinned when he remembered the reason for Linele's aggressive affection last night — he was going to be a father!

He turned to find Linele's brown eyes looking back at him.

"Hadn't you better find out what it is?" she said.

"I suppose so. I'd much rather stay here, though," he said, reaching for her.

"Didn't you get enough of that last night?" she demanded.

"Last night, perhaps. But this is now."

"Go," she said with a smile, giving him a little shove.

"Stay there," he said, swinging his legs out of the bed and reaching down to pull his trousers on.

"I was going to," she said, stretching languidly.

Conrad paused, his eyes captured by her unconscious beauty. She caught him looking and gave him a mock look of irritation. "Go and see who it is."

"Yes ma'am," he said with a smile.

Suddenly the expression on her face became one of panic, and she threw the blankets off and made a dash for bathroom. The door closed and he heard the sound of retching.

He winced in sympathy. At least, while they didn't have running water, the toilet was still working, and there was a bucket in there to flush it. "You going to be all right?" he called through the closed door as he started to lace his tunic up.

There was a muffled reply, which he took to be in the affirmative. There was another knock on the door. "This better be important," he muttered under his breath as he swung the door open.

He must have been muttering louder than he thought as the two standing outside took a hasty step back.

Sinclair, the Force Leader in charge of the 48th's troops allocated to the mission, looked particularly worried.

"What?" Conrad demanded.

"My apologies, Leader," the young Force Leader said. He had been a Squad Leader less than a year before, but promotions had been rapid as a consequence of the war. "But you were emphatic you were to be told as soon we established contact with Rufiji."

"The radio's up?" Conrad said.

"Yes Leader," Jubu said.

Jubu was the commander of the Company of the High King's Imperial Guard accompanying the expedition. A tall, suave Nguni, Linele referred to him as a 'cousin' — although Conrad wasn't sure of his exact relationship to the High King. Linele had done her best to explain the complex web of relationships that bound the ruling families together, but the way the Mmbuto é overlaid a matriarchal descent line with a kinship system similar to some Mainline Australian Aboriginals just made his head hurt. There was no doubt Jubu was a snob, his accent was the most affected of those from the ruling class Conrad had heard. If he hadn't been so good at his job Conrad would have had him replaced — unfortunately he was, so here he was.

They were interrupted by the sound of dry-retching from the bathroom.

"Is the Princess all right?" Jubu asked, trying to see around Conrad.

"It's only morning sickness," Conrad said, lifting his greatcoat up from the bench. "They've got the radio link working. I've got to go," Conrad called back over his shoulder to Linele.

"Morning sickness?" Jubu asked, standing aside to let him pass.

"We're having a baby," Conrad said. He paused, liking the sound of what he'd just said.

There was a flash of emotion across Jubu's normally impassive face, but it was gone too fast for Conrad to recognize.

"My congratulations, Leader," Sinclair said.

"Thank you."

Cornelia, one of Linele's three maids, appeared through the door at the end of the corridor, and Conrad looked at her thankfully.

"The Princess is in the toilet throwing up. When she's finished you might want to see if she wants anything to eat. Something bland perhaps."

"Of course, Leader. Valeria has just finished making some bread. I'll see if I can get her to eat some of that."

"Thank you," he said with a grateful nod.

Pulling the belt on his greatcoat tighter he started down the corridor, careful not to brush against the exposed lathes where the plaster had fallen away. It was hell to get marks left by the plaster off the greatcoat.

The two marines on duty outside came to attention as they stepped onto the porch. The sun had been up for only half an hour and it was still freezing. Jamming his hands in his pockets he tried to think positive thoughts. But all he could think of was how warm it would be in Mexico at the moment.

"I'll be glad when it starts to warm up," Sinclair said, echoing his thoughts.

Conrad nodded, taking a moment to look around as he settled the weight of his greatcoat more comfortably on his shoulders.

A stream meandered down the street towards the harbor from a pond farther up the hill where a beaver had set up a lodge. The area they were in, a short distance from the center of Choququirau, consisted of small, four-story apartments, each surrounded by a large garden. When Treik's 'biological strike' had removed humanity from the scene the gardens had run wild, the greenery quickly flowing out of the narrow sidewalks and into the road.

Below him, at the bottom of the hill, two ships rode at anchor in the harbor, surrounded by flocks of seagulls and the occasional osprey or sea eagle. The fleet's other eight vessels were berthed further upriver at Xochtl, which they'd decided was more suited for the needs of a new settlement than Choququirau. They had retained a small military garrison here, with the intention of establishing a fishing village at the mouth of the river in spring.

A pod of dolphins was playing in the surf at the mouth of the river. Conrad shook his head; the wildlife was unbelievable. There'd been a flock of geese a day after their arrival which had stretched from horizon to horizon. It almost seemed wrong that they were there to spoil it.

The distant howl of a hunting wolf brought an atavistic surge of fear, and Conrad resisted the urge to check his gun.

"Let's go," Conrad said, starting towards the closest of the three massive hexagonal stepped pyramids that dominated the city's skyline.

The pyramids had been coated with some of sort of ultra-white gloss that had resisted the ravages of time better than the concrete or brick of most of the city's other buildings, but even these once-pristine surfaces were starting to break down as moss and lichen formed on the pyramid's northern side.

They'd set the base station up at the base of the pyramid, the antenna being strung between the top of the pyramid and a nearby building. The radio hut had been made out of clapboard brought down from Xochtl, the roof covered with a tarpaulin to make it waterproof. A small coal stove warmed the room enough for him to undo the top button of his greatcoat as he entered.

"Ah Leader," the young signaler said, standing up to offer him her seat. "They're waiting for you."

"How's the signal?" Conrad asking, taking the offered seat as one of the signalers handed him a mug of coffee. He accepted it with a grateful nod.

"The signal's solid."

"Rufiji," Conrad said, pressing the transmit button. "This is Choququirau base, Clemhorn speaking."

"Please wait, Choququirau base," came the reply after a short delay.

Behind him, Sinclair pulled up a chair to share the wait.

"Where's Jubu?" Conrad asked noticing that the tall Nguni seemed to have disappeared.

"He said he needed to speak to someone," Sinclair said.

"Choququirau base, this is Rufiji." The speaker made his father's voice sound hollow, but the clarity was impressive.

"Hello Rufiji, nice to hear from you."

"Likewise. It's been a while."

"Any word from Donald?" Conrad asked. The expedition had received news about Donald's successful departure for the Mainline before leaving Muanda, at the mouth of the Congo, but that had been several months ago.

"Nothing yet."

That didn't sound good, Conrad thought. They should have had some sort of response by now.

"How's it going your end?" his father asked.

"Good," Conrad said. "As agreed we have established a base at the mouth of the Ashley River. The main settlement is about ten miles farther up river."

"And when do you think you'll be returning?"

"Another six weeks or so. I'd like to avoid the worst of the winter weather. The ships aren't exactly built for an Atlantic crossing." He didn't say the real reason was to give Linele's morning sickness the opportunity to settle down before trying the crossing.

"Understandable. I feel I should warn you there's a consortium that's just been floated to send a second fleet. All they're waiting for is your return."

Conrad suppressed a sigh. It was understandable, but he couldn't help thinking that the arrival of more humans was going to spoil the post-human paradise they found themselves in. "Roger that."

"All right, I'll speak to you tomorrow."

"Choququirau base out," Conrad said.

Stretching, Conrad stood up, allowing the signaler to reclaim her seat.

"Well that's it," Conrad told Sinclair, not admitting that finally re-establishing communications with Rufiji gave him a sense of security. Although what they could do from there if anything went wrong here he wasn't sure. He checked his watch. "I know we have a staff meeting scheduled for eight-thirty but let's reschedule it to ten. Can you let everyone know? That will let me see how the Princess is going and grab some breakfast."

"Of course, Leader."

With a nod Conrad headed outside, doing his greatcoat up again as he did so.

There wasn't any sign of the two sentries as he approached the house and he frowned unhappily. A sudden scream from inside followed by a single shot had him break into a run, his greatcoat flapping around his knees. As he ran he ripped off his gloves, his fingers struggling to open the stiff cover on his pistol holster.

He'd managed to free his pistol by the time he reached the low stone balustrade that marked the edge of the porch, and vaulting the stone work took cover by the side of the window. Peering in through the glassless opening he could see the two sentries lying sprawled on the ground inside; one's neck was clearly broken. How had Miro found them? He had to find Linele!

He pulled back the slide mechanism on his pistol and released it, waiting a moment to make sure no one had noticed the noise. There was no response from inside.

He considered the door but he was already at the window. He threw a leg over and stepped inside. Carefully, he worked his way over to the door, stepping around the two marines as he did so. Every instinct he had cried out for him to hurry but if he rushed he'd end up dead, which wouldn't help anyone.

He peered around the door; the corridor was empty. There was a heavy thud and the sound of splintering wood from the direction of the bedroom. Cautiously, he started down the corridor, pistol at the ready.

At the door to the bedroom he crouched low, peering round the edge of the door. Cornelia was standing in the center of the room, her eyes wide with fear, a knife at her throat. Conrad frowned, his eyes widening as he recognized Jubu holding the knife. A body lay sprawled in the corner in a puddle of blood, the contents of a breakfast tray scattered across the floor around her. Valeria! Just what was going on?

There was another crash from the bathroom door, and Conrad's attention snapped to the Imperial Guardsman slamming a heavy chair against the door. There was a barrage of profanities from the bathroom and Conrad smiled in relief as he recognized Linele's voice.

The first priority was Jubu, Conrad thought, as he turned his attention back to the tall Nguni. Luckily Jubu's attention was fixed exclusively on the Guardsman, but unfortunately his position behind Cornelia made it difficult for a clean shot.

There was the sound of splintering glass from the bathroom. That was it, he Conrad thought, he was out of time.

"Jubu," Conrad said.

The tall Nguni's head snapped round, and Conrad fired.

The bullet hit Cornelia in the shoulder, slamming her back against Jubu. The bullet probably slanted up through her shoulder as Jubu's arm suddenly went limp. Conrad didn't hesitate. Correcting his aim, he fired again, this time taking Jubu in the eye, then, taking a step into the room, he fired at the Guardsman. The pistol jammed, however, and Conrad swore. The Guardsman had already dropped the chair and was going for his own pistol when Conrad stepped forward. Swinging the pistol up he smashed the heavy barrel into the face of his opponent. The Guardsman dropped without a sound.

"Linele," he called, working the slide mechanism to clear the jammed cartridge. The cartridge ejected and he cocked the gun again.

"Conrad?" the Princess asked.

Conrad let out a breath, his hand starting to shake. "Are you all right? What happened?"

"I'm fine. Jubu tried to kill me."

There was the sound of the latch, then someone trying to open the door.

Conrad considered the Guardsman, unsure how long he would remain unconscious. Deciding safety was paramount he raised the pistol and put a single shot through the Guardsman's forehead.

"Conrad!" The word was a scream from the bathroom.

"Sorry," he apologized. "Accident."

There was another rattle of the door. "I could do with some help here," Linele said sharply when the door refused to open.

"Wait a moment," Conrad said, squatting down to check on Cornelia. She was unconscious, but when he examined the wound she opened her eyes and whimpered. "Hold still," he said reassuringly. He grabbed a sheet and used Jubu's knife to slice it into a strip that could be made into a pressure bandage.

The door rattled again. "Conrad?"

"Won't be a moment. Cornelia's been shot."

Efficiently, he wound the bandage round the wound. The blood staunched, Conrad turned his attention to the bathroom door. It was definitely stuck, but with the latch off maybe he could force it.

"Stand back," he called, picking up the chair the Guardsman had been using. He could feel his anger shimmering — someone had tried to kill Linele! Furiously he slammed the chair against the door. The door burst open and Linele stared back at him wide-eyed, her hair frizzing out from her head like an irate African wild cat. A large shard of glass, wrapped in a towel, was clutched in her hand as a dagger. Seeing him standing there she carefully placed the makeshift weapon on the shelf before throwing herself into his arms.

He hugged her back — hard! For a moment he could only hold her, only just realizing how close he had come to losing her.

"Well, you took your time," she said finally, looking up at him.

He raised an eyebrow. "You were lucky I turned up when I did," he said. "I had an officers' meeting scheduled for. . . " he checked his watch. "Five minutes ago."

"Jubu must have been relying on that," she said softly.

"Valeria's dead," he said, not letting her go.

She nodded into his chest. "I know, if she hadn't diverted them I'd never have escaped."

"So what was all this about?" he asked, a hand helplessly indicating the scene that surrounded them.

Slipping out of Conrad's arms, she crossed to Jubu and kicked him — hard. "It seems my cousin. . . " she kicked him again, "this piece of putrefied pus. . . " and again, "was attempting to prevent a half-breed from taking the throne."

Conrad picked up Linele's robe, but his attempt to drape it over her shoulders was prevented when Cornelia groaned.

"Cornelia's hurt," Linele said, starting towards her maid.

"I did say that," he said defensively, following her.

"I didn't think the Mmbuto é were racist," he said as Linele finally accepted the robe, slipping into it before bending to check Cornelia's bandage. Although some of the Lines in the Cross-Temporal Empire might have practiced racial discrimination before their integration into the Empire, Traek's aggressive insistence on a total meritocracy had left the Empire without any of those insidious memes.

"We're not," Linele said. "But there is still a residue of support for the Monomotapa caste system among some of the ruling families. I will need to speak to the High King. It is probably past time that its supporters were convinced of the wrongness of their beliefs. Particularly now." She patted her stomach.

She glanced back at her cousin. "It's not surprising, I guess, given his background. The Ngori family has always boasted of its impeccable credentials, and its close links to the ruling family. Still, I can remember his kindness to me when my mother died."

Cornelia moaned.

"I'd better see about a medic," Conrad said. He paused uncertainly, uneasy at the thought of leaving Linele.

Sensing his concern, Linele looked up. "I'll be fine."

Seeing the dead Guardsman's pistol lying on the ground, Conrad picked it up. He clicked the safety off, and worked the slide to make sure there was something in the breech. "Safety's off," he said, placing it on the ground next to her hand.

She glanced at it before returning her gaze to Cornelia, giving the merest of nods.

He hesitated, but she was right, someone had to get help.

Outside the building, he paused for a moment, wondering what was going to be the fastest way of getting assistance. He was startled by a yell and saw two marines running up the street towards him. Presumably someone had heard the shots. His first instinct was to raise his weapon but that might not be the best way of greeting them if they were friends. He compromised by keeping the pistol cocked but at rest.

"Leader," the first marine said coming to halt in front of him, struggling to catch his breath. "We heard shots!"

"There has been attempt on the Princess' life," Conrad said. "She is unharmed but we need a medic urgently for her maid. You," he indicated the first marine with his finger. "Get a medic and a stretcher team. And you," he added, pointing to the second. "Find Force Leader Sinclair, I need him and a Troop of the 48th here — *stat*! Now move it!"

He watched the two take off back down the hill at the sprint and returned inside where he found Linele watching Cornelia with worried eyes.

"How is she?" he asked. The bandage looked to be holding, but he was worried about what the bullet might have hit on the way through. "The medic is on the way."

She gave a small nod. "Thank you."

Conrad bent and gently kissed her forehead. "Don't ever do that to me again," he said. "I've never been so worried in my life."

"I'll try," she said.

"Good," he said sincerely.

CHAPTER 20

Unknown location (near Detroit) — Mainline
January 1981 (97AE)

Donald groggily opened his eyes as the door to his cell slammed open.
"On your feet," the guard ordered. "You're being moved."
Donald stood up as quickly as his bruises would let him.
"Outside," the guard said, slamming the door with his baton. Donald got the message.
There were already four other prisoners in the corridor, and it was with a wry smile Donald realized the pale-blue, terrycloth tracksuits they'd been issued were virtually the same color as Etu's militia uniform.
A trustee quickly attached the de rigueur leg irons, while another threaded a chain through and locked it in place. His arms were fastened behind his back as another guard appeared carrying black hoods which were placed over their heads. Donald's nostrils were immediately filled with the scent of stale sweat.
"Right, everyone forward," the guard said.
Donald heard the chain clink and cautiously started to shuffle forward. It was disorientating under the hood and progress was slow, but finally he heard the scrape of a key being inserted into a lock, and as the door was opened, a rush of cold, fresh air immediately had him shivering. It was night, and the cold, winter wind cut through the thin material of his tracksuit like a hot knife through butter.
A coach was waiting for them, its engine slowly idling as they shuffled on board and were locked into their seats. It was then Donald discovered just how stiff and sore he still was. Mercifully the trip was fairly short, and perhaps fifteen minutes later they shuffled their way off the coach. Through the thin soles of his slipper he could tell they were standing on brick, and, under the edges of the hood, he could just make out the high intensity security lights that surrounded them.
"Keep moving," one of the guards said.
Donald flinched as a baton tapped his shoulder.
Once again the prisoners started to shuffle forward, dragging their feet until he felt the familiar lurch in reality, and between one step and the next he'd stepped onto another line.
There was a strange echo in the air, as though he was standing in the center of a massive hangar. Under the hood the air smelled of diesel and stale oil. The floor was now concrete, so cold it burned through the pa-

per-thin soles of his slippers as though they didn't exist.

"Move it," someone with a strong East-European accent said, and carefully they started to shuffle forward again.

A moment later he heard the clank of the chain hitting a step. Donald had been watching his feet, and under the edge of the hood saw they were following a line marked out in yellow on the concrete apron.

He felt a baton press against his chest, and paused.

"Okay," the guard said, as the baton was removed and he stepped forward, stumbling fractionally as he ran into the step. Someone's hand on his shoulder steadied him as he felt a tug on his leg irons and quickly he stepped up onto the step. As he did so, he heard the coach's engine grind into life.

As he was locked into his seat his fingers stroked the smooth surface of his seat. It felt slickly smooth, quite unlike anything he'd felt before.

He heard the door swing shut, and with a lurch they were on their way. Gradually the air inside the coach started to warm, and mercifully for Donald's bruises the road proved smooth and the ride uneventful. Under the hood he quickly lost all track of time, but finally the noise and vibration from the tires indicated they had left the main road. After another fifteen minutes they finally stopped, and in the abrupt silence of a dying engine he could hear the leg irons being unlocked. Unexpectedly his hood was removed and he blinked in the sudden light of an early dawn.

"Everyone out," the guard said, emphasizing the order with a short jerk of his baton.

Donald was the first out, struggling to stand erect as blood returned painfully to cramped limbs. Around him rocky hills, topped with fresh snow, crowded the faint, washed-out sky.

The coach was parked in a compound surrounded by a high wire fence, topped with several rolls of new barbed wire that glinted in the weak morning light. The compound was just big enough for the coach, but beyond it was a larger enclosure also surrounded by barbed wire. Inside, rows of long, wooden huts had been constructed parallel to the slope of a low hill.

Outside the wire, guard towers squatted like giant insects on freshly plowed ground, while beyond them a forest glistened in the dawn light. The smell of conifers drifted in, faintly antiseptic over the stink of mud and fresh manure that wafted down from the main compound.

A shove brought his attention back to what awaited them beyond the wire, and the three hundred or so prisoners clustered there, listlessly watching them, clutching worn blankets around their shoulders for extra warmth. All looked half-starved, and while most wore light blue tracksuits, perhaps a third wore the tattered remains of what had once been military uniforms.

Having herded them through into the main yard, the guards closed the gates behind them and they were left standing there uncertainly. It was only for a moment, then a prisoner, wearing a shabby gray Mainliner uniform and an armband with a small embroidered star on his shoulder, stepped forward.

"Welcome to Concentration Camp 5123," he said in what Donald, who had spent four weeks in Arabia with his Battlegroup during a training exercise a couple of years before, recognized as Arabic. Unfortunately that was all he could do, the speaker's accent was so bad Donald couldn't understand what he was saying, and he wasn't the only one.

"English?" the speaker said, noticing their blank expressions.

There were answering murmurs from the group.

"Welcome to Concentration Camp 5123," he repeated, this time in English. "I am Group Leader Aleksey Slavinsky. You have all been charged with Crimes against the State and against God. If you come with me the prison committee will answer any questions you have."

As they made their way up the slight slope, the prisoners who had been watching their arrival started to drift off.

"How long have you been here?" Donald asked the Group Leader.

"Six months," Aleksey said. "I was a Group Leader in the 51st Rapid Deployment Battlegroup, stationed in England. They gave us the option of transferring off-line, or demobilizing. Well, I chose demob and ended up here." He shrugged, spitting. "So much for ten years' loyalty to the C-TE."

The three people who made up the prison committee were waiting for them, sitting on a bench on the porch of the first building. A row of wooden crates had been set up facing them. All three on the committee had beards, and wore the standard sky-blue tracksuit prison uniform. One, the youngest, was equipped with a leather-bound ledger, quill, and a small ink bottle.

The Group Leader came to attention and saluted as the clerk opened his ledger. He said something in Arabic, of which Donald picked up only the word — 'English'.

"Please sit," Aleksey said, turning back to the newcomers, indicating the crates.

Donald cautiously took his seat, uncertain about the crate's strength. It creaked, and shifted warningly, but held.

Donald was first.

"Name?" the clerk asked him.

"Donald Clemhorn."

"Clemhorn," Aleksey said uncertainly. He was obviously trying to remember where he had heard the name before. "Are you related to the

Leader of. . ." he paused trying to remember.

"Etu," Donald said for him. "Yes, my father is the World Leader. My grandfather was First Leader Griffin."

"Of course," Aleksey said. "Do they know about it?" he asked, with a jerk of his head in the direction of the main entrance, and the guards.

"I don't know," Donald said. "They may, Miro definitely does, but. . ." he shrugged.

"Bureaucracies, heh." Aleksey said with a smile. He explained something to the committee in Arabic, who leaned forward with interested. After a quick debate Aleksey nodded and turned to Donald. "Come with me."

As Donald stood up he could not stop a grimace of pain.

Aleksey studied him for a moment. "We better take you to see the physician first. This way," he said, holding the door open into the building behind them. "Dr. Malinal was a rehabilitation and trauma management specialist before he ended up here."

"I'm impressed," Donald said.

Aleksey shrugged. "We've got all sorts here, but Dr. Malinal was a real godsend. The real problem is medical supplies, but we've recently started our own gardens, and there is some trade with the guards."

They were now walking down the center of a long hall, between rows of three tiered bunks, towards a space at the far end of the hall marked off by blankets hanging from the ceiling. About half of the beds were occupied, and here and there the bunks had been pushed apart and groups of men were playing cards between them. It felt strange to Donald not to see a single female.

"How many prisoners does this place hold?" Donald asked. There must have been at least four hundred sleeping in this building alone.

"Just over two thousand, although most of them are from Sultan. Dissidents, criminals, heretics, you name it. A lot are straight political prisoners. Generally we're left pretty much to ourselves. They have roll call every morning to make sure none of us have escaped during the night, but otherwise we're left alone."

"And does anyone try to escape?" Somehow he had to get back to let his father know what was happening.

"Not anymore."

Donald looked enquiringly at him. "Why not."

"Once the guards started to randomly select twice as many prisoners as those escaping, the camp committee soon put a stop to any attempts. Through here," he said, lifting up a corner of the blanket and gesturing Donald through.

Thanks to a small stove set up in one corner, the enclosed space was slightly warmer than the rest of the barracks. Five bunks had been set up around the inside of the small space, and a couple were presently occupied. A dark, swarthy man with a large beard and thick, bushy eyebrows looked around as they came in. He nodded once as he finished filling an enameled mug from a heavy, cast-iron kettle that had been simmering on the stove.

"Morning Aleksey," he said. "What can I do for you?"

"Got a newbie for you to check out."

The doctor looked Donald up and down. "Tea?" he asked.

"Wouldn't mind one," Donald said.

"Aleksey?"

"Thanks."

The doctor retrieved another two mugs and poured them both a cup. "So, what's your story?" he asked Donald.

Donald shrugged as he accepted the cup, uncomfortable about discussing what had happened to him.

The doctor looked him understandingly. "Torture?"

Donald nodded.

"Well, you better undress. Aleksey, can you wait outside."

The physical was quite thorough, and once it was finished, and Donald was dressed again and sitting up on the bare wood table, Aleksey was called back in.

"You've received medical treatment?" Dr. Malinal said as he washed his hands in a bowl of soapy water.

Donald nodded. "Once my cousins discovered what had happened. Their father is a Continental Leader."

"Well, the bruises will disappear soon enough but in the short term I'd expect you to suffer insomnia, irritability, and flashbacks. Longer term ..." he shrugged. "A lot of torture victims suffer post-traumatic stress disorder, depression, and adjustment disorder. We do have a support group operating in the camp — if you're interested come and see me."

"Thanks," Donald said. He'd already found out how difficult it was getting to sleep.

"There may also be some physical effects," the doctor said warningly.

"Such as?" So what else could go wrong?

"Rheumatism, post-traumatic epilepsy, and possible sterility. I don't think you need to worry about that at this stage though," the doctor said with a snort. "For now, just try and rest up." He looked around the clinic with a sigh. "Not that's there's much else you can do in here."

"No," Donald agreed, feeling a sudden surge of bitterness towards

Arnold.

"Anything else?" Aleksey asked.

The doctor shook his head. "Not for the moment. Ah, hold on, you'd better have one of these," he said, handing him a neatly folded blanket.

"Right, let's take you round to see the Chief then," Aleksey said.

Outside it was still bitterly cold and, as the wind had started to pick up, Aleksey paused a moment to allow Donald to wrap the blanket round his shoulders, before starting up the hill.

There were six men playing marbles on the hard ground outside the door of the last hut and as Aleksey and Donald approached they got to their feet warningly.

Aleksey said something in Arabic and they settled back to their game. Bodyguards?

Aleksey knocked on the door and when it was opened waved Donald in.

Once again two blankets, hanging from the roof, had been used to create a smaller space inside the main building, while a third, slightly moth-eaten, had been laid over the bare wooden floorboards to serve as a carpet. Three cushions, richly and incongruously decorated given their surroundings, furnished the space. An Arab wearing a traditional white burnoose and headcloth was sitting cross-legged on one of the cushions, studying a text on the blanket in front of him.

He looked up as they entered and Donald was surprised to find himself meeting the eyes of an ancient native-American with a long white beard, and fading, Aztec-styled tattoos on both his cheeks.

"Hawiku Mohammad, I'd like you to meet Donald Clemhorn," Aleksey said in English.

Despite his age, Hawiku rose gracefully from his cushion and salaamed elegantly.

Donald, who had started to put his hand out, smoothly copied the gesture. "Allah's blessing on you and yours," Donald said in Arabic.

"You speak our language," Hawiku said.

"A little," Donald admitted. "I was in Arabia for a couple of weeks with my Battlegroup."

"Please sit," Hawiku said.

"Donald's father is the World Leader of Etu, and is presently Leader of the Empire's alternative faction," Aleksey explained.

Donald started at that, but quickly covered it with a wince as he lowered himself cautiously to the ground.

"Ah," Hawiku said with a slight widening of his eyes. "That could not have come at a better time."

"Oh?"

"Would you be able to contact your father if we were to get you out of here?" Hawiku asked.

"Once back on the Mainline, yes," Donald said.

Hawiku nodded thoughtfully. "Then your presence, Donald Clemhorn, is most fortuitous. It would almost seem, as the Sunni claim, that Allah's hand can be seen in the writing. Aleksey, I will need to change our plans so I'll leave our new guest in your care. We will talk again Donald Clemhorn," he said, as Aleksey stood up and offered Donald a hand.

"Now what?" Donald said, when they were outside again.

"Now we find you a bed," Aleksey said with a smile.

"So what's going on here?" Donald asked, as they started to head back down the hill. "I mean, it's definitely more complicated than I thought it was when I was back on the Mainline."

"You mean on Sultan? The Sultan time-line?" he explained at Donald's blank look.

"Yes."

Aleksey frowned. "Complicated only begins to explain it. Basically, Sultan is split between two major military alliances; the Etehad Sho'mali who are the First Leader's allies, and the Etehad Junoobil. The Etehad Junoobil consists of Mexico, and the Northern Caliphate, which makes up most of Central Europe. The Etehad Sho'mali consists of Peru, the Western Caliphate, which is most of Western Europe, and the Southern Caliphate which covers Africa and the Middle East. We're presently in the territory of the United Tribes of the Great Plains. As I understand it, they used to be neutral until a coup about three years ago by a small group of Hussan Scriptureese brought them into the Etehad Sho'mali."

"And Hawiku?" Donald asked.

"He was a Chief among the United Tribes before the coup. Here, you'll be bunking down with me," he said, opening the door to the barracks.

***

Two weeks later, he was awakened from a light doze by Aleksey's hand over his mouth. As he opened his eyes he could hear the wind howling around the eaves outside.

"What is it?" he asked softly when Aleksey removed his hand.

"Shh," Aleksey ordered.

There were a number of prisoners clustered by the door, and others around them had stirred at the movement.

Donald had just started to lever himself out of the bed when there was a sudden explosion, and all the lights went off. Someone in the hut yelled in alarm, as automatic fire broke out from several locations around the camp, fire that was returned at once from the guards stationed in the camp's guard towers.

"What's happening?" Donald asked.

"We're leaving," Aleksey replied.

Someone opened the door and Donald joined the surge of prisoners as they poured outside into what seemed the middle of a snowstorm.

"Stay with me," Aleksey warned him, as a flare exploded overhead and the camp was suddenly lit up in stark black and white. Donald ducked as a missile shot overhead, trailing a tail of sparks, and exploded against the leg of a nearby guard-tower. As the leg disintegrated the tower slowly collapsed like a pack of cards.

"This way," Aleksey said as he followed the small group of prisoners heading downhill, away from the fight.

They were about halfway down the hill when the flare guttered out, leaving them in darkness. No one stopped running, and lost in the rush Donald continued to stumble along, the wind almost blinding him with its snow. Not really knowing what was going on he clutched his blanket tighter around his shoulders and tried to keep up with Aleksey.

Someone whistled at them from the bottom of the hill, near the fence. Whoever it was, was wearing a thick parka and had an automatic rifle slung over their back. The group Donald was with immediately veered towards them.

Closer, Donald could see that a large hole had been cut in the wire fence, and as they scrambled through someone else was waiting to point them in the direction of the forest. At the edge of the trees he risked looking back for a moment. He could just make out the body of the guard slumped over the rail of his tower, while behind them it prisoners were breaking out through the holes cut for them in the wire, and running for the shelter of the nearby woods.

Guards were now firing indiscriminately into the mass of escaping prisoners, but their rescuers merely hurried them on, cursing and swearing at those struggling to keep up.

There were two trucks waiting for them about a hundred yards into the forest, engines idling.

"What about the others?" Donald asked, as he was bundled into the first.

"They'll have to shift for themselves," was Aleksey's blunt reply. "We've got everyone we wanted."

"Do they have much chance?"

"As much chance as a crab in a skillet, but they'll slow down any pursuit."

With twenty-five crowded in the back of the truck there was barely room to breathe, but at least they were out of the wind. As the truck started to bump its way down the track, the realization he had escaped from the camp, and was apparently among friends, started to sink in. Wrapping the thought around himself, he clutched it to his chest with all the strength at his disposal.

The truck bumped its way along the forest track for perhaps half an hour before turning onto a sealed road. Then, as Donald dozed uneasily, jostled every now and then by those around him, the truck whined along the highway in top gear. About an hour before dawn, they turned off the road again, slewing their way onto a gravel track.

As the sun started to rise above the horizon the truck finally ground to a halt, and a moment later its back hatch was dropped with a loud clang.

"Everyone out," one of the guerrillas said.

Uncertainly, everyone clambered out of the truck, to find themselves standing in the middle of a small forest glade. Trenches had been dug into the forest floor around them, and a short distance away were a number of what looked like small, earth-covered bunkers. A man emerged from one of the bunkers, saw Donald looking at him, and nodded pleasantly. He was wearing an old camouflage uniform, the trousers of which were so patched that it was difficult to know if there was any of the original cloth left.

After the last person climbed out of the truck, the hatch was swung back into place and the truck quickly driven away.

"This way," one of the guerrillas said.

Now what, Donald wondered. The what turned out to be breakfast, admittedly only cold salted meat and dried bread, but there was more than enough for everyone, and the former prisoners fell on it with enthusiasm. For some, it was their first square meal in months.

As Donald pushed his plate away, his hunger temporarily satisfied, he was surprised to realize the person who had been sitting next to him was Hawiku. Beside him was Aleksey. Then again, perhaps it wasn't surprising he hadn't recognized Hawiku without his beard, and dressed simply in a prisoner's jumpsuit.

Hawiku gave him a broad smile, and raised his mug of cordial tea in a toast. "Your good health," he said, in careful English.

"And yours," Donald said, echoing the gesture.

He looked around, but no one seemed to be moving away from the table yet. "Can we talk now?" he asked, reminding Hawiku of his promise to talk.

"Of course. I would be astonished if you didn't have any questions."

"Where are we?"

"In a guerrilla camp, near the Place of the Two Rivers. I believe it is near your Mainline Pittsburgh. It is as far east as you can go without hitting the radiation from the last war."

"Radiation? As in atomic radiation?"

Hawiku nodded. "A result of the Great War against the United Christian States."

"What happened?"

"They lost. Thirty million people dead."

Donald's breakfast turned to ashes in his stomach at the thought they might have to face something like that on the Mainline, or on Etu.

Hawiku nodded his understanding at the look that had crossed Donald's face. "You are not alone in feeling that way. Following the war there was mass revulsion at the use of atomic weapons, and international treaties have now banned their use, but. . ." he shrugged and Donald nodded. Having once had them there was nothing stopping them using them again.

"And these guerrillas? They are from the United Tribes?"

"Yes. After the coup, a number of regiments took to the forests. We have been getting some support from the Mexicans, but not enough, the Junoobil are too afraid of rocking the boat. From our perspective the Sho'mali's alliance with Miro couldn't have come at a better time. We were close to being wiped out, but with most of the Sho'mali strength now off-line we have been able reclaim some territory."

"And you are hoping I can help, how?"

"The Junoobil have obviously been concerned at how the alliance with your First Leader affects the balance of power here. With your help I hope to persuade them to adopt a more active stance."

"And how will you do that?"

"We will be traveling to Mexico to meet the Caliph."

Donald raised an eyebrow. Well he certainly seemed to have fallen in with the right people. "Just so long as it is understood I have my own interests to plead."

"Of course," Hawiku said placatingly.

And with that, knowing that he was only a pawn in a game more complex than he had imagined, Donald had to be content.

CHAPTER 21

Rufiji — Mmbuto é Line
March 1981 (97AE)

Conrad watched the mangrove swamps slip by as the ship worked its way upriver, and idly slapped at a mosquito on his arm. The beginning of the afternoon's sea breeze created small eddies on the surface of the water, while their companion vessel followed close behind. The remaining eight ships of the original fleet were still in the Caribbean.

Almost home, he thought. Now there was a thought. Who'd have ever believed he'd make Africa his home, or that he'd ever become a father. Ever *want* to become a father he quickly corrected himself. Gratefully, he slid his arm around Linele, pulling her into his side. Under her gown the bump was just starting to show.

The only cloud on the horizon was what the High King's reaction to news was going to be, and, perhaps more importantly what his reaction to the news of his cousin's death would be. He sighed. Linele had assured him that there was nothing to worry about, but unfortunately he couldn't stop.

"What was that for?" she asked, looking up at him happily.

Pregnancy seemed to suit her; he had never seen her more beautiful.

"Just thinking about what the High King is going to say."

She dimpled prettily. "How many times do I have to tell you — Don't Worry." She punctuated the last two words with a series of pokes.

He winced theatrically. "I can't help it. I just wish it was over with." Realizing that he might be spoiling Linele's spirits, he gave her a kiss.

"What was that for?" she asked.

"Because I love you."

She started to pull him down for another one, but he shook his head. "Not now," he warned her as they rounded the last bend in the river and the port of Rufiji opened out in front of them.

There was a sudden crack from one of the forts guarding the entrance, and a moment later a perfect smoke ring drifted up into the cloudless sky. Ten seconds later another shot followed the first.

"That was quick," Linele remarked.

"It was," Conrad agree. "Probably a breech loader."

"A breech loader?"

"The round is loaded from the back of the barrel. They're a lot easier to reload than muzzle loaders."

As the crew moved efficiently to furl the sails, a small launch moved out to greet them, the smoke gushing from its funnel forming a thick, dark cloud behind it.

"Someone's been busy," Conrad said, as many of the sailors moved to the rails to see this new wonder.

There was a strident oath from the boson as they started to lose way and the crew moved reluctantly back to work.

Conrad eyed the welcoming committee that was waiting for them on the pier and felt himself break out in a cold sweat. Nervously, he checked the three chests on the deck behind them, and the box at his feet which contained their personal gift for the High King. "Perhaps you should stay on board until I've had a chance to speak to your father," he suggested.

"Why? Aren't you proud of your child?" she asked, patting her stomach.

"Well yes but. . ." He stopped.

"How many times do I have to tell you —"

"Don't worry. I know, I'll try," he promised.

Chengerai was the first to greet them, stepping aboard even before they had finished tying up.

"Welcome back Princess," he said with a broad smile, bowing low before turning to Conrad. "My Lord. I understand from the King's Agent in Luanda that the expedition was even more successful than we could have hoped."

They had berthed in Luanda a month ago, on their return, but what was the 'My Lord' bit?

"I don't know about 'more successful than we could have hoped', but it was certainly very successful."

"Try telling that to the market, the semaphore from Luanda has been running hot for the past month."

Conrad smiled uncomfortably. "Papa," he said, pleased for the interruption as his father stepped on board.

"Conrad," his father said, pulling him into a hug.

"I noticed the launch and the breech loaders," Conrad said when he was released. "You've been busy."

"You've been gone a couple of months," his father said. "You didn't expect us to sit around and wait for your return did you?" He turned to Linele, and bowed. "Princess."

"First Leader," she said, in greeting.

Brian indicated the sedan chairs waiting for them on the wharf. "Your father asked me to escort you both to the palace as soon as you arrived."

So much for keeping Linele out of the way until he'd been able to talk to the High King, Conrad thought, picking the box up that contained their homecoming gift, and following his father down the plank. The four marines allocated to each chest picked up their loads. "Have you heard from Donald?" he asked.

His father shook his head. "It's only four months. Still early days."

Conrad had the feeling he was more worried than he was letting on.

"Come on," his father said, "we can talk as we go. The High King was most emphatic. I don't think we should keep him waiting any longer than necessary."

"So, how was America?" he asked, as they settled themselves into the double sedan chair behind Linele's. The chair's thin gauze curtains gave them some privacy, while still allowing the breeze to penetrate.

"Disturbing," Conrad replied truthfully as the porters shifted the chair onto their shoulders. "It's so empty it's almost scary. There's no one left at all. I felt as though I was walking on eggshells all the time. They have these massive hexagonal pyramids everywhere. Some of them still look almost pristine with these ultra-white gloss surfaces. I have to say the wildlife is pretty amazing though, especially the birds; their flocks literally fill the sky at times, but the cities, ports, and villages. . .they're just ghost-towns. Treik's 'biological strike' didn't just decimate humanity, it removed it."

"I honestly can't see how the Mmbuto é survived," he admitted, as he peered through the gauze curtains at the crowds, pulled back on both sides of the road to allow them through. "I mean, we know they were trading across the Atlantic, and we know the plagues got to Europe. Even with the strictest of quarantines, how could they have survived?"

His father shrugged. "It's possible the most virulent diseases didn't make it across the Atlantic. With a short enough infectious period, and a high enough mortality rate a three week trip is going to serve as a significant barrier."

"Something got across though?"

"I suspect it was either a mutated variety, or more likely Treik used a combination of infectious agents and it was one of the less virulent ones that got across."

"Virulent enough to virtually clear Europe out."

His father nodded. "Just for your ears at this stage," he said. "The High King has decided to rename Choququirau as Sha Ithemba."

Conrad mentally translated the term. "New Hope. It's a good name."

"I think so. I'm hoping to be able to transfer another three Battlegroups there within a couple of months. The Council allowed us to start recruiting mercenaries just after you left and I've decided to establish a base there. If things work out we can transfer them through to the Mainline direct from there."

"Three Battlegroups! Just how many troops do we have now?"

"Just over fifteen thousand."

"That's six Corps," Conrad said, unable to hide his surprise. It was the same number of Corps that they had managed to raise at the beginning of the war when his grandfather had all the resources of their allies available.

"But without heavy weapons," his father said warningly. "Although that should be changing in the near future," he added with a pleased grin.

"You *have* been busy."

"As I understand you have," he said, leaving Conrad to wonder exactly what he had heard.

The High King was waiting for them in the main hall, and it seemed to Conrad that every eye was upon them as he and Linele approached the dais before going down on their knees before him.

"My congratulations on the success of your trip," the High King said, leaning forward to grasp both their hands in his. "Both in terms of the mission, and shall we say, your proved fertility."

There was a polite titter from the court, and Conrad felt a sudden blush of embarrassment. But damn, his intelligence was good.

"Daughter," the High King said, indicating she take the stool at his feet.

While Linele settled herself on the stool Conrad opened the box he'd been carrying and carefully lifted out the small statue of a snarling jaguar that it contained. Exquisitely molded in swirling gold and platinum, it was just small enough to fit in the palm of one's hand.

"Majesty, please accept this as an indication of the wealth of your new territories," Conrad said, presenting him with the gift.

The High King nodded, his eyes widening as he felt its weight. For a moment he simply admired it. "A beautiful gift," he said finally before placing it on the armrest of his chair, rather than passing it to an attendant.

"And this," Conrad said, signaling the marines to upend the chests they still carried on their shoulders. Gold poured from the chests onto the floor: coins, goblets, plates, and miniatures.

There was a collective gasp from those gathered, and Linele gave him an approving nod.

The High King gestured with his right hand and an aide hurried forward with a cushion, resting on which was a small gold brooch. He took it and examined it critically for a moment before leaning forward to pin it on Conrad's breast.

"Let it be known that Conrad Clemhorn now bears the rank of First Noble of the Empire. He shall be titled Lord of the Eastern Lands, and his descendants shall retain the title until the end of days."

Conrad suppressed his broad smile. "Majesty," he said. Now there could no doubt of his fitness to marry Linele.

"Please," the High King said, indicating he should rise. "World Leader," he said as Brian approached.

Brian bowed his head. "Majesty."

"How goes the training of the latest two regiments?"

"Well enough, Majesty. I believe they complete their basic training in two weeks."

"I understand from the Council that with these two regiments your army is now larger than mine."

"Your Majesty knows he has nothing to fear from us," Brian said carefully.

"Exactly what I told the Council," the High King said with a tight smile. "As Living God on Earth your new regiments' primary loyalty remains to me; and it is certainly cheaper than having to supply them myself. However, the Council is naturally cautious and it will go some way to reassuring my advisors that we now have links stronger than simply friendship between us." He glanced meaningfully at his daughter who smiled beatifically back at him. "But I did want to ask you about the new portal."

Conrad glanced at his father. They had a new portal?

His father shrugged a little. "It is still several months away, but Kaito has now managed to create a team he believes understand the mechanics of the process, if not the physics."

"And the new weapons?"

"Much sooner, as Your Majesty is fully aware given that it is the Imperial Guard who will be the first to receive them." Brian didn't look very happy at that concession.

The High King grinned unrepentantly back at the World Leader.

"Which reminds me, Majesty, heavy weapons?" Brian said.

"I am aware of the need to upgrade our own defenses, World Leader, and arrangements are in hand to do precisely that in case this line is invaded," the High King said somewhat stiffly. It was obvious to Conrad this was a continuing argument. "I do have a responsibility to my people."

"Majesty," Conrad's father said, apologizing.

The High King nodded, silently accepting the apology, as his hand idly caressed the small statuette of the jaguar Conrad had given him.

"With your permission, Majesty I would like to speak to my son."

"Of course, you will join us for dinner?" he said eagerly, looking at Conrad. Suddenly he looked like the teenager he was, eager to talk about Conrad's new discoveries.

"I would be honored."

"Good. Daughter, I need to discuss a matter of some sensitivity with you." Then, with a nod, Conrad and his father were dismissed.

Outside Conrad gave a relieved sigh. That hadn't gone too badly, he thought, as his hand lightly touched the small brooch pinned to the front of his tunic. In fact, all things considered, it had gone quite well. "What did you want to talk to me about?" he asked, as his father led him away from the court towards the wing of the palace they had taken over.

"I thought you might like to be brought up to date on how our recruitment's been progressing."

"And how are the new troops turning out?" Conrad asked.

"Good. They're disciplined, and trained, and most have had some recent experience of combat. Despite the much vaunted peace this Empire boasts of, there have been any number of brush-fire conflicts in the last ten years. And they learn fast."

"Yes, that is one thing you can say about them," Conrad said thinking of the launch they had seen on the way in. "But why's he offering us so much help all of a sudden?"

His father laughed. "It's not that much of a sudden change," he explained. "You forget you've been away a couple of months. There's been endless debate in the Council, and it's really only in the last couple of weeks that he's managed to get the upper hand. You couldn't have timed your return better in that respect."

"But what does he get out of it?"

"Freedom. The High King is the Living God on Earth, remember. That means that he is virtually a prisoner to the priests, the Council, and tradition. He is only ever free during a time of war when he is required to lead his armies, and the Council has held rigorously to a policy of enlightened mercantilism for the past fifty years. But for our arrival he would probably have lived and died a prisoner of the society he rules."

Conrad nodded his understanding. "And what am I doing now?"

"I need you at Carthago as soon as you can get there. I want to be ready to move as soon as Donald returns."

"And Carthago?" Conrad asked, unsure of the link.

"The latest two Corps have been recruited from the areas around Carthago and I need you to put them through their advanced training. I really hate asking you to go, particularly with Linele's pregnancy, but there's no one else with the sort of experience at training you have."

"And if we don't hear from Donald?" Conrad asked.

"We'll worry about that at the time."

Conrad nodded, wondering if his father was trying to avoid thinking about it. "Of course," he said, not really having any choice.

CHAPTER 22

Leolie — Etu Line
June 1981 (97AE)

Arnold took his seat in the center of the reviewing stand, nodding to General Mullah Hssan already seated in the row behind him as he did so.

"Beautiful weather for the display," the General said, leaning forward.

"It does seem that way, doesn't it," Arnold replied, tilting his head back slightly to make talking easier. The sky was a beautiful, flawless blue, with just the hint of a breeze on the air. He couldn't have asked for a better day for the tattoo.

"Leader, I'd like to introduce you to Mohica," the General continued, his hand resting possessively on the arm of the young lady sitting next to him. Arnold frowned. She must have been at least half the age of the old goat.

Mohica kept her eyes demurely fixed on her lap under Arnold's gaze.

"I hope the General is treating you well," Arnold said.

Startled, she glanced up at him, before dropping her gaze to her lap again. "Very well," she said softly.

Arnold unsuccessfully tried to hide his smile as he turned back to parade ground, old goat indeed.

Red Arrow, the Commander of Arnold's Household Guard, leaned across. "On your command, Leader." Of Sioux descent, the Commander's eagle motif tattooed onto his left cheek was still new and Arnold wondered how much it had hurt.

"Proceed."

Red Arrow whispered something into his throat mic and a string of explosions rippled across the parade ground in front of them, causing the spectators to jump and a flock of pheasants to explode from the copse on the far side of the ground.

Smoke billowed into the air, creating a screen that hid what was occurring behind it. Arnold, who had known what to expect, tried to reflect an air of bored indifference. It was difficult though, knowing what was to come. Every nerve seemed to be strung as tight as a drum in anticipation.

As the smoke slowly started to drift towards them there was a sudden roar of engines and six 'Striker' Personnel Armored Carriers charged out of the smoke towards them. There was a gasp from the audience as the eight wheeled, armored vehicles slid to a halt in front of the stand, disgorging the troops they carried.

Arnold nodded, pleased, as the core of his new Household Guard quickly moved into a loose skirmish line in front of the audience, facing out towards the smoke. He had been right, he thought. The dark blue stippled uniforms with matching berets he had designed were very effective. He wondered if he should have made their cap badges slightly larger; you could barely make out the Mujahideen emblem he had designed. The emblem, a Clemhorn double-headed eagle wielding a scimitar, worked at so many levels, linking back to the tradition as well as looking to the future. But perhaps its size wasn't important — it was what it represented, a symbol that one day would be recognized across the entire Cross-Temporal Empire.

Despite his intention to remain aloof, Arnold found himself leaning forward excitedly as automatic fire rippled down the line, subtly increasing in intensity as it traveled.

The sudden, explosive detonation of automatic cannon from the PACs caused even Arnold to jump as they built towards their deafening climax. "Yes!" he whispered, allowing himself a small nod of pleasure.

He missed the signal but suddenly everyone ceased fire and in the abrupt silence the Guard snapped to attention, facing the stand.

Arnold was the first to his feet, clapping wildly, and then others were joining him, until everyone was on their feet.

A shrill whistle and the Guard raced back to the PACs before roaring off into the cover of the smoke that still eddied across the ground.

Slowly those on the stand resumed their seats as the drone of the pipes sounded out across the stands and the First Pipe Band of the Northern Lakes League marched out, turquoise sparkling against their tanned leather aprons to announce the start of the rest of the tattoo.

"What did you think?" he asked the General, leaning back without taking his eyes off the field.

"I'm sure the natives were impressed," the General said softly.

"I'm sure they were," Arnold replied pleasantly. As will you be one day, my dear General, he promised himself. The PACs might be obsolete on Sultan, but on Etu they gave him an unbeatable edge. And one day, he promised himself, they would be replaced by the very latest that Sultan could offer him.

After the band had played its requisite four tunes it marched off to the enthusiastic cheers of the crowd. Arnold noticed the bemused looks among some of the Etehad Sho'mali seated on the stand around him and hid a smile; there was no doubt the native pipes were an acquired taste. Personally he couldn't abide the sound, but they were popular, and for small things like this, he was prepared to compromise.

He almost missed the first staccato beat of the drums as the march past proper started, and the first of the newly graduated Mujahideen marched out onto the parade ground. Unable to restrain himself he leaned forward.

It was now over twelve months since he and General Mullah Hssan had planned for this moment. In the end it had taken far longer than he had expected, and recruitment and training had been slower than they had hoped for, but they now had four Battlegroups, with another two just completing basic training.

"I think the natives are impressed," he said, satisfied, leaning back as the crowd, many of whom were relatives of those now marching past in their tight blue ranks, began a slow, methodical clap in time to the drums.

The General said something in reply that was lost in the noise from the crowd, and as he tried to work out what he had said Arnold almost missed the two soldiers as they broke from those marching past and ran towards the stand, shouting as they ran.

What were they up to? This wasn't in the program. One of the soldiers threw something towards the stand, and Arnold watched it arc through the air towards him as though in slow motion.

The sudden clang as it hit the floor between the bleachers in front of him seemed to echo through the air. . . a moment's silence, then the explosion that answered the question of what it was. A grenade! Arnold started to stand up, but immediately found himself forced back into his seat by Red Arrow, who had his hand pressed over his ear, trying to hear over the sound of the screams from the crowd as they panicked and tried to force their way down the steps. Arnold watched someone driven over the rail of the step, hands frantically trying to retain their hold on the rail before they fell.

There was a burst of automatic fire, almost unheard over the screams of the crowd. What was happening?

"Right, let's go," Red Arrow said as four of his Guard materialized next to them.

"What's happening?" Arnold demanded, as the guardsmen started to force a way through the crowd and down the steps.

"The immediate threat has been nullified," Red Arrow said. "But we're getting you back to the house."

"What threat?" Arnold demanded, but Red Arrow ignored him, pistol in hand, eyes constantly scanning the crowd. Behind them the Mullah was close on their heels, his young companion's hand clutched in his own. At the foot of the stand they passed the first of two bodies sprawled on the hard earth. Blood stained the front of the corpse's uniform. Five of his Household Guard stood nervous guard on the body as Arnold stared, fascinated. It was the first time he had seen death at such close range.

With a roar of engines three PACs suddenly broke through the smoke in front of them. The back ramps came down and he was quickly bundled inside the first.

Just before he did so, he glanced back to stands. They were almost empty now except for the small group left on the bottom row. There must have been at least ten of them, clustered in a loose circle on one side, and it took Arnold a couple of seconds to realize that the crimson that splattered the front of their weekend bests was in fact blood.

Even as the ramp started to close he could see the medics racing up the steps towards them, but from the way at least three lay slumped across the bleachers their arrival would be too late for some.

The PAC started with a jerk that threw him against Red Arrow. As he pulled himself away Arnold's hand started to shake. He stared at it, amazed, only then realizing that someone had actually tried to kill him. How dare they! He frowned, there was only one person who could have ordered it — Ivy. They knew her plans to invade were nearing fruition, and now she had tried to sow confusion among her enemy by killing him.

But he had survived, and survived unscathed. As though from a distance he heard someone call for a blanket, and then he felt it wrapped around him but it couldn't touch his thoughts. His God had spoken to him and Arnold now knew, knew without a shadow of doubt, with a calm, clear certainty that the path he had chosen had been sanctified by God.

He could hear the pealing of the bells in the back of his mind and smiled. Yes, Ivy had a surprise coming, and when she attacked the trap would fall not only on her, but on hers. She had shown her true colors and when the time came he would show no mercy.

Turning his head he saw Red Arrow looking at him worriedly.

"When we arrive at the house arrange for the Corps Commanders to attend," Arnold said. "I want to finalize our plans for the invasion."

"And General Mullah Hssan?" Red Arrow asked.

It was only then that Arnold realized the General wasn't with them. "Him too, if he can separate himself from his new friend long enough."

Red Arrow gave a toothy smile. "Of course, Leader."

Now, back in his office Arnold leaned back in his chair, rocking gently in time to the soft ticking of the clock. Tick-tock, tick-tock. He lightly stroked a finger over the desk, admiring how the sun gleamed off the polished surface of the wood. In front of him a thin trail of steam rising from the tea cup caught his attention and he put his head on his side to watch.

There was a soft knock on the door. "Come in," he said, leaning forward to pick up the cup between his finger and thumb.

"Yes Abbas?" he said, looking up as he took a sip of the delicately flavored liquid.

"I have a letter for you from First Leader Miro."

Arnold frowned, replacing the cup on its saucer as he looked at the single envelope on the tray Abbas was carrying. A letter?

"And Commander Arrow asked me to tell you that the Corps Commanders will be here in two hours."

"Thank you, Abbas."

"And may I say that I am pleased you survived the attack, sir."

"So am I," Arnold said with a smile as he retrieved the letter opener from the top drawer. Carefully he slit the envelope and slid the single sheet of paper out. He unfolded it and read the letter carefully.

"Leader?" Abbas said.

Arnold put the letter on the desk, placing the knife on it to keep it open. "It seems Donald died in an attempted prison breakout from his POW camp four months ago. Miro has only just seen fit to pass the news onto me."

"My sympathies, Leader."

Arnold nodded. Miro should never have agreed to transfer him. Well, *he* had done all he could do.

"I should tell my mother," he said.

"Do you wish to see her here?"

He shook his head. "No, I'll see her in her room." He stared at the tea in his cup. It really was a beautiful color. Regretfully, he pushed his chair back.

The guard outside his mother's room was sitting on a chair, head resting against the wall, with his eyes closed. Startled by their arrival, he leaped to his feet, slamming to attention.

"When your shift is finished, report to your Squad Leader and place yourself on charge," Abbas said quietly.

"Sir."

"Who has a key?" Arnold asked, as Abbas unlocked the door.

"Just myself. I thought it better to restrict access."

"Of course."

As Abbas opened the door, Arnold was surprised by the sound of a chanted prayer and raised an eyebrow enquiringly at Abbas.

"I provided your mother with a radio. I hope that is all right? It can only pick up Jihad Radio."

Arnold nodded as he entered. The room was larger than he remembered, although admittedly the last time he had seen it, it had been filled with boxes. The boxes had been cleared out and replaced by a small desk and bunk. A single, small, round rug covered half of the floor. Nothing could be done about the cold, however, and his mother was sitting at the desk reading, a blanket wrapped around her shoulders.

"Hello Mama," Arnold said.

"Arnold," she said, turning to face him. "And to what do I owe this visit?"

Her hair had long streaks of gray in it and her skin was bleached white. She had always been a petite woman but she had lost so much weight she was starting to look almost skeletal.

"I have just received news that Donald died in an attempted mass escape from a POW camp."

Arnold would have sworn it was impossible for his mother to look even whiter, but all the blood drained from her face and there was such utter anguish on her face that his resolve not to offer any sympathy was overcome.

"I am sorry, Mama," he said sincerely, taking a step towards her.

Wordlessly she shook her head, her hand waving him away. "Just leave me alone."

"If you would just accept the word of God," Arnold said. "He will bring you such comfort you would not realize."

Wordlessly she turned away from him, and Arnold stood there, uncertainly wondering what to do. Finally he nodded. "I will leave you," he said, and with a jerk of his head, motioned Abbas outside.

CHAPTER 23

Le Havre — Etu Line
June 1981 (97AE)

Ivy struggled to keep her eyes open and her attention fixed on the speaker who was giving a report on increasing sulphuric acid production. She knew it was important. Without the acid, they couldn't produce the hydrogen needed for the airships, but why couldn't he just have said they anticipated lifting production by five per cent a month for the next twelve months and have left it at that, instead of droning on and on about how they were going to do it?

It didn't help that the weather was muggy, and she'd been up late last night reading the latest operational reports. She could feel her eyes starting to glaze over again, and stirred uneasily. The whole report seemed like an extended metaphor for the planning required for the invasion — never-ending.

It was already summer, and they still weren't ready. Despite the fact she'd wanted to be ready for April, it was now June and they hadn't even tested their first dirigible. The bottleneck had turned out to be the 800,000 ox-guts they needed for each bag. Producing the gas itself wasn't a problem, that was just a matter of adding iron filings to dilute sulphuric acid, which apparently they now had more than enough of. But ox-guts — she shuddered again at the memory of those particular debates.

She wondered, once again, if she simply shouldn't have used ships, but they needed the speed the airships would give them. Besides, it was too late to change her mind, too many resources had already been committed.

At least Arnold had left them alone, though the gods knew how many portals he might have operating that she didn't know about. There'd been no evidence of course, but the taxes her intelligence reported he was levying must be paying for something.

The speaker finally ground to a halt and Ivy checked her watch.

"Thank you, Leader, has anyone anything else to add?"

There was a moment's silence, and then before anyone could think of something she stood up. "Same time next week then," she said, dismissing them. She knew it was rude, but she was fed up with talking. That was all she seemed to do. That and hold meetings. She had meetings to discuss balloon construction, meetings to discuss supply, meetings to discuss intelligence (though no one seemed to show any), and even, it seemed, meetings to discuss meetings.

Sergeant Horsing was waiting for her outside the room.

"Ready?" she asked shortly.

"Yes, Leader," he replied with a smile. "A bad one?"

She gritted her teeth. "No worse than usual."

She led the way out the courtyard where their two mounts were waiting, a groom standing patiently holding them. Despite the heat, the overcast sky threatened rain.

"Not a good day for a ride," he remarked.

Ivy looked at the sky and shook her head. Something else to go wrong! "Come on," she said, "I'll race you." Launching herself into the saddle she sent her mount clattering out over the cobbles.

Horsing followed her out at a more sedate speed.

Ivy pulled up to wait for him at the top of the hill that overlooked the port. Her short blond hair whipped in the wind, stinging her eyes.

"What kept you?" she said with a laugh, then wheeled her mount and sent him galloping down the other side, following the coast north. Behind her, Sergeant Horsing shook his head ruefully. On the grass now he spurred his mount to follow, trying not to fall too far behind. Finally she reined in and the Sergeant was able to draw level.

"Feeling better?" he asked.

"A little," she admitted.

She slid off her mount, and holding the reins loosely in her hand, leaned back against the saddle. She stayed like that for a couple of minutes, just standing there with her eyes closed, letting the frustrations of the meeting dissolve away with the warmth of the horse against her back and the fresh, salt-laden air gusting in from the sea against her face.

"If you want to see the yards, we'd better get a move on," Horsing reminded her.

Ivy opened her eyes regretfully. "I suppose we'd better," she said. She swung herself back into the saddle, and led the way back towards the track at a gentle canter.

It was a half hour's canter out to the airfield and upon reaching the top of the hill that overlooked the construction site, she paused for a moment to admire the view.

The building laid out below that housed the balloon was gigantic, almost five stories high and three hundred yards in length. Although nestled within the cover provided by two hills, its function was not something that could be easily camouflaged. Built entirely in wood, its exterior cladding still looked glaringly new. It seemed to Ivy that anyone seeing it would immediately realize what it was for, and there were almost thirty such buildings scattered up and down the west coast.

To date there had been no indication that her brother had discovered them, but it was a recurring nightmare for both her and her security.

The grassed area in front of the building, which would serve as a takeoff and landing area when the balloon was finished, had already recovered from the trauma suffered during the construction of the building, and its green surface was now dotted with the golden blooms of late flowering dandelions.

"It's beautiful," she said.

"Even with the security?" Horsing asked, referring to the rolls of barbed wire that marked off the inner security area, and the guards with their dogs that could be seen patrolling it

Ivy shrugged. In reality she doubted anything would protect the balloon, or its hangar, from even a small raid; the material was just too flammable (and she shuddered to think of the risks when they actually started to inflate with hydrogen) but it gave her troops something to do until the balloons were finished.

The duty guards at the gate saluted as they rode up.

"Leader," the Squad Leader said, as she came over to check their passes. "Doesn't look as if you'll be able to stay long if you want to avoid the rain."

Ivy spared a glance at the clouds that were continuing to build overhead. "Probably not," she agreed regretfully.

Inside the hangar, the air was filled with the rich aroma of pine wood, bringing back reassuring memories of carpentry classes as a child.

"Leader," a voice called out to them from the gloom, and a moment later Lonce Raincloud hurried up.

"Lonce," she said, unconsciously straightening her back. "How are things going?"

"Good, another day or so and we'll have finished fitting the outer skin."

Giving Lonce the job as liaison officer between Continental Headquarters and the yard had been one of her better decisions, she thought. Not only was he where she could keep an eye on him, but he'd turned out to be an excellent liaison officer.

"When do you start inflating the bags?" Horsing asked.

The bare structure of beams and spars of the airship which had so intrigued Ivy during construction, was now almost completely sheathed in linen, emphasizing the airship's massive size. Under the airship's outer skin the gas-bags hung flaccidly from their supports.

"Next week," Lonce said. "We need to know what its balance is before we go any further, but we wanted to get as much done as we could before we added any hydrogen to the problem."

"It's beautiful," Ivy said softly.

The gondola that would serve as its keel was already in place. Running the entire length of the balloon, its polished wood surface made it an object of remarkable beauty. It was almost wrong that an object of war could look so beautiful.

"Come on," Lonce said. "I'll walk you round."

After completing their circuit she stood a while at the door, just looking; then, satisfied, she nodded to herself and led the Sergeant and Lonce outside.

"Thanks, Lonce. It's going well isn't it?" she said.

"Yes, Leader. A little slow, but we'll get there."

Ivy thought how young he looked compared to his brother. "You'll send word as soon as you start to inflate it, won't you?" she asked.

"Of course." There seemed a hint of reproach that she might believe he wouldn't.

"Thanks again, Lonce," she said, as he held the horse so that she could mount.

"That boy has got a crush on you ten miles thick," Horsing remarked as they cantered out of the gate.

"Really?" she said, surprised. "He's so young."

"You gave him a responsible job," he pointed out.

She thought about it for a moment. "I suppose I did," she said, pulling the horse back to a walk.

They walked for a while.

"So what are you going to do about it?" Horsing asked finally.

Ivy shrugged unconcernedly. "I don't know," she said. "It's kind of nice to be worshiped by your troops."

"One person isn't all your troops," Horsing pointed out.

"It's a symptom of a greater malaise," she said lightly. "Everyone's in love with me." When Horsing didn't say anything she looked at him, and was surprised to find him avoiding her eyes. She wondered what she had said to upset him.

"Come on," she said. "I'll give you a race. And a head start to make sure you try and win this time."

She slapped her hand hard down on the rump of his horse and he skittered forward, Horsing taking a moment to recover his seat before spurring into a gallop.

***

The rest of the month seemed to pass at a snail's pace. As the country-side wilted in the heat of the summer sun, the preparations for the invasion continued unabated. Recruits and militia trained endlessly, and the factories she'd established during winter poured out the weapons and ammunition required for the offensive. The only thing holding it up were the airships, and now even they approached completion.

Ivy was working her way through the monthly status report when there was a knock on the door.

"Come in!"

It was Sergeant Horsing. "A message from Troop Leader Raincloud."

"The trials are still set for tomorrow?" she asked worriedly. Lonce's dirigible was the second due to be finished, and its maiden flight had been scheduled for tomorrow.

"Yes, he just wanted to confirm your attendance."

"I hope you said yes."

"Of course."

Ivy checked the calendar on her desk. "July the third. That's a good sign."

"Leader?"

"It's the anniversary of the first flight of a dirigible on the Mainline. The Montgolfier brothers."

The Sergeant didn't look convinced, and Ivy hid a grin. "Is it still set for dawn?"

Horsing nodded. "Six a.m."

Ivy grimaced, and Horsing smiled back at her, knowing she wasn't a morning person.

***

Despite the early hour, Ivy found the field already packed with spec-tators by the time she arrived. It was a singularly beautiful morning; the air was still with not even a hint of a breeze to disturb it, with only a few clouds on the horizon. Promptly at six the huge doors on the end of the shed were opened and slowly, majestically, the giant airship was walked out onto the field. Despite its size, well over two hundred and sixty yards in length, it floated as light as a feather between the ropes that kept it tethered to the ground.

On the stand set up in the center of the field Ivy watched with more than a little trepidation as the behemoth approached; closer and closer, until its prow towered over her and the front of the gondola was less than ten feet away.

Through the gondola's front window she could see the Captain standing relaxed behind the steering wheel. Seeing her watching him, he came to attention and sketched a salute. Her lips twitched into a smile.

Above her one of the airship's crew, suspended by a harness, carefully lowered the end of a rope until it was close enough for her to touch. Cautiously she reached out and took hold of it, feeling the movement of the airship vibrating along its length. Craning her head back she could see the cloth it was attached to hanging loose from the side of the ship.

For an instant she paused, savoring the moment, then taking a secure hold on the rope she stepped forward. "I name you *Sela*," she announced, in a clear, high voice that reached to all of those on the field. "May good luck accompany all who ride with you." She swung down on the rope with all her weight. Above her, the cloth peeled away from side of the ship, displaying the massive double-headed Clemhorn eagle it had hidden.

"Good luck, Nona," she said softly to herself, wondering what her grandmother would have thought of having an airship named after her. She'd probably have enjoyed it, she thought. Nona could never have been described as modest.

Stepping back from the edge of the stand, Ivy watched the ground crew quickly dispose of the cloth. Suddenly she was startled by the explosive roar of a motor starting up just above her head, followed almost immediately by another farther along the keel, then another, as the airship's propellers were started. She wished there'd been another way of supplying the engines, as half her autogiros were now gutted, useless shells, but if she wanted her balloons to fly, she hadn't had any choice.

As though that had been a signal the airship released its ropes and, as the roar of engines rose another octave, water streamed out of ballast tanks and it lurched into the air, free!

Ivy realized she had been holding her breath, and from the sigh that echoed around her from the crowd it appeared she had not been the only one.

She watched the airship continue to climb slowly away from the field until, after gaining enough space, the Captain increased the speed of the motors and sent the monster moving out towards the sea. Once over the water he released more ballast and the airship seemed to surge into the air. Lowering the nose, and increasing the speed of its propellers, the Captain brought the *Sela* around into a shallow dive back towards the field. Coming in low he raised the nose again, and slowing the motors allowed it to find its own height.

The maneuver was met by spontaneous applause from the crowd, and as the Captain commenced a slow climb away from the field Ivy descended to join the others watching the scene from the foot of the stand.

"Can you imagine a whole fleet of those monsters?" she overheard someone say reverentially as she reached the ground.

Ah yes, Arnold, she thought, it was time for some good old-fashioned payback.

The Captain continued the test for an hour, before bringing the balloon back to the ground where it was towed back to its shed and tied in. Ivy was shocked to realize how tense she had been and finally able to relax she accepted the congratulations of those around her. Then, as the crowd dispersed back towards the town she spotted Lonce, and excusing herself, hurried over to meet him.

"Congratulations, Lonce," she said.

He turned, surprised to hear her voice. "Thank you, Leader, but I didn't really achieve all that much."

"I disagree," she said.

He looked pleased, but shrugged deprecatingly. "So when do we go?" he asked.

"Two weeks, three at the outside."

"A fortnight!"

"There's no sense in waiting. The fleet should be ready by then, and the troops certainly are."

"I suppose you're right," he said.

"Of course I am," she said, rewarding him with a dazzling smile.

CHAPTER 24

Dar es Salaam — Mainline
May 1981 (97AE)

Defella pulled a face at the stink of fish as she doubtfully surveyed the small huddle of buildings along the beach. Unfortunately, fishing villages tended to smell the same, regardless of which line they were on. Holding the hem of her long linen skirt off the ground with one hand, she clamped her pith helmet to her head with the other as she stepped up out of the boat onto the small wooden jetty that pushed out into the Indian Ocean. "This is it?" she said, disbelievingly.

"Dar es Salaam," Ade confirmed. The Makua Scout who'd brought her from the portal frowned. "It's not really as bad as it looks."

"No, it's probably worse," the Dynand medic accompanying them muttered.

Defella felt like agreeing. Even on Dynand she'd never seen anything quite so ramshackle or so . . . squalid. It was a reminder that not even the Mainline had escaped the effects of the Decimation. What had once been a proud symbol of British 'civilization' and progress, the Railway Hotel, faced them from across the potholed street. The hotel, a two story, stone and tile building, was as derelict and as dilapidated as the rest of the town. The railway, that had once given the hotel its name, lay half buried in the sand, beside the road that seemed more holes than anything else.

"Careful," she warned the medic, who had followed her ashore and had just stumbled over the hem of her skirt.

The medic grimaced, as behind her the rest of their small team followed them ashore. Unlike Defella and the medic, who were dressed in what Kaito had assured her was de rigueur for Mainline ladies in the tropics, the others (members of the Emperor's elite Personal Guard) were dressed in the more practical local garb of loose fitting trousers and short tunic, belted at the waist, that came to mid-thigh.

"Where is he, Ade?" Defella demanded.

"This way, my lady," Ade said, starting to lead the way along the road. As he did so, the four guards fell in around them carrying the chests that held their supplies on their shoulders. The medic carried her own, smaller portmanteau.

"Is it safe?" Defella asked, noticing they were simply leaving the boat tied up at the quay.

Ade looked round, puzzled, then realized she was referring to the boat and nodded. "Kaleb's watching it," he said with a jerk of his head toward the young boy fishing at the end of the pier. "Besides, no one will take it. They're all aware of what happened last time someone tried."

She restrained herself from asking what had happened last time. The scowl on Ade's face seemed answer enough.

It wasn't far to the small warehouse they'd been renting and Defella waited impatiently as Ade knocked on the door. She could hear someone talking, the door opened and all she could think about was that he was all right. He was exhausted, almost dead on his feet, and there was a wariness, a deadness in his eyes that hadn't been there before, but none of that was important — he was alive.

"Hello Defella," Donald said. "I wasn't expecting they'd send you."

"I was the bunny on the spot," she said not bothering to explain that she'd been the bunny only because his father had finally agreed for her to lead a team to try and find out what had happened to him. "What happened to you, though? You look like shit."

"Thanks, you look great," he said, standing aside to allow her to enter.

"I look like an idiot in this dress," she said, stepping into the warehouse which hardly deserved the title given it was barely larger than an outsized shed.

"It is a 'new' look for you," he agreed.

"So who's sick?" she asked. Ade had been clear it hadn't been Donald, but after seeing him, Defella wasn't sure.

"Agent Mahalia. He's over there." He gestured toward the back wall and the four canvas beds lined up against it.

As the medic pushed past to see to her patient, Defella became uncomfortably aware of how close Donald was standing.

"Who's Agent Mahalia?" she asked, as Donald turned and led the way after the medic.

"A representative of our new allies," he replied shortly.

The Agent turned out to be a small, exhausted, wiry-looking Mayan, wrapped in a blanket despite the heat.

"What's he got?" Donald demanded.

"I might be able to tell you once I've finished my examination," the medic said tartly as she inserted a thermometer under the Agent's tongue. "Is he still alternating between the fevers and the shivering?"

"Yes," Donald said. "He complains about being cold, then two days later he's burning up. Two days after that, he's shivering and asking for more blankets again. He's been like that for the last four weeks or so."

"What have you been giving him?"

"Willow bark tea," Ade said. "It's helped with the headaches he's been complaining about."

The medic rummaged in her case and pulled out a stoppered jar. "Quinine," she explained in answer to Donald's look. "Picked some up before we left, based on Ade's description of the symptoms. I need half a cup of wine," she told the scout.

"So can you tell me what he's got now?" Donald asked as the scout went to get the wine.

"Malaria."

"Malaria?" Defella said. "Why wasn't he protected by the KVirus?"

The medic shook her head at the question. "Because the Kelsor Virus was designed as a self-replicating nano-trap for *viruses*. It has some effect against bacteria, but malaria is not a virus. It's not even a bacterium. It's actually a single cell parasite. So the KVirus has absolutely no effect on it. Luckily the Mombuto E know about the disease, and the treatment." She shook the jar to indicate.

It didn't take Ade long to return with the wine, and, after stirring in a pinch of powder from the jar, she handed the cup to Mahalia, who made a face at the bitterness of the wine before drinking it down quickly.

"How long before he can travel?" Donald asked.

"Three, four weeks."

Donald looked worried. "We can't wait four weeks."

Defella looked at him.

"I've committed us to an attack on the Mainline within eight months. We've been promised arms, advanced arms, and ammunition, but we had to move within a year. We've already lost four months getting back."

Defella considered the darkening sky visible through the small window over Mahalia's bed. "It's too late to leave now, whatever we do. But if we left in the morning we could get you back to the portal, then Ade could return for Agent Mahalia once he's recovered."

"Makes sense," Donald said, although Defella could see that he still wanted to start back immediately.

"So what happened?" she said. "You were supposed to be back months ago."

"Arnold happened," Donald said bitterly.

"Arnold? Your brother Arnold?"

"Yes. It's a a long story. If we're not leaving immediately it can wait until after dinner." He glanced at the small wood stove in the corner and Defella realized that at least some of the general aroma of fish was coming from the pot simmering gently on the stove.

"What's cooking?"

"Stew."

"I can see that. I meant, what flavor."

"Whatever's available, I think."

"Oh, Donald," she said, ruefully shaking her head.

As Ade helped the other scout to finish preparing dinner, and the four guards started to set up their bedrolls for later, Defella found herself standing behind Donald in the open door watching the last of the daylight glisten off the waves.

"Did you manage to see her?" Defella asked softly.

"Matija?"

She nodded, giving him a short, uncertain smile.

Donald shook his head. "She's dead."

"Oh Donald, I'm so sorry. What happened?"

"I don't know," he said, avoiding her gaze.

"How did you find out?"

"I spoke to her father on the phone. He told me." He shrugged. "It's probably all for the good. I'm not exactly marriageable material at the moment." He gestured in a manner that encompassed his attire and the general state of his family's decline.

She began to reach out to him, but he flinched and she let her hand drop. "Food," she suggested, to cover the rejection.

They ate under building's front awning, sitting on rugs placed on the sand, listening to the soft wash of the waves breaking on the shore. Agent Mahalia joined them, wrapped in a blanket, already looking a little better although still extremely weak.

The stew, which turned out to be clams, was served in a peanut sauce with broken rice and an unleavened bread to soak up any remaining juices. It was so good Defella resolved to ask Ade for the recipe. A 'stew' Donald had said!

"I'm stuffed," she said finally, when she'd finished her meal. "What?" she demanded when she noticed Donald grinning at her.

"I'm not surprised you're stuffed, given how much you ate."

"I was starving," she said defensively. "I haven't been able to eat for the last day or so because I was so seasick." She didn't add she'd also been worried about Donald.

"So tell. What happened?" she asked, noticing the others preparing to listen. "How did you meet Arnold?"

Donald looked at his hands, then sighed. "Maku and I got as far as Cape Town. We converted the diamonds to cash and I contacted my father's ex-factor as we'd planned. And she handed us straight over to Miro."

"Why?"

"Because, apparently, Arnold is now the World Leader of Etu."

"You've got to be joking!" Defella said.

"I wish I was. Unfortunately, if my treatment was any indication, he's completely thrown in his lot with the Raputas."

"Treatment?" Defella asked. Donald's voice had gone worryingly flat when he'd used the term.

"Questioning, torture. Call it what you want, I wouldn't have survived if my cousins hadn't arrived and got me out."

"And Maku?"

"Killed when I was arrested." He took a breath. "Anyway, my cousins weren't able to get me released but did manage to get me transferred to a POW camp on Sultan."

"Sultan?"

"The line where Miro's allies come from. It turned out to be a lucky break."

Defella shook her head. Getting Donald to explain what had happened was like prying a bone out of a dog's mouth. "How was getting transferred to a POW camp — lucky?"

"Relatively speaking," he admitted wryly. "Apparently the Resistance had been planning on a mass breakout from the camp and when they found out who I was I got invited along."

"So where did these new allies come from, if Sultan is Miro's ally?" she said, increasingly frustrated by his obtuseness.

"Sultan is split between two military alliances," Agent Mahalia said, breaking in to explain. "The Etehad Joonobil and the Etehad Sho'mali. From your perspective, the Etehad Joonobil are the good guys."

"Once we got away from the camp," Donald continued, "the Resistance smuggled me across the border into the United Mexican States, which is one of the main partners in the Etehad Joonobil."

"I'm a Special Agent with the UMS Federal Police," Mahalia interjected. "I'm presently detached to act as Donald's liaison. The UMS is one of two core members of the Etehad Junoobil. The other is the Northern Caliphate, which covers most of Central Europe. There are others, but those are the two that count."

"Unless you're trying to negotiate an agreement with them," Donald said sourly. "Getting agreement from the UMS authorities didn't take that long. But I thought I'd be stuck there till next Christmas getting everyone else to sign on."

Mahalia grimaced in agreement.

"So it's the Sho'mali who are Miro's allies?" Defella asked, trying to make sure she got it straight.

"Correct," Mahalia said. "They've been fighting a cold war for nearly a decade now. The only thing preventing the war from going hot has been a precarious balance between the two blocs. That balance was badly upset by the coup in the United Tribes–" He stopped when he saw Defella's face start to glaze. "It doesn't matter, from our perspective the important thing is that the Sho'mali have now managed to establish bases on at least five Lines. The information Leader Clemhorn will give us on how to construct a portal will be of immeasurable worth, but we must attack within eight months. If we delay beyond that time it may not be possible to contain them. And the alternative . . . " he shrugged. "Well the last war killed over thirty million people and devastated much of North America." He stood up tiredly and gave Defella a small bow. "I apologize, but I need to retire. My best wishes for the trip."

The medic followed him to make sure he didn't stumble on the way back to his bed.

"So *how* did you get back?" Defella asked Donald after the Agent had disappeared inside. There seemed to be a large number of holes in his story, and he'd definitely skimmed over some areas, such as his arrest, but given what he and Mahalia had described she was starting to understand why Donald was so eager to be on his way again.

"Long story short," Donald said, "with Agent Mahalia's assistance I got smuggled back as a member of the Etehad's Shomali's security service."

"Just like that?"

"Well, not quite like that, but it did seem rather anticlimactic until Mahalia managed to catch malaria."

He paused, obviously remembering something.

"What?" she demanded.

He gave her a sudden grin that lit up his entire face. "If you could just have seen it, Defella. Their technology, their science. Bases on the moon. And space stations, I actually saw one through binoculars while we were crossing the border. " His hands emphasized what he meant. He looked as excited, and as cute as a boy getting ready for his first dance, she thought, catching herself just in time to stop from blurting that out to him.

"That sounds amazing," she said, to cover herself.

He nodded. "All I want to do is to rewrite my entire PhD thesis. This was just the evidence that would have nailed my argument. It's marvelous!" he enthused, his eyes fixed on the distance, his thoughts obviously still on the wonders he had seen.

Suddenly Defella realized how tired she was. "All right, we'll get you back tomorrow," she said, getting to her feet. "And as soon as Agent Mahalia is well enough to travel, he can follow."

"Thanks Defella," he said sincerely.

"And I am sorry about Matija."

He nodded. "I know."

CHAPTER 25

Carthago — Mmbuto é Line
July 1981 (97AE)

Conrad sat on the terrace of his house on the lower slopes of Hade-shath Mountain, watching the foam settle softly on his ale. Below him the city of Carthago, with its one million inhabitants, filled the coastal strip to the ocean. It was late morning, and the table next to him still contained the remains of his recent breakfast. It had been late when he'd got in, the night march finishing just after midnight. It had been a final 'graduation' for the two Corps who had completed their advanced training two weeks ago. The night march had been the culmination of a fortnight-long exercise that had included a simulated attack through a portal. The whole exercise had run flawlessly and, reaching for the glass, Conrad couldn't help feeling quietly satisfied at what he'd achieved.

Beyond the city, the azure waters of the Atlantic Ocean glinted in the winter sun, the surf breaking against the long curve of the coast that disappeared into the distance. Behind him, the mountain towered over its lower slopes, dominating the skyline and the city sprawled at its feet. Although he had never visited Mainline Cape Town, he was fairly sure it looked nothing like the city crowding up against the slopes below. With its cramped back-streets, wide, shaded boulevards, and ancient granite and marble temples with their gigantic statures that dwarfed any he had seen during his travels, Carthago truly had a sense of uniqueness.

Part of that was its age; it was old, parts of the city dated back to its foundation by settlers from Carthage nearly two and a half thousand years before. And there was something almost bizarre about sitting there, he mused, sipping a beer, while a legendary civilization that had long disappeared from the Mainline continued its day-to-day minutia around him.

The bell in the temple of Baal, less than a hundred yards away, started to toll its deep, ponderous call to prayer. Conrad checked his watch, twelve o'clock, regular as ever. Almost immediately it was answered from a temple down in the city, before the others all joined in. Conrad raised his glass in an ironic salute and took another swallow. That was one thing he hadn't been warned about by the owner when he had been negotiating to rent the house. At the time he'd thought the temples, clinging to the mountain side around the house, glittering in their white marble, had merely looked romantic, it hadn't occurred to him that they would all have bells, bloody big bells, that they would insist on ringing at dawn, midday, and dusk every day of the week. Every day that was except Friday, when they rang the bells five times a day, starting an hour before dusk.

When he'd complained to Linele about the noise in his first letter, she had just asked him what he had expected, they were temples after all. He had decided for the sake of matrimonial harmony not to explain that he hadn't expected bells.

He missed Linele, but the High King had been emphatic about not allowing her to accompany him during her pregnancy. Actually, he decided, as he refilled the glass from the pitcher beside it, he missed Linele a lot more than he'd expected. And then there was the constant, nagging worry about the birth.

His eyes drifted to the small portrait of Linele on the table beside him. It had been her wedding present to him, and had come as a total surprise. Apparently she'd been talking to Defella about Dynand wedding customs and had decided this was one that she wanted to start on this line. His finger reached out and gently touched the smooth shine of her cheek. By the little gods, he missed her. At least he'd finished the job he'd been sent down here for and as soon as they heard from Donald they were ready to go.

The problem was, of course, that they hadn't heard from Donald, and it was now almost eight months since he'd left. Defella had been given permission to take a squad through two months ago to see if she could find any trace of him, but Conrad feared the worst.

Below him, in the distance, a steamer had started to belch black smoke into the air as it prepared to depart. He remembered the departure of the second fleet to the Americas, just before he had left to come down here. It had been a magnificent sight, twenty ships, their sails bellowing in the wind as they caught the breeze, and then a moment of sadness as he realized this would probably be the last time anyone would see such a sight. But progress could not be stopped, and the shipyards were already working on the next generation of coal-driven carriers.

He frowned, realizing he hadn't noticed the steamer in port yesterday, so presumably it had arrived sometime during the night. He started to call for someone to find out if it had brought any news from Rufiji, when the door to the building opened and Chengerai appeared.

"Chengerai," he said, as he started to his feet. "What's wrong? Is Linele all right?"

"The Princess is fine, as are your children," Chengerai said, with a wide, toothy grin.

"Children?" Conrad said.

"Twins. A boy and a girl. The Princess wanted to come herself but the doctors felt she should wait for a couple of weeks."

"She's not ill?" Conrad asked, alarmed at the news the doctors felt she wasn't well enough to move.

"Of course not. The birth was difficult but she is mending well."

"And twins? What are their names?"

"That will wait until your return," Chengerai said. "But they are both well. The High King is very impressed, and tells me to give you his congratulations."

"And what do they look like?"

Chengerai snorted. "Like babies. If you've seen as many as I have you wouldn't ask. But the boy bears his mother's coloring, which I might add particularly pleases the High King. And how is everything here?" he asked.

"Good," Conrad said. "But if we don't get some action soon I don't know how long we can retain the fighting edge they've built up."

"Well, it is possible that we will be able to fix that," Chengerai said. "Your brother has returned."

"Donald is back?" He felt the concern that had been riding him for the past couple of months disappear.

"Yes. And your father has requested your immediate return with the two Corps."

Conrad stared at him, bemused, for a moment. His brother was all right! Suddenly the news that he was also the father of twins struck home and he pulled Chengerai into a bear hug. "Chengerai, that's the best news I've had in months."

CHAPTER 26

Rufiji — Mmbuto é Line
July 1981 (97AE)

At the knock on his door Donald lifted his head from the pillow and blearily considered the alarm clock on the bedside table beside him. Oh joy, he thought sarcastically, seven o'clock. It had been another long, sleepless night and now, just when he might actually get a couple of hours sleep, someone wanted him up.

"Who is?" he called.

"Defella."

"Hold on a moment." With a sigh, he allowed his head to collapse back against the pillow. Defella, what did she want? For a moment he simply lay there, before deciding that if he wanted to find out why she wanted to see him he'd have to get up.

With a sour look at the sleeping tablets next to the alarm clock he dragged on a shirt and shorts, before splashing some lukewarm water on his face from the bowl on the bedside table. The tablets had been prescribed by the medic, but because of the nightmares they gave him Donald had found he preferred the insomnia.

Running his fingers through his hair he checked his reflection in the mirror. Probably about time he got a haircut, he thought, checking its length. Then, unable to put it off any longer, he threw the door open.

Defella stepped back, startled by the door's sudden opening.

"Hello Defella."

"Donald," she surveyed him up and down. "You still look like shit."

"Thanks." He wished he could have said the same about her but she looked pretty good in a simple chemise and thigh-length boots. Her flawless olive skin was tanned and healthy, emphasizing the startling green of her eyes. She looked like a Dynand recruitment poster-girl. She was wearing her hair down, so that it just touched the back of her neck. He frowned as he realized he was thinking about reaching out to touch it.

"I just dropped by to see if you wanted to join me for breakfast?" she said hesitantly, concerned at the frown.

The thought of food was one of the furthest things from his mind, but he heard the hesitation in her voice and knew what it must have taken her to ask him.

"Of course," he said.

He was rewarded with a smile that lit up her entire face. "Good."

He'd just pulled the door closed behind him when he heard his name called and turned round to see Conrad, Linele happily holding onto one arm, hurrying down the passage towards them.

"Conrad," he said, as he was pulled into a massive bear hug. "When did you get in?"

"About nine last night," Conrad said releasing him to hold him at arms' length and to look him up and down through narrowed eyes. "You've lost weight."

"I haven't been sleeping well," Donald admitted, who had the feeling he wasn't going to be able to pull the wool over his brother's eyes as easily as he was doing with everyone else. Not that it seemed he was doing a good job of that, he thought, given Defella's comment that he looked like shit.

"Are you going somewhere?" Conrad asked.

"Defella just asked me to join her for breakfast," he said. He noticed her starting to back away and grabbed her arm before she could disappear.

"We'll join you then," Conrad said.

"Princess," Donald said, taking the opportunity to greet Linele as Conrad ushered them down the corridor.

"Donald," she replied gravely, a twinkle in her eye.

"So what happened?" Conrad asked.

"I got caught," Donald said simply, wishing people would stop asking.

"And?" Conrad asked, when it became obvious Donald wasn't going to say anything more.

Donald sighed. "It's a long story. But basically I ended up in Arnold's clutches."

"Arnold!"

He nodded. "Our little brother is now Etu's World Leader."

"Arnold?"

"You really need to do something about expanding your vocabulary," Donald said dryly.

Conrad frowned, his eyes suddenly narrowing. "And?"

"And what?"

"There's something else. You said in his clutches."

No, he'd been right —no pulling the wool over his brother's eyes. "I was tortured." There, he'd said it.

Conrad's eyes studied his face closely. "How are you coping?"

Donald felt his eyes start to fill with water and bit his bottom lip angrily. He was not going to cry in front of his brother. "I'm surviving."

"Papa know about it?"

"Not really."

"You want me to tell him?"

Donald shook his head, the concern in his brother's voice almost breaking his determination not to cry. "He's got enough on his plate already."

"All right."

"That's it?" Donald said.

"For the moment," Conrad said. "But if we ever get hold of Arnold. . . " his voice held the unspoken promise of further action.

"I don't think he's exactly sane," Donald said warningly.

Conrad shrugged.

"There's something else."

"What?"

"Mama. When I asked Arnold about her, he seemed. . .vague."

Conrad frowned. "In what way?"

"I'm not really sure. It's almost as though he'd forgotten about her."

"That might be a good thing, given what you've been saying."

"Perhaps," Donald said, though he wasn't sure. He had a nagging feeling that there had been something seriously wrong with Arnold's reaction.

Conrad nodded, obviously filing the information away for later. "So how did you get away?" he asked.

"Rajko and Margaret got me transferred to a POW camp on Sultan."

"Sultan?"

"Miro's new allies. Anyway, I lucked out and got contacted by the resistance. The long and the short of it is that I finally got shipped home in the uniform of an officer in the Etehad Sho'mali Intelligence Corp. A euphemism for security, which tended to dissuade anyone from asking too many difficult questions."

"So what's the situation on the Mainline?" Conrad asked.

"What do you want? The good news or the bad?"

"Start with the bad."

"The bad news is that I've committed us to moving against Miro almost immediately. The good news is that Sultan is divided into two major power blocks and while Miro is in alliance with one, we're now in alliance with the other."

"And how did you manage that?" Conrad demanded.

"As I said, it's a long story," Donald said.

"It doesn't matter," Conrad said contritely, "you can tell me later. Have you seen the twins yet? They're beautiful, aren't they?"

"They are," Donald said with a smile, pleased at the change in conversation. Although you're the last person I would have expected to have become the doting father."

"Times change," Conrad told him. "As do people," he added, casting a glance at Linele, who gave him a happy smile in return.

***

Their father had scheduled a briefing of the six Corps Commanders the next morning, to explain what he had in mind.

Donald was idly doodling on his pad, waiting for his father to start the meeting when Conrad hurried in and sat down next to him.

"You're late," Donald whispered.

"I had to help clean the twins up after breakfast. It's amazing how much mess they can make."

"Maybe we should loan them to Miro? A new secret weapon?"

"He wouldn't have a chance," Conrad agreed.

Their father gave a warning cough, to which Conrad responded with an unrepentant grin.

"Let's get this meeting started then," the World Leader said, unable to completely suppress his own smile. "You've all read Donald's report, and you've all met Agent Mahalia, the Etehad Junoobil representative." He nodded in the direction of the small Mayan sitting next to him. "Now, before Donald's return we had been planning for a two-pronged attack on the Mainline, with bridgeheads established in both the Americas, and on the European mainland. That was why we went to so much trouble establishing a base in the America's. Unfortunately that plan requires at least two portals, and after speaking to Kaito I don't think we'll get them."

"What went wrong?" Conrad asked. "I thought he'd guaranteed a second one six months ago?"

His father shook his head. "I don't understand exactly, but he's been running into problems with the solution failing to facilitate the transmutation of the substrate into its exotic form. He thinks we might getting something in a year or so but, bottom line, we've got only the one portal for the foreseeable future."

"And the weapons we've been promised from the Etehad Junoobil?" Conrad asked. "Shouldn't we wait until they start to arrive?"

His father shook his head again. "Retraining would take longer than we've got. Donald committed us to attack within eight months, and the reasons for that commitment haven't changed. Now, things aren't as bad as they seem. Agent Mahalia feels he can guarantee some direct action from the alliance once we've invaded, or at the very least access to replacement stores. And the site we've chosen on the Adige River in Italy is purposively close to the three Mainline cities of Bologna, Verona and Milano. All of whom, of course, have portals to Lines which supported my father-in-law's claim to the First Leadership. So once we've captured those we can open portals through to friendly Lines."

"We've been working on the dam we'll need to power the generators for almost six months, and Battlegroup Leader Haratan's report indicates it's progressing ahead of schedule. As a result, I'd like to start moving the army north before winter, so we're in a position to invade with spring."

Conrad looked around those gathered at the table. "I'm in favor," he said with a shrug. They were mutters of agreement from the others there.

"It's agreed then. We'll move the army to Italy."

Despite the ease with which the decision was taken, Donald was unsurprised that the actual transfer of forces north proved considerably more complicated. Although most of the army had started north by the end of September, it was early October before the two Corps that Conrad had been training arrived from the Cape and were ready to follow. Finally the last convoy containing Donald, Defella, Conrad, Linele and the twins, and their one, presently irreplaceable, portal, started north by barge.

The barges of the convoy were pulled by the new coal-driven steamers that seemed to be popping up everywhere. They were certainly faster than the horses which had previously pulled the barges. For the moment, those displaced would not have to worry about a job, as his father was still recruiting, but after the war was over Donald wondered how they would cope with the new world that was taking shape about them.

The main canal from Rufiji rose steadily through a series of locks, before passing through a tunnel that cut directly through the mountains, before descending again to Lake Kyoga, Mainline's Lake Victoria. Then down it went again, through a series of over three hundred locks, into the Nile.

Donald was sitting on the prow of the barge, legs dangling over the edge, watching the lock rise about them in the silver moonlight. It was close to midnight and the air smelled of damp wood and water. The sound of frogs filled the night around him, while overhead the stars seemed so close, so bright it was as though he could just reach out and touch them.

For an instant he had a strong feeling of déjà vu, as he remembered the trip he and Defella had taken precisely a year ago, just prior to his trip to the Mainline. As though to reinforce the feeling, a lion decided to roar his challenge into the darkness only a short distance away.

"Mind if I join you?" Defella asked, startling him from his thoughts.

"Of course not," he said, looking up at her.

Gracefully she settled herself beside him, her bare feet dangling just above the water.

"Are you cold?" he asked, starting to shrug out of his jacket. She was wearing the chemise again, and while he certainly appreciated the amount of skin she was showing it didn't look all that warm.

She shook her head. "I'm fine. It reminds me of home."

For a while they simply sat in companionable silence while the massive gates to the lock slowly opened and the barge edged its way out.

Defella let out a soft sigh.

"A penny for your thoughts," Donald said.

"I was just thinking how beautiful it was," she said.

Donald nodded silently. It was beautiful. Pity the war had to spoil it, but then he'd thought that several times before. Unfortunately, it didn't seem to make much difference.

"I wish my mother could see it," she said wistfully.

"Do you miss her?"

She nodded. "We were always a little distant while I was growing up. I don't think she really liked children, and she was pretty busy as a Continental Leader. But when I turned sixteen things started to change. Meeting Andra might have had something to do with it, she's Mom's present partner. Andra definitely brought out a different, softer side to her."

"How about your sisters? You've got, what, four?"

She nodded. "I miss them, but particularly Drysand. She was just leaving for uni when I left for the Mainline. I think you'd like her. She's a bit of an academic as well."

"Thanks," Donald said dryly, but he knew what she meant.

"Did you ever think Conrad would settle down?" she asked suddenly.

Donald couldn't help smiling. "Not really," he admitted. "He always struck me as the confirmed bachelor. Why do you ask?"

"No reason, it's just that he seems pretty settled into the role of being a father."

"He does, doesn't he?" Linele and the twins were accompanying them on the barge and Conrad seemed to spend all of his spare moments with them. Not that Donald begrudged him the time, the twins were adorable, but for a moment it reminded him of what might have been in a different world with Matija and his own child.

For a while they simply sat listening to the sound of water under the bows, and the soft chug from steamer pulling them down the river.

His eyes were starting to drift closed and he was just about to suggest it was time to hit the sack when he felt Defella's head settle against his shoulder. His senses came alive as he felt the bare skin of her arm through the cloth of his shirt and the soft curve of her breast against his arm. He froze, but as she sensed that and started to pull away, he put his arm around her and pulled her into his side, and happily she settled back into him.

He listened to her soft breathing. If only the rest of his life could be as simple, he thought. He didn't know what would happen, but for the moment he was content to simply feel the warmth of Defella sitting beside him.

***

Once at Ngoni, at the mouth of the Nile, Linele and the twins left them to return to Rufiji, while the two Corps embarked on the fleet waiting to take them to Italy.

The dam was still only half completed by the time they arrived, and the two Corps were quickly put to work assisting the other four already there before winter brought a complete stop to their endeavors. There was some grumbling at the work they had to do, but not as much as Donald had expected. The mercenaries of the Mmbuto é were a little like the ancient Romans in that respect, they built roads and canals wherever they went. After all they were employed by merchants, who were not going to pay soldiers to just sit on their butts all day and play dice when there was something useful they could be doing.

Besides, when Conrad organized it into a competition between the five Corps, with bonuses of beer to those teams which came in first during the day, most of the grumbles dropped away into good-natured bantering. Especially when Conrad ordered the Leaders to take their turn with the men, something Donald would have been happier to avoid as he surveyed his cold and bruised hands at the end of a particularly hard day.

Finally, just before the advent of the first heavy snows, the dam was finished, and Kaito was able to turn his full attention to fitting the generators they would use to power the portal.

It was a cold, wet January day as Donald allowed the outside door to his father's office to swing closed behind him, and thankfully thumped the snow off his boots as he started to undo his coat.

"Who is it?" Defella called.

"Donald."

Defella's face appeared around the side of the inside door as he shrugged the heavy greatcoat off and hung it up on its hook to dry.

He bent down to kiss her but she jumped away. "You're cold," she said.

"So warm me up."

"Later," she said, a hint of promise in her eyes, leaving Donald wondering what he had done to deserve her.

As he entered the office's ante-room, Conrad looked up from where he was ensconced next to the fire, and waved the letter he'd been reading at him in greeting. "I got a letter from Linele."

"How is she?" Donald asked

"Missing me," Conrad announced happily.

"And the twins?"

"Couldn't be better. Apparently they're running her off her feet."

"Is that you, Donald?" his father called from the other room. "I'll be out in a moment."

"No hurry," Donald said, positioning himself with his back to the fire as he gradually felt the warmth flow back into his body.

"Cold, isn't it?" his father said conversationally as he joined them.

"That's probably a bit of an understatement," Donald said.

"How do you think the troops are coping?" his father asked Conrad.

"No frostbite yet, but we've had another five cases of insubordination. It seems everyone is getting cabin fever."

"And the Dynands?" his father asked Defella.

She shook her head regretfully. "It would be better not to ask. I am having great difficulty in enforcing discipline. We've had to threaten to shift the camp if they can't control themselves. They're supposed to be in the army, not organizing a harem."

Conrad raised an eyebrow at Donald who simply ignored him, knowing he was referring to his own relationship with Defella.

There was a knock on the door. Donald looked at Conrad, who shrugged, but before Donald could get to it Kaito had already opened it from outside.

"Kaito, what brings you round?" Donald said, stepping back to let him inside.

"I thought I better tell you we've confirmed the line we opened the portal to yesterday is Sultan. Agent Mahalia wants to leave as soon as you give him the go-ahead."

Donald looked at his father, who gave him a nod.

"We better see the Agent off then, though I can't see why he wants to leave," he said sarcastically, lifting his coat off the hook. The lining hadn't even had time to warm up and cold fell off it like a physical force. "Sunny

Mexico, pshah."

He shook his head at Defella as she started to rise. "You may as well stay here," he said. "It won't take long." He looked at Kaito, who nodded his confirmation.

Conrad hoisted himself out of his seat, as their father went to get his coat. "Let's get it over with then."

Donald adjusted his scarf as he stepped outside. Snow had already started to clog the path again, even though it had been cleared only that afternoon.

"When's it going to stop?" Conrad asked, looking at the sky.

"Probably not for another month or so," Donald pulling his beanie down over his ears.

The portal was housed in a low, brick-lined building, hidden under a series of low earth embankments. Agent Mahalia was waiting for them there, a bundled figure of furs, who looked as though he was only too happy to be on his way back to Mexico.

"Ready?" Brian asked him.

"Yes Leader," he replied. "It will be good to see my home again."

"Go with God then."

The Agent bowed, nodded briefly to Donald, then, after a quick glance to Kaito stepped up to the portal. It shimmered briefly as he stepped through it, then the First Leader nodded to Kaito, who cut the power.

"We won't risk opening the portal again until spring," he told Kaito. "It's obvious when one is operating because of the power surge on the others. And the less Miro knows, or guesses, the better."

Kaito nodded his agreement.

"My thanks for your assistance," their father said. "I'll see you back in the office," he said, slapping his arms together.

"You look as if you could do with a drink," Conrad said to Kaito, after he had gone.

"I could," Kaito agreed.

"Well, there should be some warm brandy back at the office," Donald pointed out.

"Thanks," Kaito said. "I'll join you in a couple of minutes. I still have to close this up, and shut down the generator."

The two left him to follow. The snow was starting to fall again, and through the flakes the lighted rooms of the barracks shone out in front of them like beacons, attracting them back to the warmth.

CHAPTER 27

Le Havre — Etu Line
August 1981 (97AE)

Ivy yawned, pausing for one long, last look around before following the last of the troops into the airship's gondola. To the east, the sky was just lightening with the arrival of dawn. There was no doubt it was going to be a beautiful day, she thought, as the dark velvet of night warmed to the blue of the new day and the first, faint hint of a breeze set the leaves on the trees on the edge of the field dancing. There was a cough from the engines overhead and, as they blurred into life, the sudden stink of diesel made Ivy wrinkle her nose. Sergeant Horsing, standing just inside the hatch looked enquiringly at her and she nodded. Time to go, she thought.

Inside, the corridor was still crowded with infantry waiting to take their seats, their hobnailed boots sliding slightly on the gondola's hard, roughly sanded wooden floor. Eventually the passage cleared enough for her to get to the bridge.

"Permission to depart, Leader?" the Captain said, as she settled into the seat next to him, Sergeant Horsing taking up his position behind her. In front of her, the wide window gave her an unobstructed view of the field outside.

"Permission granted," she said.

"Engineer, take us to three thousand feet and bring us nor-nor-west."

"Captain," the Engineer replied, reaching for the ballast release lever.

"Gently, Mr. Kraten," the Captain reminded him. "We have passengers."

Ivy smiled to herself as the Engineer's hand slowed, before gently nudging the release. As the pitch of the engines rose she could feel the gentle shudder of the ballast being dumped, and slowly the airship gained height. She took a breath, surprised to find she'd been holding it, and let it out slowly. This was it. Donald had laughingly given her five years to make Corps Leader. Now look at her, Continental Leader after only two. It had cost more than she had expected, however, and she wondered how her mother was. She could only hope she was safe. Though it had sometimes driven her up the wall with their trivia, she missed her mother's weekly letters.

"Coffee?" Horsing asked, and Ivy realized she must have been dozing.

"Thanks," she said, rotating a shoulder to try and get rid of some its stiffness.

"Careful," he warned her, as he handed her the mug. "It's the real stuff."

She raised an eyebrow, but took her time to savor the coffee's aroma before taking a sip.

"So what's happening?" she said, checking her watch. They'd been aloft for nearly two hours now. They must be close to being able to seeing some of the other airships by now.

"Just coming up on the rendezvous point now," the Captain said. "Engineer, bring us into the wind and slow all engines."

Ivy leaned forward, peering out of the window at the coast of Brittany below as the giant airship maneuvered slowly into the breeze.

The plan called for the landing of two Corps in America within three days of each other. The schedule was pretty tight, and required the fleet to make two return trips across the Atlantic, one Corps per crossing. Regardless of how successful the initial landing was, Ivy knew that if they couldn't capture Lincoln and its portal intact, this could all turn into one very expensive disaster.

"There," Horsing said as the first of the other airships loomed into view outside, a startling white against the backdrop of the sky's perfect blue. Below them, two small shadows danced across the tops of the waves far below.

Ivy couldn't help a small intake of breath, and a surge of pride at the sight of the massive ship as it floated effortlessly towards them. The airship's outer linen skin shone a brilliant white against the light blue of the sky, and the deeper blue of the ocean below. Obviously it appeared that she wasn't the only one who thought that, as the gondola seemed to list slightly as soldiers gathered at the windows on that side to watch its approach.

As they watched the other airship turned broadside to them, and a pennant broke from its tail, the Clemhorn eagle fluttering bravely in the breeze. There was a whisper of conversation behind her as those others on the bridge took in the sight.

"Leader," the Captain said.

"Yes," Ivy said, reluctantly turning her attention away from the spectacle.

"Airships Five and Seven are now approaching from the port bow."

"Thank you Captain," Ivy said, settling herself back into her seat.

Twenty minutes later, the radio operator passed a slip to the Captain. "That's the last one," the Captain said. "The fleet's assembled."

She nodded. She'd lost an airship the day before, when a sudden gust of wind had caught it while it was landing. It was repairable, but the repairs would take at least two weeks. Still, there were now nineteen airships gathered around them, poised to begin the invasion.

"Thank you, Captain," Ivy said. "Give the order to proceed." And as the giant behemoth swung round to its new heading, leading the rest of the fleet out across the Atlantic, she leaned back, resting her head against the backrest. She'd done the best she could; whatever happened now was beyond her control.

The rest of the day seemed an anti-climax as the fleet of leviathans ground their way slowly out across the ocean. With a following wind they made good progress, and after a spectacular red sunset that had filled the entire western horizon with spun candy, Ivy took to her hammock, confident that morning would bring with it the sight of land.

She was woken from an uneasy sleep by someone shaking her shoulder.

"What is it?" she asked drowsily, trying to work out where she was.

"Captain's compliments ma'am. He'd like to see you on the bridge."

"Of course," she said throwing the blanket off and standing up. This didn't sound good she thought, as she squinted at her watch, trying to make out the time. Ten a.m.? Oh, of course, she hadn't reset her watch since they'd left.

"Leader?" Sergeant Horsing said drowsily from the next hammock over.

"It's all right Horsing, go back to sleep," she told him as she pulled her boots on, lacing them up loosely. There didn't seem any reason for them both to be up. But as she followed the steward out of the room she heard Horsing pulling his own boots on.

The air in the corridor was freezing and there was an uneasy movement to the floor that had her resting her hand on the handrail all the way to the bridge. The Captain turned as she entered the room and saluted. Behind him the windows opened onto utter blackness.

Lonce was peering out of one of the windows, and as she nodded a greeting she noticed a faint blush rise over his cheeks.

"You wanted to see me, Captain?" she said.

"We've received a message from Airship 15. She's losing hydrogen."

"What happened?"

"It looks as if a seam gave way on one of the main buoyancy chambers. Unfortunately two of the others have started to go as well. They've dumped their ballast but it hasn't helped much."

"How the hell did that happen?" she demanded.

"Losing one of the chambers could be an accident," Lonce offered, "but three. . ." He shrugged uncomfortably.

"You're saying it was on purpose?" Ivy demanded.

"More likely shoddy workmanship," the Captain said, as Horsing entered the bridge. "If it was sabotage we would have had other reports by now."

Damn, she thought angrily, incensed at the thought of someone's shoddy work putting the lives of over two hundred of her soldiers at risk.

"So where are we?" she asked. Whoever was responsible would pay, but for the moment it appeared she had other priorities.

"About a hundred miles south of Nova Scotia."

"And their location?"

The Captain pointed off their right. "About fifty miles to the north."

"Any chance of them making land?"

He shook his head. "They're dead in the air at the moment."

"So what happens if they try to put her in the drink?' she asked.

"Tricky," he said thoughtfully, "but not totally impossible."

"Um, Leader," Lonce said uneasily.

"Yes?"

"No life rafts."

She looked at him unbelievingly.

"It was a question of weight. . ."

Taking a deep breath she let it out slowly. She'd worry about how that occurred later. "All right," she said. "Tell the fleet what's happening, and let them know we're going to try a rescue at first light. We're going to need another airship, but the rest of the fleet is to continue to Lincoln. Tell Airship 15's Captain they've got to do anything they can not to lose any height. They can dump their arms, ammunition, stores, everything; we're carrying enough spares to re-arm them." It had been intended to arm the militias with it, but there didn't seem any other alternative.

"You're going to try for a midair rescue?" the Captain said, quickly grasping her intention.

"I don't think we've got any choice. If we dump hydrogen we won't have enough to make it back to Europe."

"Probably not," he agreed. "It'll be difficult, but not impossible."

Ivy rubbed at her face tiredly. "It better be," she said. "Otherwise we're going to be in a lot of trouble. You better get a message to them; tell them they have to stay up."

"Understood," the Captain said.

She checked the two clocks above the window. One, now showing five past four, was set to show the time in Lincoln, the other — Le Havre.

"How long till dawn?" she asked.

"Just under an hour," he said, after glancing at the clocks.

"Let's get everyone up and serve breakfast then," she said.

He nodded, before turning to see to the order.

She was sipping on a coffee Lonce had brought her when the first faint, hint of light broached the distant horizon. As it did so, she became aware that the sky around them was heavy with cloud, with more moving in quickly from behind them. Below them, a thick layer of clouds hid the ocean from sight. Suddenly the entire sky turned red, and as it did so, the clouds beneath them seemed to explode in flames.

"Not exactly a good omen," Horsing muttered quietly from behind her.

"No," she agreed. "Any sign of them?" she asked the Captain.

He shook his head. "We should be able to see them in a moment though," he said reassuringly.

Lonce, peering out of the window, let out a gasp.

"What?" Ivy started to say, before stopping herself as she caught sight of the airship, hanging vertically in the air below them. She imagined a string attached to its nose. A string barely able to support its a hundred and fifty tons. A string very close to breaking. Behind it, the second airship waited patiently for dawn to assist with the rescue.

A sudden gust of wind caused the bridge to shift and Lonce had to grab for the window sill to keep his balance.

"I'm worried about the weather," the Captain said. "If the storm breaks. . ."

"I know. Could we try towing them?"

Lonce shook his head. "The framework wouldn't take it," he said. "We'd rip apart."

"All right. Captain, can you get close enough for us to throw a line to them?"

"You still want to try for a midair transfer?"

"I don't think the storm gives us any choice," Ivy said regretfully. "We can't wait."

He nodded. "You'll find it easier to do it from the tail," he said.

"Right, Horsing, get a team ready."

The Sergeant disappeared and Ivy turned back to the Captain. "Where's the rest of the fleet?"

"Almost at Lincoln."

"Warn them about the storm, and tell them to start landing their troops as soon as possible."

He nodded. "Good luck," he said.

Ivy nodded absentmindedly, her mind already fixed on the task ahead of her. "Lonce, you're with me," she said.

Horsing and two squads were waiting for them in the corridor outside. "We need ropes," Ivy said.

"This way," Lonce said, leading them to the store where the necessary ropes were obtained.

Once they'd finished kitting up, Lonce took a deep breath, and Ivy gave him a reassuring smile. "You're the expert," she said.

Lonce closed his eyes for a moment, before nodding as though having decided something. "This way," he said, and led them through the gondola and up a stair to an access door that led into the body of the airship itself.

It was even colder than in the gondola and Ivy immediately started to shiver.

"Are you all right?" Horsing asked.

"Just cold."

It was eerie inside the airship. Giant sacs hung like enormous bloated fruit over their heads, while the whole airship shuddered and trembled in the wind. Light seemed to come from everywhere, diffusing unevenly through the airship's linen skin that flexed in the gusting wind. The supports creaked while the drone of the engines surged in time to the gusts.

"This way," Lonce said, leading them out onto the laddered walkway laid along the keel of the airship.

It took them a quarter of an hour to reach the stern where Lonce made them fasten their lines, before allowing them to step out through the hatch onto the walkway that led to rear port engine nacelle.

They emerged into a dim light, and the full force of the emerging storm. Drizzle stung her face, and Ivy staggered as the wind grabbed at her. Only Horsing's quick reflexes stopped her from slipping.

"Thanks," she said.

Horsing only grunted.

Looking down over the edge of the walkway, Ivy saw they were almost directly over the other airship. Faces peered up at them anxiously through the open window of the disabled airship's bridge.

"Let's see if we can get a rope down to them," Ivy said, trying to wipe the water from her eyes so she could see.

One of the squad loosened the rope he had been carrying, and fixed one end around the rail of the walkway before lowering the other over the edge. The tail of the rope whipped in the wind, moving constantly from side to side. As they played out more rope, Ivy tightened her grip on the rail and peered over the edge at the airship below them, which was moving erratically in the gathering wind. A particularly vicious gust sent the damaged craft surging towards them and desperately she grabbed hold of a walkway beam as the impending disaster unfolded before her in slow motion.

"Look out!" she shouted, but it was already too late and her voice was lost in the ripping of fabric and the hiss of escaping gas as a broken spar pierced one of the bags. The walkway they were standing on heaved suddenly as the Captain dumped ballast, drenching the ship below them with water, and Ivy frantically tightened her grip, trying to keep her feet. For a moment it seemed the Captain's actions might work, and they could avoid further damage, but even as they started to separate the wind slammed them together again, and as it did so one of the rotors churning the air behind them caught the nose of the airship, ripping the fabric and snarling the two irrevocably together.

"Back inside," Ivy shouted over the shriek of the dying craft, as the two giants crashed and mangled each other in the grip of the wind. Before they could start to retrace their steps, however, the walkway slid away from beneath her, and she saw a frayed rope snapping in the wind, just beyond her hand. She looked round frantically, and realized that somehow Lonce's lifeline had broken.

"Lonce," she called desperately.

He looked round, saw what had happened, and had just begun to struggle back up the walkway when it gave way under him. As it heaved madly in the wind Lonce lost his grip. There was an expression of bewilderment on his face as the surface slid out from underneath him.

"Lonce!" Ivy screamed, throwing herself vainly after him, to find herself jerked back by her rope. And then could do nothing but watch numbly as he cart-wheeled through the air, hit the gondola of the airship below them, bounced, and then began the long fall to the surface of the ocean far below them.

"Gods," she heard someone say in a shocked whisper, and turned to see Horsing staring after him with horrified eyes.

"We'd better get back," she said numbly, after a couple of minutes. "There's nothing more we can do here." She gazed up at their fatally damaged craft and shook her head regretfully.

It took half an hour to crawl back through the crippled ship, trying to avoid the damaged areas and the great holes which had been ripped in its side. The torn fabric flapped wildly in the gathering wind, that now howled unhindered through the interior of the airship. Towards the gondola, they encountered teams moving cautiously back to try and repair the damage, and wished them luck, but no one had much hope. The ship was finished.

"Leader," the Captain said when she entered the bridge. "I wasn't expecting to see you again."

"What's the situation?" she asked.

"I was hoping you could tell me," he said. "You've seen it."

She shook her head sadly. "It's not good," she said; looking out of the window, back along the hull to where Airship 15 still lay, impaled in their side.

"You've lost all of your rear bags," she said, "and most of the body up to the middle is just splinters. It must be playing merry hell with your control."

"It would be if I had any," he said. "I've had to cut the engines because of possible fire. And the gods know what will happen when we get hit by the full force of the storm."

Ivy looked out of the window, at the building darkness of clouds around them. "Can we get above them?" she asked.

He shook his head. "I've already dumped all the ballast I've got. We've got too much dead weight in the stern."

"We'll have to manually separate them," she said.

He looked at her for a moment before nodding, and turning to his First Officer. "Alex, break out the axes and get everyone into the airship. You're going to need to try and cut us free by hand. I'll let Captain Harking know," he said, referring to the Captain of Airship 15.

"And tell Captain Bodicao she's to proceed to Lincoln," Ivy said. "There's nothing more she can do here now." She gazed at the other airship still holding station a short distance away, rather like a whale-calf that had just lost its mother. Realizing she was wool-gathering she gave herself a mental shake and turned to follow the First Officer who had already left.

"Good luck," the Captain called after her.

"Thanks," she said, knowing they were going to need it.

She emerged from the relative calm of the bridge into the chaos of the main cabin to find troopers struggling to get axes out of packs that were not meant to be opened until landing, the floor pitching and swaying madly beneath them. Steadying herself for a moment against the wall, Ivy listened to the giant craft moaning its death throes around her, timbers creaking as it struggled to remain aloft.

It was even worse once they'd left the gondola, and re-entered the body of the airship. Now the wind could be heard as an audible shriek, whining and thrumming among the spars and strings, and she flexed her fingers against the bitter cold.

"You do realize that if we're successful in cutting it free we might have already lost structural integrity," the First Officer said, having to shout to be heard above the noise of the wind.

"Which means?" Ivy shouted back.

"The whole thing might just collapse." His hand mimed a death roll.

She looked up at the cavernous interior, dark with the approaching storm, ropes and torn canvas flapping madly in the growing wind and shrugged. "What choice do we have?"

"None," he said.

And then she was lost in the moment of Lonce's death again, and closed her eyes against the look on his face as he lost his grip and started to slide away from her.

"Ivy?" It was Horsing.

She swallowed hard and opened her eyes, struggling to focus through the picture of Lonce as cart-wheeled through the air, beginning his long fall to the surface of the ocean below.

"You all right?" Horsing asked anxiously.

She noticed the First Officer also looking at her in concern and nodded.

"We'll need ropes for lifelines," she pointed out.

Horsing looked back the way they had come, then at the sky visible through one of the holes below them. "I don't think we've got time."

She looked at the First Officer who held up his hand and crossed his fingers.

With a wry shrug, Ivy nodded. No, there wasn't time.

Within a couple of minutes soldiers had started to swarm all over the interior of the hull, hacking and sawing at the ropes and beams that held the airship's outer skin together, but it seemed as though they were losing the battle. The wind grew steadily in violence, and there was a sudden peal of thunder in the distance.

Ivy flinched at the thought of what would happen if they were hit by lightning, as those around her threw themselves back into their work with redoubled fervor.

For a time nothing seemed to happen, but then slowly the beams started to break away at the bottom of the airship, and as they did so her nose started to rise.

"She's ripping," the First Officer yelled, as her ropes and spars sang like violin strings. "Move back!" Even as he turned, the airship rolled and he was thrown, losing his balance, and falling to the floor of the airship. For a moment Ivy thought he was safe, then the airship rolled again and he disappeared through a hole in the fabric.

Several more lost their grip and fell, one tearing through the cloth and falling with an agonized scream to the ocean below.

Then, as though satisfied with the toll it had taken, the ship ripped itself free, and released from the weight that had held it captive, shook itself like a dog and surged upwards. As it did there was a flash of lightning, and burning filled the sky beneath them — a slow roiling cloud of living flame.

"There, but for the love of the gods," she heard Horsing say softly, as the remains of the other ship flared, and drifted slowly down to the gathering waters below.

Ivy closed her eyes against the pain. There were black specks in the flames, and with a shudder she released they were people.

She felt Horsing's arm rest for a moment on hers.

"Leader?" he said softly.

She shook her head, unable to speak, as she started to shake.

CHAPTER 28

Milano equivalent — Mmbuto é Line
February 1982 (98AE)

Donald adjusted his scarf before thrusting his hands deeper into the pockets of his greatcoat to try and get them warm. The snow had all but disappeared, but it was still freezing, and with the sky heavily overcast and threatening rain it was likely to get worse.

"Don't be such a boy, it's not that cold," Defella said, her gaze fixed on the long line of troops moving slowly through the portal just in front of them.

"A boy?" Donald said.

"Baby then," she said frowning, looking up at him. "It is boy, yes?"

He shook his head. "Girl."

"A girl. Hah, a girl would not be so soft," she scoffed.

Another phrase lost in translation, he thought. But on a line where there were five females to every male it was hardly surprising which sex was considered the stronger.

Defella's attention swung back to the troops passing through the portal and Donald realized that the first of her headquarters' troops had just reached the front of the line.

He frowned, wishing he didn't feel so worried about her departure. Objectively he knew there shouldn't be any trouble, they'd had scouts through the portal since yesterday morning, but a portal entry was the most difficult of bridgeheads to establish, and there was so much that could go wrong, particularly with a single portal that was so small that they could only push the troops through in single file. The real problem was, of course, that his father had given Defella the honor of leading the First Corps through. It was an honor Donald would have been happier she hadn't received, even if she had well and truly earned it.

"Looks like it's my turn," Defella said, giving one final adjustment to the straps of the heavy pack she was carrying. Satisfied, she stretched up and gave him a quick peck on his cheek before flashing him a smile. "Take care, I'll see you in a couple of hours."

He nodded. "Look after yourself."

"Of course," and stepping forward she joined the last of her headquarters' group as they passed through the portal.

The rest of the Dynands weren't scheduled to go through for another three days, but behind him stretched the apparently endless column of troops due to pass through the portal that day. All five thousand of them, each trooper bowed down under the weight of the pack they were carrying; an apparently endless line of fodder for their newly revitalized war. With a sigh, he turned away to look for Kaito.

He found his former roommate monitoring the portal from the control room built into the side of a small hill about fifty yards away from the portal.

"Everything going all right?" Donald asked, bending as he entered the room to avoid hitting his head on the low wooden beams that provided the main support to the bunker's sod-covered roof.

"Couldn't be better," Kaito said. "Defella gone through yet?"

Donald nodded as he crossed the small room to peer out of the slit window that overlooked the portal. "About five minutes ago."

Kaito looked around, saw the bunker was temporarily deserted, and lowered his voice. "So what do you think our chances are?"

Donald shrugged, wondering what it was about the line of soldiers shuffling through the portal that was worrying him. "Ask me in a week," he suggested. "At the moment I haven't the foggiest."

"That's what I thought. Do you want a cup of tea?"

"Thanks." At least it would give him something to do with his hands, Donald thought. He was on his second mug, peering out of the slit window at the portal again when he finally realized what had been bugging him.

"Damn!" he swore, checking his watch.

"What?" Kaito said, coming to his feet.

"It's taking too long. We should have already started the 14th by now. At this rate we'll still be here in a week. I need to see my father."

He sensed, rather than saw, Kaito move to peer out of the window behind him as he hurried out to find his father.

He found him, with Conrad, watching the column with three Corps Leaders, on the top of the hill behind the bunker.

"It's taking too long," Donald said as he came up behind them, breathing heavily from the steep climb.

Conrad nodded. "We know."

"Can you go and see if you can speed things up?" his father asked.

"Of course," Donald said. He made his way back down the hill again and inserted himself in the line close to the portal.

"Where's Leader Haratan?" he asked the trooper on station on the other side of the portal.

She gestured behind the portal and Donald walked round it to see that Defella had set her headquarters up on the same hill his father had been using on the Mmbuto é Line. A single row of sandbags had been laid out on the ground to mark out the walls of her future command post and a squad of soldiers were already working busily to raise the height of the wall.

"Donald," Defella said surprised, looking up from the map pinned down on the small card table in front of her as he clambered up to meet her. "What are you doing here? Is everything all right?"

"My father asked to come through to see what the delay was," he said, trying to get his breath back.

"Delay?" she asked, puzzled, then looked at her watch. "Dragon's breath! Sorry," she said shaking her head. "I didn't know we were falling that far behind."

"Can we hurry them up?" he said. "Otherwise we're only going to get through about half of what we need today."

She nodded and spoke to her radio officer. Looking down at the portal, Donald saw the line immediately speed up, the troops starting to move through at a slow trot.

"Better?" she asked.

"Better," he agreed. "So what's the situation?" he asked, looking over her shoulder at the map.

"Our perimeter is about here," she said, drawing a circle on the map with her finger.

Donald shook his head worriedly, it was far too small, only two miles in radius.

She saw his concern. "I know," she said. "I'm trying to push scouts out to give us some leeway, but it takes time to get a Force assembled and send it off."

"All right, I'll get back to Papa and let him know what's happening. I don't know there's anything else you can do, but try and keep them moving."

He scrambled back down the hill, moving to avoid a Force of ninety people moving at a quick trot along the river towards the southern perimeter. He wished they could have had some of their artillery through by now, but it wasn't due through until later that night.

He squeezed through in a gap in the line and passed back to the command post.

"How is it?" his father asked.

"Not good," Donald said. "They've speeded up a little, but the outer perimeter is still less than two miles out."

His father looked at the map on the table in front of them, a mirror image of the one Defella had been using, tracing the line of the river with his finger thoughtfully.

"Leader Himilco," he said finally, turning to the thickset, Carthagian Battlegroup Leader standing next to him whose troops were presently passing through the portal. "I want you to move your headquarters through immediately. Once through you're to move everyone you've got forward to those hills overlooking the river and dig in. I know it's a little ahead of schedule, but it will make it easier to pass the others through if they don't have to move out straight away."

Himilco nodded, saluted, and went to see to his staff.

With the troops moving through at the trot rather than a slow shuffle, by dusk Donald was able to report to his father that they had managed to move the invasion back on schedule. Nightfall brought no slackening to the transfer of troops and equipment through the portal, which was planned to continue without pause for the next two days, and shortly after seven Donald followed the first of the artillery through. On the other side he stopped for a moment to watch the crew of the first gun struggling to re-assemble it in the glare of the artificial lights. They had rehearsed the whole exercise twice, but as he watched them it occurred to Donald they should have practiced more. It had taken them five minutes to pass the gun through the portal, and another fifteen to re-assemble it in the area marked out for them to one side of the portal. Only then, groaning and panting, could the crews start to drag the gun to the positions which had been identified for them on the Mmbuto é Line.

He shook his head, they were still far too slow, and the light, misting drizzle now drifting across the valley wasn't helping.

Pulling the peak of his kepi down and hunching his shoulders against the rain, Donald took a moment to look around. At least the area was looking more settled. Sandbag walls had been erected around the portal and other troops were in the process of piling up additional earth and rocks to give greater protection. Despite the delays, there was an air of quiet professionalism about the scene. Satisfied, Donald turned away to find Defella.

Defella's headquarters were now considerably more substantial than they had been the last time he'd been there. The sandbag walls had been raised to shoulder height and roughly-hewn wooden beams were in the process of being lifted into position to support the roof. In the meantime, two large tents had been erected within the walls to provide some shelter against the elements. As he was ushered in he found that folding chairs had been brought through as well and Defella was sitting on one, sipping from a mug while she checked the map in front of her.

"Want some soup?" she asked, waving the mug at him.

"Thanks," he said, taking the mug from her before she spilled it. He took a sip, vegetable and beef, heavy on the beef.

"How do you think things are going?" he asked.

"About as well as we expected. We've got the perimeter out to five miles but we're still awfully exposed."

"I know," he agreed. "I'm worried about the artillery. They seemed to be taking a hell of a long time to get that first one assembled."

"They'll get faster," she said reassuringly, accepting a replacement mug from one of her aides.

"Any sign of hostiles?"

"Nothing."

"Well, at least something's going right."

Despite his concerns, Defella proved correct, and they managed to pull slightly ahead of schedule during the night. By the time his father came through the portal at eleven the next day Donald was almost starting to feel confident. Even the weather had started to improve as the clouds disappeared.

"Any contact yet?" his father asked, as he joined Donald and Defella looking over the latest information being transferred to the main map.

Donald shook his head.

"Nothing," Defella confirmed.

"I am not unthankful," his father admitted. "But it is starting to get a bit suspicious. I would have thought there should have been something by now." He tapped his chin thoughtfully. "Get a Force moving out in the direction of Padua," he told Defella. "Another couple of hours and the First Corps will be able to move out, but I'd like to know if there is anything there as soon as possible."

"I'll lead it myself," she volunteered.

He shook his head. "Thank you, but no. I need you here."

Defella had the Force on its way within five minutes. They had just reported in on leaving the outer perimeter, when the sound of distant gunfire brought Donald's head round with a snap.

"What's happening?" his father demanded.

Defella shrugged, already on her way next door to the radio.

She returned less than two minutes later, a copy of the message slip in her hand. "The reconnaissance Force was ambushed. We lost contact before we could get any information."

"Did we get anything at all?" the World Leader asked. "Numbers, types of troops?"

"No, nothing," Defella said, shaking her head regretfully.

"Leaders." It was a Force Leader standing by the entrance to the bunker. "I think you should see this."

"What?" Donald demanded, joining her in the entrance.

The Force Leader simply pointed down the hill towards the portal where something had obviously gone wrong. No one was coming through, and those that had were now milling around aimlessly.

Donald swore under his breath. "Send someone down there to find out what's going on," he told the Force Leader quietly. "We can't afford have any trouble now."

Even as he spoke a messenger came pounding up the hill to gasp out his message to disbelieving ears.

"Leaders, they've have been attacked! On the Mmbuto é Line."

"Attacked!" Defella said, stunned. "But how?"

Donald's father's face had gone completely white. "They must have known we were coming," he said.

Oh gods, Donald thought, looking at his father, who looked as though he'd aged twenty years.

Suddenly his father shook himself, like a dog coming out of the water. "Donald, I need you back there. Tell Conrad it's a trap. Tell him I'm bringing everyone back, and he is to hold the portal area for as long as possible."

Donald saluted, gesturing for the messenger who had brought the news to lead the way out of the bunker. Behind him he could hear his father giving the orders that signaled the end of the attack and start their withdrawal.

"Pull everyone back in alternate Groups," he was saying. "Evens first, get orders out to the odd numbers that they're going to have to be ready to take up the slack. And get everyone not on the perimeter back through the portal immediately. I don't think we're going to have much time." As though to punctuate his words a plane screamed low over the hill in front of them. Donald threw himself flat, to watch mesmerized as the five bombs it released somersaulted slowly through the air. They hit the ground, and as he buried his face in his arms, the ground around the portal erupted, everything in the hollow disappearing into a fine mist.

He had just started to raise his head when he heard the unmistakable whine of incoming shells and pulled himself tighter against the ground, as the area at the foot of the hill was engulfed in a series of explosions.

He could hear the thud, thud, thud of their own artillery returning fire, but returning salvos quickly smashed the guns into silence, pounding their positions to mud. And all Donald could do was to pray he survived. Finally the bombardment began to ease as the enemy guns turned their attention to other targets.

In the eerie silence he could hear the panicked voices on the radio from the bunker behind, and it was obvious that their entire front was under attack by superior forces. Every message begged reinforcements, or for permission to withdraw.

"Donald?" It was his father.

Shakily Donald got to his feet. "I'm all right."

"I need that message to get through to Conrad."

"Sir."

Unsteadily Donald started down the hill. Halfway down, he had to pick his way carefully over ground ripped and splatted into mud, laced with blood and the last of the snow. At the bunker he found that part of the roof had collapsed, blocking the main entrance, and he had to clamber over a collapsed wall to get into the bunker. Inside, he felt a surge of relief when he realized the portal was undamaged, and taking a deep breath he stepped through the portal's shimmering surface.

He emerged to the sound of small arms fire in the distance, and the sight of eight nervous Dynand training their weapons on him. Instinctively, Donald raised his hands and as he was recognized the Force Leader came to attention and the squad lowered their weapons.

"What's the situation?" Donald asked.

"I'm not sure, Leader," the Force Leader admitted, her eyes wide with worry. "I was simply told to ensure the safety of the portal."

"I need to get a message to my brother," Donald said. "You're to tell him it's a trap. Our father is bringing everyone back, but he is to hold the portal area for as long as possible."

She nodded, nervously.

"And I need a couple of people with a radio."

She nodded. "Maccree, Donza, Shubatta. You're with the Leader."

Stepping back through the portal Donald found Defella just clambering over the collapsed wall.

"What are you doing here?" he demanded.

"Your father sent me down to help you."

Donald opened his mouth to ask who was helping his father when the first of the walking wounded appeared and further discussion had to be put aside to concentrate on helping them over the obstacle of the collapsed wall and through the portal to the relative safety of the Mmbuto é Line. Fortunately, artillery fire remained sporadic, presumably concentrating on other targets, and for fifteen minutes they worked frantically to pass as many as they could back through the portal. But the numbers were pitifully small and finally as the bombardment started to intensify again there was nothing

Donald could do but take shelter behind the remains of the wall under the continuous pounding and pray that a shell would avoid landing directly on them.

"Donald!"

It was Defella, and he realized she was shouting at him to attract his attention.

"Radio!" she yelled, holding the handpiece out to him. "It's your father."

"Donald here," he said, pressing the transmit button.

"Donald, I want you to return to Mmbuto é," his father said.

"Papa?" The stink of death, mud, and high explosive filled his nostrils, and the thunderous pounding and continuous concussion of the barrage made it difficult for him to concentrate.

"Your brother will need you. As soon as you've gone I'll try and find someone to surrender to. Now move, and take Defella with you. That's an order!"

"We can't leave you."

"There's no choice, and no time to argue. Now go!"

Donald glanced at Defella who avoided his eyes.

How could he leave his father, but what choice did he have? It wouldn't be long before a lucky shell blew the portal to hell and back. And without the portal all their hopes, and plans would be dust. "We'll be back for you," he said.

"Do so, I'll be expecting you. As soon as you're through kill the portal. Now move!"

"You heard!" he snapped bitterly to the few remaining. "Let's go!"

Defella had just passed through the portal, the silvery surface still shimmering around her outline when he heard the whistle of another incoming shell, and threw himself frantically after her.

The ensuring blast was muted by the portal, but its surface bulged with the force of the explosion, red and black lines crackling across its surface in a manner Donald had never seen before.

"I don't know how much more of this it can take?" Kaito shouted when he noticed that it was Donald who had come through. "Can't you do something?"

"Turn it off," Donald ordered, realizing he was the last and no one else was going to make it.

Kaito looked at him, shocked.

"Cut the power," Donald repeated.

"But what about everyone else?" Kaito said.

"They can't get through," Donald said. "Papa's going to surrender."

Kaito looked as though he was going to say something, then shaking his head he moved to carry out Donald's order.

"Can you dismantle the portal and get it ready for moving?" Donald asked, as soon as Kaito had returned.

"Of course, I'm getting quite good at that. I *was* looking forward to getting home though," he said, looking mournfully back through the now dead portal.

"Well, we still may," Donald said, but even as he said it he realized he didn't really believe it. They'd be lucky to escape with their lives after this debacle.

Kaito gestured to the two technicians waiting for his command, and went to undo the clamps holding the portal in place.

"Come on," Donald said to Defella, "we better find my brother, and see what's happening." And let him know about Papa he thought.

They had put two Corps, or just under six thousand troops through the portal, and had perhaps managed to save fewer than fifty. Conrad would still have three Corps, but they wouldn't have been expecting an attack, and none of their artillery would have been set up. Gods, it was a shambles, he thought, as he hurried to find his brother and find out exactly how bad the situation was.

CHAPTER 29

Milano equivalent — Mmbuto é Line
February 1982 (98AE)

Conrad was desperately trying to find out what was happening at A Barracks when he realized that Donald and Defella were waiting to talk to him.

"What are you doing here?" he demanded. Their trousers and boots were both coated with mud and Defella had what looked like blood smeared down the right side of her face. The three Dynands with them didn't seem any better.

"Papa sent us back," Donald said. "He ordered us to close the portal."

"Papa!" Conrad said. "Where is he?"

"Still on the Mainline. He's going to surrender."

"And you left him there?" Conrad said accusingly.

"I didn't have any choice, Conrad," Donald said. "They were waiting for us. It was murder."

"But you got away," Conrad said accusingly. "You should have brought him with you."

"I know I should have," Donald said, his voice rising hysterically. "But he was cut off and we were taking heavy fire. The portal couldn't take anymore, Conrad. Damn it, I didn't know what to do! He told me to come back; ordered it! What else could I do?"

Conrad looked at him for a moment, before abruptly remembering there was still a battle to fight.

"We'll have this out afterwards," he said. "At the moment, I need to find out what's happening at A Barracks. We lost contact with the Dynands when they started to jam the radios about ten minutes ago. Can you get over there and do a sitrep?"

"Of course." For a moment Donald looked as though he was going to say something else, but then he simply saluted, spun on his heel, and left.

Defella looked after him. "He tried," she said simply.

Conrad sighed; he had never really doubted it. "Look after him for me," he said.

"Of course," and waving her escort to follow she headed after Donald, unslinging her rifle as she did so.

Conrad turned back to his war just as Kerensha, the acting Leader of the First Corps, appeared. The Corps had been in the middle of transposing through the portal when the attack had started, and its senior command team were now on the other side of the portal. Despite his lack of combat experience, Kerensha had been a civil engineer before enlisting, he appeared reassuringly unflustered by the chaos that had enfolded them.

"How did you go?" Conrad asked.

"As you suspected, it appears they planned on the river being a sufficient obstacle by itself, and they've got less than a Force on the other side."

Conrad nodded. "Good. Get your Corps across then. I'll arrange for everyone else to follow. If you come across a portal, destroy it. There's got to be more than one of them though, given the speed with which they've built up."

Kerensha saluted, and turned to go. "And quickly," Conrad called after him.

Forcing the river was going to be messy, Conrad thought. But they didn't have any choice, not if they wanted to get out of there. Now for Kaito.

The portal had indeed been closed down as Donald had told him, and Kaito had already placed it in its cushioned case ready for transport. The technicians were now just clearing up the area.

"Ready to go?" Conrad asked.

"Ready," Kaito said, looking up from whatever he had been doing.

"Good, I'll arrange an escort for you. We'll be breaking out in about fifteen minutes and I wouldn't want you, or the portal, left behind."

"Thanks," Kaito said, wiping his forehead with the back of his sleeve as he straightened his back.

Conrad found Hannibal, the Fourth Corps' Leader, at his headquarters just outside the main compound. A coffee-colored Carthagian who was almost as large as Conrad, he was chewing on a mouthful of khat which he spat out as Conrad appeared.

"Any idea what's happening?" Hannibal asked. Despite the color of his skin, he claimed a direct lineal relationship to the famous leader who had fought the Romans during the Second Punic War.

"We're pulling out. Kerensha is going to force the river. I want your Corps ready to follow him across in fifteen minutes."

Hannibal nodded, unsurprised.

"I also need you to detail a Force to escort Kaito and the portal."

"And the World Leader?"

Conrad froze for a moment, unable to think what to say. Finally he managed to find his voice. "He was unable to return."

Hannibal surveyed him unblinkingly for a moment before nodding. "Then let us, how you say, rock and roll."

Conrad found his eyebrow rising at that. "You better make sure your troops are carrying their packs," he said. It was one of the first things troops dumped when they went into combat, but the supplies intended for their move onto the Mainline would now have to do for their retreat.

"Of course."

"Carry on then."

Outside the building, the firing appeared to be intensifying from the direction of A Barracks, and he hoped Donald would be safe.

Moving down to the river he was just in time to see the first Force wade out into the river, holding their rifles at arm's length above their heads. He hoped the water wasn't too cold, but this early in spring it would probably be freezing.

Bullets were striking the water all around the line, but no one hesitated. If they'd been facing the Etehad Sho'mali this might not have worked, even outnumbering them as much as they did, but they were facing Mainline regulars. One of Kerensha's troops was hit, his head disappearing in a fountain of blood, but the rest continued to press on. And the enemy were certainly not getting it easy, as there were well over a thousand troops lining this side of the bank, eager to clear the opposing shore before they had to enter the water themselves.

As the line reached the middle of the river, the Second Force slid into the water to commence their crossing, and as the First dragged itself out of the river the Third had already followed them in. Shaking themselves out into a skirmish line the First wormed its way into the scrub to provide cover for those following. Within minutes the Second had reinforced the line, and then the Third. By this time the Corps' collapsible rafts had been assembled, and the main part of the Corps started to ferry over. Things were well under control so, telling Kerensha to keep him informed of progress, he moved on to try and find out what was happening at the barracks.

He had almost reached them when a trooper rose out of the ground in front of him.

"Careful, Leader," he warned. "They're pushing around the buildings at the moment."

"Have you seen my brother?" he asked, worriedly.

"He should be in there," he said, gesturing towards the barracks.

"Thanks," Conrad said, and getting down onto his stomach he wormed his way quickly forward. Once in the shelter of the buildings he stood up and moved inside. There was a Dynand crouching cautiously in the doorway, and Conrad was almost shot before she recognized him.

"Leader!"

"I'm looking for my brother."

She looked worried. "I think he's back there," she said, indicating the headquarters room with her head.

"Thanks." Without lights, and filled with smoke, the corridors were dim, eerily deserted places that echoed strangely to the sound of battle from outside.

He found Donald lying in the corridor outside the map room, Defella kneeling next to him while a medic crouched over his head holding an IV tube.

"What happened?" he demanded.

Defella looked up, and he felt his heart lurch as he saw the tears coursing down her cheeks.

"Is he — ?" He broke off, afraid to ask the question.

She shook her head and looked at the medic.

"He's stable for the moment," the medic said. "And I've given him a shot of morphine so he's not in any pain but it's a stomach wound and he needs more attention than I can give him here."

"Can we move him?" Conrad asked.

The medic shrugged. "I don't see we've got any choice."

"You have to pull back now," Conrad told Defella, "otherwise you'll be cut off. Can you?"

"Just watch," she said bitterly, rubbing her eyes. "We're getting so good at it that pretty soon we won't even bother to advance in the first place."

He gave her a weary smile. "It is starting to feel that way isn't it? Make for the river. Kerensha has managed to force a path for us. Get your wounded across first, then everyone else. And Defella, don't leave anyone behind."

Bending, he touched a hand to Donald's cheek. "Don't you dare die on me," he said fiercely.

Donald's eye's flickered open. "Hi bro — I have no intention of dying on you," he whispered. "I promised Papa we'd be back for him." He winced and closed his eyes again. "Just get us out of here."

As Conrad squeezed his shoulder someone pushed past him to put a stretcher on the ground next to his brother. Straightening up, Conrad realized the smoke was coming from the map room where three Dynands were busy burning papers. For a moment, Conrad wished he'd been the one to remember to order their destruction, but there was only so much he could do. He massaged the bridge of his nose.

"Good luck," he told Defella. Donald didn't open his eyes, and without looking back Conrad headed for the entrance, knowing he now had one more thing to worry about.

By the time he got back to the door, the trooper on guard there was engaged in a desultory fire fight with a sniper who had pushed forward to harass them.

"Keep your head down," she told Conrad when she saw that he was intent on leaving.

"You keep his down," he told her.

She smiled fiercely.

"You got a spare grenade?" he asked.

She nodded and unclipped one from her belt.

He waited until the first of the Dynands had moved up behind him, then he got down on his stomach and crawled as quickly as he could towards the shelter of his own line. It was probably all very heroic, he thought as a bullet smacked the ground a short distance away, burying itself in the soil; but if it was the only way of getting his brother out nothing was going to stand in his way.

The Dynands behind him had opened fire now, and as the sniper took cover, Conrad pulled the pin, released the handle and counted to three before hurling the grenade as far as he could. Throwing himself flat, he hoped it was far enough. A second later the explosion ripped overhead.

It seemed to have worked as the sniper didn't fire again, and crawling on, Conrad made the best speed he could through the low shelter until he saw a trooper crouching behind a tree.

Cautiously he got to his knees and looked behind him. The Dynands had already established a skirmish line out from the door and were pushing forward to create a corridor for the wounded to get down. As he watched the first of the wounded were started to come down the line, and Conrad knew he might have already wasted too much time.

"What Battlegroup are you with?" he asked the trooper.

"The 75th, Leader."

Conrad nodded. "Any idea where your Battlegroup HQ is?"

"Force headquarters would be that way," the trooper said, pointing slightly behind him, and to the right. "No idea where the Battle Headquarters is though."

"Thanks," Conrad said and moved back away from the line before heading off to find Hannibal.

The Corps Leader was in the middle of receiving a briefing when Conrad arrived.

"What's the situation?" Conrad demanded, looking at the map.

"We're holding," the Corps Leader said. "But the enemy are pushing us strongly, and it's becoming difficult. Most of the wounded are across the river, with sufficient forces to act as protection."

"Good," Conrad said. "Pull back those units which have the most problem with ammunition and get them across the river, they can resupply from there. The others will just have to cover them. The line will be shorter anyway so they shouldn't have as much problem."

"Leader."

"I'll cross now and see what we can do for the wounded. Transport's going to be a bastard, but don't let anything hold you up."

Hannibal nodded in understanding, and Conrad made his way down to the river, crossing over with a boat of wounded.

The withdrawal across the river continued for the next two hours, with the enemy pushing steadily closer all the time. Conrad wished he had some artillery; it would have been ideal for supporting fire across the river, but they didn't have the time to get it across. Even so, he couldn't have been prouder of the way the three Corps handled the retreat.

The last units came across with a rush, with almost the entire Second Corps lining the bank to provide cover for them. Conrad, studying a map as he watched the final moves of the battle straightened stiffly as Hannibal approached.

"Hannibal," Conrad said, greeting his Corps Leader.

Hannibal came round to look at the map. "What's the situation?" he asked.

"We lost fewer troops than I was expecting when we forced the river, but losses have still been higher than I hoped. We've probably got fewer than six thousand operatives left."

Hannibal frowned, calculating the figures in his head. "That's fifty per cent what we started with."

"I know. The biggest losses were from the two Corps when we closed the portal, but our remaining three Corps have still lost close to twenty per cent each."

"So what are we doing?"

"The first thing we have to do is to warn the High King. Now Miro has the coordinates for the line he's in danger. As soon as the evening window comes in we'll get a radio message off. The second is to try and evacuate as many people as I can south. To do that I've already started to move the wounded downstream to the port."

"It's still under our control?"

"It appears to be." And for that small mercy Conrad was extremely thankful.

Hannibal was shaking his head. "We don't have the ships. Even if you pack everyone in until there's only standing room you wouldn't be able to get everyone out."

"I know," Conrad admitted. "This is why I intend to leave a reinforced Corps here with as much ammunition as I can spare to harass the enemy. The remaining two will sail with the wounded. Once we've reached Ngoni I'll send the fleet back for them.

"Which Corps are you leaving?"

"Yours, the Fourth. Kerensha's took heavy losses forcing the river."

"Makes sense," Hannibal said. He straightened himself, coming to a slow salute. "Then with your permission Leader, I will see to my orders."

"Permission granted," Conrad said, wishing he hadn't had to give the order. He suspected that by the time the fleet returned there might not be many left for it to pick up. "And good luck."

Hannibal grinned at him, a lean, wolfish smile that for some reason made Conrad think of his ancestor and namesake, the Carthaginian General who had master-minded the greatest defeat Rome had ever suffered. "Don't worry, we'll make our own luck," he said.

As Hannibal headed back down the hill, Conrad, now with one less thing to worry about, turned back to arranging the retreat of his remaining two Corps.

CHAPTER 30

Western hemisphere — Etu Line
August 1981 (97AE)

Ivy surveyed the catastrophe of the landing site. Despite their efforts over the past couple of hours, the remains of the airship still seemed to cover everything in sight, festooning the beach in acres of fabric. The white cloth shone in the moonlight, the perfect sign for any aircraft searching for them.

"Leader," Horsing said, attracting her attention.

"What," she snapped. It didn't help that her clothes were stiff with dirt and stank of sweat, and that she hadn't been able to wash for nearly a week.

"Food," he said, holding a plate out to her.

Hot food! Her mouth watered. While drifting they'd subsisted on a diet of biscuits and water due to the risks of igniting the hydrogen.

"Sorry," she apologized, accepting the plate and the roll that went with it. She took a sniff and pulled a face.

"What?" he said.

"I hate fish chowder." She took a mouthful, trying not to breath as she did so.

"Is everyone else getting some?" she asked, after she'd finished about half of it.

"Yes, I just put some pressure on the cook to get yours early."

She followed his gaze to see the first group already lining up for their meal.

"Here you are, you'd better finish it," she said, holding the plate out to him.

"I'm fine."

"Take it Sergeant, or I'm tipping it away. I don't like fish that much."

He looked as if he was going to argue for a moment, but then nodded and accepted the plate. "Thank you," he said.

Cautiously he took a mouthful and Ivy watched pleasure suffuse his face, and for some reason found herself relaxing at his obvious enjoyment.

"What?" he demanded, catching her watching.

"Nothing," she said, unwilling to explain, knowing it would only make him uncomfortable.

"Any idea where we might be?" he asked, as he took another mouthful.

"With luck, somewhere in Florida."

"And without?"

"The Caribbean."

He looked confused, and she realized he didn't understand. "The Caribbean — we could be on an island."

And it could quite easily be either. They'd been drifting for three days without power, and although it had been in a generally southern direction most of it had been over water.

"So how do you think they went at Lincoln?" he asked.

"I don't know," she admitted. "But that storm wouldn't have done any them good. The sooner we can get a radio working the better."

He nodded understandingly.

"Leader." It was the Force Leader.

"Yes."

"Some of the scouts are back."

About time, at least one of the questions might be answered.

The scouting party waited to make their report in the gondola's dining room. There was something a little disquieting for Ivy to be standing so solidly on a floor that had once recently drifted, constantly shifting underfoot as they struggled to remain aloft.

The Force Leader made the introductions. "Continental Leader, this is Squad Leader Acaroho, Trooper Sani, and Menhapoceck Donera," he said, presenting the only civilian in the group.

Menhapoceck stepped forward, inclining his head politely. His face was almost totally covered in blocky Mayan tattoos.

"Menhapoceck is a merchant from Tahatopeck," the Force Leader continued.

So they were on the mainland. Ivy felt a sudden sense of relief. Tahatopeck was near the equivalent of Mainline Miami.

"I am pleased to meet you," Ivy told him sincerely.

"The pleasure is mine," Menhapoceck responded.

"Please be seated," she said. She felt Horsing take up his normal position behind her. "I take it we're on the mainland?"

The Force Leader nodded. "About twenty miles south of Tahatopeck."

"You're a long way from home," she said smiling at Menhapoceck.

"I was visiting relatives when I was picked up by your scouts."

"My apologies for any inconvenience this may cause."

"Oh, no inconvenience," he assured her. "I am pleased to be of service."

"My thanks then," Ivy told him, leaning forward. "Now, tell me, what is the situation in Tahatopeck?"

He shrugged. "Much the same as everywhere I suppose. Most of the people have accepted your brother; and for those that haven't, well there's not a lot that they can do about it."

"And yourself?"

He scowled. "With his taxes, and foreign troops he isn't exactly my favorite person. But as I said, there's not a lot we can do. The first thing he did was to disarm the militia, and with your mother a hostage, well, there's some talk, but not much else."

"And are there any of my brother's troops stationed at Tahatopeck?"

"About fifty. But there's a Battlegroup of Malac Line infantry near Jacksonville."

And that was what, fifty miles away. Oh if only they hadn't been forced to dump their cargo. With the militia armed she could have taken the Battlegroup on and driven all the way to Lincoln. But there wasn't all that much she could do with just a Force. Especially one in the condition hers was.

Moodily, she stared at the table between them. Finally she stood up. "My thanks Menhapoceck," she told him with a tired smile. "I'm sure Force Leader Hague has some more questions for you, but I appreciate your honesty and assistance."

"It has been my pleasure, Leader, I just wish I could do more."

Outside, she stood a moment, listening to the surf breaking gently on the shore, the waves glistening in the moonlight. There wasn't a hint of a breeze, and the warm, salty air seemed to enfold her in its embrace. For a moment she considered just walking into the water and letting the waves rinse off her sweat, but until they were secure she'd forbidden anyone to bath.

With a sigh she turned away to find Horsing standing there, and gave him a half smile.

"I could sleep for a week," she said stretching, trying to ease the kinks out of her shoulders.

"Why don't you grab some then?" he asked.

"I might be needed."

"I doubt it. And if you are I'll wake you."

"You sure?" she said, looking hopefully in the direction of her blankets. No one had been able to do more than catch the merest hint of rest while the airship had drifted south. The noise, and the constant shifting as the envelope threatened to split had kept everyone awake.

"Of course."

"Thanks Horsing," she said gratefully, and within a minute of her head touching the pillow she was fast asleep.

***

There was a feeling of rain in the air, the impending storm causing the outer fabric of the airship to flex uneasily. Below her, Ivy could see the small rescue party making its way out onto the walkway that led to one of the rear engine nacelles. Below them she could see those waiting to be rescued peering worriedly up at her through the gondola's windows.

One of the squad loosened the rope he had been carrying, and fixing one end to the walkway lowered the other over the edge. It whipped in the wind, moving constantly from side to side so that it was impossible to see if it would reach them. Suddenly, as they peered over the edge Ivy became aware of the shadow moving in on them.

To the sound of ripping fabric, and the hiss of escaping gas, she saw Raincloud, struggling to hold on as the frayed end of his safety rope snapped in the wind.

As though from a distance she heard her call his name. There was an expression of utter bewilderment on his face as the surface slowly slid out from underneath him, and she could only watch numbly as he slid off into space.

Suddenly she became aware that Lonce had been standing next to his brother, and as the walkway slid out from beneath him he lost his hold and she watched as he followed his brother. Another body followed, tumbling into space, then another, until there appeared an endless trail of bodies sliding into the darkness below her.

She screamed, trying frantically to untie the rope that held her to life, while all around her everyone she had ever known fell to their death. Suddenly, she became aware that it wasn't a rope, but arms that held her imprisoned, and that someone was calling her name, trying to calm her.

Hesitantly, as reality slowly broke the dream's hold on her, she opened her eyes to find Horsing's face looking worriedly down on hers.

"Horsing?" she asked, not willing to believe it had just been a dream.

He nodded, immediately letting her go.

"I was dreaming about the accident," she said, feeling some need to explain, and trying to cover the sudden feeling of loss she had felt when Horsing had released her.

"No need to explain, Leader," he said. "There will be many of us who have nightmares of that for some time to come."

"What's the time?" she asked. It was too dark to see her watch.

"Just gone two. We've just established contact with Europe via the short wave."

"Thanks," she said, struggling out of the blankets that had somehow wound themselves around her.

The three officers on duty in the gondola's radio room snapped to attention as Ivy entered, the Force Leader just behind her.

"You've got Europe?" she said.

"Yes, Leader," the radio operator said, handing her the microphone.

She pressed the transmit button. "Rosebud here," she said, giving her codename.

"Leader, we were worried about you." The Governor's voice although faint, was still quite clear.

"So was I. Do you have any news on the rest of the fleet?"

There was a pause. "Yes, but it's not good. They were expected, lost half the ships before they could even try to land; then, when they tried to break off, were hit by the storm."

"Did any make it back?"

"Negative."

Ivy felt physically sick. A Corps, a full Corps lost because of her incompetence.

"What's your location?" the Governor asked.

"Florida. Any chance of arranging a pick up?"

"I'm afraid not, or at least not for a while. Things are pretty hectic over here at the moment. Your brother just opened four portals on the continent."

Gods! As if things could get any worse. "Where?"

"Lundon, Roma, Neu Brest, and somewhere on the Jutland Peninsula. We're still trying to pin that one down."

"How are you holding?"

"With difficulty."

"Understood. We need to minimize radio contact then. I'll contact you in a week, Rosebud out."

And that just about summed the situation up, she thought dryly as she handed the transmitter back to the radio operator. O.U.T.!

The Force Leader raised any eyebrow. "Looks like we were the lucky ones."

"Lucky!" she exclaimed.

"We could have been with the rest of the fleet at Lincoln."

"We should have been with the rest of the fleet at Lincoln," she pointed out.

He shrugged, unapologetically.

"I'll see you in the morning," she said. "It looks like we're going to be stuck here for the foreseeable future."

He nodded.

Outside the gondola, she paused for a moment to listen to the breaking waves. Just what had she been thinking to join the first wave, she thought angrily. She should have stayed in Europe. Now she was stuck here without troops, while Europe fought a war for its very existence.

"Leader?" Horsing sounded worried.

"Go to bed, Sergeant," she said, without looking at him.

She could hear him standing there uncertainly for a moment, before turning and heading up the shore to his sleeping bag. She waited a couple of minutes before following him up the beach. She was too wired to sleep but she had to try; tomorrow was going to be a hell of a day.

CHAPTER 31

Leolie — Etu Line
February 1982 (98AE)

Arnold took a carefully calculated sip of his tea as he turned the next page on the report over. He wanted to shout with joy and dance through the house at what he was reading, but to that was to lose control — and control was what separated him from the others, so he simply took another sip of his tea as he caressed the paper with the tip of his finger. Finally he finished reading the report and carefully positioned it exactly in the center of the desk. Satisfied, he leaned back in his chair. Behind him he could hear the gentle tick-tock of a clock marking time.

"It appears the First Leader has been even more successful than we have been," he said, giving General Mullah Hssan and Red Arrow a precisely calculated smile.

Red Arrow, the Commander of Arnold's Household Guard, returned the smile. "Perhaps the World Leader may be too polite given his own success; the entire invasion fleet destroyed, your sister killed, and Europe conquered."

"You're still sure of her death?" the General Mullah asked, leaning forward. "There have been rumors . . . "

Red Arrow nodded. "Quite sure. I spoke to those who personally witnessed the destruction of her airship."

"And Europe?" the General Mullah asked. "While our drones allowed us to precisely identify their deployments before the attack, the way they were dispersed meant we were able to take out less than ten per cent of their strength in the first wave. And we certainly don't have the strength to occupy all of Europe."

"It is only a matter of time," Arnold said, dismissing the warning. "Particularly after my father's death." He paused, uncertain how he felt about his father's execution. . . what he should feel about it. But Miro had assured him that his father had been offered the opportunity to retire to some backwater of a line in exchange for a simple public statement in support of the First Leader. Unfortunately his father had chosen not to accept the offer.

Red Arrow nodded his agreement. "With the World Leader's death the rebellion must collapse."

"Former World Leader," Arnold corrected him gently. But the news was really too good for him to be concerned at the slip.

"My apologies. The *former* World Leader," Red Arrow said, as Arnold swung his chair round to stare out of the window. Outside, the heat from the late summer sun shimmered off the gravel.

Arnold steepled his fingers. There would probably be no better time.

"I have been thinking," he said.

"Oh?" the General Mullah said.

"It is written that *those who raise a place of abode for our God will be triply blessed.*"

"Indeed."

Swinging round, Arnold stood up. "I'd like to show you something."

Without waiting for a reply he led them to the studio he had had constructed inside the building's former greenhouse. Unlocking the double doors, he waved them in.

All the plants had been removed and the shelving and irrigation stripped out. A large worktable had been set up in the center of the room. On the table was the three foot high model of the mosque he had been working on for the past couple of months. The model was constructed in the shape of a gigantic four-sided pyramid with the top third of its structure sliced off level to the ground. Traditional Muslim architecture would have had a large dome covering this central opening but Arnold had decided to leave it open to the air, in a style that owed more to a traditional Roman atrium. In addition to allowing light to enter the interior it also reduced the weight to be borne by the foundations.

Four minarets, one on each of the four corners of the central pyramid, soared gracefully into the air over the structure, their gold roofs gleaming in the light. The gardens and ponds surrounding the mosque suggested a cool retreat from the summer heat.

"This will be the place of abode I raise for our God," Arnold said, momentarily aware of the way the steady ticking of the clock was drowned out by the triumphant peal of bells.

Unaware of Arnold's loss of attention, the General Mullah prowled round the table, peering at it.

"An interesting concept," he said finally.

"And impossible without the use of a steel framework and lightweight, precast reinforced concrete panels," Arnold said dryly. "I haven't quite decided on the outer covering yet, but it will probably be mother of pearl. You will also note that it is nearly ten per cent larger than the Al-Masjid al-Ḥarām in Mecca. The building itself covers an area of just over a hundred acres."

The General Mullah winced and Arnold hid a smile. It was definitely time that the 'natives' showed what they were capable of. And building a mosque larger than anything the Caliph possessed, and many times larger than any other in the Cross-Temporal Empire would create a religious heart for the new order he would bring in God's name.

"How many worshippers will it house?" the General Mullah asked.

"Approximately six hundred thousand. Three hundred thousand in the main prayer hall, courtyard and porticoes and another three hundred thousand in its adjoining grounds."

"And where do you intend to build it?"

"At Leolie. The eastern sector is still in ruins. It will serve as an ideal location."

"And just how do you intend to pay for its construction?"

"I was hoping the Caliph could be persuaded to pay for it." He hid a smile at the shock on Hssan's face. As he had found out, the Caliph was as stingy a miser as any penny-pinching merchant. That was perhaps not totally surprising, given the military's call on his purse.

"A joke," Arnold told him. "I propose to levy a new land tax."

Hssan seemed to relax. "It will not be cheap. And your tax rates are already high," he warned.

"I agree. But capturing Europe will enable us to recover the taxes they haven't been paying, and we can also impose a penalty for their failure to pay tax for the past year or so. That will enable us to lower the cost on those who have been meeting their liabilities.

"Yes, Red Arrow?" he said, the Commander of his Household Guard looked as though he had swallowed an apple.

"It will be an impressive building, Leader, but is it perhaps not a little too impressive. Would it not be better, perhaps, to start a little smaller?"

Arnold shook his head. "It is written that: *reach for the grape and Allah will deliver it onto your hand, but wait and it will ferment on the vine.*"

He noticed Hssan nodding his agreement, and smiled — he had them. The room suddenly darkened, and he looked up, startled. It was only a cloud passing in front of the sun, but momentarily the steady tick-tick of the clock in his ears stilled and he was alone.

CHAPTER 32

Habesh — Mmbuto é Line
July 1982 (98AE)

Conrad carefully surveyed the burned-out remains of the farmhouse through his binoculars. Nothing — just like all the others they'd seen. Burned stubble covered the abandoned fields around the building; the fields marked out with the local, low, dry-stone walls. Beyond the fields, the bare foothills of Mount Entoto rose into the distance.

At least it wasn't as bad as it had been yesterday. Then they had come across a dairy farm on the outskirts of a deserted village. Each of the farm's small herd of unmilked cows had been in agony, standing paralyzed in the middle of the field to avoid any movement which would make her udder swing. Some of the troops had milked them straight onto the ground to ease the pressure, but no one knew what would happen without the return of those who had lived there.

Kerensha, the Corps Leader, who was standing beside him, sighed. "Still no sign of the High King."

"No," Conrad said, and no sign of Linele either, he thought, looking up at the sun. From its angle he guessed it was probably about three o'clock. "That's it then, we'll make camp here. Tell the Battlegroup Leaders that unless something else comes up we won't move for a day or so. I want to give our scouts a chance to report back before we decide whether to move north, or south. We can't just keep marching inland in the hope of finding someone. We're just as likely to march right into an ambush."

Kerensha nodded and headed back down the hill to give the necessary orders. Conrad watched him go. There was no doubt the former engineer's unflappability and organizational skills had proved vital during their long retreat. But all his ability would mean nothing if they couldn't find the High King.

Turning back to survey the mountain, Conrad struggled to hide his unease. Where were they?

The burned-out farmhouse seemed to symbolize the devastation they had found ever since they'd disembarked. Even Rufiji had been deserted, except for a small garrison of Etehad Sho'mali troops. It had taken time, and persistence, to find someone who could tell them what had happened. Certainly there had been no shortage of refugees roaming the plains, but no one who could give them the complete story.

In time they had started to build up a picture of what had occurred.

It had begun with a series of massive explosions in the center of the port; which had started a number of fires, and killed or wounded hundreds of people. Then, while authorities were trying to control the situation, an army had appeared out of nowhere, killing everyone who resisted.

It had been a massacre, and only a last ditch defense of the palace had allowed the High King to escape. What Conrad didn't know, and no one could tell him, was whether Linele and the twins had managed to escape with him, or whether they had perished in the sacking of the city.

What he did know was that over the last six months the High King had fought a number of pitched battles. Each battle had had the same outcome — the defeat and retreat of the King's forces. Now they were fighting some form of guerrilla war from the Ethiopian highlands, which was where Conrad was trying to join up with them.

"Leader." It was a messenger, breathing heavily from his run up the hill.

"Yes," Conrad said.

"Good news Leader, a messenger from the High King."

"The High King?" Conrad's face broke into a grin. They'd found him!

The courier, an officer wearing the red tipped ostrich plumes of the High King's Imperial Guard, was waiting with Kerensha at the bottom of the hill.

"Lord," the man said, bowing his head, as Conrad reached him.

"Captain," Conrad said. "We are glad to see you. I believe you come from the High King. Where is he?"

"At Koela, Lord."

Conrad thought for a moment. That was north of their present location, near Lake Victoria on the Mainline. Probably only about fifty miles away. "And he is well?" he asked.

"Very," the Captain reassured him.

"Kerensha," Conrad said. "I want the Corps ready to move in ten minutes."

The Corps Leader snapped to attention and saluted. "Ten minutes," he promised.

"So Captain, how did you find us?" Conrad asked.

"We had word there was a large party of soldiers moving inland from the sea. The High King believed it might be you, and dispatched me to contact you." He paused uncertainly for a moment, then added, "The Princess desired me to tell you to hurry home."

They could hear some muted sounds of cheering as the word spread, and Conrad found himself grinning inanely — Linele was alive!

It took them two days to reach Koela, and by the time they arrived Conrad's stomach had tied itself into knots in anticipation of what their welcome might be. Finally, shortly around midnight, the Corps marched in through the city's old, massive stone gates. The city's dry-stone, megalithic walls, high and curving, were crowded with spectators. Their path was strewn with flowers and under the smoldering glare of pitch-covered torches, the drone of native bagpipes, and the watchful gaze of a small detachment of the Imperial Guard they were welcomed home with barbaric splendor.

The army, now consisting of fewer than two thousand souls came to a halt in the center of the Great Courtyard, and Conrad marched forward to face the High King alone. The High King sat surrounded by his Personal Guard on a four legged-stool placed on the dais at the foot of a massive stone tower.

As he made his way forward, Conrad saw Linele in the crowd off to the King's right. For a moment his steps faltered, before recovering as he turned to face the High King.

Gone was the youth Conrad remembered from the first time they had met, replaced by a ruler who weighed him deliberatively through heavy, hooded eyes. There was no doubt Chaka had fully grown into the role, and his great-grandfather's heavy gold necklace now appeared to have been made for him.

"It seems your venture has brought calamity down upon the Empire," the High King said calmly.

"I'm afraid so," Conrad agreed.

"And your own mission?"

"Destroyed. My father captured or killed. It appears they knew about our plans and were waiting."

"And your brother?"

"Wounded during the retreat. I left him in Ngoni." He had hated doing that, but what choice had he had? Donald had only just survived the operation to remove his left kidney, and was going to take months to recover. He had left Defella and the Dynands with him, though.

"It is good that you managed to escape."

Conrad felt a sense of relief. "Majesty," he said with a low bow.

"How many troops do you have?"

"With me, Majesty, just these — slightly under two thousand. We left a Corps in Italy to harass the enemy, and the Dynands in Ngoni."

"You will retain command." the High King directed him. "Given the hour, we will defer detailed conversation of what has occurred until tomorrow. My General will arrange quarters for your troops." He rose, and with just a slight tilt of his head, departed.

Linele dashed forward, and Conrad enveloped her in his arms. "I thought you were dead," he admitted.

"And I you," she murmured into his chest.

He heard Kerensha say something about arranging for the Corps to be dismissed, and nodded vaguely in his direction. All he cared about was that Linele was in his arms, and he was never going to let her go again, ever.

They stayed that way until Conrad realized that they were alone, except for the guards.

"Would my husband care to see his children?" Linele asked.

"If my wife would care to take me," he said quietly.

Without letting go of him she swung herself around and under his arm, and, snuggling into his side, led him in the direction of her rooms.

The twins were sleeping, cherubic faces against the sheets that covered their bunks. To Conrad's surprise, they had grown enormously since he had left them. There was something familiar about them, perhaps something Clemhorn, although they still resembled their mother much more than him. He drew Linele closer to show that he was pleased.

"Which one's which?" he asked after a while.

She looked askance at him. "The closest is Ngori, the furthest is Sipewe," she said when she realized he was serious.

He shrugged helplessly. "It has been a while, love," he explained.

"Are you pleased to be back?" she asked doubtfully, as though seeking confirmation.

"Very pleased," he said. "Are you pleased to have me?"

"Of course," she said, horrified that he might imply that she wasn't.

"Then you shouldn't ask such questions," he said.

Sipewe stirred uneasily in her sleep, moved her thumb to give comfort to her mouth, and settled again.

Linele drew him away from them, though Conrad would have stood there all night.

"Come husband," she told him. "There are other concerns that need your attention."

"What?" he said, suddenly worried that she might be sending him away.

"Me, you idiot," she told him fiercely with a whack to his arm.

The next day Conrad awoke with Linele nestled into his side and he smiled inanely as he realized it hadn't been a dream. When he finally rolled over to face her, he found her watching him.

"Good morning," he said. "How long have you been awake?"

"About an hour."

As he leaned over to kiss her, her stomach rumbled and he laughed. "Come on, we'd better feed you. I expect the High King will want to see me soon anyway."

"He does," she admitted regretfully. "His messenger has already requested our presence."

Conrad raised an eyebrow.

"I told him we would be there once you woke."

"Well, I'm awake now," he said, his fingers lightly stroking her back.

She purred, then with a regretful sigh pushed his arm away and sat up. Conrad watched the play of the sunlight on the side of her soft skin.

"We could just pretend I'm still asleep?" he suggested.

"You wouldn't be any good to me asleep," she said with smile.

"I did say pretend," his said, gaze drawn to the smooth curve of her breasts.

"I thought you had enough of that last night."

"I'll never have enough."

She threw a pillow at him. "Move, husband. The High King is waiting for us."

Regretfully, he sat up and looked around for his clothes, not quite remembering where they'd got to last night.

The High King was cloistered with the commander of his Imperial Guard and Kerensha when Conrad and Linele found him.

"Come in," Chaka said, without looking up from the map laid on the table before them.

Conrad raised an eyebrow as he followed Linele into the room.

Chaka caught the look and smiled, reminding Conrad of the youth he had first met. "Given the circumstances My Lord, you will find we are a little less concerned with appearances nowadays."

Conrad acknowledged the rebuke with a slight nod, remembering what his father had said about their arrival freeing the High King from the ritual and tradition that had made him a prisoner of the role.

"What is your wish, Majesty?" Conrad asked, looking at the map of Africa that was held down on the table by four small golden paperweights.

He felt Linele worm her way into his side, and, looking down on her, gave her a small smile. It was wasted as her attention was focused on the map.

Chaka sighed. "What I wish for, My Lord, is for you to sweep these invaders out of my country and into the sea. What I propose is considerably less."

His finger tapped the area surrounding the Cape. "I ask you and the remainder of your army to move south to Carthago and deny the enemy control of the area."

Conrad nodded, acknowledging the sense of the order. Both he and the Corps were already familiar with the Cape thanks to the training they had undertaken there before their abortive attack on the Mainline.

"I will not let my husband go this time without me," Linele said.

"I do not ask you to," Chaka said with a small smile. "I need you to hold the southern states to my cause. This war will not be a short affair, and before the end, my people must do more than they might otherwise consider possible."

"If I can suggest something, Majesty?" Conrad said.

"Of course."

"I am concerned regarding the portal. If Miro captures it. . ." He trailed off.

"You have it with you?"

Conrad nodded.

"And you still have hopes of attacking them through it?"

"Shouldn't we? Simply driving them into the sea will not win this war. To do so we must destroy them on their own line. It is not an impossible dream. We were betrayed, but if we can rebuild, well then the shoe will be on the other foot."

Chaka gave him a feral smile. "Indeed." But then he sobered. "Although we first have to survive."

"Of course."

Chaka looked at the commander of his Guard. "Where do you suggest?"

Without hesitation the commander placed his finger on the Ivory Coast. "Our intelligence indicates no enemy activity in this area."

Chaka looked at Conrad, who nodded.

"I will arrange for an escort," Conrad said.

Chaka held out his hand and Conrad grasped it. "Take care, Majesty," he said.

An hour later, to the beat of drums and the wail of the pipes, Conrad led the Corps out of the city.

CHAPTER 33

Rome — Mainline
February 1982 (98AE)

Matija sat numbly, gently rocking Artos in her lap. In the background the rhythmic click of her aunt's knitting competed with the voice of the news reader as he droned on about the victory the First Leader's allies had just won against the 'usurper's forces'. The 'usurper', she snorted — that was the pot calling the kettle black!

She wanted to scream, to cry, do something, but all she could do was sit there rocking her son. It had been two years since Donald had disappeared. Two years without a single word from him to let her know if he was even still alive. And now this — an army destroyed — his father captured, then executed.

She looked across at her aunt, calmly knitting a new shawl next to the fire. Last week as she had watched her aunt knitting her fingers had itched, wanting a release from their prolonged rest. She'd recognized it as the need to create, welcomed it as a friend she long thought lost. She hadn't noticed it when it had first disappeared as she had struggled to come to grips with Donald's disappearance and the realization of how dangerous her world had become. Then she'd been lost in a haze as she cared for her new baby without its father. But last week she'd relished the return of that itch knowing that, finally, she was ready to create, and now it was gone again.

She looked at her fingers, wondering at their smoothness. The calluses from her weaving had almost gone.

Tears filled her eyes, and she blinked them back angrily. She — would — not — cry.

Her aunt ignored her, her attention still fixed on her knitting. Matija rested her chin on Artos' head, smelling the shampoo in his hair and the fresh scent of talc from his last change, and listened to the gentle click of the needles.

"Matija, phone call for you," one of her cousins called from the floor below.

Matija glanced uncertainly at her aunt, who looked up from her knitting. "Go," she was told. "I'll let you know if there's any news."

Both knew that the only news Matija was interested in was if it involved Donald.

"Coming," Matija called to her cousin. She put Artos down and gave him a hug, which he tried to shrug out of, planted a kiss on the top of his head, which he ignored, and watched him toddle off to his great-aunt — completely unaware that the world had changed once again, and that his father was probably even now lying wounded or dead on the battlefield just outside Bologna.

Her cousin had disappeared by the time she'd got there, leaving the telephone dangling from its cable.

"Hello," she said doubtfully, picking it up.

"Matija?"

"Papa," she said, surprised. They'd only spoken on Sunday. "Is anything wrong?"

"You've heard the news?"

"Aunt Rosa and I were just listening to it."

"I'm sorry."

"What for, Papa? You haven't done anything. It's this bloody war!"

"Is there any news on Donald? The news here is still a bit bare."

Her eyes pricked. "No Papa, but he must be dead."

There was a silence. She remembered her last day at home in Charleston, when the news had reached them of Miro's surprise attacks across the Empire. Foreign troops had stormed through their portals as the Progressive's forces retreated before them. She remembered looking out of the window at the garden's single maple tree in its autumn wardrobe. And now it would be bare, or perhaps with the first hints of spring — buds. She was aware of a sudden surge of homesickness.

"I want to come home, Papa."

"It's not safe."

"And when will it be safe, Papa? No one has come looking for me. And they certainly won't now, because there is no one left to hold me as a hostage against. I want you to see your grandson grow up. I want to see my father again. I want to come home."

There was silence on the other end of the phone and Matija wondered if the line had gone dead. Finally she heard a deep breath.

"I'll send you the money for the tickets," he said.

CHARACTERS

Abbas: appointed by General Mullah Hssan of the Etehad Sho'mali (*see Glossary)* in 96AE to ensure Arnold Clemhorn's continued safety and loyalty to the First Leader.

Achicauhtli: Conrad's personal secretary at Cempoala, Etu.

Aleksey: a member of the prisoner co-ordination committee of Concentration Camp 5123. Before his arrival at CC 5123 Aleksey had been a Group Leader in the Fifty First Rapid Deployment Battlegroup, stationed in Mainline England.

Annette: A leader of the Anarchist Collective in Mainline New York in 95AE. Nedo's girlfriend.

Archos: A young Squad Leader at Fort Larsa, Ivy's first independent command. Archos is the son of a local chief.

Arnold Clemhorn: Second son of the World Leader of Etu. In 95AE was one of the leaders of an artistic commune in Mainline New York with his cousin Nedo.

Aris Arcaos: A Pegoni war leader. The Pegoni are a barbarian alliance centered on Etu's European Alps.

Brian Clemhorn: World Leader of Etu.

Cador Horsing: A Sergeant in Etu's armed forces. Born in Spain, transferred to Fort Larsa in 95AE where he first came under Ivy's command.

Chaka: the young, High King of the Mmbuto é (born 79AE).

Chengerai: a diplomat and story-teller of the Mmbuto é.

Clemhorn *see Arnold, Brian, Conrad, Donald, Elam, Ivy*

Conrad Clemhorn: Heir and son of the World Leader of Etu. Continental Leader for South America.

Constantine MacKenzie: Son and heir to the World Leader of Huis. A year younger than Conrad they were roommates at the Academy.

Cudomix: Clemhorn Corps Leader on Etu. Before returning to front-line service in 95AE he been seconded to Etu Officer's Academy where he had been Ivy's instructor on military history.

Daniels: Senior Troop Leader at Fort Larsa, Ivy's first independent command.

Dennis Domov: World Leader of Domov. His son Mark is one of Conrad's close, personal friends, he is also Mary's father and Hayden's father-in-law.

Defella Haratan: Daughter of a Continental Leader on Dynand, and in 95AE an aide to the World Leader in Naisre. Subsequently accompanied the Clemhorn's during their retreat to the Mmbuto é Line.

Donald Clemhorn: Third son of the World Leader of Etu. Completed his PhD in Alternate History at Mainline's Charleston University.

Elem Clemhorn: Wife of the World Leader of Etu, and daughter to the First Leader of Notway (Griffin Windsor).

Elk: *see Yellow Elk.*

Ferai, Colonel: a Colonel of the Mmbuto é Imperial Marines when he met Conrad Clemhorn, Sirom Ferai's career subsequently includes military special-forces roles.

George Harnich: World Leader of Kleng.

Griffin Windsor: World Leader of Notway and leader of the progressive faction in the Council of World Leaders. Following the death of Manek in 96AE was contender for the position of First Leader.

Hannibal: the Mmbuto é, Carthagian, Fourth Corps' Leader during the C-T E civil war. Claimed a direct lineal relationship to the famous leader who had fought the Romans during the Second Punic War.

Hayden McArthur: The second son of the World Leader of Clyde. A Continental Leader Hayden is a close friend of Conrad's, as a result of their period together at the Academy. He is married to Mary, daughter of the World Leader of Domov, and their eldest child, Felicity is Conrad's godchild.

Hssan, General Mullah: of the Etehad Sho'mali *(see Glossary).* Commanded Etehad Sho'mali forces on Etu during the Cross-Temporal War, serving as military advisor to Arnold Clemhorn from 96AE.

Isobel Peric: Sister of Brian Clemhorn, and married to Roland, North American Continental Leader on Dontfrey.

Ivy Clemhorn: Only daughter of the World Leader of Etu. A career officer in Etu's armed forces.

Jon Raincloud: A Force Leader in Etu's Clemhorn Rangers. In 95 AE he was stationed at Fort Lanegan, 150 miles west of Leolie. A member of the Oneida tribe, one of the six founding nations of the Iroquois Confederacy on Etu and Ivy's first lover. Died at the Battle of Bapaume in 96AE. *See also Lonce Raincloud.*

Jubo Ngori: cousin to Linele, Princess of the Mmbuto é.

Jules McKenzie: Force Leader in the Clemhorn 72nd Battle Group. Commander of Fort Perusia, where Ivy spent two years as a Troop Leader.

Kaito Langley: Inventor of the first re-usable portal. Shared an apartment with Donald during their time together at Mainline's University of Charleston.

Kerensha: the acting Leader of the Mmbuto é, First Corps during the Clemhorn's abortive invasion of the Mainline.

Kurslow: a senior medic with Etu's 48th Light Infantry, led the initial efforts to disseminate the Kelsor Virus *(see Glossary)* as widely as possible in an effort to mitigate the typhoid-Mary effect that accompanied the Clemhorn's arrival on the Mmbuto é Line.

Lawrence McArthur: Third son of the World Leader of Clyde, and a commander in the C-TE's Imperial Security. Conrad's godfather.

Leanne Daer: Designated heir of the World Leader of D'daer.

Linele: 'daughter' of Chaka, High King of the Mmbuto é. Linele is the first to agree to be inoculated with the Kelsor Virus on the Clemhorn's arrival on the line, and subsequently marries Conrad Clemhorn.

Lindsay Byre: Heir and son of the World Leader of Chikyù. A friend of Conrad's as a consequence of their time at the Academy together.

Lonce Raincloud: younger brother to Jon Raincloud. *See also Jon Raincloud.*

Louise Peric: Youngest daughter of Isobel and Roland.

Manek: First Leader died 96 AE. His death triggered the first war of succession.

Mahalia: of Mayan descent, Special Agent Mahalia with Sultan's UMS Federal Police was appointed to act as the Clemhorn's point of contact with the Etehad Junoobil *(see Sultan)*.

Maku: the Mmbuto é scout who accompanied Donald to Mainline Cape Town and who was killed during Donald's arrest.

Maras: Professor of Time-line Theoretics at the Mainline University of Charleston. Developed the unified theory of time at the age of twenty *(see Matija Maras)*.

Margaret Peric: Eldest daughter of Isobel and Roland she is commissioned as a Battle-Group Leader on Dontfrey during the Charterists' Uprising (see Glossary).

Marshia: Troop Leader at Fort Larsa, Ivy's first independent command.

Mathilda: A Senior Troop Leader in the Clemhorn 72nd Battle Group at Fort Perusia, where Ivy spent two years as a Troop Leader.

Matija Maras: Studied textile design at the Rome Institute of Fine Arts (Mainline). Postgraduate student at the Charleston's Industrial College. Met Donald Clemhorn in 95AE via her father, Professor Maras. Subsequently had a son with Donald.

Melanie Seaforth: formerly the Clemhorn's factor on the Mainline until she resigned to move to Cape Town where she runs Universal Imports.

Metztli (Governor): Etu's Military Governor of Neu Stuttgart / Western Europe.

Michelle Peric: Second daughter of Isobel and Roland.

Miro Raputa: World Leader of Dontfrey. Leader of the conservative faction in the Council of World Leaders, and following the death of Manek in 96AE contender for the position of First Leader.

Movak: Born on Sultan in approx. 1355AD, to a Moorish conquistador and an Incan Princess, Crucified in 1388 Movak became revered and the founder of a new sect of Islam.

Nedo Peric: Second son of Isobel and Roland Peric. A close friend of Arnold, and a co-founder of the Mainline New York commune.

Nezahual: Tlatcani and head of Cempoala's City Council. Cempoala is the continental capital of South America. Father of Papanzin.

Ngori: Son to Conrad Clemhorn and Linele, princess of the Mmbuto é. Twin to Sepewe; designated heir to Chaka, High King of the Mmbuto é.

Papanzin: Conrad's lover at Cempoala during his time as Etu' South American Continental Leader. Their breakup in 95AE caused Conrad's early departure from the city.

Peric: *see Isobel, Louise, Margaret, Michelle, Nedo, Rajko, Roland*

Petro Raputa: A compatriot and rival of Conrad's as a consequence of their time together at the Academy. Son and heir to Miro Raputa, World Leader of Dontfrey.

Rajko Peric: Eldest son of Isobel and Roland, and heir presumptive to the position of North American Continental Leader on Dontfrey.

Raputa *see Miro, Petro*

Roland Peric: North American Continental Leader on Dontfrey.

Romonav: World Leader of Neu-Moscow.

Running Bear: Battle Group Leader of the Clemhorn Rangers.

Sepewe: Daughter to Conrad Clemhorn and Linele, princess of the Mmbuto é. Twin to Ngori.

Shicowe: Battle Group Leader (retired) in Etu's armed forces.

Sitting Crow: Former head of the Etu World Leader's Intelligence Service and Ivy's mentor. He retired to take over his family's import and export business.

Tenda: Chairman of the Ngoni City Council, a major city of the Mmbuto é on the north coast of Africa. At the time of meeting the Clemhorn's, Ngoni was suffering the plague.

Treik: Son of First Leader Manek. Died 94 AE leaving the Empire without a designated heir. The death of his father set the Empire on the path of war.

Tsitsho: Force Leader in the 48th Clemhorn Light Infantry.

Yellow Elk: Troop Leader at Fort Larsa, Ivy's first independent command.

GLOSSARY

ACADEMY: The Academy was established by the Empire's first, First Leader, Traek the Elder, in 25AE. The Academy provides 12 years of formal, military education to the heirs of World and selected Continental Leaders. Attendance at the Academy provides the First Leader with hostages, as well as a means by which the Empire's dominant culture is passed onto its next generation of leaders.

AE (After Empire): Measured from the creation of the Cross-Temporal Empire in 1884 CE (see CROSS-TEMPORAL EMPIRE).

AIRSHIPS: The predominant means of fast passenger transport on the Mainline before the First Trans-temporal War. A typical airship of the period was Her Majesty's Airship Britannia, which had the following statistics:

> Length: 804 feet
> Diameter: 135 feet
> Gas Volume:7,063,000 cu. feet
> Engines: Four 1200 hp diesel engines
> Maximum Speed: 84.4 mph (136km/hr)
> Lifting Gas Type : Hydrogen
> Gross Lift:242.2 tons
> Useful Lift: 112.1 tons
> Crew: 40 to 61
> Passengers: 50-72

When re-configured as a troop carrier, which was capable of being undertaken in under 24 hours, HMA Britannia could carry 180 infantry and their equipment, or a troop of thirty mounted infantry including their mounts.

ALERT STATUS: The Etu Line's security alert system. Created in 62 AE by Charles Clemhorn the system defines four levels of threats represented by four colors: yellow, orange, red, and crimson.

AUROCHS: A breed of early cattle now extinct on the Mainline. Aurochs stand about 5.7 feet tall, while domesticated cows are generally smaller than 4.9 feet. Aurochs have several features rarely seen in modern Mainline cattle, such as lyre-shaped horns set at a forward angle, a pale stripe down the spine, and sexual dimorphism of coat color. Males are black with a pale eel stripe or finching down the spine, while females and calves are reddish (colors now still found in a few Mainline domesticated cattle breeds, such as Jersey cattle).

CHARTERISTS' UPRISING: The Charterists' Uprising on Dontfrey in 95AE lasted for over five years and resulted in the documented death of over 750,000 people on the Northern American continent. The war was a particularly bitter one with atrocities committed by both sides. The beginning of the war was marked by the Louisville Massacre when loyalist forces were ordered to use poison gas against the city's civilian population as a means to hold the city pending the arrival of reinforcements.

CLASSIFICATION: Lines are generally classified by Mainline ethnographers in terms of their predominant culture. This is generally derived from religious, geographic or language groupings. For example, Aryan-Transpacific refers to an offshoot of the main Aryan-Oriental. In Aryan-Oriental speakers of the Indo-Iranian group of languages, on most Lines moved south and west, migrating east into China. In the Aryan-Transpacific subsector, some continued east, finally settling in America with their horses and cattle, and either exterminating or integrating the Amerinds into their own culture. (also see HALLOW SCALE).

COUNCIL OF LEADERS: Supreme policymaking and administrative body of the Empire. It meets quarterly, or when summoned by the First Leader, and consists of World Leaders, or their deputies. It is often simply referred to as the Council.

CROSS-TEMPORAL EMPIRE: usually abbreviated to the C-TE. Established in 0 AE by Traek the Elder, former Historian of a Nayarit Research Station, and 2IC to Iapura who led the invasion of the Mainline. Its creation has remained a contentious issue between the two schools of Historical Inevitability, and Individual Causation ever since. The conquest of an entire line by only fifty-three people within a space of six months is worthy of note, regardless of whatever school of thought one seeks to justify it by. It was not until 17 AE that a second line was discovered and the term Cross-Temporal came into official use. After that the Empire expanded quickly, and by 46 AE included over 31 Lines. Presently there are fifty-four World Leaders, although many more Lines have been discovered (see EDICT).

The three dominant cultures of the C-TE are: British, Slavic, and Nayarit. The first two representing the dominant cultures of the Mainline immediately prior to the Nayarit invasion.

DECIMATION: the term used for the period 1 AE to 11 AE when a series of plagues devastated the Mainline, resulting in the death of over 65 percent of the world's population. The plagues continued to occur until 27 AE with reducing force; until sufficient of the population had been inoculated with the KVirus to provide the necessary level of protection (see KELSOR VIRUS). The successful establishment of the Empire on so many worlds has often been linked to the plagues which accompany the arrival of Cross-Temporal Empire forces on a line, and which leaves the indigenous inhabitants too weak to resist absorption into the Empire (see HRAFFOR).

EDICT: An order proclaimed by the Council of Leaders. The most important was that proclaimed in 21 AE, which prohibits contact with a line once it is determined to possess a technology level of 6.4, or higher, on the Hallow Scale (see HALLOW SCALE).

EMPIRE (see CROSS-TEMPORAL EMPIRE)

ETEHAD JUNOOBIL: one of two major military alliances on Sultan (*see Sultan*). In 98AE the Etehad Junoobil consisted of: Mexico (predominately Movak Islam), and the Northern Caliphate (Shia). The Northern Caliphate, a successor to the Ottoman Empire, covered all of Central Europe and was the primary military power on the time-line. Until 95AE the United Tribes of the Great Plain was also a member of the alliance.

ETEHAD SHO'MALI: : one of two major military alliances on Sultan (*see Sultan*). In 95AE the Etehad Shomali consisted of: Peru (Movak Renewed); the Western Caliphate (Western Europe - Sunni), including the Angevin Empire of England, Wales, Scotland and France; the Southern Caliphate (Africa and the Middle East, both of which demonstrated strong Ibadi and Sufism traditions). In 95AE, following a military coup by a minority grouping of Hussan Koranese, the alliance was joined by the United Tribes of the Great Plains.

ETU: Home World of the Clemhorn family, it was seised to Charles Clemhorn in 48 AE in exchange for support provided to the then First Leader, Traek the Elder. The main indigenous civilization (the Northern Lakes League) had arisen around the Great Lakes of North America several thousand years previously, but had remained static for much of that time. However, as a result of the introduction of horses onto the American mainland about three hundred years previously by League merchants trading across the Atlantic the League was no longer the static society it had once been.

FESTIVAL OF LIVAS: An indigenous celebration of thanksgiving for the harvest among the inhabitants of the Northern Lakes League on Etu.

GATE: see TRANS-TEMPORAL PORTAL

HALLOW SCALE: a formula used to establish a particular culture's technology level against an open-ended scale. The formula measures over 200 variables, although quite often a key indicator may be used instead. For example: 6.4 on the Hallow Scale is generally taken to be the introduction of gunpowder.

HISTORICAL INEVITABILITY: a school of thought that holds that history is created by the effect of vast, impersonal cultural forces. In this theory the split between two Lines is caused by the buildup over an extended period of a series of paradox that cannot be relieved in any other manner. (also see INDIVIDUAL CAUSATION).

HOWTACHI LINES: A collection of three Lines discovered by Howard Howtachi which split off early in human prehistory when a genetic mutation resulted in a prevalence to female births (one male to every ten females). There is no real explanation as to why only three Lines have developed since the split, given the period they have had to develop.

HRAFFOR: A Nayarit term which translates as 'Soldiers of the Empire'. The title also signifies the right of leadership through conquest. They have often been compared to the Mainline Conquistadors of Spanish and South American history.

INDIVIDUAL CAUSATION: a school of thought which holds that history can be shaped by the effect of a decisive individual. In this theory the split of two Lines is dependent on the actions of one special individual (also see HISTORICAL INEVITABILITY).

KELSOR VIRUS: also known as the KVirus, is a single stranded DNA synthetic virus created on the Nayarit Line during the early decades of the last Nayarit civil war. It was designed as a self-replicating nano-trap to provide enhanced resistance against viral attack vectors, a necessity once the *Natrecyl Accord* was breached and both sides escalated their use of biological weapons.

The KVirus does not seek to identify and attack cells infected by attacking viruses, it simply attracts, traps, and destroys those circulating in the blood stream. As a result, viruses in a latent/dormant phase within a cell are able to avoid detection. The consequence of this is the typhoid-Mary effect where those infected remain carriers, but fail to exhibit any symptoms of the disease. Upon contacting a virgin population without the protection of the KVirus the consequences can be devastating with death rates of over 99% having been recorded. The use of this as a strategy to facilitate integration of a new line into the C-TE became the accepted modus operandi during the early years of the C-TE's establishment.

LEADER a translation of a Nayarit term, it is a designation of rank, and a title of respect used by any person to a superior. Within the Empire generally recognized civilian and military ranks are as follows:

Civilian
First Leader, Leader of the Empire.
World Leader, the person controlling a time-line.
Continental Leader, a person placed in charge of either a continent, or a major cultural grouping, on a line.
Military
Squad Leader, commands 9.
Troop Leader, commands 30.
Force Leader, commands 95.

Group Leader, commands 300.

Battlegroup Leader, commands 915 (Each Battlegroup is responsible for the recruitment, training and administration of its members, and over time tends to develop its own unique esprit de corps.)

Corps Leader, commands 2750.

LINE: (see TIME LINE).

MAINLINE: (Romano — Balkan-Renaissance) the seat of the Cross Temporal Empire. Research indicates that the pivotal creation point occurred in 1389AD when the Serbian King crushingly defeated the Turks at the Battle of Kosovo, thus firmly establishing Serbian independence and the potential for a Balkan based renaissance. Immediately prior to the conquering of the Mainline in 1884AD (0AE) by First Leader Traek (a military refugee from the Nayarit cataclysm) the Russian and British Empires were on the verge of outright war.

MMBUTO É: (Romano — sub-Saharan) a mercantilist culture dominated by the Ghanian and Mapungubwe peoples of Africa. The establishment of Carthago following the fall of Cathage in the Fourth Punic war established an early civilisation in the Cape Area, with trading links throughout the entire African continent and into southern Europe. With the arrival of the Mapungubwe (Bantu speaking) peoples soon after 600AD the Carthagian city state fell under the influence of the proto-Zimbawean civilisation, and the fushion of these two great civilisations soon resulted in an expansion northwards. In Europe, due to a failure of the Chinese to expel the Jsiung-nu from China in 48AD, the Roman Empire was spared the Huns. Despite that it eventually collapsed into a series of successor states. While Christianity did form, Peter never made it to Rome, and with the collapse of the Roman Empire it fractured into a series of feuding cults that was never able to form a coherent church.

NAYARIT: Little is now known of this line, following the total destruction of its ecosphere in 0 AE after 80 years of total war. A war which involved both biological, chemical, and nuclear weapons; and is now popularly referred to within the C-TE as the Nayarit cataclysm. The first trans-temporal portal was developed on Nayarit at Chiqu, a small training and research facility in the western foothills off the mountains that define the eastern boundary of the great central plains of the North American continent. The only survivors of the Nayarit Line were believed to be the fifty-three Hraffor who followed Iapura through the portal.

One of the three dominant cultures of the Cross-Temporal Empire (the other two being Russian and English). Its influence has become steadily more diffused with time. The language appears to have affinities with Mainline Nahuatl languages.

POISON GAS: Two main variants are used across the C-TE:

Geranium: so-called because of its distinctive odor, which has been described as similar to scented geraniums, but sometimes called by the name of its discoverer Dr. Phillipa Lewisite (i.e. Lewisite). It is an organoarsenic compound, specifically an arsine, and was developed by the British for use after the last Sino-British war as a vesicant (blister agent) and lung irritant.

Nerve gas: Developed by the Nayarit, and brought with them when they invaded the Mainline the gas is an organophosphorus compound with the formula $[(CH3)2CHO]CH3P(O)F$. It is a colorless, odorless liquid with a relatively high volatility relative to similar nerve agents. The gas is estimated to be over 500 times more toxic than cyanide.

PORTAL: (see TRANS-TEMPORAL PORTALS)

SEAGUS: the Russian linguist who developed a simplified form of English consisting of 1,000 key words. His work was used to create a 'First Contact Pack' of five picture books which were used by the Hraffor during the initial expansion of the Empire to simplify the integration of multiple Lines into its structure.

SULTAN: (American — Islamic) in 98AE Sultan is divided between two major, military alliances; the *Etehad Junoobil*, and the *Etehad Sho'ma-li*. It is suspected that the pivotal creation point occurred in 735AD when the Arabs crushed the Franks at the battle of Bourges, gaining control over France up to the Rhine, and leading to a collapse of other Christian powers. In 1252AD a Spanish fleet from the Southern Caliphate reached South American and established the first Muslim colony in the new world.

SYNCLAIR'S SYNDROME: an inevitably fatal reaction by the body's defenses against the KVirus.

TAHLTAN BEAR DOGS: the Tahltan Bear Dog is a breed of dog indigenous to Canada. Primarily black, dark brown or blue, with some white patches on the chest and sometimes the feet. They stand 14 to 17 inches high at the shoulder, with relatively large, erect pointed ears, and a refined, pointed muzzle. The glossy coat is of average length, with guard hairs covering a thicker undercoat. Paws are somewhat webbed and relatively large for the size of the dog. Foxy in appearance, they possess a peculiar yodel. Their main distinction among dogs is their novel tail. Short, bushy and carried erect, it has been described variously as a shaving brush or a whisk broom.

TIME-FRONT: a term used to describe that point on a number of time lines which exist concurrently at the same moment of relative time (see TIME LINE).

TIME LINE: a multiple reality caused by time splitting into a number of component parts. It's creation is not fully understood (see HISTORICAL INEVITABILITY and INDIVIDUAL CAUSATION).

TLATCANI: the C-TE prefer to work through existing authorities when absorbing a line, simply superimposing their own authority over the top of the original. In Mexico, the Clemhorns found a culture that while loosely based on earlier Mayan social types was unique to the Etu Line, and based around individual city-states. Generally each city was administered by a council made up of representatives of each calpulli or group of families. Each council would elect four members who would act as an executive council, with the four then choosing a Tlatcani, or council leader.

TRANS-TEMPORAL PORTALS: are a specific occurrence of a 'wormhole' or a Einstein Rosen-Podolsky bridge that link two non-contiguous space-time points between parallel universes (or in this case — time lines). The portal allows people and objects to pass through this gateway from one parallel dimension to another. The selection of the 'linked' Lines depends on how the quantum state of the exotic matter making up gate has been 'tuned'. Travel through a portal does not change the person's relative position in either time or space.

The first trans-temporal portal was developed by Tou Azulai at Chiqu — a small, secret research facility — during the last years of the Nayarit civilization. Azulai, an expert on string theory, had been attempting to create anti-gravity by means of the controlled application of dark energy to an underlying substrate of mono-planular-charhdian-silica (MPCS). Although the anti-gravity experiment failed, the exotic matter he had accidentally created resulted in the chance creation of the first trans-temporal portal. One of the more unusual characteristics of the exotic matter he had created was its ability to transmute normal MPCS into its exotic form when placed in contact with the substrate when in a complex, aqueous solution.

When operating, the portal requires a constant supply of electrical energy which grows exponentially with the number of simultaneous portals established between two Lines. If the energy falls below a certain level the portal will collapse with a catastrophic shattering of the underlying substrate. This weakness was addressed by Dr. Kaito Langley of the Mainline's University of Constantinople, who developed the first re-usable portal in 96 AE.

While operating the surface of a gate resembles the shimmering surface of a soap bubble because of thin-film interference.

Due to random quantum effects within the event horizon, coherent energy cannot pass through the gate. This prevents electrical signals from passing through the portal. As a result, it is necessary to place telex and fax machines in close proximity to the portal, allowing a physical representation of the message to be passed through the gate, before being re-encoded and passed on.

Despite the transfer being virtually instantaneous, the quantum effects previously noted have resulted in individuals using the portal reporting auditory, visual, and other hallucinatory effects during the transfer. One portal traveler describing the effect as "… similar to being consumed by chaos, before being spat out the other end".

FIRST FAMILIES OF THE C-TE (95AE)

(view on web at: http://andrewjharvey.com/CTEwiki/doku.php?id=people:first-families-95ae)

First Families of the Cross Temporal Empire (96 AE)

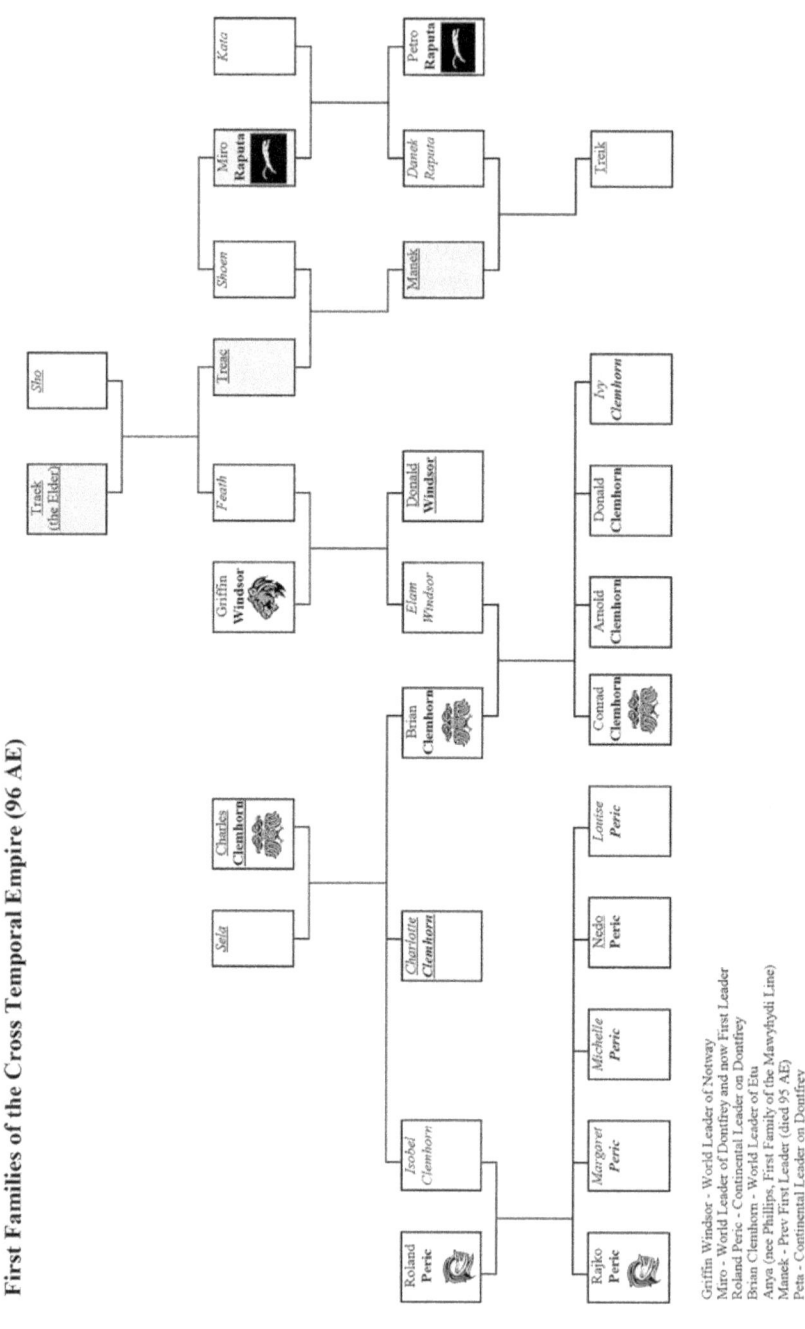

Griffin Windsor - World Leader of Notway
Miro - World Leader of Dontfrey and now First Leader
Roland Peric - Continental Leader on Dontfrey
Brian Clemhorn - World Leader of Etu
Anya (nee Phillips, First Family of the Mawyhydi Line)
Manek - Prev First Leader (died 95 AE)
Peta - Continental Leader on Dontfrey
Conrad Clemhorn - Continental Leader on Etu

Underlined = deceased
Italics = female
Shaded = Current and former First Leaders

LINES OF THE C-TE (95AE)

Ah Kinchil

Alignment: Conservative
Ruling Family: Moyle
Symbol: a Western dragon

Anhui

Alignment: Nonaligned
Ruling Family: Hefei
Symbol: a sea eagle

Atdhe

Alignment: Nonaligned
Ruling Family: Hoxha
Symbol: an olive tree

Chaac

Alignment: Nonaligned
Ruling Family: Polkinghorn
Symbol: the Castle of Chaec

Changsi

Alignment: Conservative
Ruling Family: Treithick
Symbol: a Californian redwood

Chikyù

Alignment: Progressive
Ruling Family: Byre
Symbol: the Phoenix emerging from the flames

Ch'olan

Alignment: Nonaligned
Ruling Family: Couch
Symbol: a tiger

Chujean

Alignment: Nonaligned
Ruling Family: Medina
Symbol: a single flame

Clyde

Alignment: Progressive
Ruling Family: McArthur
Symbol: a sailing junk

Colletta

Alignment: Conservative
Ruling Family: Thompson
Symbol: a winged rifle

D'daer

Alignment: Progressive
Ruling Family: Daer
Symbol: the ruined city of Anphor Tor

Domov

Alignment: Progressive
Ruling Family: Domov
Symbol: an ankh

Domovina

Alignment: Conservative
Ruling Family: Novak
Symbol: a thrush

Dontfrey

Alignment: Conservative
Ruling Family: Raputa
Symbol: the snarling head of a jaguar

Dynand

Alignment: Nonaligned
Ruling Family: Yanez

Symbol: a Bhutan cypress

Effling

Alignment: Conservative
Ruling Family: Ortiz
Symbol: a red Greek cross

Ekahau

Alignment: Conservative
Ruling Family: Poblete
Symbol: a coptic ankh

Etu

Alignment: Progressive
Ruling Family: Clemhorn
Symbol: a double-headed Mayan eagle

Fitzmorton

Alignment: Progressive
Ruling Family: Stirling
Symbol: a round tower

Fujian

Alignment: Nonaligned
Ruling Family: Fuzhou
Symbol: a spinning wheel

Gansu

Alignment: Conservative
Ruling Family: Castillo
Symbol: a blue marble sphere

Guangdong

Alignment: Nonaligned
Ruling Family: Guangzhou
Symbol: a scimitar

Gwizhou

Alignment: Nonaligned
Ruling Family: Fuentes
Symbol: a griffin

Gwlad

Alignment: Conservative
Ruling Family: Morris
Symbol: an oak tree

Hainan

Alignment: Nonaligned
Ruling Family: Haikous
Symbol: a mace

Hocawi

Alignment: Conservative
Ruling Family: Ahler
Symbol: the Southern Cross

Huis

Alignment: Progressive
Ruling Family: MacKenzie
Symbol: a ten-sided star

Ix Chel

Alignment: Conservative
Ruling Family: Borup
Symbol: a Chinese dragon

Ixbalanque

Alignment: Nonaligned
Ruling Family: Ege
Symbol: a wolf

Ixtab

Alignment: Nonaligned
Ruling Family: Buck

Symbol: a coconut palm

Jerek

Alignment: Progressive
Ruling Family: Giesing
Symbol: a cedar tree

Kinich Ahau

Alignment: Nonaligned
Ruling Family: Han
Symbol: an eight rayed sun

Kleng

Alignment: Progressive
Ruling Family: Harnich
Symbol: a crescent

Mainline

Alignment: Nonaligned

Malac

Alignment: Conservative
Ruling Family: Espersen
Symbol: a yellowfin tuna

Marke

Alignment: Conservative
Ruling Family: Boulay
Symbol: a blue star

Maun

Alignment: Progressive
Ruling Family: Lorge
Symbol: a zebra

Mawyhydi

Alignment: Conservative
Ruling Family: Phillips

Symbol: a Tudor rose

Milawe

Alignment: Progressive
Ruling Family: Riendeau
Symbol: a yellow lotus

Nebo

Alignment: Conservative
Ruling Family: Turk
Symbol: a hand — palm outwards

Neu-Moscow

Alignment: Progressive
Ruling Family: Romanov
Symbol: a brown bear

Neydd Gymanwlad

Alignment: Conservative
Ruling Family: Morgan
Symbol: a chrysanthemum

Notway

Alignment: Progressive
Ruling Family: Windsor
Symbol: a cougar

O'Brien

Alignment: Nonaligned
Ruling Family: O'Brien
Symbol: a harp

Q'anjobalan

Alignment: Nonaligned
Ruling Family: Vannier
Symbol: a golden pearl

Rolfe

Alignment: Conservative
Ruling Family: Rolfe
Symbol: a red lion rampant on a black background

Styphon

Alignment: Conservative
Ruling Family: Morrison
Symbol: a cannon

Velican

Alignment: Conservative
Ruling Family: Kos
Symbol: four stars on a circle

Vinogradov

Alignment: Nonaligned
Ruling Family: Morozob
Symbol: a kernel of rice

Vorobyov

Alignment: Nonaligned
Ruling Family: Vazilyev
Symbol: a glass crown

Yucatecan

Alignment: Conservative
Ruling Family: Lachance
Symbol: a macaw

Yum Cimil

Alignment: Progressive
Ruling Family: Arthur
Symbol: a coyote

Yumil Kaxob

Alignment: Nonaligned
Ruling Family: Myricks

Symbol: a black lion

Zajendnic

Alignment: Nonaligned
Ruling Family: Krajnc
Symbol: an Andean condor

About the Author

Andrew spent his high-school years in the school's library lost in the worlds of Andre Norten, Robert Heinlein, and Isaac Asimov. His first commercially accepted series of novels (the Garden Adventures) was originally completed to read to his two sons at night. Now his children have left home he lives in Perth with his wife, one dog, and sixty four gold fish. Andrew can be contacted at www. andrewjharvey.com.

In addition to writing, Andrew is also the Principal of Hague Publishing. Established in 2011 as an independent publisher of Science Fiction and Fantasy, Hague Publishing is registered in Western Australia, and publishes original work by Australian and New Zealand authors.

Previously Principal for the Davies Literary Agency, Andrew was also editor and publisher of The Western Australian Year Book for a number of years, in addition to being the editor and a writer for 'Afterlife - the on-line magazine for Atmosphere users'.

Andrew's first published short story (A Messenger to the Dragon) appeared in Aurealis - Australian Fantasy and Science Fiction in 1992.

A passionate reader of Alternate History Andrew is presently working on completing further books set in the Cross-Temporal Empire.

www.ingramcontent.com/pod-product-compliance
Lightning Source LLC
Chambersburg PA
CBHW041751010726
47507CB00009B/354

enchanted with the light. I wanted the camera to capture what stunned my eyes and tickled my other senses. A million photos later, the shot still eludes me. The camera still fails me. No shot seems to capture what my eye sees, what my mind grasps, what my heart and soul feels.

So with Washington and the north in my rear view mirror now I make the beach my life. I lie in the hot sand and let each tiny kernel cling to me. I frolic in water like a child and try to surf its waves like a dolphin. I kayak on its tumultuous sea.

YOU'LL ALWAYS BE A PART OF ME
by Georgia Jansson

I ran inside the cabin even though I knew I was too late,
And there you lay on the cold, hard floor, death no longer a debate.
Your fingers fisted from holding the gun; blood where it had run.
JJ, your suffering is now over, my heartbreak has just begun.

I kneel down beside you and hold your hand,
For the first time in our life, you couldn't really understand
That my pain was way beyond any description,
This time my dearest comrade, you couldn't fix my situation.

I cried, "JJ, why'd you do this, I was taking care of you?"
Onto his bloodied body my tears rolled, more than a few.
"We were going to beat this cancer," my voice leaving me now.
He whispered, "We did. You just refuse to remember how."

I sit back on my heels and study his handsome face.
How will I go on each day without you to give me grace?
Without you to make me laugh at the tough times in my life,
Without us to sing with your guitar and the fireplace light?

You never shared Vietnam with anyone else but me
I am so proud you loved me enough to let me see.
So today I find my brave soldier dead off the field of battle
I must stand proud and go on without you, as life's sabers rattle.

You taught me so much over our twenty-five years
Birthing foals in muddy paddocks, facing my fears,
Landing an arrow in the target at 80 long yards
How to cheat charmingly with marked poker cards.

I still can't turn the light out in the cabin for long
It would be admitting my JJ really is gone.
My brave heart, you will never truly leave
For death cannot kill love, only cause me to grieve.

The cabin is sold, it's time to let go.
I sit in the darkness with memories and woe.
Finally I sighed, tears streaming down my face,
"You're not here anymore are you, JJ? Not in this space."

"That's right GA, my sweet friend, and neither are you."
We are but a memory, never let it make you feel blue.
I leaned on him one more time, his cheek I kissed
And then I watched him walk away into the mist.

Friend, Tovarish, Tomadachi, Bon Ami

GOING SOUTH
by Mike Casey

As a long time Yankee, I was always concerned about going south. Growing up in New York City, I had heard horror stories first from my mother, Alice, about the way she had been mistreated on a railroad trip through Georgia during World War II. She had been on her way to meet her husband my father Joe in Florida. During an overnight stay in Atlanta, somebody reminded her that she was not in Kansas or New York anymore. Apparently some local got nasty with Alice. Big mistake. Nobody messed with my mother and left unscathed.

She told me many times how she handled that person. After he had insulted her for being from the north, she set him straight. Atlanta had been a southern city destroyed by General Sherman during his infamous march to the sea. To remind the ill-mannered man of this point, Alice sang " Marching through Georgia." She laughed every time she repeated the tale ending with "that sure shut him up."

Being fearless had to be in her family's genes. Before she reminded the southerner about Sherman's destruction of Georgia, two of her three brothers, serving in the American Army in the European theater, during WW II, were wounded in battles against the Nazi's.

As a result, I had some trepidation when I first ventured below the Mason Dixon line as a young boy. I first did so, during a trip to the nation's capital, Washington D.C. to visit my mother's brother Jack, my godfather. He had survived his serious war injuries and worked for some unnamed, secretive federal agency. During the decade of the 1950's, Washington remained a segregated southern city. While on a bus trip around the capitol area I witnessed something that still stays with me to this day. My mother, from a blue-collar Irish/Catholic family, had cardinal rules not to be violated on pain of severe punishment. One had been to be courteous, unless someone else isn't. The other, don't be prejudice. Consequently she argued often with her husband, my father a NYC policeman. This time she turned her wrath on a white man and her brother, whom she felt had disrespected a black commuter. What happened on the bus to her dismay occurred when this gentleman hopped onto a front seat while we were riding around the capital. Immediately a white man yelled at him "Nigger get to the back of the bus." The black man meekly complied.

My mother erupted. She said something very loudly about "stupid" and gave my uncle a dirty look because he seemed to agree with the prejudice person.

My next visit south would not come until decades later. By that time I had seen the horrors of the civil rights struggles in the

1960's and lived through the assassinations of Medgar Evers, Jack Kennedy, Martin Luther King and Robert Kennedy. All the crimes, save RFK's killing had taken place in the South. I had also read voraciously about our nations worst conflict, the Civil War. My reason for heading south had been to visit my best friends home. John had moved to the Tampa area of Florida.

My drive down route 95 from Long Island proved to be a long and mostly uneventful trip made in single long day.

Because of a traffic problem in northern Florida, I decided to take an alternative route across the sunshine state south and west towards the Gulf Coast. Somewhere in the middle of the Florida, I decided to stop to pick up a six-pact of beer to share with John. That turned out to be a big mistake, as I entered into a bar/ package store located in the middle of nowhere. I should have been forewarned by the pickups parked out front. All had gun racks filled with rifles and shotguns prominently displayed. Missing these signs of redneck regalia, I stepped into the establishment. Almost at once I knew I could be in trouble.

"Looks like we gotts us a New York Jew in our place," I heard some patron say, referring to my license plates..

Because I had my wife and my elementary aged daughter in my car, I just smiled at the bar tender, ignoring the stupid statement. After placing my order and starting to exit the store, I heard another customer say: "he's got a Chinese girl with him," obviously referring to my Asian American wife.

As I drove away into the darkening night and the surrounding swamp, I told Bonnie, "this place is nothing like New York. Hope we can get away safely."

Some five years later I returned south, this time to Dennis van Der Meer's Tennis camp in Sweetbriar Virginia. Throughout the ensuing week I was subjected to the taunts and jeers from some of my camp mates concerning my northern background. After winning the end of the program singles tennis tournament, Dennis asked me to give a speech. Channeling my inner Alice I said: "I won the tournament and we won the war."

After that my family and I started to visit the south more regularly. We drove down route 95 for visits to colleges my daughter might attend, tennis camps on Hilton Head Island in South Carolina and vacations trips to Ocean Isle North Carolina. The latter had been a place some friends of ours from Long Island either had retired to or were planning to do so.

We liked everything about Ocean Isle, except the lack of tennis. The local areas had few courts, none of which were of the har-true variety. The clay-like surface is slower and easier to play on then cement surfaces. Consequently, we kept looking for our dream retirement community mostly along the Atlantic coast. Vacations were spent exploring options including the east and west coasts of Florida, the Atlantic islands of Georgia and coastal communities of both North and South Carolina.

During another visit to our friend's beach house on Ocean Isle, we decided to drive south towards Charleston and the nearby Isle of Palms. We had previously spent a delightful week on that island playing tennis and taking lessons at its first class facilities.

Looking at a map of South Carolina, I decided to stay along the coast by driving south along route 17. By so doing I would avoid the boring drive on route 95. When we were approximately 60 miles south of Ocean Isle, my hunger pangs announced lunch. Looking for a place to eat, we entered into a shopping center in Pawleys Island, South Carolina. Seeing no obvious eating establishments, my wife went into a Piggly Wiggly supermarket. There she found extensive luncheon offerings, including a sushi bar, sandwiches and hot food plates.

After we left Pawley's Island, I determined to further investigate the community.

What I found out really excited me. The area had some of the best beaches along the Grand Strand, an area which stretched from southern NC to Georgetown SC. In addition to the numerous golf courses, a game I had just begun to play, Pawleys Island is home to the Litchfield Tennis Club. This facility had 17 har-true courts and a six-day a week round robin competition. The area also had many excellent eating establishments.

Before moving to the south we considered our options. These included Hilton Head Island in the southern part of South Carolina and the Isle of Palms near Charleston. All were eventually eliminated for one reason or another. Hilton Head was too far south of New York for a one-day ride. Additionally the real estate was old, expensive and the beaches full of shells. The Isle of Palms, just north of Charleston offered much. We were very tempted until we discovered that it had been severely devastated by Hurricane Hugo in 1989. We determined to give Ocean Island another look before deciding on our retirement destination.

While riding around the area with my friend Lenny, a former tennis player, who lives in the area of Sunset Beach NC, we stopped at the beautiful Sea Pines Golf Community. I went up to the front desk in clubhouse and innocently asked, "if there were any tennis courts on the facility."

A rather large overweight man sitting at the counter said: "tennis, what's tennis?"

I replied instantly "it's a game for athletes." Lenny commented as we exited the door, "you sure answered him, Mike."

"Just Alice coming out once again," I said.

I felt good about my put-down of the obnoxious golfer. When Bonnie asked what about the tennis facilities, I replied "not in this place."

Before making our final choice concerning Pawley's Island, we also considered the Grand Dunes in Myrtle Beach. As area called Sienna Park offered some Spanish-style colonial homes with many amenities including a private beach, a tennis club, and an outstanding golf course. All were first class facilities. Two problems prevented us from buying, the cost and the traffic.

After deciding to move to Pawley's Island, our next step to purchase a piece of land. Then we would have our first ever-new house built. We found a site in a development called the Reserve, located at the west end of Willbrooke Boulevard. The gated community made up of both private homes and attached villas is secluded yet very accessible to all the businesses located on Route 17. Once we bought our half-acre plot, we became members of the Litchfield Beach Association. As a result we were now able to enjoy the private beach and bathhouse facilities.

We spent the next few years going south to vacation near our plot of land along the Grand Strand. During one trip south, an unexpected hurricane struck the coast closing the roads into Myrtle Beach. We decided to head west and spent a delightful two nights in Asheville NC visiting for the first time the Biltmore estate. This, the largest house in the U.S. and its surrounding grounds, proved to be spectacular. The city of Asheville is fascinating. It's an art deco lover's paradise that would call us back on many occasions.

After we left Asheville for the ride towards Pawleys Island, I wondered how our property faired through the tropical storm. Knowing that route 501 into Myrtle Beach would still be closed, I looked at a road map-before the days of GPS and Garman-and found that I could approach our property from the south via Georgetown. This colonial era municipality, the third oldest in South Carolina, founded in 1729 is a commercial center dominated by the paper and steel industries. About a hundred years earlier the Georgetown rice producing industry, once vast and very lucrative had finally succumbed for a variety of reasons. Slavery ended and along with it cheap labor. Some powerful unnamed hurricanes in the 1890's had devastated the region. Finally competition from mechanically harvested rice coming from Texas, Louisiana, and Arkansas ended commercial rice growing in South Carolina.

Our property turned out to have survived the storm with only a few tree branches littered around the ground. We decided to build our house as soon as we retired. A few years later we did so, taking advantage of the fabulous beach, the tennis, the golf and the restaurants. One other feature attracted Bonnie and me to Pawleys, Brookgreen Gardens. This former rice plantation and one time Huntington's estate consists of over 9,000 acres. It contains beautiful plants and America's largest collection of sculptures.

Brookgreen provided us with the necessary cultural attraction. I liked the place so much I have been volunteering at Brookgreen since 2007, in a variety of capacities, most recently for the education department.

Living in the South, I tried to put my mother's philosophy to use; that is to be courteous until someone else isn't. During my first year playing tennis at the Litchfield Club, a member referred to me as "a damn Yankee." Instead of taking immediate umbrage at the remark, I asked, "What's a damn Yankee?"

I was told, "it's a Yankee who came and stayed."

Fine I thought to myself, I would just show them. I did very often helping my team win the South Carolina State championship, the following year.

After receiving the congratulations from some of the same people, who I think initially, resented my northern origins, I replied, "that I'm not southern born but I got here as soon as I could."

LIVING OUTSIDE THE LINES
by Georgia Jansson

The last ten years had taken a grand toll on me and then retirement came riding in on a white horse to save the day.

Leaving my beloved Red Stallion farm, the Antietam Battlefield and the beautiful mountains of western Maryland wasn't exactly the easiest thing I had done but it was the best thing.

I needed a big change. I was worn out. The last ten years had been filled with grief and heartache.

I steered the rented cargo van onto the highway.

My mind wanted to take me back to where I came from and why, but I fought it off by reading license plates, waving to kids and flirting with a couple of truck drivers as I sang along with the radio. Loud!

As soon as I arrived in Petersburg I pulled the car into a rest stop and slid the rented van into the parking space cutting the engine. I simply let my head fall back and stretched my legs as far under the dash as I could. And took a deep breath of different air.

After a few minutes of shuteye and listening to garden-fresh sounds from new folks, I felt less fatigued. I wasn't used to driving long distances.

Outside I walked a bit. The air still held a pinch of a northern clip. I looked around, chatted with a few people enjoying the diverse accents, some slight, some nearly unintelligible. For the very first time in my life, I was in no hurry. Imagine that. I sat down on one of the benches and simply sighed. The breeze was enough to turn the leaves on the trees. I lifted my face to the sun and closed my eyes. As it warmed my cheeks and left its taste on my lips, I felt it. The taste of freedom.

Walking to the van, my cell phone rang. That infuriated me. Who would dare call me after I said all my good-byes and explained I would call them when I was at my destination and that might be months from now. Purely out of habit, I looked to see who it was. None of my immediate family! A number I didn't even recognize. I walked to the trashcan, took on the stance of a NBA player, jumped and literally threw the cell phone in so hard I could hear the thud on the bottom. Score! I never wanted to hear a phone ring again. I picked up a couple of shouts of approval and some applause. I took a bow.

Back in the van, I slipped my shoes off while I munched on a ham sandwich and chips. I expect I'll be that way a good part of the time from now on. Barefoot and snacking.

I decided to rummage through one of the boxes marked "closet" and find some different shoes. I no longer needed the footwear designed to plod through snow and ice or simply keep toes warm during cold weather. I slipped on my old penny loafers and thought about living the rest of my life in the fanciest, silliest flip flops I could find when I got to Myrtle Beach and the Wings Stores.

I was traveling light. I sold all my very new furniture, paintings, silver ware, dishes, pots and pans. I left my king sized bed in my senior apartment because I couldn't physically move it. The apartment people threatened me and I just laughed. They could go to hell. For some reason, the staff that ran the Senior Citizen Apartment complex was young and condescending. Boy, could I tell you some stories but that's another story.

About the cargo van. It was something I had never driven before so that in itself was an adventure. I had left my car in Myrtle Beach and flown back up to make the final transfer. Moving companies wanted a king's ransom to haul my things down south so instead of giving in I told them to take a hike. Although normally I would have had to do business their way I didn't HAVE to do anything I don't want to anymore. I can take care of it myself because I have the time to. It was emancipating not having to say "oh, okay, take all my money, you surely have me over a barrel." Like I said, I got rid of everything except my toothbrush and personal belongings.

I felt the selfishness moving in. It wasn't a pleasant feeling and those were the only postures I had room for. Shaking my head to clear it and concentrating on the scenery that whizzed by the car,

I decided self-centered was exactly what I wanted to be from now on. Might take some work, but I am sure I can get there.

Back on the road again, driving further toward warm, sweet air and beautiful oceans I could sense the humidity of the air increasing, as did the heat. Sweeter. Softer environment. Yes, my mountain air was an entity all its own but I was so ready for change. I welcomed every swamp, every flash of sunlight through the trees lining the road and the promise of a stress-free, more restful life ahead.

Without thinking much about it, I stomped the accelerator and changed to the center lane falling into running over the speed limit with the rest of the drivers. WooHoo, I got braver and changed to the fast lane. I love this. And so did the cops that were flagging car after car to the side of the road. At first, I felt that sinking feeling in my stomach but it quickly disappeared. Now this old Granny is going to have a rap sheet! I proudly accepted the ticket and then the fine. I didn't know that I would get two more citations once I got to Myrtle Beach for not wearing a seat belt. Made the rap sheet even better since this good girl always wore her belt but who needed one when everyone drove so slowly there? I learned that lesson quickly. I had always lived my life within the lines. Beginning today, I would live outside the lines as I chose. Being the "good little girl, good wife, good mother, good friend, good helper, good nursemaid, good good good...... done done done!

Crossing the North Carolina State Line and driving past Roanoke Rapids I knew I was making good time. The air was even warmer and by the time I reached Rocky Mount I really felt the effect of the sun. Glorious. Every mile that rolled beneath the tires set me free. Freer than I ever thought possible. Rolling, rolling rolling...

Now, South of the Border is a place you just can't drive through. You have to get out and walk around and buy all kinds of useless crap you'll throw away in two weeks. Even though I would wear tank tops in the summer in Maryland, it would only be around the farm. Where I worked I wouldn't dare show flabby arms. I bought several tops in bright colors with flamingos and starfish blazoned on the front. In the car I slipped one on throwing my t-shirt in the back. I was determined to arrive with flab flying, never to hide it again. Like me or don't, I couldn't care less. And right then and there I changed my name. Don't really know why since I would never introduce myself to anyone, but I did it. And I have kept it all these years.

One last stop before cruising down Rte. 17 business, I purchased a bathing suit I would have to strain to fit into and had no intention of wearing. I picked up two pairs of shorts, one of which I wore out of the dressing room. Outside, I simply threw the jeans I was wearing in a trashcan along with the t-shirt from the floor of the van. So there.

The excitement of my new reality was filling me up like helium in a balloon. Emancipated. Set loose from self-imposed chains. No accounting to anyone or listening to somebody's latest excuse. Driving away from the past was bringing forth much more than I had thought about before. Some of that comes from my Catholic upbringing. Guilt. That was the first rule of order I learned on Saturday morning catechism. You must do this or that or the church roof will fall in. I remember being terrified I'd forget to genuflect and be struck by a car on the way out of church. And standing in those confessional lines…oh no, no more Good Lord no more. Of course, over the years since I left the church I made sure God and me had a good line of conversations going. But the guilt I was taught to live with is hard to shake.

The actual glorious thing I'm going to accomplish right from the get-go is being anonymous. Meet no one. If I'm somewhere individuals gather and talk I will simply listen. I will not speak to a soul. I am going to stay out all night without telling anyone where I am. I'll pick up a penny that's tails up! Maybe go to a bar since I'd never been inside of one. I'll be responsible for no one and to no one. I will care for nobody and nobody will care for me. Not a New Year's resolution, just the way it's going to be.

The difference in union and confederacy, allow me my writer's leeway, was exhilarating. Myrtle Beach, being a tourist town, I immediately picked up on the restful and fun-loving vibes right away. I pulled into the parking lot of a restaurant that stood high on stilts and offered a great view of the edge of my new world. The sea. The Atlantic Ocean. I ordered a burger and fries with a side order of hot-fudge sundae. I ate the ice cream first.

Feeling satisfied and naughty, I walked out on the deck and took a seat. I leaned back in my chair, propped my feet up on the railing as if I'd been here forever and watched the general public playing ball, building sand castles, brushing their backsides clean, and balancing on skim boards.

I stood up, my bare feet loving the feeling of the deck boards. I was being drawn to the waves that splashed up on the sand. I moved down the steps, my shoes dangling from my fingers. Hypnotically, I let my heart and mind respond to the allure of all that spread out before me.

Slowly, I approached shore and moved closer, my toes finally in the sand. I was home. No, home was in the north. No, the north was reminiscence. I was home. And I deserve it!

P.S. I kept my vow to remain anonymous for two years, and then turned right around and made wonderful friends. I found I needed that after all.

.

MOVING SOUTH KICKING AND SCREAMING
by Gail Ritrievi

"How long did you say we had to stay here?" I whined after a three-minute inspection of the condo rental at Island Green Golf Club in Murrells Inlet, South Carolina. My husband winced at the tone of the question and responded with a " we can look for something else if you wish, Gwen. (His name for me when he wants to get my full attention.) It didn't work this time. I was already thinking of possible alternatives in spite of the rather late hour.

"You know that Kelly (one of our daughters) is at a health care conference in Myrtle Beach and has a suite at the Radisson Hotel. She did invite us to stay if any of your reservations did not work out." I suggested.

"Fine", he snorted." Call her and I will re-pack the car."

I must admit I felt very guilty and bratty but I made the call and Kelly clearly understood her mother's problem and welcomed us willingly. The drive north on route 17 was quiet and chilly but we entered the tenth floor suite on the beach side pleased to have such a sweetheart of a child. (I knew she would come in handy one of these days.) We sipped some wine and slept soundly with the ocean below supplying the lullaby. The

next morning we relaxed at the pool and enjoyed the attention
of Carlos, the pool boy, in his attention-getting Speedo, who
periodically sprayed us with a cooling solution to make us more
comfortable- as if that would be possible.

That afternoon my travel agent/companion for life (I hope)
announced that he had a realtor ready to lead us to several
possible locations suitable for ideal retirement and endless golf,
his ultimate dream. I promised I would behave and try to open
my mind to the possibilities, but I had my fingers crossed as I
agreed to his terms.

The Chicora agent picked us up at the hotel somewhat
surprised that we had left the condo so quickly, but she happily
drove us to a series of developments and senior citizen
establishments. Each location had some feature that reminded
me of a bad episode of HGTV's House hunters and I was the
negative spouse who found a flaw in everything. The Lakes was
too watery, Woodlake Village residents were too old, Jensens
was too doublewide, Prestwick was too much tennis, Wachesaw
was too expensive, and the beach house was too much upkeep.
What a pain I was... until we drove into Indigo Creek Golf
Plantation and our patient guide gladly handed us over to an
agent overseeing the model homes. I stopped complaining and
paid close attention to the details. We walked the areas of empty
available lots, then sat down with our very southern hostess to
hear the details. As we left the tour, I said, " You know, I think I

could live here." My husband turned us around and the rest is history. I actually thought of someone else other than myself and made him a happy man. Twenty years later he is still smiling and I have turned into a rather reasonable partner. He's such a lucky guy!

ARE WE THERE YET?
by Rebecca Bridges

I took a long and winding road to reach the retirement paradise of my dreams. Let me walk you through my journey. The first twenty-one years of my life I lived in one state, Oklahoma, with fifteen of those years in the same city, the next forty years I inhabited seven more states and one country other than the United States.

Yes, I married an Army man. My first marriage, that is. Oh, and the second one too. Did that comment make it sound like I had a dozen? I didn't, just the two. Being an Army wife explains *some* of the moves. But it doesn't explain *all* of them.

I did mislead you a bit. Shortly after my second birthday my family moved to Alaska – for six months. Since I don't recall a moment of that adventure I find it hard to count it as one of my many living locations. I don't use the term state since we lived there before Alaska entered the union. Hey, I'm not *that* old, it didn't become a state until 1959. We lived there during the summer months, which meant the sun didn't set for many hours. I remember Mom talking about the green shades on all the windows to help block out the light. She had a tough time getting us to go to sleep while the sun still shone. Since my sister is a mere eighteen months older than me, she doesn't have many memories either while we lived there. There is one image still vivid in her mind. The day she opened a closet door and a polar bear rug fell on top of her. Now that I think about it maybe that explains a few things.

We returned to Oklahoma where I spent a traditional childhood going to parochial school, taking piano and ballet lessons and going to camp in the summer. For those who know me they may be shocked to discover I took piano lessons for six years. You wouldn't know it if you happened to hear me play. Yes, I'm dreadful.

I lived at home while completing a Bachelor degree in Business at the local University. My first *real* move away from Oklahoma lead me to nearby Wichita Falls, Texas, where I accepted a full-time job as a computer programmer after graduation. My time spent there ended after a short ten months because I married the first of the two soldiers in my life. Marrying a soldier didn't surprise anyone since my hometown stood outside Ft. Sill and most of the eligible bachelors were in the service. We were promptly sent to Germany, a little town outside Frankfurt. We spent the next three years traveling Europe and enjoying the diverse cultures. The cold war prevented us from traveling to the Eastern European countries. I couldn't find a job as a computer programmer but I did acquire a secretarial job with civil service. Learning the art of being an officer's wife was fun and daunting. I enjoyed playing hostess at dinner parties, baby showers and ladies luncheons. Not fun was the mandatory *volunteer work* and awareness that my participation would reflect in my husband's efficiency report.

The Army transferred us to California, my husband's home state. We rented a condo right on the beach in Monterey. We were able to watch the migration of the humpback whales from our balcony. The year round cool weather didn't make sunbathing on the beach a frequent event but we could walk down the beach to the pier in five minutes. I enjoyed watching the organ grinder complete with a small monkey as he plied his trade at the end of the pier. Such divine tranquility was short lived. The Army didn't need as many Cobra helicopter pilots now that the war in Viet Nam had ended. He became a victim of the Reduction In Force (RIF). With his unusual skill set jobs were scarce. A former Army buddy started a business flying geologists to the less inhabited locales in the U.S. This new work initially took us to Moab, Utah. The culture in the beehive state contrasted sharply with our previous locations of California and Europe. Frequent travels to small cities would be the norm with this career so we purchased a fifth wheel trailer to ensure livable conditions. The Arches National Park is located near Moab. A great place to visit. I'd like to stress the word *visit*. I don't recommend it as a place to live unless you adore camping since that's the main form of entertainment. Did I mention I hate to camp? After two really, really *long* months we received word of our next work/home site. North Dakota. Thanksgiving loomed. Oh. My. God. Wintering in such a cold climate in a house made of metal didn't appeal to either of us. He quit. Without a job between us we made our way to Las Vegas.

A close friend lived on an acre of land on the outskirts of Las Vegas. He and his wife allowed us to park our temporary home on their property while we each looked for work. Their house stood less than a mile from the grounds owned by Wayne Newton also known as Mr. Las Vegas. I never did spot him but I enjoyed watching his fabulous horses. It took no time at all for me to find a job with a government contractor. I worked with nuclear physicists on projects associated with the Nevada Nuclear Test Site. It turned out to be the most interesting job I've ever had. My computer programming skills had previously been geared toward business applications. I now worked as a scientific programmer. That's very different and challenging work. I loved it. We bought a *real* house and settled into our new life. My husband found a job, actually two of them, while we lived for two years in Sin City. Then a new opportunity came knocking. The Army wanted him back as an Active Reservist.

We pulled up stakes and started over, again, in St. Louis. Having spent most of my young life in Oklahoma, I wasn't a stranger to tornadoes and the destruction they could cause. I'd seen them on the horizon many times but I'd never been in the middle of one. Until I moved to Missouri. Go figure. We were lucky, the damage included our wooden fence being flattened and a couple of really big walnut trees felled across the driveway. The neighbors across the street lost their roof. My first employment in St. Louis occurred at a local phone company. In those days there were dozens of small phone companies around the country and I landed a job only two miles from home. The best thing about the job was the short commute. After a year I managed to land a job as a programmer with the federal government. The long-term employment options trumped the additional time commuting. A decision I made while there had some unexpected consequences later. I joined the Army Reserve.

For various reasons my life with my husband became unbearable to me. We divorced and I moved to an apartment. I'm sure the circumstances colored my view of St. Louis. I never did enjoy living there. It took me a year after the divorce but I managed to transfer to another federal job in San Antonio, Texas. When I arrived I felt as if a giant weight had been lifted from my shoulders. The mild weather and friendly people cured my blues and energized me. I bought a house and enjoyed the freedom of doing what I wanted when I wanted. I remember having dinner the week before Thanksgiving with a co-worker on the River Walk. We ate outside and even when the sun went down the weather stayed pleasant. She originally hailed from Minnesota and had to call friends that evening to tell them about our little adventure.

As a reservist I participated in physical training (PT) during my annual two-week commitment. One day while running two miles, something I hated to do, a smart-ass soldier ran with me for a few moments asking if he could join me. The comment seemed to me to be a jibe at my slow pace. I smiled but thought to myself, "what a jerk". You guessed it, this is how I met my new husband. Obviously, we saw each other again in more pleasant surroundings. He really wasn't a jerk. A year later I married him and acquired an instant family. He had two children, a girl and a boy. It took some adjustments on everyone's part that first year but we survived and I can't imagine my life without them.

Two weeks after we married the Army sent us to Ft. Leavenworth, Kansas. Ed had the honor of attending the Command and General Staff College, which is a ten-month course. We lived in Army quarters about a mile from his classroom. The children loved it. They could ride their bikes to the Post Exchange (PX) where they could play video games, walk to school; lots of children their age living on the same street and a park within one block that held a basketball court. Let's just say the grownups were not as enthralled with the small town life. They rolled up the sidewalks at dark. The baggers at the Commissary were trustees from Ft. Leavenworth prison. Remember my earlier comments about tornados? As Dorothy and Toto can attest they are common in Kansas too. My newly acquired children were terrified of tornados. So what's a mother to do when the tornado siren goes off? Of course you make them come inside. It so happens the tornado siren and the warning of escaped prisoners is the same. We had a lot of escaped prisoners that year.

Ed asked to be assigned to Redstone Arsenal, Alabama, following the school assignment. His request was granted and we set off on the new adventure. Although I'd attended a military school in Ft. Rucker, Alabama, when I first joined the Army Reserves, I'd never been to the northern part of the state. Huntsville is the city that surrounds Redstone Arsenal. There were many federal offices on the Arsenal even a segment of NASA. As an employee of the federal government it turned out to be an excellent move for my career. We settled in and raised our family. Huntsville was the perfect size city for us, not too big and not too small. After thirteen years of living no more than three years in one spot, usually less than a year, I looked forward to growing roots. And we did, for fourteen years. Remember those tornadoes I keep talking about? When I lived in Oklahoma it had the distinction of being the state with the most tornadoes. When I moved to Alabama that dubious title moved from Oklahoma to Alabama. Was someone trying to tell me something? No matter, we managed to avoid being struck by the sometimes deadly events.

The children were grown, Ed had long since retired from the Army, and I wanted to move. Not just anywhere. I wanted to live in Europe again. As a federal employee I had an opportunity to request a transfer. I applied for a lot of jobs and finally in 2001 I obtained a position in Heidelberg, Germany. I'd visited Heidelberg many years earlier when I lived in that small town outside Frankfurt. It was a gem. I couldn't wait.

We lived in a suburb of Heidelberg for the next five years – no tornadoes. Ed found a job with a government contractor for a couple of years then decided to become a federal employee for the final three years. During the time we lived there we visited more than a dozen countries including some of the former east-bloc variety. The cold war ended years ago and the boarders opened up making travel even easier. My plan to shop my way through Europe came to fruition! The experiences were incredible. Some of the trips we took were sponsored by the USO, others were mapped out by us. I remember one group outing with several other civil servants. We flew to Berlin where we arranged for a bus and a local person for a tour guide. Among the usual stops like Check Point Charlie and the Holocaust Museum she showed us Potts Dam and the Spy Bridge – where spies were exchanged between the Communists and the Western world. The quiet and foggy day fueled my imagination to conjure up an exchange happening right before our eyes. Our guide then showed us a town where, prior to WWII, the *rich* civil servants lived. The laughter that comment generated puzzled her.

But there is no place like the United States. After five years we were ready to come home. As a civil servant I had return rights to my old job at Redstone Arsenal, Alabama. We returned and built a home to house all our fabulous finds from Europe. Our children were both married and we had one grandchild. In the next few years three more grandchildren made their appearance much to our delight. Retirement loomed. Did we want to stay in Huntsville? Neither of the children had settled there. We had a vacation home in Myrtle Beach, South Carolina. We enjoyed our visits there so we figured living there full time would be fun. We decided to give it a try.

Ed retired first and waited impatiently for me. The day after my retirement we loaded up a U-Haul trailer and drove to the beach. Our house in Alabama had a For Sale sign out front. So started our life of retirement. In a small house. A *really* small house. So small we didn't have room to display all those treasurers we'd found in Europe. They sat gathering dust in a storage unit. Naturally, we decided to build a bigger house. Just a few weeks ago we moved in to that house. Are we there yet? At our final home? We think so.

I'm currently planning my next trip to Europe. This time with a couple of my girlfriends. What about Ed, you ask? He and our son are contemplating a pilgrimage to St. Andrews, Scotland, home of golf.

MEETING OUR NEW NEIGHBORS
by Carole O'Neill

Leaving New England meant not only leaving family, but also some very dear neighbors. Still, the excitement of eventually enjoying similar gatherings with new neighbors in South Carolina gave us new hope for an enjoyable retirement.

We moved into a new townhouse just north of the waterway. The neighborhood was only two years old and the opportunity to meet new neighbors, probably migrating from somewhere as cold as our former hometown, was exciting.

Our second month in the townhouse, while standing in line at Wal-Mart, we met our neighbors from across the street. Karen and Tommy were hurricane Katrina victims with many stories to share. It was a good feeling to get to enjoy our new life in the south with nice neighbors.

A few weeks later, at nearly midnight, there was a banging on our front door at the same time our phone began ringing.

"Don't open that door until you look through the peephole," I yelled to my husband, Jim. We had turned off Letterman in the middle of his monologue not more than a half hour earlier so we could get enough sleep before my early morning class at the university. It was exam week.

"Carole, we need your help out front," Karen was yelling into my ear, when I answered the phone.

"What's going on?" I asked.

"It's our neighbor, Sherry." "She can't find her husband, and she's hysterical."

Tommy told my husband the same story when he answered the door, and Jim was already putting on a jacket and heading across the street. As I followed behind, I could see someone sitting on the ground. Her moans got louder as we approached. It took all four of us to get her into a lawn chair in order to try to calm her down.

We had never met Sherry before this, but we did see her husband Fred walking their dog a few times over the past few weeks. This was not the best way to meet.

"Sherry came to our door and said Fred was missing," Karen began. "We got dressed and went through their entire townhouse with her, but there was no sign of Fred," Karen continued. "Sherry wasn't making much sense between sobs, however, she noticed that the key to the mailbox was gone from the hook. Tommy took Sherry in our car to drive up to the mailboxes to see if Fred might have had a heart attack on his way back to the townhouse."

The townhouses in our neighborhood had groupings of mailboxes at the entrance to each development. Woods surrounded our grouping, and the lighting was poor. When Tommy pulled his car up to the mailboxes he tried to block her full view, but knew she saw Fred's glasses on the cement slab under the mailboxes. When her screams got louder he knew she also saw the blood, just inches away. That's when Sherry's hysteria began.

Tommy drove her back to her driveway, and while he was putting his car in his garage next door, Sherry began walking up the street crying. She was dressed in a nightgown and robe. She got only a couple of driveways from her own when she sat down in the road. She was moaning and sobbing at the same time and calling Fred's name. She rolled herself into a ball on the ground. That's when Tommy ran across the street to our townhouse and Karen called me on her cell.

As we waited for the police to arrive, we found ourselves wondering how anything like this could happen to someone here in Berkshire Forest. This was such a quiet community. At least we thought so when we moved here.

The detectives came and called for the dogs that they hoped would sniff the blood and lead them to some clue about Fred's whereabouts. Soon the fire engine and ambulance rolled up to the end of the street and sat in wait for whatever would be found.

For the next several hours we went from her open garage to her living room and back out to her driveway. Trying to reassure her that Fred would be fine when they found him, was not working. At least four times she got on her cell phone and between sobs told Fred she was worried about him and needed him to call her as soon as he got her message. There was no doubt in my mind that he was not getting her messages. I didn't know how to comfort her. I couldn't imagine what I would do if Jim were missing overnight.

By five-thirty in the morning, I apologized to Sherry, but said I needed to sleep for a few hours so that I would be able to make some sense in the class I would be teaching at the university at ten o'clock that morning. Tommy and Karen agreed to stay with Sherry until the detectives either left the neighborhood, or came in with some information that gave everyone reason to relax.

We didn't even get a chance to change our clothes when the phone rang again. "Jim, the detectives just spoke with me in Sherry's driveway. They say she will need us. Can you guys come back?" Tommy asked.

"Jim, I think he's dead." I whispered, as we once again crossed the street in the dark.

We sat in the empty space on the sectional sofa in Sherry's living room. Karen was sitting next to Sherry and Tommy was standing with the two detectives.

The lead detective sat down next to Sherry and began, "I'm sorry, Mrs. Engel, but we found Fred and he is dead."

There was the beginning of a noise out of Sherry's mouth just before she fainted.

Both detectives worked on her until she was revived.

"Where is he?" she sobbed. "I want to see him now." She tried to get up off the sofa.

"Do you know anyone who would want to hurt Fred?" the detective asked.

"Everyone loved Fred," she sobbed. He was a loving husband and gentle man to everyone who knew him," she continued.

"I'm sorry, Mrs. Engel, but Fred was murdered."

She started to get up from the sofa and collapsed again. The two detectives pushed the coffee table away from the sofa and on their knees worked to bring her around while calling for the ambulance at the end of the block

"Hurry, I'm getting no pulse," the lead detective said into the microphone attached to his left shoulder.

"Oh my God," I said to Jim. "We just met her, her husband is dead, and now she may not make it." "What's going on?"

The ambulance attendants placed her in the ambulance and Karen agreed to ride to the hospital with her. Tommy agreed to stay in her townhouse so the detectives could go through Fred's computer and office desk.

We went back to our townhouse, but sleep never came. I headed off to the university and somehow got through my class and returned to the neighborhood with a very different feeling than the day we moved in. The HOA hired the services of Excalibur for hourly checks throughout the entire development. The extra security didn't convince many of us that we were safe.

There were calling hours at the end of the week at a funeral home. Jim and I felt we needed to be there for Sherry's sake. We were all so new in the area and not many people had even met the Engels.

Sherry was sitting in the front row of the chapel. Her hair was long and she actually looked like a movie star from the forties. Fred's coffin was up in front and we knelt and said a prayer while checking his neck for signs of the marks from the shoelace the detectives said was used to kill him.

We sat in the back of the chapel just before a man walked up, closed the lid and stood behind Fred's body in the coffin. He was wearing overalls over a white t-shirt.

"I'm a mechanic and a preacher," the man began. We learned later that he was Sherry's brother from Kentucky. "I usually preach for seven hours," he continued.

Jim looked at me and pointed to his watch. "This funeral

home closes in an hour," he said, "He'll have to cut it short."

"Fred would call me and want to discuss the bible," the preacher began. "I talked with him several times each week. Even when he was traveling." "I am certain it was the DEVIL who did this," he stated with emphasis on the evil word.

Things came to a grinding halt a few minutes later when the funeral home attendants walked up to the front of the room and stood at either side of the coffin.

The few people in attendance went up to Sherry to offer their condolences.

"I'm so sorry we had to meet under these circumstances," I told Sherry as she hugged so tight I thought my breath would stop. "If I can do anything when you get back, please don't hesitate to ask."

She was taking Fred's body to Kentucky for another service before he was cremated.

For the next week, each time I saw the cars driving by I checked the locks on all our windows and made sure the chairs I placed under the doorknobs in front and in back were still secure. For the next few days I hardly slept. The newspaper account of the death drew reporters to our doors at all hours of the day and night. Sherry called Karen from Kentucky to ask if the detectives had given any of us any update on their case.

By the end of the next week, we were all just a bundle of nerves. How could there be a murderer in our neighborhood without some clues found.

It was dinnertime on Friday when I saw the BREAKING NEWS graphic on the television. I grabbed for the remote to turn up the sound when I saw a picture of Fred on the screen. The words knocked me down on my sofa.

"THE HORRY COUNTY DETECTIVES HAVE JUST INFORMED US THAT TWO PEOPLE HAVE BEEN ARRESTED FOR THE MURDER OF FRED ENGEL. ONE IS HIS WIFE, SHERRY, AND THE OTHER IS HER LOVER, TIM."

THE STORY OF PAWLEYS ISLAND TOLD THROUGH ART
by Kay Nelson

The town and actual island known as Pawleys doesn't have boardwalks or beachy town trappings. It's slow, private and classy. The people live on island time, a little to the right of bohemian I imagine; relaxed, down to earth, and spiritual. Yes, with the tides, winds, sand, ocean smells and sounds, the soul is soothed.

But, I've found Pawleys Island can be a frightening place to visit because once you spend time here you can't get the romance of the Lowcountry out of your mind. I know this as a fact because it happened to me. After visiting my friends in Pawleys for one week we bought a home and one year later lived here. Some say there are ghosts and spirits among us. Maybe one of these spirits cast a spell and won't let go.

After moving here I wanted to know everything there was to know about the Lowcountry. I spent months exploring, learning the lore and falling in love. I took classes in art, and it became a passion. I would like to tell my experiences of Pawleys Island through my paintings.

Brookgreen Gardens is one of the wonders of the world, so beautiful, and a relic from the past. I took this picture our first Christmas here. I developed the photo on canvas and then enhanced the image with acrylic paint to add a little mystery and southern charm.

Despite the pull of the tides, or the spell of the ghosts, the move would have been impossible if it didn't have a hook to reel the children and grandchildren to visit each year. Our garage is refashioned with surfboard shelves, and eleven hooks for bogy boards (of course each grandchild had to choose their own). The lure worked and the families visit often.

I hoped to capture the smell of the ocean, a leisurely life and surf friendly waves. Pawleys Island is a laid back paradise. I welcome you to bring a book and sit in the sun in one of my chairs.

An abstract of the grandkids on the beach. Painted in acrylics.

Of course Pawleys Island has more than waves. The grandkids love to go to the dock and crab, or fish. They have an ongoing contest to see who can catch the most crabs. With nets and cages, umbrellas, coolers, chairs and lotion in hand, we make a day of crabbing.

This is an 8 X 10 watercolor painting I made for the grandson that caught the most crabs. Every year another grandchild tries to beat the record.

And then, there are the marshes, parks, and wildlife,

Pluff mud is a new word in my life. This is also a great area for kayaking.

Went to lunch with the family. My granddaughter said, "Mimi, can I borrow your phone? I want to take a picture of that pirate ship." I looked across the harbor following her extended finger. The ship she saw did look like a pirate ship.

I painted this 12 X 14 watercolor from the photo image my granddaughter took during our lunch outing. Where else could you sit on the wharf, eat shrimp, burgers and fries and see a pirate ship across the waterway?

The wild life is amazing.

We protect the endangered loggerhead turtles.

This frog lives in our back yard and makes so much noise...

I sent this watercolor painting of a snowy egret to my friend.

.

Ready for flight. Acrylic painted of a gull from a photo by Vino Paul.

Brookgreen Gardens butterfly exhibit. This is a photo of a Monarch on canvas, overlaid with acrylic paint to give highlights and color.

This proud pelican didn't fly away when Vino Paul took his picture. The guide said he must be sick and ready to die. I wanted to immortalize the old bird by putting a little pink in his gray cracked beak, and a glisten in his eye. He's painted on canvas in acrylic paints.

This is an acrylic painting of one of the original slave quarters still featured on a local plantation tour. I've lived here four years and still have only begun to experience the history of the lowcountry.

The wall of a dilapidated motel is all that remains of the most popular black beach resort of its time. McKenzie Beach stretches twenty-three acres from the ocean to the highway. Built in 1936 to provide a place where blacks could visit without fear of racial discrimination. Here they were fed and entertained with live music provided by the likes of Count Basie and Duke Ellington.

And, everywhere you go there is fabulous food…..

This painting was inspired by a table cover at one of the local restaurants.

Seashells can be found on the beaches in the morning before the sun lovers invade with their umbrellas and ocean gear.

In this acrylic painting I wanted to capture, God's grace. An actual sunset in the Lowcountry certainly reveals God's awe much brighter and leaves you feeling there is a grand plan in the hands of the master.

Oh, yes. And, Pawleys Island has fabulous golf, but that's a story for someone else.

THE MAGIC RED BOAT
by Rebecca Bridges

The fully furnished beach house that became our vacation home and eventually our retirement home held one surprising trophy. Since the cottage stood a mere block from the Garden City South Carolina Pier, the storage shed held an array of beach toys along with the usual lawn mower and weed eater. Over the years some items disappeared and new ones purchased. However, there was one item all the grandchildren treasured and made sure it was never left behind at the beach. The magic red boat. So named for the spell it seemed to cast over the grandchildren.

The plastic boat stretched about twenty-four inches long and eight inches wide. There was about eight inches of flat surface in the middle with each end having about six inches of graduated *smoke stacks*. The first grandchild gathered it close as his chubby toddler legs raced to the shore. He sat on it perched at the edge of the tide then floated out to ocean when the water receded. Good thing his mom and dad stood sentinel catching them both before they traveled too far. Time after time he squealed with delight as the water floated the miniature vessel he clung to toward the open ocean. That first time he was a mere two and a half years old. The next year when he came to visit he specifically requested the red boat. "Red boat," I asked. "Yes, I think it's still here." Rummaging through the storage shed to locate it as we gathered the chairs and umbrellas.

This time he weighed too much for the boat to float out to sea with him aboard. That didn't stop him from sitting on it and using his legs to push as the water came and went. It was still his favorite. As the years went by his use of the boat transformed but it was always the first to be chosen. Until his little brother discovered it. As any good steward of a family heirloom he allowed the new regime to take possession as he sought out the delights of new treasures.

The third grandchild is a girl. Her use of the magic red boat differed greatly from her male cousins. When turned upside down and filled with sand it makes an amazing sand castle. The plastic fairies that adorn the castle wall have fantastical adventures.

This year our fourth and final grandchild, another boy, will have the delightful role of Captain of the ship. If his sister will relinquish the title. Or perhaps they'll share; they're pretty good at that.

The scruffy plastic boat has faded over the years and is now more orange than red. But it still holds the title of The Magic Red Boat.

KEEP ON CLIMBIN'
by Kay Nelson

When I was in grade school I loved to hike. The harder it was to walk the terrain, the better I felt. I fancied myself a Robin Hood, or an Indian, or one of the explorers who first crossed the North West Passage. I would spend hours in the woods, wading the creeks and climbing trees for a glimpse of who might be trailing me. Of course, this was in the old days, when no fear of predators invaded the minds of child or parent. In the treetops I looked for the dreaded Sheriff of Nottingham, or the cowboys, or whomever I fancied the enemy at the moment.

As I matured, (well I don't think I've reached that point yet), but, as I aged the adventure and the love for excitement never diminished. When I was seven months pregnant with my first child I climbed Mt. Monadnock, in Keene, New Hampshire. I don't remember ever being winded. At the top of the Mountain, my friend told me on a clear day you could see Boston Harbor. It wasn't a clear day, so I can't attest to the hundred-mile view.

The day my second child was born I was on a speedboat being the lookout for the skiers we towed. Later a group of us were on an island in the middle of the lake having lunch when I felt the first pain. I thought at the time, "I'm glad we came in a speed boat." I made it home, changed clothes and headed immediately to the hospital. My precious son was born two hours after arrival.

When the kids were old enough to have steady footing I took them hiking and mountain climbing. Just yesterday my son called and said, "Hey, mom. I'm taking the kids to Dinosaur State Park to hike and climb the rocks." That's where I took the boys when they were the age of my grandchildren.

Fifty years later I guess I'm still climbing mountains. I've retired from a full career. Am married to the love of my life, have four children, four step-children and eleven beautiful, loving grandchildren. My biggest setback in life was when my Multiple Sclerosis kicked in about four years ago, like a hornet after a hive intruder; my disease is now being labeled progressive. I haven't walked in three years. I can stand and pivot and sit, which is enough to land me on equipment that meets my needs. I streak across parking lots in my high-speed scooter. People in the cross walks have been known to yell, "Hey, slow down."

Crazy as it sounds; in my mind I feel I'm still climbing mountains. Just looking at a picture of my children or grandchildren keeps me climbing. In the past three years I've gone back to school at Coastal Carolina. I dabble in painting. My friends send me pictures of their vacations and I paint their memories. For Christmas this year several friends asked me to paint their family pets. When I finish a painting and see a beautiful likeness of what I intended to paint, well, it's like I've just climbed to the top of Mt. Kilimanjaro.

I've taken up writing too and have two books published, one an e-book. Again, when I see my name on the final project, well it feels like I've concurred another mountain.

My most recent climb came in the form of a trip to see my children and grandchildren. My husband couldn't get the time off I needed for a decent reunion. You see I decided I was going to stay in Texas a month. My husband and I drove to Ft. Worth, in my incredibly magic handicapped, hand controlled van. Of course, my speedy scooter sat in the back waiting for the ramp to be lowered. My husband left after three days and I stayed in a log cabin in Jelly Stone Park for the remainder of the month. I receive energy from my children, and grandchildren. I just want to eat them up I love them so much. I had more company in that log cabin than Santa at Christmas. The park adventure was definitely more fun and rewarding than climbing Mt. Monadnock, pregnant.

So, I think I have a bright future. No matter where life takes us we all have hypothetical mountains to climb. I still get the rush when I reach the top. Life is good, and I'm waiting for my next adventure.

NOSTALGIC WEEKEND
by John Kenny

I checked all of the categories on Fodor's and Trip Advisor, even Google for Nostalgic Weekend.   There was a travel company with that name located in the middle of the Aegean Sea. There were weekends related to classic cars and young adventures, but not what I was looking for.

You see, my NOSTALGIC WEEKEND seemed to epitomize the Merriam Webster definition: "a wistful or excessively sentimental yearning for return to or of some past period or irrecoverable condition."

My return was to the 1950s and 1960s and to a place that still exists, but that I had not visited in almost 50 years. The impetus for my weekend was an invite to an aptly named party: WE'RE NOT DEAD YET! The party was arranged by two 66 year old friends that I had grown up with me in the Bronx, New York in the 50s and 60s. Although born in 1947, all frames of reference that were able to be recalled by me were in those two decades. Those were the grammar school and high school years. For many of us in the Bronx, they were the ***Glory Days*** that Springsteen would immortalize in his hit single. Unlike his lyrics, for me they actually were glory days.

Yeah, just sitting back trying to recapture
a little of the glory of, well time slips away

and leaves you with nothing mister but
boring stories of glory days

Not much boring about them for me. After all, I lived in the
greatest city in the world with the best baseball and football teams
in the world. This 2013 party would give me a chance to see if I
had grown up with some of the best friends in the world and if they
really were glory days or just boring stories of days gone by.

WE'RE NOT DEAD YET was what the invitation said, when
it arrived at my home in South Carolina. The party was triggered
by our chronological age. The invitation indicated that one needed
a Medicare card to attend, and we all qualified, at least the ones
that were still alive. About 30 of us would show. I suspect many
of us showed because we knew we had experienced glory days but
also that time was catching up to all of us. Each of us had already
lost a spouse or child or friend who had died too soon. All of us
had ailments that were way too obvious and minds that were way
to addled.

But the party was a chance to return to that irrecoverable past
period when we were Boy Scouts and star athletes and young
lovers and kids in parochial school uniforms. There among the 30
of us, we had Marines who had survived Viet Nam, Cops who
survived the World Trade Center bombing, mothers who had borne
tens of babies, a couple of guys who spent some time behind bars,
but most of all we had fond memories of a time gone by, maybe
wistful or sentimental, but surely heartfelt.

It was especially surreal for me. Unlike ALL of the others at the party, I was the only one that had moved away and not returned for almost 50 years. The others had remained in New York, not necessarily in the Bronx, but within a 30 mile radius and most had stayed in close contact over the years. I was the aberration in the group. When I graduated High School, I went off to college in New England and essentially would never live in New York again. Suffice it to say, that that is a story for another day.

Today's story is about Nostalgic Weekend 2013. It was autumn in our lives.

New York City immediately after World War II became the unquestioned leader among major cities of the world. It was experiencing an economic boom. Wall Street was driving the free world in entertainment, fashion and finance. For me, the most important world leadership was in sports and World Series. We had two major league football and two major league baseball teams.

My world view was much narrower. It was a four block radius that was anchored by a grammar school on one end, a playground on another, the ball field a bit further and the railroad tracks. It was this narrow world view that made me an inveterate New Yorker. Try as I might for the next 60 years, I was firmly rooted in the Bronx. The city was deeply ingrained in me, like a habit. Being Bronx was chronic.

What I am today, was rooted in those ten to fifteen years of being brought up in New York. When people ask why I am

Yankee fan or Giants football fan, to me it is a moot question. My world only consisted of New York teams, to be more specific, only teams that played in my borough of New York, the Bronx. My ingrained habit in the 1950s and 1960s was to live and die around Yankees and Giants and sports in general. My dad would not start a day without reading the New York papers and regaling us kids on the stats for what he said were the world's best players, playing on the world's best teams. Of course, they were both housed in the world's biggest and best stadium, the incomparable Yankee Stadium.

My early years were those when true sports titans played the stadium. Mantle and Maris and Yogi on the Yanks and Gifford and Tittle and Tarkenton on the Giants. These legends were just a few neighborhoods away and my dad made certain that we would live the games with them, mostly on the ubiquitous live radio broadcasts, but often in person.

You see it was in my youth that the only perfect game in a World Series ever took place., and I was there. It was 1956, I was 9 and the Yanks had Mickey Mantle in the outfield and Yogi Berra catching and Casey Stengel coaching. The Brooklyn Dodgers, our cross town rivals, had hall of famers, Jackie Robinson, Pee Wee Reese and Roy Campanella. But on that day, the only Yankee that counted was Don Larsen, our pitcher. He was scorching hot. No runs, no hits and his team had no errors to give the Yanks the win and that only perfect World Series ever. Mantle and Bauer would give the Yanks a couple of homers, but only one run was necessary. My dad had me cut school that day. My education at the hands of the nuns at St. Raymond's was clearly less important than any World Series game involving the Yankees and Dodgers. It turned out to be the best history lesson I ever got!

Two years later, the National Football League Championship game would also be played at Yankee Stadium with the N.Y. Giants taking on the Baltimore Colts with big names like Johnny Unitas and Pat Summerall. The Colts would win the NFL Championship, but the game won over new fans, and set the stage for the NFL's explosion in popularity. To this day many experts still believe it to be the greatest game ever played.

You can see how easily I digress. How memories flood in and overtake the WE AINT DEAD weekend story. So my wife and I flew up from Myrtle Beach, from deep in the Confederacy, to rekindle old memories and to re touch old friends.

Landing at La Guardia, was different on this trip. I had done so on tens of business trips, but this day, my mind was filled with memories of the glory days. Out the plane window I could see Parkchester, the sprawling apartment complex where I spent my first 18 years. I could sense those elevators and stairways and playgrounds and ballfields that were my youth. We never owned a car.....who needed one? Our transportation was walking and city buses and the labyrinthine N.Y. Subway System.

Just then, a flash occurred. It was me and five or six annoying punks, with ice skates hanging from our shoulders, terrorizing normal adults on the Lexington Avenue subway line heading to Central Park and its gigantic Wollman outdoor ice skating rink. It was one of our winter playgrounds. I closed my eyes and could see the zoo on one side, and the New York skyline surrounding us as we froze our asses off, chasing each other and generally terrorizing those who came to just skate. From Central Park we would always head to the world's greatest toy store, F.A.O. Schwartz, to ogle and try out toys, we could not afford. You see, the ice rink immortalized in **LOVE STORY** and the toy store brought to life in **BIG** were our playgrounds. We lived cheap, but we lived large. From there we would pick a major department store, where real rich folks came to shop and it was our venue for hide and seek, or chase or some other totally engaging kid game. Eventually, a security guard would catch up with us and throw us out, but what a day we had. All for the cost of a 15 cent subway token, each way of course. That is, if we didn't decide to jump the turnstile when the station attendant wasn't watching.

Spirit landed. Enterprise rental awaited and the real adventure would begin. WE AINT DEAD YET would begin in about 5 hours, so we had some time to kill. Unfortunately, our party was scheduled for foreign territory, Staten Island instead of the Bronx The only nostalgia for me on that Island was a Ferry ride from Manhattan, that as a youth, was a mandatory, albeit fun ritual. For a quarter, you could ride round trip and see the majestic cityscape from the water, and ogle at the Statue of Liberty. Never once, did I get off that Ferry and never did my feet touch that foreign island. So what awaited me as a 66 year old was all virgin territory.

So, I had to plot my drive to that Island carefully. The only nostalgia on the map in the Boroughs of Queens, Brooklyn and Staten Island, was another Island.....at least by name. It was Coney Island. "It ain't an island, stupid, it's an amusement park" was how I remembered being told as a kid. Now, I know it is a neighborhood in the south of Brooklyn looking out at the Atlantic Ocean. For me, as a kid, it was the largest amusement park in the world with the scariest roller coaster, the Cyclone, the highest parachute drop and the best hot dogs at Nathan's. As a family, Coney Island was a mandatory spring trip. We could not hop in the car and get there, because my parents never owned a car, or even had driver's licenses. We would always take a series of subways from the top of the Bronx, through Manhattan and then deep into Brooklyn. It felt like it took all day to get there. But it was worth it. Rides, games, noise, junk food, glory days for sure! What could be better?

Well, it was all still there on this autumn day in 2013. Tired, smaller, smellier. But it was there and the memories overwhelmed the reality and I could feel my dad's hand walking me on the boardwalk, or see my mom's smile when I finally got the gold ring on the Steeplechase. We made the mandatory Nathan's stop and ordered the chili dog. It was a perfect kick off to NOSTALGIC WEEKEND. The sun shone on the Atlantic. The air was crisp and clean. Kids were screaming and frolicking and my mood was set for a reunion with my youth.

WE AINT DEAD YET was in the basement of a clubhouse at a swim club in a corner of Staten Island. It was perfect! Not because it was swank, or classy or even pretty. It was perfect because it was so New York. It was just like the Knights of Columbus halls that my parent's took us to for a hundred gatherings of the ethnics in the Bronx. The Italians and Irish all gathered in halls like this in post war city life. It was a full bar without a bar tender. It was fold out tables and chairs and brought in food on Bunsen burners. This could have been the Italian-American Club on Zarega Avenue in the Bronx in the 50s or a thousand other similar venues. You saw them in the Sopranos or in Fort Apache the Bronx. My friends weren't trying to capture a by gone look or feel or ambiance. This was their city and this continued to be their style. It was not a $1,000 rented tent behind a gate in the Debordieu Colony with valet parking. This was life in the city, as it was, and still is.

I had butterflies coursing through my intestines. They had landed somewhere between Coney Island and the swim club. Now they were in full flutter.

I had seen only 2 of the 30 or so people in 55 years. I had flown the coop. Lived in New England and Washington, DC and South Carolina and traveled to many of the world's capitals. What the hell was I thinking? Coming back. Stepping into their world. There was a moment, as I took the first step down into the basement, that I wanted to turn back. The lighting was fairly dim, or was it just my old eyes? I hesitated. There at the bar was a lifeline. A big smiling Irish red face. The one I knew. The one whose wedding I had been best man in. "So the witness protection program gave you a weekend pass?" One cheap shot, led to another. I knew I was back home. The guys showed no mercy. They raised the painful taunts that were part and parcel of our youth. I could sense all eyes on us, but the ice was already broken.

Over the next 3 hours it was like being in GOODFELLAS or A BRONX TALE. My whole neighborhood was either Italian or Irish and we reverted back to childhood form. Most of the stories felt as if they had happened yesterday, but others were long forgotten, maybe repressed. A track meet, the high school dances, the arrests in the playground. There wasn't enough time, but it was grand. Then there was the food! There was enough for a small village in Sicily. The Italian momma who put the spread on spared no expense. Lasagna, shells, meatballs, antipasto, bread, cold cuts, on and on.. The table had to have been 10 feet long. All I had had to eat was a Nathan's hotdog, so it was chow down time. Loved every heartburn moment of it. Maybe it was the free flowing Chianti or the shots of Jameson, but life was good. The stories continued. Maybe a little maudlin as the evening progressed. A child buried way too soon. A spouse passed. A soldier maimed for life. We talked Vietnam and our teenage buddy KIA, Kennedy brother's assassinations and Twin Towers violated and desecrated and how each had affected our lives.....forever. As the night wore down, it was promises to meet again and vows to stay in touch and maybe another reunion down the road. All in all, for me it was the epitome of nostalgia, pleasure and sadness caused by remembering something from the past and wishing that I could experience it again. At least most of it.

"As I've aged, it seems I have come to the autumn of my life;
Where I'm left with remnants of dreams & things that lag behind,
Yet what remains is a mellow feeling of contentedness,
Its liken to autumn-that brings a pause in time;
When life comes to rest,
And one is given a chance to reflect upon the journey.
Jean Dament, IN THE AUTUMN OF MY LIFE

The party was so impactful that Mary Lou and I scrapped our plans for a traditional Big Apple weekend to continue to trip down memory lane. I chose five of the most critical landmarks in my early life: the church, the diner, the "hood", the library and the station. The next day and half promised to be a nostalgic whirlwind.

Sunday morning and being practicing Catholics, Mass was in order. Staten Island churches wouldn't do. It was back to the Bronx and the mother church of my youth. We drove across four of the five boroughs and showed up in the nick of time for a standing room only Mass at Saint Raymonds. This was no ordinary church. It was the size of a cathedral and had the ornate trappings of a basilica. After all, this was the first Catholic Church in the Bronx. Built in 1845 at a time when Catholics and immigrants were hated and feared by many, especially those "dirty Irish papists." The temporary church had been in a wooden barn, but the 2000 or so parishoners could not be served. We have been to churches throughout North America and Europe. St. Raymonds does not pale in comparison. I was stunned. Having not been back there since age 18, I had no sense of its beauty and regalness. But most stunning was its liveliness. Every seat was filled. Every aisle was packed with standers. There were eight priests serving the mass. Twenty altar servers in attendance. A choir supported by the magnificent pipe organ. This was the sanctuary of my youth. Where I had been baptized and confirmed and been an altar boy. Where my oldest sister had been married in a grand wedding, with me as the ring bearer. It was there that my mother had her funeral mass and it was in St. Raymond's cemetery that she would be laid to rest.

My memories were of playing chase as a 12 year old through the pews and climbing the massive sides of the church or of hiding in the confessionals during hide and seek. As a youth, this was not the holy basilica, but just another one of our neighborhood acqaintances. We went to school for 9 years at St. Raymonds. We had our school plays there. We raced on the street that abutted the school and church. We threw baseballs and basketballs and footballs at every building and surface imaginable. St Rays was an extension of our immigrant families. It was the focal point of our lives.

For that hour of mass, Jesus got little of my attention. A flood of memories and flashbacks filled the air and rushed through my veins.

Across the street from church was the diner. Not just any diner, but the epitome of the city diners spread through every neighborhood of the Bronx. It was open 24 hours a day, because, as you know, New York doesn't sleep....at least not the cops and firemen and bookies and gamblers and subway workers and sundry other blue collar folks. They were the sons and daughters of immigrants in the Bronx of the 50s and 60s.

The diner was a go to place in my youth. Now it was an overdose of nostalgia. There's a review on Yelp that says: "The décor is old school and the wait staff are seriously old school. They look like they've been there when they broke ground on the place." When we arrived, it was déjà vu. Nothing had changed in the 50 years since I had last eaten there. The booths, the counters, the bathroom, the plates and "silver" all seemed the same. Pictures on the wall showed history dating back a hundred years. We reveled in the hearty, greasy breakfast and the smells and sounds. I closed my eyes and saw my dad with two eggs over easy, home fries and white toast. My dad would have been there at 2 a.m. on a Saturday, after the poker game broke up at the Knights of Columbus hall, down the block. For him it was a mandatory stop. For me on that particular day, it was a moment of sheer pleasure.

Having consumed communion for our souls and immigrant soul food for our bellies, it was now time to give Mary Lou a drive by into the "hood". Parkchester was my neighborhood. It was a mini city. Built in 1939, it was designed to house 12,000 families in 51 groups of 7 and 12 story buildings. It was a working family dream. Low rent, safe, clean and designed with access to the subway, abundant food stores, Laundromats, movie theatres and of course Catholic churches and public and private schools. First generation immigrant families flocked to it and remained in their same rent controlled apartments for decades and in some cases generations.

Mary Lou was able to marvel at the art deco beauty of the old buildings and the abundance of amenities that truly made this a neighborhood. I, on the other hand, wanted to point out the playground with its urban basketball "court" with steel nets. I shared the vignettes of kisses on park benches and flirtations in elevators and first loves. For me it was memories of racing to grammar school, late as usual, knowing it would lead to a ruler set of 20 whacks on the behind. There were fights with bullies and ghost in the grave yard chases for hours on end. Over there was the forbidden railroad tracks that were a guaranteed allure to us as teens. A racing locomotive with 20 passenger cars arriving from New England was always ample reason to violate parental restrictions. For twenty minutes that Sunday, we drove up and down almost twenty years of my life. I left with a lump in my throat and a smile in my eye.

The final two stops the next day, were to grand edifices of the greatest city in the world. We left the Bronx and headed to Manhattan and what the rest of the world thinks of as New York

City. As a kid, we must have made a hundred treks on the subway down to two of the most magnificent buildings I had ever seen: Grand Central Station and the New York Public Library. These were places of epic proportion, both in terms of size and in terms of what they contained.

My memories of Grand Central are of family trips to New England to visit my mother's relatives. The ceilings were magnificent. The windows were resplendent. The locomotives were immense. The throngs of people were overwhelming. Grand Central rivaled the biggest and best of the world's train stations, but for me, as a kid, it was the biggest and best and the only train station in the world. Arriving back that Sunday, it was just as breathtaking. Sun was streaming through the windows and arches, I could sense the movie, THE DARK KNIGHT, arriving from the basement labyrinth. We strolled through and soaked up a sense of its grandeur. Just then, I had a flashback to a February day in 1962, age 15. My sister Joan and I had taken the subway from the Bronx to meet my dad who worked in Manhattan. We were to take a Penn Central train up to Providence for a holiday weekend. There, on the largest television screen in the world, hanging from the rafters of the station, was John Glenn, a Marine pilot in a space suit. Walter Cronkite was telling the world that Glenn was the first American to orbit the earth in space. It was surreal for me in 1962 and was on this day as well. Trains had given way to flight and now to space ships. Grand Central was a dreamscape.

From there we strolled over to our final stop of the nostalgia weekend, the New York Public Library. Here was the inner sanctum of my youth. As parochial school kids it was mandatory that we make a pilgrimage to "the greatest library of the world", at least, our world. This 1895 masterpiece would come to house 53 million items. For us, it was the all the books of the world in a single place. Its Dewey decimal card system was the roadmap to the world's written word. Its stacks and cubicles housed every imaginable subject. We were led into the sanctum with hushed tones and threats and dire consequences for any bad behavior. In here we would research any topic we wanted to do our term papers on. Here, as a child, I learned to love books for their own sake. Not for their words or pictures, but for what they stood for. These were monuments to intelligence and knowledge and greatness. Who knew, I would learn to love to read them and maybe even try writing one or two.

The weekend would end, but not be forgotten. My Bronx friends would now become social network buddies. I would follow their triumphs and tragedies with pictures of grandkids and trips and would reach out in person for the bigger moments. The church, the diner, the hood, the station and the library all reinforced why I am like I am here in South Carolina. I still am an unapologetic Yankee fan, still love greasy diner food, have become an adult altar boy and still love trains and books and read the New York Times. The Yankee in me has now grown to be a low country lover. The beach and the salt marsh the sun and surf give me comfort and let me revel in the reminiscences of a blessed youth. The friendships of sixty years now have a chance to blossom in the sun and salt of this glorious low country called South Carolina.

THE EIGHT BEDS OF CHRISTMAS
by Carole O'Neill

It's a month before Christmas, and all thru our house

Wrapped presents sit piled for their trip from the south

Merged families, ten children, eighteen grandchildren to see

But the eight beds we'll sleep on could cripple Hubby and Me.

It's the agreement we made with one another when we decided to retire in Myrtle Beach. While the southern paradise keeps us content for most of each year, when the holidays approach we prepare to keep our commitment and head north.

With a merged family, Hubby and I will have to travel to both Massachusetts and North Carolina. It takes several felt laundry bags decorated in Christmas colors to hold the presents we need to arrange in our Toyota sleigh.

It was foolish of us to continue our pattern of bestowing several gifts on each child and grandchild after we retired. Each year we say, "This year we're going to cut down on the amount of presents we buy." One of these years we will.

Packing the car is always a challenge. The presents bought

for the family living in the last house we stop at, need to be loaded first. In our advancing years, this is a greater challenge than you might think. We will spend the first part of our month in Massachusetts and celebrate an early Christmas with my family. The challenge grows greater when we decide to drop off all the gifts for the offspring living in North Carolina at Hubby's daughter's in the western part of the state of North Carolina on our way north.

With the car packed to the brim with enough clothes and boots to satisfy the possibility of snow and ice in New England and making sure we have plenty of cooler apparel for the south, we begin our holiday journey. For this first part of the trip, my legs are straddling the snow shovel that extends back between the captains seats. As the days pass the shovel will be given a permanent space in the way back.

The first bed of Christmas belongs to grandchild number three

It sits in the basement without lamps to help see

The double bed mattress has seen better days

But the NASCAR front seat offers an alternative way

We arrive at the home of Hubby's oldest daughter by mid-afternoon and back up the car to her Carolina Room around the side near the creek. Since everyone is working, it takes us some time to unload and separate the gifts into piles for the other kid's take.

When the family arrives we enjoy dinner for eight and spend hours just catching up on what's happened since we were last together. When they decided they needed more room as the children grew, they finished off their basement with bedrooms and a bath for the kids. We will spend our first night downstairs in our grandson's room – a museum dedicated to the North Carolina Tarheels with a dash of NASCAR memorabilia.

Who would think to bid on the former front seat from Jimmy Johnson's racecar at that auction last summer? I guess the fact that it fits perfectly next to our grandson's double bed, as long as a nightstand isn't needed and the bed can be pushed up against the exterior wall, keeps him happy. Who needs a lamp to read by when you can squint from the shadow of the recessed bulbs in the ceiling? Sunglasses help with the glare. Maybe if there were a window in the room, there would be a windowsill to place our medications on.

Letting Hubby use the bed, I settle onto the car seat and attach my book light to it's side to serve as a nightlight for the many trips we will make to the bathroom before dawn.

The pain in my side wakes me up. I'm not sure what time it is because my book light has blown out and there are no windows to give away a dawn. It's only when I feel my way to the door and use the light switch in the bathroom that I find my phone and realize it's time to shower and dress for our day on the road.

I wake Hubby and he's not happy that the dark room has allowed him to sleep into what would have been hour number two on the road to our next stop. It's raining this morning. Where did we put those umbrellas?

The trip from the south goes from rain to light snow

Making travel a challenge to stay in line with the flow

As nightfall arrives we have made it half way

And bed number two is in the hotel where we'll stay.

Getting off the highway at the Marriott suites in Delaware is a welcome relief from the day of travel. The rain changed from freezing to snow before we stopped. We don't look forward to unpacking the sleigh to prevent any temptation from those searching for bargains. It takes two rolling luggage carts to hold our overnight bag and the presents going north. The only suite left sports a microwave, fridge and a queen bed with four fluffy pillows. We can hardly wait to finish our dinner and tuck ourselves in for a long winters night.

It doesn't take long before we realize that the pillows are stuffed with feathers. My sneezing tips us off that there is something amiss. I'm sure the allergy pills are packed for the trip, but locating just where that bag is stuffed takes two trips down to the car and the rearrangement of northern and southern clothing piled between shovels and snowshoes we plan to use with grandchildren number four and seven.

By the time they are found, my nostrils have plugged up to the point of needing time in the bathroom with the hot shower running high to fill the room with steam.

The manager sends up new foam pillows and takes away the culprits. It's only two o'clock; we still have four or five hours before we need to pack up and continue our trek north. Hubby falls asleep before his head reaches the new pillows. By four o'clock I can breathe again and join him for a short nap. At least there is room on the bed.

Morning comes fast and the snow has stopped but the temperature has dropped and the roads are now crunchy with ice. The plows worked overnight and the main highways seem treated and usable. The struggle to get to the luggage carts before the other guests takes some creativity.

Eight hours more driving finds us at the exit to my oldest daughter's Massachusetts town. The ice on the roads and trees has resulted in a "State of Emergency" announcement by the Governor. Electricity has been out all over the northeast. Our only saving grace is that these children live among the "yuppies" that believe in buying up all the open spaces and building their own electric company. While other friends and relatives in New England wait for days to get their utilities back, we thankfully enjoy tucking ourselves into bed under many layers of quilts with a good book to read.

The presents are unpacked for their final destination,

And we enjoy a hot toddy to calm our frustrations.

Bed number three at the top of the stairs,

Awaits our tired bodies among the dog hairs.

With two dogs shedding heavily, our daughter spends hours vacuuming before we arrive. And shutting the door to our room helps my allergies during sleep. But medication is needed for our time in the rest of the house. We wake each morning hoping that it would be the day our bodies would adjust to the below freezing temperatures. Instead we add another Eddie Bauer woolen blanket to the covers we sit beneath in front of the television as we watch another version of *It's A Wonderful Life*.

The ten days we stay with them are filled with annual visits to our primary care physicians we still can't bear to replace with new doctors in the retirement community we now call home, and appearances at grandchildren's hockey games at indoor facilities we find colder than the outside air.

The Christmas gathering of my offspring culminates this stop. And, the car is now getting loaded with gifts we will enjoy for years to come.

The sleigh is much lighter for this leg of our trip

To bed number four, not one we should skip

No feathers, no dog hair, no snow and no ice,

Just revelers with noisemakers who are not very nice.

The hotel bed is on the other end of the spectrum from the one we just left. Our backs spend the first few hours adjusting to the softer mattress as we listen to the partygoers passing outside our door.

Morning comes fast and we leave right away.
Our destination is North Carolina by the end of the day.
Bed number five is three levels above ground.
Stopping half way helps our breathing we found.

Thank goodness Hubby's oldest daughter delivered the gifts we dropped at her house on our way north. The guest room on the third floor has its own ensuite. Once we get up there we stay for the night. The next day is spent with the youngest grandchildren of our eighteen. Our concentration goes from finding the cartoon character, Waldo, on large pages in activities books, to completing the 12,000-piece transformer made completely from LEGO's. We are made aware of new parts of our bodies as we move in several positions on the floor and use one another for stability when we finally get ourselves upright. Soon it is time for yet another exchange of gifts and the children take turns playing the role of Santa's helper until all three hundred gifts are unwrapped. .

Bed number six is a familiar sight.

The same one we slept in on our first night.

The NASCAR backseat hasn't changed, not a bit.

This time we're prepared with the lamps that we lit.

Christmas Eve is a wonder and special to us 'cuz we spend it with our oldest grandchildren – never a fuss. After lunch Christmas Day, we pack up and head east to bed number seven and another holiday feast.

The drive across the state of North Carolina is quiet today. Most families are at home sharing a holiday meal with one another. We find one McDonald's open and we buy tall iced teas for the trip and listen to the new book on tape we just received. Before we know it we are pulling into the driveway at our next stop.

This second floor bedroom belongs to grandson number five. The brass headboard sports a football helmet hanging from one post and Mardi Gras beads from the other. With the slightest movement the rattling begins, and the life size cardboard cutout of Tony Stewart at our feet reminds us of the southerners affinity to racing. After exchanging presents with Hubby's oldest son and his family we drive across town for the last of our family celebrations.

Bed number eight is pushed up against a wall,

And the mattress is higher in the middle allowing us to fall.

Hubby's hand hits the floor before his body leaves the bed,

But, my lips kiss the wall, just before I hit my head.

We begin to unwind because we realize our trip is coming to an end. A movie sounds good and dinner at the local Mexican restaurant fills us with good food and is a great change from all the Christmas fare we've been eating over the last few weeks. The present exchange even felt different this time. Maybe we were finally getting the knack of this holiday road trip. Just in time for it to end.

We drive south with a sense of relief. Our responsibility for holiday giving has been fulfilled. As we approach the South Carolina line I notice the sign for a travel agency. Why not just see what they have to offer. After only ten minutes, I notice the beautiful pictures of an Island called Margarita. They even have an excursion leaving for the holidays next year. My breathing changes and I am left with visions of sun and sand. The beds are luxurious and have room size fans that spin non-stop.

Maybe, just maybe.

LOW COUNTRY LONGINGS
by Mike Casey

During the long flight back east from the golden state of California, I had time to reflect upon my residence in the state of South Carolina. I had journeyed across the nation in March of 2014, this time by jet. Dare I say that this "damn Yankee" missed the low country? Damn right I did.

While California, at this time home to my grandson Casey Wheeler and his wonderful parents, my daughter Michelle and her husband Nolan, South Carolina is still the place I want to be.

As we left Oakland's airport Monday night for the red eye flight east, first to New York's JK, and then on to Charleston, South Carolina, I realized why we moved to the south – weather and taxes. The residence where our daughter lives our west is Pleasanton, located in the Liveamour Valley. It is a San Francisco suburb. As such it benefited from the central, usually fine weather, the ongoing drought lifted temporarily by some unusual colder and wetter weather, the proximity to three wine regions, the city by the bay and the Sierra Nevada Mountains.

The downside of the golden state is its very Big Apple style tax system – 13% state income fee, and the ultra high cost of housing. During our almost month-long stay in our daughter's near million-dollar very nice modest residence, we had a great time. Besides enjoying our nine-month old grandson, we sampled some of the wine country's delights. Expensive is an understatement. So called wine flights provided us consumers with samples of the vineyards products. Most were fine and the attractive atmosphere worth the modest fees. The purchase price of the products however, sent us scurrying to our car looking for an impossible to find bargain in the region.

Some critics may justifiably claim that I'm no connoisseur of fine wines. True. I do know however what I like and paying nearly a hundred dollars for a bottle of some never before heard of vintage just wasn't going to happen. Instead we opted for the supermarket offered wines, sold at much more affordable prices We took our modestly priced fermented grape juice back to our hotel and enjoyed it outside by the gas-lit fire pit. Delightful. We were in our element. To hell with the wine snobs.

Throughout our California stay, I suffered through a very painful leg injury, which finally sent me running – not very fast – to a doctor for some strong medication. My younger, somewhat hypochondriac brother, a trained nurse, had become convinced that I was suffering from a blood clot. He thought I would expire on the long flight home from deep vein thrombosis. The diagnosis by a California physician turned out to be somewhat less troubling. I had overextended my leg muscles surrounding my replacement knees by overusing our recently purchased elliptical exercise machine. I still suffer but will live. My estate will not be divided at this time. Sorry Joe.

After the late night flight, we left JFK for the short hour and a half jet ride south to Charleston. I gaze out of my window seat at the metropolitan New York region that once had been my long time home. Mostly fond memories filled my thoughts. I was happy however to be leaving. Delighted in fact not to be driving the 700 plus highway miles back to my South Carolina residence.

Southerners, according to local writer, John Brock, "have an overwhelming proclivity toward verbosity." We talk too much, I must admit. Guilty as charged. That carries over to my writings. Brock continues; "Southerners became consummate story-tellers." Again I fit the stereotype. American literature is filled with writers from Dixie. Hopefully, I can make my contribution.

Shortly thereafter we approached Charleston. The moniker of low country became very evident as our jet slowly rounded towards the Holy City's airport. Water is the regions lifeblood. That was very evident as we glided over the Ravenel Bridge and the peninsula. I thought immediately of the area's literary star, Pat Conroy. This gifted stylist, as some have described him, paints a beautiful portrait of the region. His " tide-carried" and "tide-possessed" phrases aptly apply to the rivers surrounding the city. Conroy considers the low country a national treasure. His powerful writings bring many of his readers to the region. In some of his best selling books, he portrays southern sunsets and the low country marine life such as shrimp, crabs and oysters, all found in the marshy area filled with smells he loves. The famous author's descriptions of destructive family dynamics also hit home in books like The Prince of Tides and South of Broad. The latter book's portrayal of a "dazzling older brother" who died before his time reminded me somewhat of my deceased brother, Dennis. He was very bright, well liked, an altar boy and very involved in the Catholic Church during his abbreviated lifetime.

For me perhaps the most fascinating part of Charleston is its history. History is its legacy. I thought of all the battles that took place in and around the area first with the native Americans, then the British, Sherman's Yankees and finally for black civil rights. I smiled as we made our final approach to the airport excited to soon be landing.

An article I recently read said Pawleys Island was on the National Geographic's International List of "Best Summer Family Vacation." And I live here.

Writing this memoir is like an expedition in search of lost valuable items. I mined my experiences in an attempt to better understand myself.

EPILOGUE

We always count on our own "Poet Laureate"
To help us understand what we wrote
This anthology leaves no exception to that
So, for a moment, on her, we shall dote.

Gail says:

Reaction to Georgia's poem "You'll Always be part of me"

What strength it took to write those words
Expressing such love is not for nerds.
Such beauty, happiness, so much to cherish
With memories that will never perish.

Reaction to Carole's Meeting Our New Neighbors

A neighborhood adventure could only be told
By Carole whose life does unfold
Into drama, fun, unexpected turns
For the reader whose interest burns
For more surprises in the stories she tells
Thrilling us as her character rebels
Or changes into a horrible creature.
Dull is not her prominent feature.

Reaction to Kay's Keep on Climbin'

Living life to the fullest seems Kay's aspiration
In spite of huge challenges that get in the way.
Her readers gain great inspiration
Learning how she lives each day.

Reaction to Mike Casey's Going South

An Irish temper and a happy smile,
Loves tennis and goes the extra mile
To obey the rules his mother set
That respect and tolerance are the best bet.

Reaction to Rebecca's Are We There Yet?

Never realized such a life well spent
Resulted in a writer confident
With writing both memoir and romance.
Always productive, always thinking,
Well-traveled, this violet is non-shrinking

Reaction to John's writing

As a leader, most willing,
His wisdom is thrilling.
As a teacher, most effective,
No facts are defective.
He's blessed with a community mind
For Georgetown, he's quite a find.
Even John's writing is right on the mark
With a perfect bite that matches the bark.

Reaction to Gail's Moving South

You'd never know she resisted moving,
Since her life today is really grooving
She's finally accepted the southern style.
And will stay in the Inlet for quite awhile.

ABOUT THE AUTHORS

Rebecca Bridges

Growing up in Oklahoma
I could see for miles across the plains where buffalo grass, paint
brush flowers and mesquite trees grew. My view today includes
ocean waves, dolphins, pelicans and palmetto trees.

Mike Casey

Born and raised in the Big
Apple's Queens County. Life-long Yankee fan and long time Long
Island resident, teacher, coach and volunteer most recently at
Brookgreen Gardens in South Carolina. Founding member of the
Coastal Author's Network. Published author of Chyna, a children's
book about the death of a beloved pet.

Georgia Jansson

Leaving my farm in the mountains of western Maryland means I'll have to do without the snow and the ice and the cold wind that blew down my civil war barn like the big bad wolf. Instead, I'll have to learn to put up with that big ole sun, the warm silky sand and the mesmerizing sound of ocean waves washing ashore. Damn!

John Kenny

Born in the Bronx, moved through New England and Washington. Was a little slow getting south, but thrilled I made it. I love to teach, write, kayak and take photos. My passion is working with the boys at Tara Hall Home for Boys in Georgetown.

Kay Nelson

I have four children and eleven grandchildren. They provide the light that keeps me going. Four years ago my husband and I moved to Pawleys Island, South Carolina where I fell in love with the Lowcountry. I am an artist and author.

Carole O'Neill

This was the view from my academic office in Boston, where I taught film and television for twenty years. My view today looks out over the South Carolina coast where I sit with my husband, Jim, and read the latest novels.

Gail Ritrievi

Born and carefully groomed in Bethlehem, Pennsylvania many years ago. I am very proud of the Keystone State roots. My greatest loves are my four adult children, my loyal friends both north and south, golfing and writing.

Other writings by these authors and their pseudonyms, Many can be found at Amazon.com.

Lucy Austin

The Only Lonely Tree. A children's book that teaches the dangers of forest fires from the point of view of the Tree and a Rabbit.

Rebecca Bridges

The Beach House Butcher. A romantic suspense. An eastern seaboard serial killer selects Garden City, South Carolina, as his new hunting ground. A suspended FBI agent seeks redemption by locating the maniac before he tortures and kills another woman.

Mike Casey

Chyna. A children's book about the death of a beloved pet.

A Bronx Boomer. A historical novel concerning the life of a boy from the Bronx, born after World War II, who survives his dysfunctional family, the Vietnam War, and the 9/11 terrorist attack as a fireman – one of New York City's bravest.

Travelin' Man. A memoir of my hectic year of 2013. It includes a trip to Boston as a spectator at the finish line, another to welcome our first grandchild in July, four summer weddings on Long Island, and a cross-country road trip in the company of a large, overly-protective, Swiss Mountain dog named Moose.

JD Franklin

Ten Things to Know to Survive Type II Diabetes.

Georgeann Jansson

Veteran's Day. A romance novel. Running from the law until he can prove his innocence, a Vietnam vet kidnaps a beautiful young woman to help him. Together they save each other.

Joey Light

Daddy for Hire. A romance novel. His daughter needs a woman's touch in her life and the heroine's two boys need a male influence. They form an unusual alliance and despite their resolve to keep it business only the kids work their magic.

High-Riding Heroes. A romantic suspense novel about a young Virginia woman inheriting half of her grandfather's tourist Wild West Town. She finds herself forced to work with a genuine cowboy who doubts that she can run the western town properly and sets out to point her in the right direction. Sparks fly.

Sterling's Reasons. A romantic suspense novel featuring a cop who accidentally kills his partner in a drug bust, and the woman sent by a secret someone to get him interested in living again.

Trisha Moriarty

The Secrets She Kept. A memoir about my mother's affair with our parish priest, and her secret family we discovered after her death.

Kay Nelson

A Political Philosophy is Born. A Political History Autobiography. This book outlines how former speaker Jim Wright developed his political convictions.

Spilled Blood. Historical fiction. Two women develop an unexpected friendship and become involved in a software designed voter fraud scheme. The book is filled with intrigue and suspense.

Women of the Plantation. Historical fiction. As the Civil War looms, time honored traditions crumble. The wars growing turbulence brings harrowing dangers close to home. The brave decisions and courageous actions of women both slave and free, change the course of history. The lively Gullah culture rich in knowledge, chants, trickster lore, and spiritualism is introduced.

Carole O'Neill

Women in Media Careers – Success Despite the Odds. The book, co-authored by Lee Bollinger, takes an in-depth look at women's careers in mass media by outlining job descriptions and providing insider tips on ways to begin a career.

Gail Ritrievi

Women's Voices by The Write Sisters

Women's Voices, Only Louder by the Write Sisters

Both books were a collaborative effort of a writing group consisting of all women (of course).

The Life of Don Hamacher as told to Gail Ritrievi. This memoir was ghost written at the request of the subject who was ninety-one at the time.